"Most of us imagine totalitarianism as something imposed upon us—but what if we're complicit in our own oppression? That's the scenario in Eggers's ambitious, terrifying, and eerily plausible new novel. . . . Brave and important and will draw comparisons to *Brave New World* and *1984*. Eggers brilliantly depicts the Internet binges, torrents of information, and endless loops of feedback that increasingly characterize modern life. But perhaps most chilling of all is his notion that our ultimate undoing could be something so petty as our desperate desire for affirmation."

—*Booklist* (starred review)

"With *The Circle*, Eggers has given us everything. . . . When you put down the book and go to check your email, you might just realize that we are living the fiction. . . . [*The Circle*] takes place before a fall that we might really be approaching, and it's this compelling sense of impending, unpredictable doom that makes this work of fiction feel very real, and very necessary."

—Flavorwire

"Page-turning. . . . An elegantly told, compulsively readable parable for the twenty-first century. . . . What may be the most haunting discovery about *The Circle*, however, is readers' recognition that they share the same technology-driven mentality that brings the novel's characters to the brink of dysfunction. We too want to *know everything* by watching, monitoring, commenting, and interacting, and the force of Eggers's richly allusive prose lies in his ability to expose the potential hazards of that impulse."

—*Vanity Fair*

"You may find yourself so engrossed in Dave Eggers's futuristic novel, *The Circle*, that you forget about Facebook entirely. And by the last pages, you may think twice before logging on again."

—*O, The Oprah Magazine*

"A stunning work of terrifying plausibility."

—*Publishers Weekly* (starred review)

"Eggers has a keen eye for context, and the great strength of *The Circle* lies in its observations about the way instant, asynchronous communication has damaged our personal relationships. . . . We go on using the social media platforms that have been used against us; we post geo-tagged photos that could lead potential criminals straight to our private homes and our children's pre-schools, and we do all of this with full knowledge of the possible consequences. We have closed our eyes and given our consent. Everyone else is doing it. In the digital age, it is better to be unsafe than to be left out."

—*San Francisco Chronicle*

"Dave Eggers wrote the best business book of the year. . . . It challenged me deeply. . . . That's what a good business book should do: challenge your assumptions, and make you think in new ways. . . . Putting into words what many of us intuitively sense, Eggers demands us to confront the now well-researched idea that increasing digital connectedness is actually making us more isolated. . . . [*The Circle*] asks us to imagine an enterprise with the aspiration to know it all, but also forces us to ask whether we should want to play a role in making that happen."

—*Harvard Business Review*

"*The Circle* is intelligent and quirky, engaged and affecting and confirms Eggers's place as one of the most interesting novelists currently writing."   —*The Scotsman*

"Eggers's writing is so fluent, his ventriloquism of tech-world dialect so light, his denouement so enjoyably inevitable."
                                                —*The Observer* (London)

"What fuels this novel is its thunderbolt of an idea: digital culture is suffocating us and, what's more, is doing so under the duplicitous guise of widespread human beneficence. . . . This is a novel about the silence inside your head. . . . A powerful argument for turning off your iPhone and going for a walk."   —*Newsweek*

"The particular charm and power of Eggers's book . . . could be described as 'topical' or 'timely,' though those pedestrian words do not nearly capture its imaginative vision. . . . Simply a great story, with a fascinating protagonist, sharply drawn supporting characters and an exciting, unpredictable plot. . . . As scary as the story's implications will be to some readers, the reading experience is pure pleasure."   —*The New York Times Magazine*

"We need a legion of Dave Eggers in the world today, calling out the dangers."   —*Salon*

"Timely and potent. We have met Big Brother, and he is us."
                                                —*TIME* magazine

Dave Eggers

THE CIRCLE

Dave Eggers grew up near Chicago and graduated from the University of Illinois at Urbana-Champaign. He is the founder of McSweeney's, an independent publishing house in San Francisco that produces books, a quarterly journal of new writing (*McSweeney's Quarterly Concern*), and a monthly magazine (*The Believer*). McSweeney's also publishes Voice of Witness, a nonprofit book series that uses oral history to illuminate human rights crises around the world. In 2002, he cofounded 826 Valencia, a nonprofit youth writing and tutoring center in San Francisco's Mission District. Sister centers have since opened in seven other American cities under the umbrella of 826 National, and like-minded centers have opened in Dublin, London, Copenhagen, Stockholm, and St. Paul/Minneapolis, among other locations. His work has been nominated for the National Book Award, the Pulitzer Prize, and the National Book Critics Circle Award, and has won the Dayton Literary Peace Prize, France's Prix Médicis, Germany's Albatross Prize, the National Magazine Award, and the American Book Award. Eggers lives in Northern California with his family.

mcsweeneys.net

voiceofwitness.org

826national.org

valentinoachakdeng.org

believermag.com

scholarmatch.org

BOOKS BY THIS AUTHOR

NOVELS

The Circle

A Hologram for the King

What Is the What

You Shall Know Our Velocity!

STORIES

How We Are Hungry

How the Water Feels to the Fishes

NONFICTION

Zeitoun

FOR ALL AGES

The Wild Things

ORAL HISTORY (AS CO-EDITOR)

Surviving Justice: America's Wrongfully Convicted and Exonerated

Teachers Have It Easy: The Big Sacrifices and Small Salaries of America's Teachers

AS EDITOR

The Best American Nonrequired Reading

The Best of McSweeney's

MEMOIR

A Heartbreaking Work of Staggering Genius

THE
CIRCLE
a novel

DAVE EGGERS

Vintage Books
Random House LLC
New York

FIRST VINTAGE OPEN-MARKET EDITION, MAY 2014

All rights reserved. Published in the United States by Vintage Books,
a division of Random House LLC, New York, and in Canada by
Random House of Canada Limited, Toronto, Penguin Random House
companies. Originally published in the United States in hardcover by
McSweeney's Books, San Francisco, and Alfred A. Knopf,
a division of Random House LLC, New York, in 2013.

Vintage and colophon are registered trademarks of Random House LLC.

The Library of Congress has cataloged the Knopf edition as follows:
Eggers, Dave.
The circle : a novel / Dave Eggers.
pages cm
1. Fiction—Literary. 2. Fiction—Technological. I. Title.
PS3605.G48 C57 2013 813'.6—dc23 2013032894

Vintage Open-Market ISBN: 978-0-8041-7229-5
eBook ISBN: 978-0-385-35140-9

www.vintagebooks.com

Printed in the United States of America
10 9 8 7 6 5 4 3 2 1

There wasn't any limit, no boundary at all, to the future. And it would be so a man wouldn't have room to store his happiness.

JOHN STEINBECK
East of Eden

MY GOD, MAE thought. It's heaven.

The campus was vast and rambling, wild with Pacific color, and yet the smallest detail had been carefully considered, shaped by the most eloquent hands. On land that had once been a shipyard, then a drive-in movie theater, then a flea market, then blight, there were now soft green hills and a Calatrava fountain. And a picnic area, with tables arranged in concentric circles. And tennis courts, clay and grass. And a volleyball court, where tiny children from the company's daycare center were running, squealing, weaving like water. Amid all this was a workplace, too, four hundred acres of brushed steel and glass on the headquarters of the most influential company in the world. The sky above was spotless and blue.

Mae was making her way through all of this, walking from the parking lot to the main hall, trying to look as if she belonged. The walkway wound around lemon and orange trees and its quiet red cobblestones were replaced, occasionally, by tiles with imploring messages of inspiration. "Dream," one said, the word laser-cut into the red stone. "Participate," said another. There were dozens: "Find Community." "Innovate." "Imagine." She just missed stepping on the hand of a young man in a grey jumpsuit; he was installing a new stone that said "Breathe."

On a sunny Monday in June, Mae stopped in front of the main door, standing below the logo etched into the glass above. Though the company was less than six years old, its name and logo—a circle surrounding a knitted grid, with a small 'c' in the center—were already among the best-known in the world. There were more than ten thousand employees on this, the main campus, but the Circle had offices all over the globe, and was hiring hundreds of gifted young minds every week. It had been voted the world's most admired company four years running.

Mae wouldn't have thought she had a chance to work at such a place, but for Annie. Annie was two years older and they'd roomed together for three semesters in college, in an ugly building made habitable through their extraordinary bond, something like friends, something like sisters or cousins who wished they were siblings and would have reason never to be apart. Their first month living together, Mae had broken her jaw one twilight, after fainting, flu-ridden and underfed, during finals. Annie had told her to stay in bed, but Mae had gone to the 7-Eleven for caffeine and woke up on the sidewalk, under a tree. Annie took her to the hospital, and waited as they wired her jaw, and then stayed with Mae, sleeping next to her, in a wooden chair, all night, and then at home, for days, had fed Mae through a straw. It was a fierce level of commitment and competence that Mae had never seen from someone her age or

2

near her age, and Mae was thereafter loyal in a way she'd never known she could be.

While Mae was still at Carleton, meandering between majors, from art history to marketing to psychology—getting her degree in psych with no plans to go further in the field—Annie had graduated, gotten her MBA from Stanford and was recruited everywhere, but particularly at the Circle, and had landed here days after graduation. Now she had some lofty title—Director of Ensuring the Future, Annie joked—and had urged Mae to apply for a job. Mae did so, and though Annie insisted she pulled no strings, Mae was sure that Annie had, and she felt indebted beyond all measure. A million people, a billion, wanted to be where Mae was at this moment, entering this atrium, thirty feet high and shot through with California light, on her first day working for the only company that really mattered at all.

She pushed open the heavy door. The front hall was as long as a parade, as tall as a cathedral. There were offices everywhere above, four floors high on either side, every wall made of glass. Briefly dizzy, she looked downward, and in the immaculate glossy floor, she saw her own face reflected, looking worried. She shaped her mouth into a smile, feeling a presence behind her.

"You must be Mae."

Mae turned to find a beautiful young head floating atop a scarlet scarf and white silk blouse.

"I'm Renata," she said.

"Hi Renata. I'm looking for—"

"Annie. I know. She's on her way." A sound, a digital drop-let, came from Renata's ear. "She's actually . . ." Renata was looking at Mae but was seeing something else. Retinal interface, Mae assumed. Another innovation born here.

"She's in the Old West," Renata said, focusing on Mae again, "but she'll be here soon."

Mae smiled. "I hope she's got some hardtack and a sturdy horse."

Renata smiled politely but did not laugh. Mae knew the company's practice of naming each portion of the campus after a historical era; it was a way to make an enormous place less impersonal, less corporate. It beat Building 3B-East, where Mae had last worked. Her final day at the public utility in her hometown had been only three weeks ago—they'd been stupefied when she gave notice—but already it seemed impossible she'd wasted so much of her life there. Good riddance, Mae thought, to that gulag and all it represented.

Renata was still getting signals from her earpiece. "Oh wait," she said, "now she's saying she's still tied up over there." Renata looked at Mae with a radiant smile. "Why don't I take you to your desk? She says she'll meet you there in an hour or so."

Mae thrilled a bit at those words, *your desk,* and immediately she thought of her dad. He was proud. *So proud,* he'd said on her voicemail; he must have left the message at four a.m. She'd gotten it when she'd woken up. *So very proud,* he'd said, choking up. Mae was two years out of college and here she was, gainfully employed by the Circle, with her own health insurance, her own apartment in the city, being no burden to her parents, who had plenty else to worry about.

Mae followed Renata out of the atrium. On the lawn, under dappled light, a pair of young people were sitting on a manmade hill, holding some kind of clear tablet, talking with great intensity.

"You'll be in the Renaissance, over here," Renata said, pointing across the lawn, to a building of glass and oxidized copper. "This is where all the Customer Experience people are. You've visited before?"

Mae nodded. "I have. A few times, but not this building."

"So you've seen the pool, the sports area." Renata waved her hand off toward a blue parallelogram and an angular building, the gym, rising behind it. "Over there there's the yoga studio, crossfit, Pilates, massages, spinning. I heard you spin? Behind that there's the bocce courts, and the new tetherball setup. The cafeteria's just across the grass . . ." Renata pointed to the lush rolling green, with a handful of young people, dressed professionally and splayed about like sunbathers. "And here we are."

They stood before the Renaissance, another building with a forty-foot atrium, a Calder mobile turning slowly above.

"Oh, I love Calder," Mae said.

Renata smiled. "I know you do." They looked up at it together. "This one used to hang in the French parliament. Something like that."

The wind that had followed them in now turned the mobile such that an arm pointed to Mae, as if welcoming her personally. Renata took her elbow. "Ready? Up this way."

They entered an elevator of glass, tinted faintly orange. Lights flickered on and Mae saw her name appear on the walls, along with her high school yearbook photo. WELCOME MAE HOLLAND. A sound, something like a gasp, left Mae's throat. She hadn't seen that photo in years, and had been happy for its absence. This must have been Annie's doing, assaulting her with it again. The picture was indeed Mae—her wide mouth, her thin lips, her olive skin, her black hair, but in this photo, more so than in life, her high cheekbones gave her a look of severity, her brown eyes not smiling, only small and cold, ready for war. Since the photo—she was eighteen then, angry and unsure—Mae had gained much-needed weight, her face had softened and curves appeared, curves that brought the attention of men of myriad ages and motives. She'd tried, since high school, to be more open, more accepting, and seeing it here, this document of a long-ago era when she assumed the worst of the world, rattled her. Just when she couldn't stand it anymore, the photo disappeared.

"Yeah, everything's on sensors," Renata said. "The elevator reads your ID, and then says hello. Annie gave us that photo. You guys must be tight if she's got high school pictures of you. Anyway, hope you don't mind. We do that for visitors, mostly. They're usually impressed."

As the elevator rose, the day's featured activities appeared on every elevator wall, the images and text traveling from one panel to the next. With each announcement, there was video, photos, animation, music. There was a screening of *Koyaanisqatsi* at noon, a self-massage demonstration at one, core strengthening at three. A congressman Mae hadn't heard of, grey-haired but young, was holding a town hall at six thirty. On the elevator door, he was talking at a podium, somewhere else, flags rippling behind him, his shirtsleeves rolled up and his hands shaped into earnest fists.

The doors opened, splitting the congressman in two.

"Here we are," Renata said, stepping out to a narrow catwalk of steel grating. Mae looked down and felt her stomach cinch. She could see all the way to the ground floor, four stories below.

Mae attempted levity: "I guess you don't put anyone with vertigo up here."

Renata stopped and turned to Mae, looking gravely concerned. "Of course not. But your profile said—"

"No, no," Mae said. "I'm fine."

"Seriously. We can put you lower if—"

"No, no. Really. It's perfect. Sorry. I was making a joke."

Renata was visibly shaken. "Okay. Just let me know if anything's not right."

"I will."

"You will? Because Annie would want me to make sure."

"I will. I promise," Mae said, and smiled at Renata, who recovered and moved on.

The catwalk reached the main floor, wide and windowed and bisected by a long hallway. On either side, the offices were fronted by floor-to-ceiling glass, the occupants visible within. Each had decorated his or her space elaborately but tastefully—one office full of sailing paraphernalia, most of it seeming airborne, hanging from the exposed beams, another arrayed with bonsai trees. They passed a small kitchen, the cabinets and shelves all glass, the cutlery magnetic, attached to the refrigerator in a tidy grid, everything illuminated by a vast hand-blown chandelier aglow with multicolored bulbs, its arms reaching out in orange and peach and pink.

"Okay, here you are."

They stopped at a cubicle, grey and small and lined with a material like synthetic linen. Mae's heart faltered. It was almost

7

precisely like the cubicle she'd worked at for the last eighteen months. It was the first thing she'd seen at the Circle that hadn't been rethought, that bore any resemblance to the past. The material lining the cubicle walls was—she couldn't believe it, it didn't seem possible—burlap.

Mae knew Renata was watching her, and she knew her face was betraying something like horror. *Smile,* she thought. *Smile.*

"This okay?" Renata said, her eyes darting all over Mae's face.

Mae forced her mouth to indicate some level of satisfaction. "Great. Looks good."

This was not what she expected.

"Okay then. I'll leave you to get yourself acquainted with the workspace, and Denise and Josiah will be in soon to orient you and get you set up."

Mae twisted her mouth into a smile again, and Renata turned and left. Mae sat, noting that the back of the chair was half-broken, that the chair would not move, its wheels seeming stuck, all of them. A computer had been placed on the desk, but it was an ancient model she hadn't seen anywhere else in the building. Mae was baffled, and found her mood sinking into the same sort of abyss in which she'd spent the last few years.

Did anyone really work at a utility company anymore? How had Mae come to work there? How had she tolerated it? When people had asked where she worked, she was more inclined to lie and say she was unemployed. Would it have been any better if it hadn't been in her hometown?

After six or so years of loathing her hometown, of cursing her

8

parents for moving there and subjecting her to it, its limitations and scarcity of everything—diversion, restaurants, enlightened minds—Mae had recently come to remember Longfield with something like tenderness. It was a small town between Fresno and Tranquillity, incorporated and named by a literal-minded farmer in 1866. One hundred and fifty years later, its population had peaked at just under two thousand souls, most of them working in Fresno, twenty miles away. Longfield was a cheap place to live, and the parents of Mae's friends were security guards, teachers, truckers who liked to hunt. Of Mae's graduating class of eighty-one, she was one of twelve to go to a four-year college, and the only one to go east of Colorado. That she went so far, and went into such debt, only to come back and work at the local utility, shredded her, and her parents, though outwardly they said she was doing the right thing, taking a solid opportunity and getting started in paying down her loans.

The utility building, 3B-East, was a tragic block of cement with narrow vertical slits for windows. Inside, most of the offices were walled with cinderblock, everything painted a sickly green. It was like working in a locker room. She'd been the youngest person in the building by a decade or so, and even those in their thirties were of a different century. They marveled at her computer skills, which were basic and common to anyone she knew. But her coworkers at the utility were astounded. They called her the *Black Lightning,* some wilted reference to her hair, and told her she had *quite a bright future* at the utility if she played her cards right. In four or five years, they told her, she could be head of IT for the whole sub-station! Her exasperation was unbounded. She had not gone to college, $234,000 worth of elite liberal arts education, for a job like that. But it was work, and she needed the money. Her student loans were voracious and demanded monthly feedings, so she took the job and the paycheck and kept her eyes open for greener pastures.

Her immediate supervisor was a man named Kevin, who served as the ostensible technology officer at the utility, but who, in a strange twist, happened to know nothing about technology. He knew cables, splitters; he should have been operating a ham radio in his basement—not supervising Mae. Every day, every month, he wore the same short-sleeved button-down, the same rust-colored ties. He was an awful assault on the senses, his breath smelling of ham and his mustache furry and wayward, like two small paws emerging, southwest and southeast, from his ever-flared nostrils.

All this would have been fine, his many offenses, but for the fact that he actually believed that Mae cared. He believed that Mae, graduate of Carleton, dreamer of rare and golden dreams, cared about this job at the gas and electric utility. That she would be worried if Kevin considered her performance on any given day subpar. It drove her mad.

The times he would ask her to come in, when he would close his door and sit at the corner of his desk—they were excruciating. *Do you know why you're here?* he would ask, like a highway cop who'd pulled her over. Other times, when he was satisfied with whatever work she'd done that day, he did something worse: he *praised* her. He called her his *protégée*. He loved the word. He introduced her to visitors this way, saying, "This is my protégée, Mae. She's pretty sharp, most days"—and here he'd wink at her as if he were a captain and she his first mate, the two of them veterans of many raucous adventures and forever devoted to each other. "If she doesn't get in her own way, she has a bright future ahead of her here."

She couldn't stand it. Every day of that job, the eighteen months she worked there, she wondered if she could really ask Annie for a favor. She'd never been one to ask for something like that, to be rescued, to be lifted. It was a kind of neediness, pushiness—*nudginess,* her dad called it, something not bred into her. Her parents were quiet people who did not like to be in anyone's way, quiet and proud people who took nothing from anyone.

And Mae was the same, but that job bent her into something else, into someone who would do anything to leave. It was sickening, all of it. The green cinderblocks. An actual water cooler. Actual punch cards. The actual *certificates of merit* when someone had done something deemed special. And the hours! Actually nine to five! All of it felt like something from another time, a rightfully forgotten time, and made Mae feel that she was not only wasting her life but that this entire company was wasting life, wasting human potential and holding back the turning of the globe. The cubicle at that place, *her* cubicle, was the distillation of it all. The low walls around her, meant to facilitate her complete concentration on the work at hand, were lined with burlap, as if any other material might distract her, might allude to more exotic ways of spending her days. And so she'd spent eighteen months in an office where they thought, of all the materials man and nature offered, the one their staff should see, all day and every day, was burlap. A dirty sort of burlap, a less refined form of burlap. A bulk burlap, a poor man's burlap, a budget burlap.

Oh god, she thought, when she left that place she vowed never to see or touch or acknowledge the existence of that material again.

And she did not expect to see it again. How often, outside of the nineteenth century, outside a general store of the nineteenth century, does one encounter burlap? Mae assumed she never would, but then here it was, all around her in this new Circle workspace, and looking at it, smelling its musty smell, her eyes welled up. "Fucking burlap," she mumbled to herself.

Behind her, she heard a sigh, then a voice: "Now I'm thinking this wasn't such a good idea."

Mae turned and found Annie, her hands in fists at her sides, posing like a pouting child. "Fucking burlap," Annie said, imitating her pout, then burst out laughing. When she was done, she managed, "That was incredible. Thank you so much for that, Mae. I knew you'd hate it, but I wanted to see just how much. I'm sorry you almost cried. Jesus."

Now Mae looked to Renata, whose hands were raised high in surrender. "Not my idea!" she said. "Annie put me up to it! Don't hate me!"

Annie sighed with satisfaction. "I had to actually *buy* that cubicle from Walmart. And the computer! That took me ages to find online. I thought we could just bring that kind of stuff up from the basement or something, but we honestly had nothing on the entire campus ugly and old enough. Oh god, you should have seen your face."

Mae's heart was pounding. "You're such a sicko."

Annie feigned confusion. "Me? I'm not sick. I'm awesome."

"I can't believe you went to that much trouble to upset me."

"Well, I did. That's how I got to where I am now. It's all

about planning and it's all about follow-through." She gave Mae a salesman's wink and Mae couldn't help but laugh. Annie was a lunatic. "Now let's go. I'm giving you the full tour."

As Mae followed her, she had to remind herself that Annie had not always been a senior executive at a company like the Circle. There was a time, only four years ago, when Annie was a college student who wore men's flannel housepants to class, to dinner, on casual dates. Annie was what one of her boyfriends, and there were many, always monogamous, always decent, called a *doofus*. But she could afford to be. She came from money, generations of money, and was very cute, dimpled and long-lashed, with hair so blond it could only be real. She was known by all as effervescent, seemed incapable of letting anything bother her for more than a few moments. But she was also a doofus. She was gangly, and used her hands wildly, dangerously, when she spoke, and was given to bizarre conversational tangents and strange obsessions—caves, amateur perfumery, doo-wop music. She was friendly with every one of her exes, with every hookup, with every professor (she knew them all personally and sent them gifts). She had been involved in, or ran, most or all of the clubs and causes in college, and yet she'd found time to be committed to her coursework—to everything, really—while also, at any party, being the most likely to embarrass herself to loosen everyone up, the last to leave. The one rational explanation for all this would have been that she did not sleep, but this was not the case. She slept decadently, eight to ten hours a day, could sleep anywhere—on a three-minute car ride, in the filthy booth of an off-campus diner, on anyone's couch, at any time.

Mae knew this firsthand, having been something of a chauffeur to Annie on long rides, throughout Minnesota and Wisconsin and Iowa, to countless and largely meaningless cross-country contests. Mae had gotten a partial scholarship to run at Carleton, and that's where she met Annie, who was effortlessly good, two years older, but was only intermittently concerned with whether she, or the team, won or lost. One meet Annie would be deep in it, taunting the opponents, insulting their uniforms or SATs, and the next she'd be wholly uninterested in the outcome but happy to be along for the ride. It was on the long rides, in Annie's car—which she preferred Mae to drive—that Annie would put her bare feet up or out the window, and would riff on the passing scenery, and would speculate, for hours, on what went on in the bedroom of their coaches, a married couple with matching, almost military, haircuts. Mae laughed at everything Annie said, and it kept Mae's mind off the meets, where she, unlike Annie, had to win, or at least do well, to justify the subsidy the college had provided her. They would invariably arrive minutes before the meet, with Annie having forgotten what race she was meant to run, or whether she really wanted to run at all.

And so how was this possible, that this scattershot and ridiculous person, who still carried a piece of her childhood blanket around in her pocket, had risen so quickly and high through the Circle? Now she was part of the forty most crucial minds at the company—the Gang of 40—privy to its most secret plans and data. That she could push through the hiring of Mae without breaking a sweat? That she could set it all up within weeks of Mae finally swallowing all pride and making the ask? It was a testament to Annie's inner will, some mysterious and core sense of destiny. Outwardly, Annie showed no signs of garish ambition, but Mae was sure that there was something within Annie that insisted upon this, that she would have been here, in this position, no matter where she'd come from. If she'd grown up in the Siberian tundra, born blind to shepherds, she still would have arrived here, now.

"Thanks Annie," she heard herself say.

They'd walked past a few conference rooms and lounges and were passing through the company's new gallery, where a half-dozen Basquiats hung, just acquired from a near-broke museum in Miami.

"Whatever," Annie said. "And I'm sorry you're in Customer Experience. I know that sounds shitty, but I will have you know that about half the company's senior people started there. Do you believe me?"

"I do."

"Good, because it's true."

They left the gallery and entered the second-floor cafeteria—"The Glass Eatery, I know it's such a terrible name," Annie said—designed such that diners ate at nine different levels, all of the floors and walls glass. At first glance, it looked like a hundred people were eating in mid-air.

They moved through the Borrow Room, where anything from bicycles to telescopes to hang gliders were loaned, for free, to anyone on staff, and onto the aquarium, a project championed by one of the founders. They stood before a display, as tall as themselves, where jellyfish, ghostly and slow, rose and fell with no apparent pattern or reason.

"I'll be watching you," Annie said, "and every time you do

something great I'll be making sure everyone knows about it so you won't have to stay there too long. People move up here pretty reliably, and as you know we hire almost exclusively from within. So just do well and keep your head down and you'll be shocked at how quickly you'll be out of Customer Experience and into something juicy."

Mae looked into Annie's eyes, bright in the aquarium light. "Don't worry. I'm happy to be anywhere here."

"Better to be at the bottom of a ladder you want to climb than in the middle of some ladder you don't, right? Some shitty-ass ladder made of shit?"

Mae laughed. It was the shock of hearing such filth coming from such a sweet face. "Did you always curse this much? I don't remember that part of you."

"I do it when I'm tired, which is pretty much always."

"You used to be such a sweet girl."

"Sorry. I'm fucking sorry, Mae! Jesus fucking Christ, Mae! Okay. Let's see more stuff. The kennel!"

"Are we working at all today?" Mae asked.

"Working? This *is* working. This is what you're tasked with doing the first day: getting to know the place, the people, getting acclimated. You know how when you put new wood floors into your house—"

"No, I don't."

"Well, when you do, you first have to let them sit there for ten days, to get the wood acclimated. Then you do the installation."

"So in this analogy, I'm the wood?"

"You are the wood."

"And then I'll be installed."

16

"Yes, we will then install you. We'll hammer you with ten thousands tiny nails. You'll love it."

They visited the kennel, a brainchild of Annie, whose dog, Dr. Kinsmann, had just passed on, but who had spent a few very happy years here, never far from his owner. Why should thousands of employees all leave their dogs at home when they could be brought here, to be around people, and other dogs, and be cared for and not alone? That had been Annie's logic, quickly embraced and now considered visionary. And they saw the nightclub—often used during the day for something called ecstatic dancing, a great workout, Annie said—and they saw the large outdoor amphitheater, and the small indoor theater—"there are about ten comedy improv groups here"—and after they saw all that, there was lunch in the larger, first-floor cafeteria where, in the corner, on a small stage, there was a man, playing a guitar, who looked like an aging singer-songwriter Mae's parents listened to.

"Is that . . . ?"

"It is," Annie said, not breaking her stride. "There's someone every day. Musicians, comedians, writers. That's Bailey's passion project, to bring them here to get some exposure, especially given how rough it is out there for them."

"I knew they came sometimes, but you're saying it's every day?"

"We book them a year ahead. We have to fight them off."

The singer-songwriter was singing passionately, his head tilted, hair covering his eyes, his fingers strumming feverishly, but the vast majority of the cafeteria was paying little to no attention.

"I can't imagine the budget for that," Mae said.

"Oh god, we don't *pay* them. Oh wait, you should meet this guy."

Annie stopped a man named Vipul, who, Annie said, would soon be reinventing all of television, a medium stuck more than any other in the twentieth century.

"Try nineteenth," he said, with a slight Indian accent, his English precise and lofty. "It's the last place where customers do not, ever, get what they want. The last vestige of feudal arrangements between maker and viewer. We are vassals no longer!" he said, and soon excused himself.

"That guy is on another level," Annie said as they made their way through the cafeteria. They stopped at five or six other tables, meeting fascinating people, every one of them working on something Annie deemed *world-rocking* or *life-changing* or *fifty years ahead of anyone else*. The range of the work being done was startling. They met a pair of women working on a submersible exploration craft that would make the Marianas Trench mysterious no more. "They'll map it like Manhattan," Annie said, and the two women did not argue the hyperbole. They stopped at a table where a trio of young men were looking at a screen, embedded into the table, displaying 3-D drawings of a new kind of low-cost housing, to be easily adopted throughout the developing world.

Annie grabbed Mae's hand and pulled her toward the exit. "Now we're seeing the Ochre Library. You heard of it?"

Mae hadn't, but didn't want to commit to that answer.

Annie gave her a conspiratorial look. "You're not supposed to see it, but I say we go."

They got into an elevator of plexiglass and neon and rose through the atrium, every floor and office visible as they climbed five floors. "I can't see how stuff like that works into the bottom line here," Mae said.

"Oh god, I don't know, either. But it's not just about money here, as I'm guessing you know. There's enough revenue to support the passions of the community. Those guys working on the sustainable housing, they were programmers, but a couple of them had studied architecture. So they write up a proposal, and the Wise Men went nuts for it. Especially Bailey. He just loves enabling the curiosity of great young minds. And his library's insane. This is the floor."

They stepped out of the elevator and into a long hallway, this one appointed in deep cherry and walnut, a series of compact chandeliers emitting a calm amber light.

"Old school," Mae noted.

"You know about Bailey, right? He loves this ancient shit. Mahogany, brass, stained glass. That's his aesthetic. He gets overruled in the rest of the buildings, but here he has his way. Check this out."

Annie stopped at a large painting, a portrait of the Three Wise Men. "Hideous, right?" she said.

The painting was awkward, the kind of thing a high school artist might produce. In it, the three men, the founders of the company, were arranged in a pyramid, each of them dressed in their best-known clothes, wearing expressions that spoke, cartoonishly, of their personalities. Ty Gospodinov, the Circle's boy-wonder visionary, was wearing nondescript glasses and an enormous hoodie, staring leftward and smiling; he seemed to be enjoying some moment, alone, tuned into some distant frequency. People said he was borderline Asperger's, and the picture seemed

19

intent on underscoring the point. With his dark unkempt hair, his unlined face, he looked no more than twenty-five.

"Ty looks checked out, right?" Annie said. "But he couldn't be. None of us would be here if he wasn't a fucking brilliant management master, too. I should explain the dynamic. You'll be moving up quickly so I'll lay it out."

Ty, born Tyler Alexander Gospodinov, was the first Wise Man, Annie explained, and everyone always just called him Ty.

"I know this," Mae said.

"Don't stop me now. I'm giving you the same spiel I have to give to heads of state."

"Okay."

Annie continued.

Ty realized he was, at best, socially awkward, and at worst an utter interpersonal disaster. So, just six months before the company's IPO, he made a very wise and profitable decision: he hired the other two Wise Men, Eamon Bailey and Tom Stenton. The move assuaged the fears of all investors and ultimately tripled the company's valuation. The IPO raised $3 billion, unprecedented but not unexpected, and with all monetary concerns behind him, and with Stenton and Bailey aboard, Ty was free to float, to hide, to disappear. With every successive month, he was seen less and less around campus and in the media. He became more reclusive, and the aura around him, intentionally or not, only grew. Watchers of the Circle wondered, *Where is Ty and what is he planning?* These plans were kept unknown until they were revealed, and with each successive innovation brought forth by the Circle, it became less clear which had originated from Ty himself and which were the products of the increasingly vast group of inventors, the best in the world, who were now in the company fold.

Most observers assumed he was still involved, and some insisted that his fingerprints, his knack for solutions global and elegant and infinitely scalable, were on every major Circle innovation. He had founded the company after a year in college, with no particular business acumen or measurable goals. "We used to call him Niagara," his roommate said in one of the first articles about him. "The ideas just come like that, a million flowing out of his head, every second of every day, never-ending and overwhelming."

Ty had devised the initial system, the Unified Operating System, which combined everything online that had heretofore been separate and sloppy—users' social media profiles, their payment systems, their various passwords, their email accounts, user names, preferences, every last tool and manifestation of their interests. The old way—a new transaction, a new system, for every site, for every purchase—it was like getting into a different car to run any one kind of errand. "You shouldn't have to have eighty-seven different cars," he'd said, later, after his system had overtaken the web and the world.

Instead, he put all of it, all of every user's needs and tools, into one pot and invented TruYou—one account, one identity, one password, one payment system, per person. There were no more passwords, no multiple identities. Your devices knew who you were, and your one identity—the *TruYou,* unbendable and unmaskable—was the person paying, signing up, responding, viewing and reviewing, seeing and being seen. You had to use your real name, and this was tied to your credit cards, your bank, and thus paying for anything was simple. One button for the rest of your life online.

To use any of the Circle's tools, and they were the best tools, the most dominant and ubiquitous and free, you had to do so as yourself, as your actual self, as your TruYou. The era of false identities, identity theft, multiple user names, complicated passwords and payment systems, was over. Anytime you wanted to see anything, use anything, comment on anything or buy anything, it was one button, one account, everything tied together and trackable and simple, all of it operable via mobile or laptop, tablet or retinal. Once you had a single account, it carried you through every corner of the web, every portal, every pay site, everything you wanted to do.

TruYou changed the internet, in toto, within a year. Though some sites were resistant at first, and free-internet advocates shouted about the right to be anonymous online, the TruYou wave was tidal and crushed all meaningful opposition. It started with the commerce sites. Why would any non-porn site want anonymous users when they could know exactly who had come through the door? Overnight, all comment boards became civil, all posters held accountable. The trolls, who had more or less overtaken the internet, were driven back into the darkness.

And those who wanted or needed to track the movements of consumers online had found their Valhalla: the actual buying habits of actual people were now eminently mappable and measurable, and the marketing to those actual people could be done with surgical precision. Most TruYou users, most internet users who simply wanted simplicity, efficiency, a clean and streamlined experience, were thrilled with the results. No longer did they have to memorize twelve identities and passwords; no longer did they have to tolerate the madness and rage of the anonymous hordes; no longer did they have to put up with buckshot marketing that guessed, at best, within a mile of their desires. Now the messages they did get were focused and accurate and, most of the time, even welcome.

And Ty had come upon all this more or less by accident. He was tired of remembering identities, entering passwords and his credit-card information, so he designed code to simplify it all. Did he purposely use the letters of his name in TruYou? He said he realized only afterward the connection. Did he have any idea of the commercial implications of TruYou? He claimed he did not, and most people assumed this was the case, that the monetization of Ty's innovations came from the other two Wise Men, those with the experience and business acumen to make it happen. It was they who monetized TruYou, who found ways to reap funds from all of Ty's innovations, and it was they who grew the company into the force that subsumed Facebook, Twitter, Google, and finally Alacrity, Zoopa, Jefe and Quan.

"Tom doesn't look so good here," Annie noted. "He's not quite that sharky. But I hear he loves this picture."

To the lower left of Ty was Tom Stenton, the world-striding CEO and self-described *Capitalist Prime*—he loved the Transformers—wearing an Italian suit and grinning like the wolf that ate Little Red Riding Hood's grandmother. His hair was dark, at the temples striped in grey, his eyes flat, unreadable. He was more in the mold of the eighties Wall Street traders, unabashed about being wealthy, about being single and aggressive and possibly dangerous. He was a free-spending global titan in his early fifties who seemed stronger every year, who threw his money and influence around without fear. He was unafraid of presidents. He was not daunted by lawsuits from the European Union or threats from state-sponsored Chinese hackers. Nothing was worrisome, nothing was unattainable, nothing was beyond his pay grade. He owned a NASCAR team, a racing yacht or two, piloted his own plane. He was the anachronism at the Circle, the flashy CEO, and created conflicted feelings among many of the utopian young Circlers.

His kind of conspicuous consumption was notably absent from the lives of the other two Wise Men. Ty rented a ramshackle two-bedroom apartment a few miles away, but then again, no one had ever seen him arrive at or leave campus; the assumption was that he lived there. And everyone knew where Eamon Bailey lived—a highly visible, profoundly modest three-bedroom home on a widely accessible street ten minutes from campus. But Stenton had houses everywhere—New York, Dubai, Jackson Hole. A floor atop the Millennium Tower in San Francisco. An island near Martinique.

Eamon Bailey, standing next to him in the painting, seemed utterly at peace, joyful even, in the presence of these men, both of whom were, at least superficially, diametrically opposed to his values. His portrait, to the lower right of Ty's, showed him as he was—grey-haired, ruddy-faced, twinkly-eyed, happy and earnest. He was the public face of the company, the personality everyone associated with the Circle. When he smiled, which was near-constantly, his mouth smiled, his eyes smiled, his shoulders even seemed to smile. He was wry. He was funny. He had a way of speaking that was both lyrical and grounded, giving his audiences wonderful turns of phrase one moment and plainspoken common sense the next. He had come from Omaha, from an exceedingly normal family of six, and had more or less nothing remarkable in his past. He'd gone to Notre Dame and married his girlfriend, who'd gone to Saint Mary's down the road, and now they had four children of their own, three girls and finally a boy, though that boy had been born with cerebral palsy. "He's been touched," Bailey had put it, announcing the birth to the company and the world. "So we'll love him even more."

Of the Three Wise Men, Bailey was the most likely to be seen on campus, to play Dixieland trombone in the company talent show, most likely to appear on talk shows representing the Circle, chuckling when talking about—when shrugging off—this or that FCC investigation, or when unveiling a helpful new feature or game-changing technology. He preferred to be called Uncle Eamon, and when he strode through campus, he did so as would a beloved uncle, a first-term Teddy Roosevelt, accessible and genuine. The three of them, in life and in this portrait, made for a strange bouquet of mismatched flowers, but there was no doubt that it worked. Everyone knew it worked, the three-headed model of management, and the dynamic was thereafter emulated elsewhere in the Fortune 500, with mixed results.

"But so why," Mae asked, "couldn't they afford a real portrait by someone who knows what they're doing?"

The more she looked at it, the stranger it became. The artist had arranged it such that each of the Wise Men had placed a hand on another's shoulder. It made no sense and defied the way arms could bend or stretch.

"Bailey thinks it's hilarious," Annie said. "He wanted it in the main hallway, but Stenton vetoed him. You know Bailey's a collector and all that, right? He's got incredible taste. I mean, he comes across as the good-time guy, as the everyman from Omaha, but he's a connoisseur, too, and is pretty obsessed with preserving the past—even the bad art of the past. Wait till you see his library."

They arrived at an enormous door, which seemed and likely was medieval, something that would have kept barbarians at bay. A pair of giant gargoyle knockers protruded at chest level, and Mae went for the easy gag.

"Nice knockers."

Annie snorted, waved her hand over a blue pad on the wall, and the door opened.

Annie turned to her. "Holy fuck, right?"

It was a three-story library, three levels built around an open atrium, everything fashioned in wood and copper and silver, a symphony of muted color. There were easily ten thousand books, most of them bound in leather, arranged tidily on shelves gleaming with lacquer. Between the books stood stern busts of notable humans, Greeks and Romans, Jefferson and Joan of Arc and MLK. A model of the *Spruce Goose*—or was it the *Enola Gay*?—hung from the ceiling. There were a dozen or so antique globes lit from within, the light buttery and soft, warming various lost nations.

"He bought so much of this stuff when it was about to be auctioned off, or lost. That's his crusade, you know. He goes to these distressed estates, these people who are about to have to sell their treasures at some terrible loss, and he pays market rates for all this, gives the original owners unlimited access to the stuff he's bought. That's who's here a lot, these grey-hairs who come in to read or touch their stuff. Oh you have to see *this*. It'll blow your head off."

Annie led Mae up the three flights of stairs, all of them tiled with intricate mosaics—reproductions, Mae assumed, of something from the Byzantine era. She held the brass rail going up, noting the lack of fingerprints, of any blemish whatsoever. She saw accountants' green reading lamps, telescopes crisscrossed and gleaming in copper and gold, pointing out the many beveled-glass windows—"Oh look up," Annie told her, and she did, to find the ceiling was stained glass, a fevered rendering of countless angels arranged in rings. "That's from some church in Rome."

They arrived at the library's top floor, and Annie led Mae through narrow corridors of round-spined books, some of them as tall as her—Bibles and atlases, illustrated histories of wars and upheavals, long-gone nations and peoples.

"All right. Check this out," Annie said. "Wait. Before I show you this, you have to give me a verbal non-disclosure agreement, okay?"

"Fine."

"Seriously."

"I'm serious. I take this seriously."

"Good. Now when I move this book . . ." Annie said, removing a large volume titled *The Best Years of Our Lives*. "Watch this," she said, and backed up. Slowly, the wall, bearing a hundred books, began to move inward, revealing a secret chamber within. "That's High Nerd, right?" Annie said, and they walked through. Inside, the room was round and lined with books, but the main focus was a hole in the middle of the floor, surrounded by a copper barrier; a pole extended down, through the floor and to unknown regions below.

"Does he fight fires?" Mae asked.

"Hell if I know," Annie said.

"Where does it go?"

"As far as I can tell, it goes to Bailey's parking space."

Mae mustered no adjectives. "You ever go down?"

"Nah, even showing me this was a risk. He shouldn't have. He told me that. And now I'm showing you, which is silly. But it shows you the kind of mind this guy has. He can have anything, and what he wants is a fireman's pole that drops seven stories to the garage."

The sound of a droplet emitted from Annie's earpiece, and she said "Okay" to whomever was on the other end. It was time to go.

"So," Annie said in the elevator—they were dropping back to the main staff floors—"I have to go and do some work. It's plankton-inspection time."

"It's what time?" Mae asked.

"You know, little startups hoping the big whale—that's us—will find them tasty enough to eat. Once a week we take a series of meetings with these guys, Ty-wannabes, and they try to convince us that we need to acquire them. It's a little bit sad, given they don't even pretend to have any revenue, or even potential for it, anymore. Listen, though, I'm going to hand you off to two company ambassadors. They're both very serious about their jobs. Actually, beware of just *how* into their jobs they are. They'll give you a tour of the rest of the campus, and I'll pick you up for the solstice party afterward, okay? Starts at seven."

The doors opened on the second floor, near the Glass Eatery, and Annie introduced her to Denise and Josiah, both in their late-middle-twenties, both with the same level-eyed sincerity, both wearing simple button-down shirts in tasteful colors. Each shook Mae's hand in two of theirs, and almost seemed to bow.

"Make sure she doesn't work today," were Annie's last words before she disappeared back into the elevator.

Josiah, a thin and heavily freckled man, turned his blue unblinking eyes to Mae. "We're so glad to meet you."

Denise, tall, slim, Asian-American, smiled at Mae and closed her eyes, as if savoring the moment. "Annie told us all about you two, how far back you go. Annie's the heart and soul of this place, so we're very lucky to have you here."

"Everyone loves Annie," Josiah added.

Their deference to Mae felt awkward. They were surely older than her, but they behaved as if she were a visiting eminence.

"So I know some of this might be redundant," Josiah said, "but if it's okay we'd like to give you the full newcomer tour. Would that be okay? We promise not to make it lame."

Mae laughed, urged them on, and followed.

The rest of the day was a blur of glass rooms and brief, impossibly warm introductions. Everyone she met was busy, just short of overworked, but nevertheless thrilled to meet her, so happy she was there, any friend of Annie's . . . There was a tour of the health center, and an introduction to the dreadlocked Dr. Hampton who ran it. There was a tour of the emergency clinic and the Scottish nurse who did the admitting. A tour of the organic gardens, a hundred yards square, where there were two full-time farmers giving a talk to a large group of Circlers while they sampled the latest harvest of carrots and tomatoes and kale. There was a tour of the mini-golf area, the movie theater, the bowling alleys, the grocery store. Finally, deep in what Mae assumed was the corner of the campus—she could see the fence beyond, the rooftops of San Vincenzo hotels where visitors to the Circle stayed—they toured the company dorms. Mae had heard something about them, Annie mentioning that sometimes she crashed on campus and now preferred those rooms to her own home. Walking through the hallways, seeing the tidy rooms, each with a shiny kitchenette, a desk, an overstuffed couch and bed, Mae had to agree that the appeal was visceral.

"There are 180 rooms now, but we're growing quickly," Josiah said. "With ten thousand or so people on campus, there's always a percentage of people who work late, or just need a nap during the day. These rooms are always free, always clean—you just have to check online to see which ones are available. Right now they book up fast, but the plan is to have at least a few thousand rooms within the next few years."

"And after a party like tonight's, these are always full," Denise said, with what she meant to be a conspiratorial wink.

The tour continued through the afternoon, with stops to sample food at the culinary class, taught that day by a celebrated young chef known for using the whole of any animal. She presented Mae with a dish called roasted pigface, which Mae ate and discovered tasted like a more fatty bacon; she liked it very much. They passed other visitors as they toured the campus, groups of college students, and packs of vendors, and what appeared to be a senator and his handlers. They passed an arcade stocked with vintage pinball machines and an indoor badminton court, where,

Annie said, a former world champion was kept on retainer. By the time Josiah and Denise had brought her back around to the center of the campus, the light was dimming, and staffers were installing tiki torches in the grass and lighting them. A few thousand Circlers began to gather in the twilight, and standing among them, Mae knew that she never wanted to work—never wanted to be—anywhere else. Her hometown, and the rest of California, the rest of America, seemed like some chaotic mess in the developing world. Outside the walls of the Circle, all was noise and struggle, failure and filth. But here, all had been perfected. The best people had made the best systems and the best systems had reaped funds, unlimited funds, that made possible this, the best place to work. And it was natural that it was so, Mae thought. Who else but utopians could make utopia?

"This party? This is nothing," Annie assured Mae, as they shuffled down the forty-foot buffet. It was dark now, the night air cooling, but the campus was inexplicably warm, and illuminated by hundreds of torches bursting with amber light. "This one's Bailey's idea. Not like he's some Earth Mother, but he gets into the stars, the seasons, so the solstice stuff is his. He'll appear at some point and welcome everyone—usually he does at least. Last year he was in some kind of tanktop. He's very proud of his arms."

Mae and Annie were on the lush lawn, loading their plates and then finding seats in the stone amphitheater built into a high grassy berm. Annie was refilling Mae's glass from a bottle of Riesling that, she said, was made on campus, some kind of new concoction that had fewer calories and more alcohol. Mae looked across the lawn, at the hissing torches arrayed in rows, each row leading revelers to various activities—limbo, kickball, the Electric Slide—none of them related in any way to the solstice. The seeming randomness, the lack of any enforced schedule, made for a party that set low expectations and far exceeded them. Everyone was quickly blitzed, and soon Mae lost Annie, and then got lost entirely, eventually finding her way to the bocce courts, which were being used by a small group of older Circlers, all of them at least thirty, to roll cantaloupes into bowling pins. She made her way back to the lawn, where she joined a game the Circlers were calling "Ha," which seemed to involve nothing more than lying down, with legs or arms or both overlapping. Whenever the person next to you said "Ha" you had to say it, too. It was a terrible game, but for the time being, Mae needed it, because her head was spinning, and she felt better horizontal.

"Look at this one. She looks so peaceful." It was a voice close by. Mae realized the voice, a man's, was referring to her, and she opened her eyes. She saw no one above her. Only sky, which was mostly clear, with wisps of grey clouds moving swiftly across the campus and heading out to sea. Mae's eyes felt heavy, and she knew it was not late, not past ten anyway, and she didn't want to do what she often did, which was fall asleep after two or three drinks, so she got up and went looking for Annie or more Riesling or both. She found the buffet, and found it in shambles, a feast raided by animals or Vikings, and made her way to the nearest bar, which was out of Riesling and was now offering only some kind of vodka-and-energy drink concoction. She moved on, asking random passersby about Riesling, until she felt a shadow pass before her.

"There's more over here," the shadow said.

Mae turned to find a pair of glasses reflecting blue, sitting atop the vague shape of a man. He turned to walk away.

"Am I following you?" Mae asked.

"Not yet. You're standing still. But you should if you want more of that wine."

She followed the shadow across the lawn and under a canopy of high trees, the moonlight shooting through, a hundred silver spears. Now Mae could see the shadow better—he was wearing a sand-colored T-shirt and some kind of vest, leather or suede, over it—a combination Mae hadn't seen in some time. Then he stopped and was crouching down near the bottom of a waterfall, a manmade waterfall coming down the side of the Industrial Revolution.

"I hid a few bottles here," he said, his hands deep in the pool that received the falling water. Not finding anything, he kneeled down, his arms submerged to the shoulder, until he retrieved two sleek green bottles, stood up and turned to her. Finally she got a good look at him. His face was a soft triangle, concluding in a chin so subtly dimpled she hadn't seen it before that moment. He had the skin of a child, the eyes of a much older man and a prominent nose, crooked and bent but somehow giving stability to the rest of his face, like the keel of a yacht. His eyebrows were heavy dashes rushing away, toward his ears, which were rounded, large, princess-pink. "You want to go back to the game or . . . ?" He seemed to be implying that the "or" could be far better.

"Sure," she said, realizing that she didn't know this person, knew nothing about him. But because he had those bottles, and because she'd lost Annie, and because she trusted everyone

33

within these Circle walls—she had at that moment so much love for everyone within those walls, where everything was new and everything allowed—she followed him back to the party, to the outskirts of it anyway, where they sat on a high ring of steps over-looking the lawn, and watched the silhouettes run and squeal and fall below.

He opened both bottles, gave one to Mae, took a sip from his, and said his name was Francis.

"Not Frank?" she asked. She took the bottle and filled her mouth with the candysweet wine.

"People try to call me that and I . . . I ask them not to."

She laughed, and he laughed.

He was a developer, he said, and had been at the company for almost two years. Before that he'd been a kind of anarchist, a provocateur. He'd gotten the job here by hacking further into the Circle system than anyone else. Now he was on the security team.

"This is my first day," Mae noted.

"No way."

And then Mae, who intended to say "I shit you not," instead decided to innovate, but something got garbled during her verbal innovation, and she uttered the words "I fuck you not," knowing almost instantly that she would remember these words, and hate herself for them, for decades to come.

"You fuck me not?" he asked, deadpan. "That sounds very conclusive. You've made a decision with very little information. You fuck me not. Wow."

Mae tried to explain what she meant to say, how she thought, or some department of her brain thought, that she would turn the phrase around a bit . . . But it didn't matter. He was laugh-

34

ing now, and he knew she had a sense of humor, and she knew he did, too, and somehow he made her feel safe, made her trust that he would never bring it up again, that this terrible thing she said would remain between them, that they both understood mistakes are made by all and that they should, if everyone is acknowledging our common humanity, our common frailty and propensity for sounding and looking ridiculous a thousand times a day, that these mistakes should be allowed to be forgotten.

"First day," he said. "Well, congratulations. A toast."

They clinked bottles and took sips. Mae held her bottle up to the moon to see how much was left; the liquid turned an otherworldly blue and she saw that she'd already swallowed half. She put the bottle down.

"I like your voice," he said. "Was it always that way?"

"Low and scratchy?"

"I would call it *seasoned*. I would call it *soulful*. You know Tatum O'Neal?"

"My parents made me watch *Paper Moon* a hundred times. They wanted me to feel better."

"I love that movie," he said.

"They thought I'd grow up like Addie Pray, streetwise but adorable. They wanted a tomboy. They cut my hair like hers."

"I like it."

"You like bowl cuts."

"No. Your voice. So far it's the best thing about you."

Mae said nothing. She felt like she'd been slapped.

"Shit," he said. "Did that sound weird? I was trying to give you a compliment."

There was a troubling pause; Mae had had a few terrible experiences with men who spoke too well, who leaped over any number of steps to land on inappropriate compliments. She turned to him, to confirm he was not what she thought he was—generous, harmless—but actually warped, troubled, asymmetrical. But when she looked at him, she saw the same smooth face, blue glasses, ancient eyes. His expression was pained.

He looked at his bottle, as if to lay the blame there. "I just wanted to make you feel better about your voice. But I guess I insulted the rest of you."

Mae thought on that for a second, but her brain, addled with Riesling, was slow-moving, sticky. She gave up trying to parse his statement or his intentions. "I think you're strange," she said.

"I don't have parents," he said. "Does that buy me some forgiveness?" Then, realizing he was revealing too much, and too desperately, he said, "You're not drinking."

Mae decided to let him drop the subject of his childhood. "I'm already done," she said. "I've gotten the full effect."

"I'm really sorry. I sometimes get my words in the wrong order. I'm happiest when I don't talk at something like this."

"You are really strange," Mae said again, and meant it. She was twenty-four, and he was unlike anyone she'd ever known. That was, she thought drunkenly, evidence of God, was it not? That she could encounter thousands of people in her life thus far, so many of them similar, so many of them forgettable, but then there is this person, new and bizarre and speaking bizarrely. Every day some scientist discovered a new species of frog or waterlily, and that, too, seemed to confirm some divine showman, some celestial inventor putting new toys before us, hidden but hidden poorly, just where we might happen upon them. And this Francis person, he was something entirely different, some new frog. Mae turned to look at him, thinking she might kiss him.

But he was busy. With one hand, he was emptying his shoe, sand pouring from it. With the other he seemed to be biting off most of his fingernail.

Her reverie ended, she thought of home and bed.

"How will everyone get back?" she asked.

Francis looked out at a scrum of people who seemed to be trying to form a pyramid. "There's the dorms, of course. But I bet those are full already. There are always a few shuttles ready, too. They probably told you that." He waved his bottle in the direction of the main entrance, where Mae could make out the rooftops of the minibuses she'd seen that morning on her way in. "The company does cost analyses on everything. And one staffer driving home too tired or, in this case, too drunk to drive—well, the cost of shuttles is a lot cheaper in the long run. Don't tell me you didn't come for the shuttle buses. The shuttle buses are awesome. Inside they're like yachts. Lots of compartments and wood."

"Lots of wood? Lots of wood?" Mae punched Francis in the arm, knowing she was flirting, knowing it was idiotic to flirt with a fellow Circler on her first night, that it was idiotic to drink this much on her first night. But she was doing all those things and was happy about it.

A figure was gliding toward them. Mae watched with dull curiosity, realizing first that the figure was female. And then that this figure was Annie.

"Is this man harassing you?" she asked.

Francis moved quickly away from Mae, and then hid his bottle behind his back. Annie laughed.

"Francis, what are you so squirrelly about?"

"Sorry. I thought you said something else."

"Whoa. Guilty conscience! I saw Mae here punch you in the arm and I made a joke. But are you trying to confess something? What have you been planning, Francis Garbanzo?"

"Garaventa."

"Yes. I know your name."

"Francis," Annie said, dropping herself clumsily between them, "I need to ask you something, as your esteemed colleague but also as your friend. Can I do that?"

"Sure."

"Good. Can I have some alone time with Mae? I need to kiss her on the mouth."

Francis laughed, then stopped, noticing that neither Mae nor Annie was laughing. Scared and confused, and visibly intimidated by Annie, he was soon walking down the steps, and across the lawn, dodging revelers. Halfway across the green he stopped, turned back and looked up, as if making sure Annie intended to replace him as Mae's companion that night. His fears confirmed, he walked under the awning of the Dark Ages. He tried to open the door, but couldn't. He pulled and pushed, but it would not budge. Knowing they were watching, he made his way around the corner and out of view.

"He's in security, he says," Mae said.

"That's what he told you? Francis Garaventa?"

"I guess he shouldn't have."

"Well, it's not like he's in security-security. He's not Mossad. But did I interrupt something you definitely shouldn't be doing on your first night here, you idiot?"

"You didn't interrupt anything."

"I think I *did*."

"No. Not really."

"I did. I know this."

Annie located the bottle at Mae's feet. "I thought we ran out of everything hours ago."

"There was some wine in the waterfall—by the Industrial Revolution."

"Oh, right. People hide things there."

"I just heard myself say, 'There was some wine in the waterfall by the Industrial Revolution.' "

Annie looked across the campus. "I know. Shit. I know."

At home, after the shuttle, after a Jell-O shot someone gave her on board, after listening to the shuttle driver talk wistfully about his family, his twins, his wife, who had gout, Mae couldn't sleep. She lay on her cheap futon, in her tiny room, in the railroad apartment she shared with two near-strangers, both of them flight attendants and rarely seen. Her apartment was on the second floor of a former motel and it was humble, uncleanable, smelling of the desperation and bad cooking of its former residents. It was a sad place, especially after a day at the Circle, where all was made with care and love and the gift of a good eye. In her wretched low bed, Mae slept for a few hours, woke up, recounted the day and the night, thought of Annie and Francis, and Denise and Josiah, and the fireman's pole, and the *Enola Gay,* and the waterfall, and the tiki torches, all of these things the stuff of vacations and dreams and impossible to maintain, but then she knew—and this is what was keeping her up, her head careening with something like a toddler's joy—that she would be going back to that place, the place where all these things happened. She was welcome there, employed there.

She got to work early. When she arrived, though, at eight, she realized she hadn't been given a desk, at least not a real desk, and so she had nowhere to go. She waited an hour, under a sign that said LET'S DO THIS. LET'S DO ALL OF THIS, until Renata arrived and brought her to the second floor of the Renaissance, into a large room, the size of a basketball court, where there were about twenty desks, all different, all shaped from blond wood into desktops of organic shapes. They were separated by dividers of glass, and arranged in groups of five, like petals on a flower. None were occupied.

"You're the first here," Renata said, "but you won't be alone for long. Each new Customer Experience area tends to fill pretty quickly. And you're not far from all the more senior people." And here she swept her arm around, indicating about a dozen offices surrounding the open space. The occupants of each were visible through the glass walls, each of the supervisors somewhere between twenty-six and thirty-two, starting their day, seeming relaxed, competent, wise.

"The designers really like glass, eh?" Mae said, smiling.

Renata stopped, furrowed her brow and thought on this notion. She put a strand of hair behind her ear and said, "I think so. I can check. But first we should explain the setup, and what to expect on your first real day."

Renata explained the features of the desk and chair and screen, all of which had been ergonomically perfected, and could be adjusted for those who wanted to work standing up.

"You can set your stuff down and adjust your chair, and— Oh, looks like you have a welcoming committee. Don't get up," she said, and made way.

Mae followed Renata's eyeline and saw a trio of young faces making their way to her. A balding man in his late twenties extended his hand. Mae shook it, and he put an oversized tablet on the desk in front of her.

"Hi Mae, I'm Rob from payroll. Bet you're glad to see *me*." He smiled then laughed heartily, as if he'd just realized anew the humor in his repartee. "Okay," he said, "we've filled out everything here. There's just these three places you need to sign." He pointed to the screen, where yellow rectangles flashed, asking for her signature.

When she was finished, Rob took the tablet and smiled with great warmth. "Thank you, and welcome aboard."

He turned and left, and was replaced by a full-figured woman with flawless, copper skin.

"Hi Mae, I'm Tasha, the notary." She held out a wide book. "You have your driver's license?" Mae gave it to her. "Great. I need three signatures from you. Don't ask me why. And don't ask me why this is on paper. Government rules." Tasha pointed to three consecutive boxes, and Mae signed her name in each.

"Thank you," Tasha said, and now held out a blue inkpad. "Now your fingerprint next to each. Don't worry, this ink won't stain. You'll see."

Mae pushed her thumb into the pad, and then into the boxes next to each of her three signatures. The ink was visible on the page, but when Mae looked at her thumb, it was absolutely clean.

Tasha's eyebrows arched, registering Mae's delight. "See? It's invisible. The only place it shows up is in this book."

This was the sort of thing Mae had come for. Everything was done better here. Even the *fingerprint ink* was advanced, invisible.

When Tasha left she was replaced by a thin man in a red zippered shirt. He shook Mae's hand.

"Hi, I'm Jon. I emailed you yesterday about bringing your birth certificate?" His hands came together, as if in prayer.

Mae retrieved the certificate from her bag and Jon's eyes lit up. "You brought it!" He clapped quickly, silently, and revealed a mouth of tiny teeth. "*No one* remembers the first time. You're my new favorite." He took the certificate, promising to return it after he'd made a copy.

Behind him was a fourth staff member, this one a beatific-looking man of about thirty-five, by far the oldest person Mae had met that day.

"Hi Mae. I'm Brandon, and I have the honor of giving you your new tablet." He was holding a gleaming object, translucent, its edges black and smooth as obsidian.

Mae was stunned. "These haven't been *released* yet."

Brandon smiled broadly. "It's four times as fast as its predecessor. I've been playing with mine all week. It's very cool."

"And I get one?"

"You already did," he said. "It's got your name on it."

He turned the tablet on its side to reveal that it had been inscribed with Mae's full name: MAEBELLINE RENNER HOLLAND.

He handed it to her. It was the weight of a paper plate.

"Now, I'm assuming you have your own tablet?"

"I do. Well, a laptop anyway."

"Laptop. Wow. Can I see it?"

Mae pointed to it. "Now I feel like I should chuck it in the trash."

Brandon paled. "No, don't do that! At least recycle it."

"Oh, no. I was just kidding," Mae said. "I'll probably hold on to it. I have all my stuff on it."

"Good segue, Mae! That's what I'm here to do next. We should transfer all your stuff to the new tablet."

"Oh. I can do that."

"Would you grant me the honor? I've trained all my life for this very moment."

Mae laughed and pushed her chair out of the way. Brandon knelt next to her desk and put the new tablet next to her laptop. In minutes he had transferred all her information and accounts.

"Okay. Now let's do the same with your phone. Ta-da." He reached into his bag and unveiled a new phone, a few significant steps ahead of her own. Like the tablet, it had her name already engraved on the back. He set both phones, new and old, on the desk next to each other and quickly, wirelessly, transferred everything within from one to the other.

"Okay. Now everything you had on your other phone and on your hard drive is accessible here on the tablet and your new phone, but it's also backed up in the cloud and on our servers. Your music, your photos, your messages, your data. It can never be lost. You lose this tablet or phone, it takes exactly six minutes to retrieve all your stuff and dump it on the next one. It'll be here next year and next century."

They both looked at the new devices.

"I wish our system existed ten years ago," he said. "I fried two different hard drives back then, and it's like having your house burn down with all your belongings inside."

Brandon stood up.

"Thank you," Mae said.

"No sweat," he said. "And this way we can send you updates for the software, the apps, everything, and know you're current. Everyone in CE has to be on the same version of any given software, as you can imagine. I think that's it . . ." he said, backing away. Then he stopped. "Oh, and it's crucial that all company devices are password protected, so I gave you one. It's written here." He handed her a slip of paper bearing a series of digits and numerals and obscure typographical symbols. "I hope you can memorize it today and then throw this away. Deal?"

"Yes. Deal."

"We can change the password later if you want. Just let me know and I'll give you a new one. They're all computer-generated."

Mae took her old laptop and moved it toward her bag.

Brandon looked at it like it was an invasive species. "You want me to get rid of it? We do it in a very environmentally friendly way."

"Maybe tomorrow," she said, "I want to say goodbye."

Brandon smiled indulgently. "Oh. I get it. Okay then." He gave a bow and left, and behind him she saw Annie. She was holding her knuckle up to her chin, tilting her head.

"There's my little girl, grown up at last!"

Mae got up and wrapped her arms around her.

"Thank you," she said into Annie's neck.

"Awww." Annie tried to pull away.

Mae grabbed her tighter. "Really."

"It's okay." Annie finally extricated herself. "Easy there. Or maybe keep going. It was starting to get sexy."

"Really. Thank you," Mae said, her voice quaking.

"No, no, no," Annie said. "No crying on your second day."

"I'm sorry. I'm just so grateful."

"Stop." Annie moved in and held her again. "Stop. Stop. Jesus. You are such a freak."

Mae breathed deeply, until she was calm again. "I think I have it under control now. Oh, my dad says he loves you, too. Everyone's so happy."

"Okay. That's a little strange, given I've never met him. But tell him I love him, too. Passionately. Is he hot? A silver fox? A swinger? Maybe we can work something out. Now can we get to work around here?"

"Yup, yup," Mae said, sitting down again. "Sorry."

Annie arched her eyebrows mischievously. "I feel like school's about to start and we just found out we got put in the same homeroom. They give you a new tablet?"

"Just now."

"Let me see." Annie inspected it. "Ooh, the engraving is a nice touch. We're going to get in such trouble together, aren't we?"

"I hope so."

"Okay, here comes your team leader. Hi Dan."

Mae rushed to wipe any moisture from her face. She looked past Annie to see a handsome man, compact and tidy, approaching. He wore a brown hoodie and a smile of great contentment.

"Hi Annie, how are you?" he said, shaking her hand.

"Good, Dan."

"I'm so glad, Annie."

"You got a good one here, I hope you know," Annie said, grabbing Mae's wrist and squeezing.

"Oh I *do* know," he said.

"You watch out for her."

"I will," he said, and turned from Annie to Mae. His smile of contentment grew into something like absolute certainty.

"I'll be watching *you* watch *her*," Annie said.

"Glad to know it," he said.

"See you at lunch," Annie said to Mae, and was gone.

Everyone but Mae and Dan had left, but his smile hadn't changed—it was the smile of a man who did not smile for show. It was the smile of a man who was exactly where he wanted to be. He pulled up a chair.

"So good to see you here," he said. "I'm very glad you accepted our offer."

Mae looked into his eyes for signs of disingenuousness, given there was no rational person who would have declined an invitation to work here. But there was nothing like that. Dan had interviewed her three times for the job, and had seemed unshakably sincere each time.

"So I assume all the paperwork and fingerprints are done?"

"I think so."

"Like to take a walk?"

They left her desk and, after a hundred yards of glass hallway, walked through high double doors and into the open air. They climbed a wide stairway.

"We just finished the roofdeck," he said. "I think you'll like it."

46

When they reached the top of the stairs, the view was spectacular. The roof overlooked most of the campus, the surrounding city of San Vincenzo and the bay beyond. Mae and Dan took it all in, and then he turned to her.

"Mae, now that you're aboard, I wanted to get across some of the core beliefs here at the company. And chief among them is that just as important as the work we do here—and that work is very important—we want to make sure that you can be a human being here, too. We want this to be a workplace, sure, but it should also be a *human*place. And that means the fostering of community. In fact, it *must* be a community. That's one of our slogans, as you probably know: *Community First*. And you've seen the signs that say *Humans Work Here*—I insist on those. That's my pet issue. We're not automatons. This isn't a sweatshop. We're a group of the best minds of our generation. Genera*tions*. And making sure this is a place where our humanity is respected, where our opinions are dignified, where our voices are heard—this is as important as any revenue, any stock price, any endeavor undertaken here. Does that sound corny?"

"No, no," Mae rushed to say. "Definitely not. That's why I'm here. I love the 'community first' idea. Annie's been telling me about it since she started. At my last job, no one really communicated very well. It was basically the opposite of here in every way."

Dan turned to look into the hills to the east, covered in mohair and patches of green. "I hate hearing that kind of thing. With the technology available, communication should never be in doubt. Understanding should never be out of reach or anything but clear. It's what we do here. You might say it's the mission of the company—it's an obsession of mine, anyway. Communication. Understanding. Clarity."

Dan nodded emphatically, as if his mouth had just uttered, independently, something that his ears found quite profound.

"In the Renaissance, as you know, we're in charge of the customer experience, CE, and some people might think that's the least sexy part of this whole enterprise. But as I see it, and the Wise Men see it, it's the foundation of everything that happens here. If we don't give the customers a satisfying, human and *humane* experience, then we have no customers. It's pretty elemental. We're the proof that this company is human."

Mae didn't know what to say. She agreed completely. Her last boss, Kevin, couldn't talk like this. Kevin had no philosophy. Kevin had no ideas. Kevin had only his odors and his mustache. Mae was grinning like an idiot.

"I know you'll be great here," he said, and his arm extended toward her, as if he wanted to put his palm on her shoulder but thought against it. His hand fell to his side. "Let's go downstairs and you can get started."

They left the roofdeck and descended the wide stairs. They returned to her desk, where they saw a fuzzy-haired man.

"There he is," Dan said. "Early as always. Hi Jared."

Jared's face was serene, unlined, his hands resting patiently and unmoving in his ample lap. He was wearing khaki pants and a button-down shirt a size too small.

"Jared will be doing your training, and he'll be your main contact here at CE. I oversee the team, and Jared oversees the unit. So we're the two main names you'll need to know. Jared, you ready to get Mae started?"

"I am," he said. "Hi Mae." He stood, extending his hand, and Mae shook it. It was rounded and soft, like a cherub's.

Dan said goodbye to both of them and left.

Jared grinned and ran a hand through his fuzzy hair. "So, training time. You feel ready?"

"Absolutely."

"You need coffee or tea or anything?"

Mae shook her head. "I'm all set."

"Good. Let's sit down."

Mae sat down, and Jared pulled his chair next to hers.

"Okay. As you know, for now you're just doing straight-up customer maintenance for the smaller advertisers. They send a message to Customer Experience, and it gets routed to one of us. Random at first, but once you start working with a customer, that customer will continue to be routed to you, for the sake of continuity. When you get the query, you figure out the answer, you write them back. That's the core of it. Simple enough in theory. So far so good?"

Mae nodded, and he went through the twenty most common requests and questions, and showed her a menu of boilerplate responses.

"Now, that doesn't mean you just paste the answer in and send it back. You should make each response personal, specific. You're a person, and they're a person, so you shouldn't be imitating a robot, and you shouldn't treat them like they're robots. Know what I mean? No robots work here. We never want the customer to think they're dealing with a faceless entity, so you should always be sure to inject humanity into the process. That sound good?"

Mae nodded. She liked that: *No robots work here.*

They went through a dozen or so practice scenarios, and Mae polished her answers a bit more each time. Jared was a patient trainer, and walked her through every customer eventuality. In the event that she was stumped, she could bounce the query to his own queue, and he'd take it. That's what he did most of the day, Jared said—take and answer the stumpers from the junior Customer Experience reps.

"But those will be pretty rare. You'd be surprised at how many of the questions you'll be able to field right away. Now let's say you've answered a client's question, and they seem satisfied. That's when you send them the survey, and they fill it out. It's a set of quick questions about your service, their overall experience, and at the end they're asked to rate it. They send the questions back, and then you immediately know how you did. The rating pops up here."

He pointed to the corner of her screen, where there was a large number, 99, and below, a grid of other numbers.

"The big 99 is the last customer's rating. The customer will rate you on a scale of, guess what, 1 to 100. That most recent rating will pop up here, and then that'll be averaged with the rest of the day's scores in this next box. That way you'll always know how you're doing, recently and generally. Now, I know what you're thinking, 'Okay, Jared, what kind of average is average?' And the answer is, if it dips below 95, then you might step back and see what you can do better. Maybe you bring the average up with the next customer, maybe you see how you might improve. Now, if it's consistently slumping, then you might have a meet-up with Dan or another team leader to go over some best practices. Sound good?"

"It does," Mae said. "I really appreciate this, Jared. In my previous job, I was in the dark about where I stood until, like, quarterly evaluations. It was nerve-wracking."

"Well, you'll love this then. If they fill out the survey and do the rating, and pretty much everyone does, then you send them the next message. This one thanks them for filling out the survey, and it encourages them to tell a friend about the experience they just had with you, using the Circle's social media tools. Ideally they at least zing it or give you a smile or a frown. In a best-case scenario, you might get them to zing about it or write about it on another customer-service site. We get people out there zinging about their great customer service experiences with you, then everyone wins. Got it?"

"Got it."

"Okay, let's do a live one. Ready?"

Mae wasn't, but couldn't say that. "Ready."

Jared brought up a customer request, and after reading it, let out a quick snort to indicate its elementary nature. He chose a boilerplate answer, adapted it a bit, told the customer to have a fantastic day. The exchange took about ninety seconds, and two minutes later, the screen confirmed the customer had answered the questionnaire, and a score appeared: 99. Jared sat back and turned to Mae.

"Now, that's good, right? Ninety-nine is good. But I can't help wondering why it wasn't a 100. Let's look." He opened up the customer's survey answers and scanned through. "Well, there's no clear sign that any part of their experience was unsatisfactory. Now, most companies would say, Wow, 99 out of 100 points, that's nearly perfect. And I say, exactly: it's *nearly* perfect, sure.

But at the Circle, that missing point nags at us. So let's see if we can get to the bottom of it. Here's a follow-up that we send out."

He showed her another survey, this one shorter, asking the customer what about their interaction could have been improved and how. They sent it to the customer.

Seconds later, the response came back. "All was good. Sorry. Should have given you a 100. Thanks!!"

Jared tapped the screen and gave a thumbs-up to Mae.

"Okay. Sometimes you might just encounter someone who isn't really sensitive to the metrics. So it's good to ask them, to make sure you get that clarity. Now we're back to a perfect score. You ready to do your own?"

"I am."

They downloaded another customer query, and Mae scrolled through the boilerplates, found the appropriate answer, personalized it, and sent it back. When the survey came back, her rating was 100.

Jared seemed briefly taken aback. "First one you get 100, wow," he said. "I knew you'd be good." He had lost his footing, but now regained it. "Okay, I think you're ready to take on some more. Now, a couple more things. Let's turn on your second screen." He turned on a smaller screen to her right. "This one is for intra-office messaging. All Circlers send messages out through your main feed, but they appear on the second screen. This is to make clear the importance of the messages, and to help you delineate which is which. From time to time you'll see messages from me over here, just checking in or with some adjustment or news. Okay?"

"Got it."

"Now, remember to bounce any stumpers to me, and if you need to stop and talk, you can shoot me a message, or stop by. I'm just down the hall. I expect you to be in touch pretty frequently for the first few weeks, one way or the other. That's how I know you're learning. So don't hesitate."

"I won't."

"Great. Now, are you ready to get *started*-started?"

"I am."

"Okay. That means I open the chute. And when I release this deluge on you, you'll have your own queue, and you'll be inundated for the next two hours, till lunch. You ready?"

Mae felt she was. "I am."

"Are you sure? Okay then."

He activated her account, gave her a mock-salute, and left. The chute opened, and in the first twelve minutes, she answered four requests, her score at 96. She was sweating heavily, but the rush was electric.

A message from Jared appeared on her second screen. *Great so far! Let's see if we can get that up to 97 soon.*

I will! she wrote.

And send follow-ups to the sub-100s.

Okay, she wrote.

She sent out seven follow-ups, and three customers adjusted their scores to 100. She answered another ten questions by 11:45. Now her aggregate was 98.

Another message appeared on her second screen, this one from Dan. *Fantastic work, Mae! How you feeling?*

Mae was astonished. A team leader who checked in with you, and so kindly, on the first day?

Fine. Thanks! she wrote back, and brought up the next customer request.

Another message from Jared appeared below the first.

Anything I can do? Questions I can answer?

No thanks! she wrote. *I'm all set for now. Thanks, Jared!* She returned to the first screen. Another message from Jared popped up on the second.

Remember that I can only help if you tell me how.

Thanks again! she wrote.

By lunch she had answered thirty-six requests and her score was at 97.

A message from Jared came through. *Well done! Let's follow up on any remaining sub-100s.*

Will do, she answered, and sent out the follow-ups to those she hadn't already handled. She brought a few 98s to 100 and then saw a message from Dan: *Great work, Mae!*

Seconds later, a second-screen message, this one from Annie, appeared below Dan's: *Dan says you're kicking ass. That's my girl!*

And then a message told her she'd been mentioned on Zing. She clicked over to read it. It was written by Annie. *Newbie Mae is kicking ass!* She'd sent it out to the rest of the Circle campus—10,041 people.

The zing was forwarded 322 times and there were 187 follow-up comments. They appeared on her second screen in an ever-lengthening thread. Mae didn't have time to read them all, but she scrolled quickly through, and the validation felt good. At the end of the day, Mae's score was 98. Congratulatory messages arrived from Jared and Dan and Annie. A series of zings followed, announcing and celebrating what Annie called *the highest score of any CE newb ever of all time suck it.*

By her first Friday Mae had served 436 customers and had memorized the boilerplates. Nothing surprised her anymore, though the variation in customers and their businesses was dizzying. The Circle was everywhere, and though she'd known this for years, intuitively, hearing from these people, the businesses counting on the Circle to get the word out about their products, to track their digital impact, to know who was buying their wares and when—it became real on a very different level. Mae now had customer contacts in Clinton, Louisiana, and Putney, Vermont; in Marmaris, Turkey, and Melbourne and Glasgow and Kyoto. Invariably they were polite in their queries—the legacy of TruYou—and gracious in their ratings.

By midmorning that Friday, her aggregate for the week was at 97, and the affirmations were coming from everyone in the Circle. The work was demanding, and the flow did not stop, but it varied just enough, and the validation was frequent enough, that she settled into a comfortable rhythm.

Just as she was about to take another request, a text came through her phone. It was Annie: *Eat with me, fool.*

They sat on a low hill, two salads between them, the sun making intermittent appearances behind slow-moving clouds. Mae and Annie watched a trio of young men, pale and dressed like engineers, attempting to throw a football.

"So you're already a star. I feel like a proud mama."

Mae shook her head. "I'm not at all. I have a lot to learn."

"Of course you do. But a 97 so far? That's insane. I didn't get above 95 the first week. You're a natural."

A pair of shadows darkened their lunch.

"Can we meet the newbie?"

Mae looked up, shielding her eyes.

"Course," Annie said.

The shadows sat down. Annie jabbed her fork at them. "This is Sabine and Josef."

Mae shook their hands. Sabine was blond, sturdy, squinting. Josef was thin, pale, with comically bad teeth.

"Already she's looking at my teeth!" he wailed, pointing to Mae. "You Americans are *obsessed*! I feel like a horse at an auction."

"But your teeth *are* bad," Annie said. "And we have such a good dental plan here."

Josef unwrapped a burrito. "I think my teeth provide a necessary respite from the eerie perfection of everyone else's."

Annie tilted her head, studying him. "I'm sure you *should* fix them, if not for you for the sake of company morale. You give people nightmares."

Josef pouted theatrically, his mouth full of carne asada. Annie patted his arm.

Sabine turned to Mae. "So you're in Customer Experience?" Now Mae noticed the tattoo on Sabine's arm, the symbol for infinity.

"I am. First week."

"I saw you're doing pretty well so far. I started there, too. Just about everyone did."

"And Sabine's a biochemist," Annie added.

Mae was surprised. "You're a biochemist?"

"I am."

Mae hadn't heard about biochemists working at the Circle. "Can I ask what you're working on?"

"Can you *ask*?" Sabine smiled. "Of course you can *ask*. But I don't have to tell you anything."

Everyone sighed for a moment, but then Sabine stopped.

"Seriously though, I can't tell you. Not right now, anyway. Generally I work on stuff for the biometric side of things. You know, iris scanning and facial recognition. But right now I'm on something new. Even though I'd like to—"

Annie gave Sabine an imploring, quieting look. Sabine filled her mouth with lettuce.

"Anyway," Annie said, "Josef here is in Educational Access. He's trying to get tablets into schools that right now can't afford them. He's a do-gooder. He's also friends with your new friend. Garbonzo."

"Garaventa," Mae corrected.

"Ah. You *do* remember. Have you seen him again?"

"Not this week. It's been too busy."

Now Josef's mouth was open. Something had just dawned on him. "Are you Mae?"

Annie winced. "We already said that. Of course this is Mae."

"Sorry. I didn't hear it right. Now I know who you are."

Annie snorted. "What, did you two little girls tell each other all about Francis's big night? He's been writing Mae's name in his notebook, surrounded by hearts?"

Josef inhaled indulgently. "No, he just said he'd met someone very nice, and her name was Mae."

"That's so sweet," Sabine said.

"He told her he was in security," Annie said. "Why would he do that, Josef?"

"That's not what he said," Mae insisted. "I told you that."

Annie didn't seem to care. "Well, I guess you could call it security. He's in child safety. He's basically the core of this whole program to prevent abductions. He actually could do it."

Sabine, her mouth full again, was nodding vigorously. "Of course he will," she said, spraying fragments of salad and vinaigrette. "It's a done deal."

"What is?" Mae asked. "He's going to prevent all abductions?"

"He could," Josef said. "He's motivated."

Annie's eyes went wide. "Did he tell you about his sisters?"

Mae shook her head. "No, he didn't say he had siblings. What about his sisters?"

All three Circlers looked at each other, as if to gauge if the story had to be told there and then.

"It's the worst story," Annie said. "His parents were such fuck-ups. I think there were like four or five kids in the family, and Francis was youngest or second-youngest, and anyway the dad was in jail, and the mom was on drugs, so the kids were sent all over the place. I think one went to his aunt and uncle, and his two sisters were sent to some foster home, and then they were abducted from there. I guess there was some doubt if they were, you know, given or sold to the murderers."

"The what?" Mae had gone limp.

"Oh god, they were raped and kept in closets and their bodies were dropped down some kind of abandoned missile silo. I mean, it was the worst story ever. He told a bunch of us about it when he was pitching this child safety program. Shit, look at your face. I shouldn't have said all this."

Mae couldn't speak.

"It's important that you know," Josef said. "This is why he's so passionate. I mean, his plan would pretty much eliminate the possibility of anything like this ever happening again. Wait. What time is it?"

Annie checked her phone. "You're right. We gotta scoot. Bailey's doing an unveiling. We should be in the Great Hall."

The Great Hall was in the Enlightenment, and when they entered the venue, a 3,500-seat cavern appointed in warm woods and brushed steel, it was loud with anticipation. Mae and Annie found one of the last pairs of seats in the second balcony and sat down.

"Just finished this a few months ago," Annie said. "Forty-five million dollars. Bailey modeled the stripes off the Duomo in Siena. Nice, right?"

Mae's attention was pulled to the stage, where a man was walking to a lucite podium, amid a roar of applause. He was a tall man of about forty-five, round in the gut but not unhealthy, wearing jeans and blue V-neck sweater. There was no discernible microphone, but when he began speaking, his voice was amplified and clear.

"Hello everyone. My name is Eamon Bailey," he said, to another round of applause that he quickly discouraged. "Thank you. I'm so glad to see you all here. A bunch of you are new to the company since I last spoke, one whole month ago. Can the newbies stand up?" Annie nudged Mae. Mae stood, and looked around the auditorium to see about sixty other people standing, most of them her age, all of them seeming shy, all of them quietly stylish, together representing every race and ethnicity and, thanks to the Circle's efforts to ease permits for international staffers, a dizzying range of national origins. The clapping from the rest of the Circlers was loud, a sprinkling of whoops mixed in. She sat down.

"You're so cute when you blush," Annie said.

Mae sunk into her seat.

"Newbies," Bailey said, "you're in for something special. This is called Dream Friday, where we present something we're working on. Often it's one of our engineers or designers or visionaries, and sometimes it's just me. And today, for better or for worse, it's just me. For that I apologize in advance."

"We love you Eamon!" came a voice from the audience. Laughter followed.

"Well, thank you," he said, "I love you back. I love you as the grass loves the dew, as the birds love a bough." He paused briefly, allowing Mae to catch her breath. She'd seen these talks online, but being here, in person, seeing Bailey's mind at work, hearing his off-the-cuff eloquence—it was better than she thought possible. What would it be like, she thought, to be someone like that, eloquent and inspirational, so at ease in front of thousands?

"Yes," he continued, "it's been a whole month since I've gotten up on this stage, and I know my replacements have been unsatisfying. I am sorry to deprive you of myself. I realize there is no substitute." The joke brought laughter throughout the hall. "And I know a lot of you have been wondering just where the heck I've been."

A voice from the front of the room yelled "surfing!" and the room laughed.

"Well, that's right. I have been doing some surfing, and that's part of what I'm here to talk about. I love to surf, and when I want to surf, I need to know how the waves are. Now, it used to be that you'd wake up and call the local surf shop and ask them about the breaks. And pretty soon they stopped answering their phones."

Knowing laughter came from the older contingent in the room.

"When cell phones proliferated, you could call your buddies who might have gotten out to the beach before you. They, too, stopped answering their phones."

Another big laugh from the audience.

"Seriously, though. It's not practical to make twelve calls every morning, and can you trust someone else's take on the conditions? The surfers don't want any more bodies on the limited breaks we get up here. So then the internet happened, and here and there some geniuses set up cameras on the beaches. We could log on and get some pretty crude images of the waves at Stinson Beach. It was almost worse than calling the surf shop! The technology was pretty primitive. Streaming technology still is. Or was. Until now."

A screen descended behind him.

"Okay. Here's how it used to look."

The screen showed a standard browser display, and an unseen hand typed in the url for a website called SurfSight. A poorly designed site appeared, with a tiny image of a coastline streaming in the middle. It was pixilated and comically slow. The audience tittered.

"Almost useless, right? Now, as we know, streaming video has gotten a lot better in recent years. But it's still slower than real life, and the screen quality is pretty disappointing. So we've solved, I think, the quality issues in the last year. Let's now refresh that page to show the site with our new video delivery."

Now the page was refreshed, and the coastline was full-screen, and the resolution was perfect. There were sounds of awe throughout the room.

"Yes, this is live video of Stinson Beach. This is Stinson right at this moment. Looks pretty good, right? Maybe I should be out there, as opposed to standing here with you!"

Annie leaned into Mae. "The next part's incredible. Just wait."

"Now, many of you still aren't so impressed. As we all know, many machines can deliver high-res streaming video, and many of your tablets and phones can already support them. But there are a couple new aspects to all this. The first part is how we're getting this image. Would it surprise you to know that this isn't coming from a big camera, but actually just one of these?"

He was holding a small device in his hand, the shape and size of a lollipop.

"This is a video camera, and this is the precise model that's getting this incredible image quality. Image quality that holds up to this kind of magnification. So that's the first great thing. We can now get high-def-quality resolution in a camera the size of a thumb. Well, a very big thumb. The second great thing is that, as you can see, this camera needs no wires. It's transmitting this image via satellite."

A round of applause shook the room.

"Wait. Did I say it runs on a lithium battery that lasts two years? No? Well it does. And we're a year away from an entirely solar-powered model, too. And it's waterproof, sand-proof, wind-proof, animal-proof, insect-proof, everything-proof."

More applause overtook the room.

"Okay, so I set up that camera this morning. I taped it to a stake, stuck that stake in the sand, in the dunes, with no permit, nothing. In fact, no one knows it's there. So this morning I turned it on, then I drove back to the office, accessed Camera One, Stinson Beach, and I got this image. Not bad. But that's not the half of it. Actually, I was pretty busy this morning. I drove around, and set up one at Rodeo Beach, too."

And now the original image, of Stinson Beach, shrunk and moved to a corner of the screen. Another box emerged, showing the waves at Rodeo Beach, a few miles down the Pacific coast. "And now Montara. And Ocean Beach. Fort Point." With each beach Bailey mentioned, another live image appeared. There were now six beaches in a grid, each of them live, visible with perfect clarity and brilliant color.

"Now remember: no one sees these cameras. I've hidden them pretty well. To the average person they look like weeds, or some kind of stick. Anything. They're unnoticed. So in a few hours this morning, I set up perfectly clear video access to six locations that help me know how to plan my day. And everything we do here is about knowing the previously unknown, right?"

Heads nodded. A smattering of applause.

"Okay, so, many of you are thinking, Well, this is just like closed-circuit TV crossed with streaming technology, satellites, all that. Fine. But as you know, to do this with extant technology would have been prohibitively expensive for the average person. But what if all this was accessible and affordable to anyone? My friends, we're looking at retailing these—in just a few months, mind you—at fifty-nine dollars each."

Bailey held the lollipop camera out, and threw it to someone in the front row. The woman who caught it held it aloft, turning to the audience and smiling gleefully.

"You can buy ten of them for Christmas and suddenly you have constant access to everywhere you want to be—home, work, traffic conditions. And anyone can install them. It takes five minutes tops. Think of the implications!"

The screen behind him cleared, the beaches disappearing, and a new grid appeared.

"Here's the view from my backyard," he said, revealing a live feed of a tidy and modest backyard. "Here's my front yard. My garage. Here's one on a hill overlooking Highway 101 where it gets bad during rush hour. Here's one near my parking space to make sure no one parks there."

And soon the screen had sixteen discrete images on it, all of them transmitting live feed.

"Now, these are just *my* cameras. I access them all by simply typing in Camera 1, 2, 3, 12, whatever. Easy. But what about sharing? That is, what if my buddy has some cameras posted, and wants to give me access?"

And now the screen's grid multiplied, from sixteen boxes to thirty-two. "Here's Lionel Fitzpatrick's screens. He's into skiing, so he's got cameras positioned so he can tell the conditions at twelve locations all over Tahoe."

Now there were twelve live images of white-topped mountains, ice-blue valleys, ridges topped with deep green conifers.

"Lionel can give me access to any of the cameras he wants. It's just like friending someone, but now with access to all their live feeds. Forget cable. Forget five hundred channels. If you have one thousand friends, and they have ten cameras each, you now have ten thousand options for live footage. If you have five thousand friends, you have fifty thousand options. And soon you'll be able to connect to millions of cameras around the world. Again, imagine the implications!"

The screen atomized into a thousand mini-screens. Beaches, mountains, lakes, cities, offices, living rooms. The crowd applauded wildly. Then the screen went blank, and from the black emerged a peace sign, in white.

"Now imagine the human rights implications. Protesters on the streets of Egypt no longer have to hold up a camera, hoping to catch a human rights violation or a murder and then somehow get the footage out of the streets and online. Now it's as easy as gluing a camera to a wall. Actually, we've done just that."

A stunned hush came over the audience.

"Let's have Camera 8 in Cairo."

A live shot of a street scene appeared. There were banners lying on the street, a pair of police in riot gear standing in the distance.

"They don't know we see them, but we do. The world is watching. And listening. Turn up the audio."

Suddenly they could hear a clear conversation, in Arabic, between pedestrians passing near the camera, unawares.

"And of course most of the cameras can be manipulated manually or with voice recognition. Watch this. Camera 8, turn left."

On-screen, the camera's view of the Cairo street panned left. "Now right." It panned right. He demonstrated it moving up, down, diagonally, all with remarkable fluidity.

The audience applauded again.

"Now, remember that these cameras are cheap, and easy to hide, and they need no wires. So it hasn't been that hard for us to place them all over. Let's show Tahrir."

Gasps from the audience. On-screen there was now a live shot of Tahrir Square, the cradle of the Egyptian Revolution.

"We've had our people in Cairo attaching cameras for the last week. They're so small the army can't find them. They don't even know where to look! Let's show the rest of the views. Camera 2. Camera 3. Four. Five. Six."

There were six shots of the square, each so clear that sweat on any face could be seen, the nametags of every soldier easily read.

"Now 7 through 50."

Now there was a grid of fifty images, seeming to cover the entire public space. The audience roared again. Bailey raised his hands, as if to say "Not yet. There's plenty more."

"The square is quiet now, but can you imagine if something happened? There would be instant accountability. Any soldier committing an act of violence would instantly be recorded for posterity. He could be tried for war crimes, you name it. And even if they clear the square of journalists, the cameras are still there. And no matter how many times they try to eliminate the cameras, because they're so small, they'll never know for sure where they are, who's placed them where and when. And the not-knowing will prevent abuses of power. You take the average soldier who's now worried that a dozen cameras will catch him,

66

for all eternity, dragging some woman down the street? Well, he should worry. He should worry about these cameras. He should worry about SeeChange. That's what we're calling them."

There was a quick burst of applause, which grew as the audience came to understand the double-meaning at play.

"Like it?" Bailey said. "Okay, now this doesn't just apply to areas of upheaval. Imagine any city with this kind of coverage. Who would commit a crime knowing they might be watched any time, anywhere? My friends in the FBI feel this would cut crime rates down by 70, 80 percent in any city where we have real and meaningful saturation."

The applause grew.

"But for now, let's go back to the places in the world where we most need transparency and so rarely have it. Here's a medley of locations around the world where we've placed cameras. Now imagine the impact these cameras would have had in the past, and will have in the future, if similar events transpire. Here's fifty cameras in Tiananmen Square."

Live shots from all over the square filled the screen, and the crowd erupted again. Bailey went on, revealing their coverage of a dozen authoritarian regimes, from Khartoum to Pyongyang, where the authorities had no idea they were being watched by three thousand Circlers in California—had no notion that they *could* be watched, that this technology was or would ever be possible.

Now Bailey cleared the screen again, and stepped toward the audience. "You know what I say, right? In situations like this, I agree with the Hague, with human rights activists the world over. There needs to be accountability. Tyrants can no longer hide. There needs to be, and will be, documentation and account-ability, and we need to bear witness. And to this end, I insist that all that happens should be known."

The words dropped onto the screen:

ALL THAT HAPPENS MUST BE KNOWN.

"Folks, we're at the dawn of the Second Enlightenment. And I'm not talking about a new building on campus. I'm talking about an era where we don't allow the majority of human thought and action and achievement and learning to escape as if from a leaky bucket. We did that once before. It was called the Middle Ages, the Dark Ages. If not for the monks, everything the world had ever learned would have been lost. Well, we live in a similar time, when we're losing the vast majority of what we do and see and learn. But it doesn't have to be that way. Not with these cameras, and not with the mission of the Circle."

He turned again toward the screen and read it, inviting the audience to commit it to memory.

ALL THAT HAPPENS MUST BE KNOWN.

He turned back to the audience and smiled.

"Okay, now I want to bring it back home. My mother's eighty-one. She doesn't get around as easily as she once did. A year ago she fell and broke her hip, and since then I've been concerned about her. I asked her to have some security cameras installed, so I could access them on a closed circuit, but she refused. But now I have peace of mind. Last weekend, while she was napping—"

A wave of laughter rippled through the audience.

"Forgive me! Forgive me!" he said, "I had no choice. She

wouldn't have let me do it otherwise. So I snuck in, and I installed cameras in every room. They're so small she'll never notice. I'll show you really quick. Can we show cameras 1 to 5 in my mom's house?"

A grid of images popped up, including his mom, padding down a bright hallway in a towel. A roar of laughter erupted.

"Oops. Let's drop that one." The image disappeared. "Anyway. The point is that I know she's safe, and that gives me a sense of peace. As we all know here at the Circle, transparency leads to peace of mind. No longer do I have to wonder, 'How's Mom?' No longer do I have to wonder, 'What's happening in Myanmar?'

"Now, we're making a million of this model, and my prediction is that within a year we'll have a million accessible live streams. Within five years, fifty million. Within ten years, two billion cameras. There will be very few populated areas that we won't be able to access from the screens in our hands."

The audience roared again. Someone yelled out, "We want it now!"

Bailey continued. "Instead of searching the web, only to find some edited video with terrible quality, now you go to SeeChange, you type in Myanmar. Or you type in your high school boyfriend's name. Chances are there's someone who's set up a camera nearby, right? Why shouldn't your curiosity about the world be rewarded? You want to see Fiji but can't get there? SeeChange. You want to check on your kid at school? SeeChange. This is ultimate transparency. No filter. See everything. Always."

Mae leaned toward Annie. "This is incredible."

"I know, right?" Annie said.

"Now, do these cameras have to be stationary?" Bailey said, raising a scolding finger. "Of course not. I happen to have a dozen helpers all over the world right now, wearing the cameras around their necks. Let's visit them, shall we? Can I get Danny's camera up?"

An image of Machu Picchu appeared on-screen. It looked like a postcard, a view perched high above the ancient ruins. And then it started moving, down toward the site. The crowd gasped, then cheered.

"That's a live image, though I guess that's obvious. Hi Danny. Now let's get Sarah on Mount Kenya." Another image appeared on the great screen, this one of the shale fields high on the mountain. "Can you point us toward the peak, Sarah?" The camera panned up, revealing the peak of the mountain, enshrouded in fog. "See, this opens up the possibility of visual surrogates. Imagine I'm bedridden, or too frail to explore the mountain myself. I send someone up with a camera around her neck, and I can experience it all in real time. Let's do that in a few more places." He presented live images of Paris, Kuala Lumpur, a London pub.

"Now let's experiment a bit, using all of this together. I'm sitting at home. I log on and want to get a sense of the world. Show me traffic on 101. Streets of Jakarta. Surfing at Bolinas. My mom's house. Show me the webcams of everyone I went to high school with."

At every command, new images appeared, until there were at least a hundred live streaming images on the screen at once.

"We will become all-seeing, all-knowing."

The audience was standing now. The applause thundered through the room. Mae rested her head on Annie's shoulder.

"All that happens will be known," Annie whispered.

"You have a glow."

"You do."

"I do not have a glow."

"Like you're with child."

"I know what you meant. Stop."

Mae's father reached across the table and took her hand. It was Saturday, and her parents were treating her to a celebratory dinner commemorating her first week at the Circle. This was the kind of sentimental slop they were always doing—at least recently. When she was younger, the only child of a couple who long considered the possibility of having none at all, their home was more complicated. During the week, her father had been scarce. He'd been the building manager at a Fresno office park, working fourteen-hour days and leaving everything at home to her mother, who worked three shifts a week at a hotel restaurant and who responded to the pressure of it all with a hair-trigger temper, primarily directed at Mae. But when Mae was ten, her parents announced they'd bought a parking lot, two stories near downtown Fresno, and for a few years, they took turns manning it. It was humiliating to Mae to have her friends' parents say, "Hey, saw your mom at the lot," or "Tell your dad thanks again for comping me the other day," but soon their finances stabilized, and they could hire a couple guys to trade shifts. And when her parents could take a day off, and could plan more than a few months ahead, they mellowed, becoming a very calm, exasperatingly sweet older couple. It was as if they went, in the course of a year, from being young parents in over their heads to grandparents, slow-moving and warm and clueless about what exactly their daughter wanted. When she graduated from middle school, they'd driven her to Disneyland, not quite understanding that she was too old, and that her going there alone—with two adults, which was effectively alone—was at cross-purposes with any notion of fun. But they were so well-meaning that she couldn't refuse, and in the end they had a mindless kind of fun that she didn't know was possible with one's parents. Any lingering resentment she might direct at them for the emotional uncertainties of her early life was doused by the constant cool water of their late middle age.

And now they'd driven to the bay, to spend the weekend at the cheapest bed and breakfast they could find—which was fifteen miles from the Circle and looked haunted. Now they were out, at some fake-fancy restaurant the two of them had heard about, and if anyone was aglow, it was them. They were beaming.

"So? It's been great?" her mother asked.

"It has."

"I knew it." Her mother sat back, crossing her arms.

"I don't ever want to work anywhere else," Mae said.

"What a relief," her father said. "We don't want you working anywhere else, either."

Her mother lunged forward, and took Mae's arm. "I told Karolina's mom. You know her." She scrunched her nose—the closest she could come to an insult. "She looked like someone had stuck a sharp stick up her behind. Boiling with envy."

"Mom."

"I let your salary slip."

"Mom."

"I just said, 'I hope she can get by with a salary of sixty thousand dollars.' "

"I can't believe you told her that."

"It's true, isn't it?"

"It's actually sixty-two."

"Oh jeez. Now I'll have to call her up."

"No you won't."

"Okay, I won't. But it's been very fun," she said, "I just casually slip it into conversation. My daughter's at the hottest company on the planet and has full dental."

"Please don't. I just got lucky. And Annie—"

Her father leaned forward. "How *is* Annie?"

"Good."

"Tell Annie we love her."

"I will."

"She couldn't come tonight?"

"No. She's busy."

"But you asked her?"

"I did. She says hi. But she works a lot."

"What does she do exactly?" her mother asked.

"Everything, really," Mae said. "She's in the Gang of 40. She's part of all the big decisions. I think she specializes in dealing with regulatory issues in other countries."

"I'm sure she's got a lot of responsibility."

"And stock options!" her father said. "I can't imagine what she's worth."

"Dad. Don't imagine that."

"Why is she working with all those stock options? I'd be on a beach. I'd have a harem."

Mae's mother put her hand on his. "Vinnie, stop." Then to Mae she said, "I hope she has time to enjoy it all."

"She does," Mae said. "She's probably at a campus party as we speak."

Her father smiled. "I love that you call it a campus. That's very cool. We used to call those places *offices*."

Mae's mother seemed troubled. "A party, Mae? You didn't want to go?"

"I did, but I wanted to see you guys. And there are plenty of those parties."

"But in your first week!" her mother looked pained. "Maybe you should've gone. Now I feel bad. We took you away from it."

"Trust me. They have them every other day. They're very social over there. I'll be fine."

"You're not taking lunch yet, are you?" her mother asked. She made the same point when Mae had started at the utility: don't take lunch your first week. Sends the wrong message.

"Don't worry," Mae said. "I haven't even used the bathroom."

Her mother rolled her eyes. "Anyway, let me just say how proud we are. We love you."

"And Annie," her father said.

"Right. We love you and Annie."

They ate quickly, knowing that Mae's father would soon tire. He'd insisted on going out to dinner, though back at home, he rarely did anymore. His fatigue was constant, and could come on suddenly and strong, sending him to near-collapse. It was important, when out like this, to be ready to make a quick exit, and before dessert, they did so. Mae followed them back to their room and there, amid the B&B owners' dozens of dolls, spread about the room and watching, Mae and her parents were able to relax, unafraid of eventualities. Mae hadn't gotten used to her father having multiple sclerosis. The diagnosis had come down only two years earlier, though the symptoms had been visible years before that. He'd been slurring his words, had been overshooting when reaching for things and, finally, had fallen, twice, each time in the foyer of their house, reaching for the front door. So they'd sold the parking lot, made a decent profit, and now spent their time managing his care, which meant at least a few hours a day poring over medical bills and battling with the insurance company.

"Oh, we saw Mercer the other day," her mother said, and her father smiled. Mercer had been a boyfriend of Mae's, one of the four serious ones she'd had in high school and college. But as far as her parents were concerned, he was the only one who mattered, or the only one they acknowledged or remembered. It helped that he still lived in town.

"That's good," Mae said, wanting to end the topic. "He still makes chandeliers out of antlers?"

"Easy there," her father said, hearing her barbed tone. "He's got his own business. And not that he'd brag, but it's apparently thriving."

Mae needed to change the subject. "I've averaged 97 so far," she said. "They say that's a record for a newbie."

The look on her parents' faces was bewilderment. Her father blinked slowly. They had no idea what she was talking about. "What's that, hon?" her father said.

Mae let it go. When she'd heard the words leave her mouth, she knew the sentence would take too long to explain. "How are things with the insurance?" she asked, and instantly regretted it. Why did she ask questions like this? The answer would swallow the night.

"Not good," her mother said. "I don't know. We have the wrong plan. I mean, they don't want to insure your dad, plain and simple, and they seem to be doing everything they can to get us to leave. But how can we leave? We'd have nowhere to go."

Her father sat up. "Tell her about the prescription."

"Oh, right. Your dad's been on Copaxone for two years, for the pain. He needs it. Without it—"

"The pain gets . . . ornery," he said.

"Now the insurance says he doesn't need it. It's not on their list of pre-approved medications. Even though he's been using it two years!"

"It seems unnecessarily cruel," Mae's father said.

"They've offered no alternative. Nothing for the pain!"

Mae didn't know what to say. "I'm sorry. Can I look up some alternatives online? I mean, have you seen if the doctors could find another drug that the insurance will pay for? Maybe a generic . . ."

This went on for an hour, and by the end, Mae was wrecked. The MS, her helplessness to slow it, her inability to bring back the life her father had known—it tortured her, but the insurance situation was something else, was an unnecessary crime, a piling-on. Didn't the insurance companies realize that the cost of their obfuscation, denial, all the frustration they caused, only made her father's health worse, and threatened that of her mother? If nothing else, it was inefficient. The time spent denying coverage, arguing, dismissing, thwarting—surely it was more trouble than simply granting her parents access to the right care.

"Enough of this," her mother said. "We brought you a surprise. Where is it? You have it, Vinnie?"

They gathered on the high bed covered with a threadbare patchwork quilt, and her father presented Mae with a small wrapped gift. The size and shape of the box suggested a necklace, but Mae knew it couldn't be that. When she got the wrapping off, she opened the velvet box and laughed. It was a pen, one of the rarefied kind that's silver and strangely heavy, requiring care and filling and mostly for show.

"Don't worry, we didn't buy it," Mae's father said.

"Vinnie!" her mother wailed.

"Seriously," he said, "we didn't. A friend of mine gave it to me last year. He felt bad I couldn't work. I don't know what kind of use he thought I'd have for a pen when I can barely type. But this guy was never so bright."

"We thought it would look good on your desk," her mother added.

"Are we the best or what?" her father said.

Mae's mother laughed, and most crucially, Mae's father laughed. He laughed a big belly laugh. In the second, calmer phase of their lives as parents, he'd become a laugher, a constant laugher, a man who laughed at everything. It was the primary sound of Mae's teenage years. He laughed at things that were clearly funny, and at things that would provoke just a smile in most, and he laughed when he should have been upset. When Mae misbehaved, he thought it was hilarious. He'd caught her sneaking out of her bedroom window one night, to see Mercer, and he'd practically keeled over. Everything was comical, everything about her adolescence cracked him up. "You should have seen your face when you saw me! Priceless!"

But then the MS diagnosis arrived and most of that was gone. The pain was constant. The spells where he couldn't get up, didn't trust his legs to carry him, were too frequent, too dangerous. He was in the emergency room weekly. And finally, with some heroic efforts from Mae's mom, he saw a few doctors who cared, and he was put on the right drugs and stabilized, at least for a while. And then the insurance debacles, the descent into this health care purgatory.

This night, though, he was buoyant, and her mother was feeling good, having found some sherry in the B&B's tiny kitchen, which she shared with Mae. Her father was soon enough asleep in his clothes, over the covers, with all the lights on, with Mae and her mother still talking at full volume. When they noticed he was out cold Mae arranged a bed for herself at the foot of theirs.

In the morning they slept late and drove to a diner for lunch. Her father ate well, and Mae watched her mother feign nonchalance, the two of them talking about a wayward uncle's latest bizarre business venture, something about raising lobsters in rice paddies. Mae knew her mother was nervous, every moment, about her father, having him out for two meals in a row, and watched him closely. He looked cheerful but his strength faded quickly.

"You guys settle up," he said. "I'm going to the car to recline for a moment."

"We can help," Mae said, but her mother hushed her. Her father was already up and headed for the door.

"He gets tired. It's fine," her mother said. "It's just a different routine now. He rests. He does things, he walks and eats and is animated for a while, then he rests. It's very regular and very calming, to tell you the truth."

They paid the bill and walked out to the parking lot. Mae saw the white wisps of her father's hair through the car window. Most of his head was below the windowframe, reclined so far he was in the back seat. When they arrived at the car, they saw that he was awake, looking up into the interlocking boughs of an unremarkable tree. He rolled down the window.

"Well, this has been wonderful," he said.

Mae made her goodbyes and left, happy to have the afternoon free. She drove west, the day sunny and calm, the colors of the passing landscape simple and clear, blues and yellows and greens. As she approached the coast, she turned toward the bay. She could get a few hours of kayaking in if she hurried.

Mercer had introduced her to kayaking, an activity that until then she'd considered awkward and dull. Sitting at the waterline, struggling to move that strange ice-cream-spoon paddle. The constant twisting looked painful, and the pace seemed far too slow. But then she'd tried it, with Mercer, using not professional-grade models but something more basic, the kind the rider sits on top of, legs and feet exposed. They'd paddled around the bay, moving far quicker than she'd expected, and they'd seen harbor seals, and pelicans, and Mae was convinced this was a criminally underappreciated sport, and the bay a body of water woefully underused.

They'd launched from a tiny beach, the outfitter requiring no training or equipment or fuss; you just paid your fifteen dollars an hour and in minutes were on the bay, cold and clear.

Today, she pulled off the highway and made her way to the beach, and there she found the water placid, glassine.

"Hey you," said a voice.

Mae turned to find an older woman, bowlegged and frizzy-haired. This was Marion, owner of Maiden's Voyages. She was the maiden, and had been for fifteen years, since she'd opened the business, after striking it rich in stationery. She'd told Mae this during her first rental, and told everyone this story, which Marion assumed was amusing, that she'd made money selling stationery and opened a kayak and paddle-board rental operation. Why Marion thought this was funny Mae never knew. But Marion was warm and accommodating, even when Mae was asking to take out a kayak a few hours before closing, as she was this day.

"Gorgeous out there," Marion said. "Just don't go far."

Marion helped her pull the kayak across the sand and rocks and into the tiny waves. She clicked on Mae's life preserver. "And remember, don't bother any of the houseboat people. Their living rooms are at your eye level, so no snooping. You want footies or a windbreaker today?" she asked. "Might get choppy."

Mae declined and got into the kayak, barefoot and wearing the cardigan and jeans she wore to brunch. In seconds she had paddled beyond the fishing boats, past the breakers and paddle-boarders, and was in the open water of the bay.

She saw no one. That this body of water was so seldom used had confounded her for months. There were no jetskis here. Few casual fishermen, no waterskiers, the occasional motorboat. There were sailboats, but not nearly as many as one would expect. The frigid water was only part of it. Maybe there were simply too many other things to do outdoors in Northern California? It was mysterious, but Mae had no complaint. It left more water to her.

She paddled into the belly of the bay. The water did indeed get choppier, and cold water washed over her feet. It felt good, so good she reached her hand down and scooped a handful and drenched her face and the back of her neck. When she opened her eyes she saw a harbor seal, twenty feet in front of her, staring at her as would a calm dog whose yard she'd walked into. His head was rounded, grey, with the glossy sheen of polished marble.

She kept her paddle on her lap, watching the seal as it watched her. Its eyes were black buttons, unreflective. She didn't move, and the seal didn't move. They were locked in mutual regard, and the moment, the way it stretched and luxuriated in itself, asked for continuation. Why move?

A gust of wind came her way, and with it the pungent smell of the seal. She had noticed this the last time she had kayaked, the strong smell of these animals, a cross between tuna and unwashed dog. It was better to be upwind. As if suddenly embarrassed, the seal ducked underwater.

Mae continued on, away from shore. She set a goal to make it to a red buoy she spotted, near the bend of a peninsula, deep in the bay. Getting to it would take thirty minutes or so, and en route, she would pass a few dozen anchored barges and sailboats. Many had been made into homes of one kind or another, and she knew not to look into the windows, but she couldn't help it; there were mysteries aboard. Why was there a motorcycle on this barge? Why a Confederate flag on that yacht? Far off, she saw a seaplane circling.

The wind picked up behind her, sending her quickly past the red buoy and closer to the farther shore. She hadn't planned to land there, and had never made it across the bay, but soon it was in sight and coming quickly upon her, eelgrass visible beneath her as the water went shallow.

She jumped out of the kayak, her feet landing on the stones, all rounded and smooth. As she was pulling the kayak up, the bay rose up and engulfed her legs. It wasn't a wave; it was more of a sudden uniform rising of the water level. One second she was standing on a dry shore and the next the water was at her shins and she was soaked.

When the water fell again, it left a wide swath of bizarre, bejeweled seaweed—blue, and green, and, in a certain light, iridescent. She held it in her hands, and it was smooth, rubbery, its edges ruffled extravagantly. Mae's feet were wet, and the water was snow cold but she didn't mind. She sat on the rocky beach, picked up a stick and drew with it, clicking through the smooth stones. Tiny crabs, unearthed and annoyed, scurried to find new shelters. A pelican landed downshore, on the trunk of a dead tree, which had been bleached white and leaned diagonally, rising from the steel-grey water, pointing lazily to the sky.

And then Mae found herself sobbing. Her father was a mess. No, he wasn't a mess. He was managing it all with great dignity.

But there had been something very tired about him that morning, something defeated, accepting, as if he knew that he couldn't fight both what was happening in his body and the companies managing his care. And there was nothing she could do for him. No, there was too much to do for him. She could quit her job. She could quit and help make the phone calls, fight the many fights to keep him well. This is what a good daughter would do. What a good child, an only child, would do. A good only child would spend the next three to five years, which might be his last years of mobility, of full capability, with him, helping him, helping her mother, being part of the family machinery. But she knew her parents wouldn't let her do all that. They wouldn't allow it. And so she would be caught between the job she needed and loved, and her parents, whom she couldn't help.

But it felt good to cry, to let her shoulders shake, to feel the hot tears on her face, to taste their baby salt, to wipe snot all over the underside of her shirt. And when she was done, she pushed the kayak out again and she found herself paddling at a brisk pace. Once in the middle of the bay, she stopped. Her tears were dry now, her breathing steady. She was calm and felt strong, but instead of reaching the red buoy, which she no longer had any interest in, she sat, her paddle on her lap, letting the waves tilt her gently, feeling the warm sun dry her hands and feet. She often did this when she was far from any shore—she just sat still, feeling the vast volume of the ocean beneath her. There were leopard sharks in this part of the bay, and bat rays, and jellyfish, and the occasional harbor porpoise, but she could see none of them. They were hidden in the dark water, in their black parallel world, and knowing they were there, but not knowing where, or really anything else, felt, at that moment, strangely right. Far beyond, she could see where the mouth of the bay led to the ocean and there, making its way through a band of light fog, she saw an enormous container ship heading into open water. She thought about moving, but saw no point. There seemed no reason to go anywhere. Being here, in the middle of the bay, nothing to do or see, was plenty. She stayed there, drifting slowly, for the better part of an hour. Occasionally she would smell that dog-and-tuna smell again, and turn to find another curious seal, and they would watch each other, and she would wonder if the seal knew, as she did, how good this was, how lucky they were to have all this to themselves.

By the late afternoon, the winds coming from the Pacific picked up, and getting back to shore was trying. When she got home her limbs were leaden and her head was slow. She made herself a salad and ate half a bag of chips, staring out the window. She fell asleep at eight and slept for eleven hours.

The morning was busy, as Dan had warned her it would be. He'd gathered her and the hundred-odd other CE reps at eight a.m., reminding them all that opening the chute on Monday morning was always a hazardous thing. All the customers who wanted answers over the weekend certainly expected them on Monday morning.

He was right. The chute opened, the deluge arrived, and Mae worked against the flood until eleven or so, when there was something like respite. She'd handled forty-nine queries and her score was at 91, her lowest aggregate yet.

Don't worry, Jared messaged. *Par for the course on Monday. Just go after as many follow-ups as you can.*

Mae had been following up all morning, with limited results. The clients were grumpy. The only good news that morning came from the intra-company feed, when a message from Francis appeared, asking her to lunch. Officially she and the other CE staff were given an hour for the meal, but she hadn't seen anyone else leave their desk for more than twenty minutes. She gave herself that much time, though her mother's words, equating lunch with a monumental breach of duty, rattled in her mind.

She was late getting to the Glass Eatery. She looked around, and up, and finally saw him sitting a few levels above, his feet dangling from a high lucite stool. She waved, but couldn't get his attention. She yelled up to him, as discreetly as she could, to no avail. Then, feeling foolish, she texted him, and watched as he received the text, looked around the cafeteria, found her, and waved.

She made her way through the line, got a veggie burrito and some kind of new organic soda, and sat down next to him. He was wearing a wrinkled clean button-down shirt and carpenter's pants. His perch overlooked the outdoor pool, where a group of staffers was approximating a game of volleyball.

"Not such an athletic group," he noted.

"No," Mae agreed. As he watched the chaotic splashing below, she tried to overlay this face in front of her with the one she remembered from her first night. There were the same heavy brows, the same prominent nose. But now Francis seemed to have shrunk. His hands, using a knife and fork to cut his burrito in two, seemed unusually delicate.

"It's almost perverse," he said, "having so much athletic equipment here when there's no athletic aptitude at all. It's like a family of Christian Scientists living next to a pharmacy." Now he turned to her. "Thanks for coming. I wondered if I'd see you again."

"Yeah, it's been so busy."

He pointed to his food. "I had to start already. Sorry about that. To be honest, I didn't totally expect you to show up."

"I'm sorry for being late," she said.

"No, believe me, I get it. You need to handle the Monday flow. The customers expect it. Lunch is pretty secondary."

"I have to say, I've felt bad about the end of our conversation that night. Sorry about Annie."

"Did you guys actually make out? I tried to find a spot where I could watch from, but—"

"No."

"I thought if I climbed a tree—"

"No. No. That's just Annie. She's an idiot."

"She's an idiot who happens to be in the top one percent of people here. I wish I was that kind of idiot."

"You were talking about when you were a kid."

"God. Can I blame it on the wine?"

"You don't have to tell me anything."

Mae felt terrible, already knowing what she did, hoping he would tell her, so she could take the previous, secondhand, version of his story and write over it with the version directly from him.

"No, it's fine," he said. "I got to meet a lot of interesting adults who were paid by the government to care for me. It was awesome. What do you have left, ten minutes?"

"I have till one."

"Good. Eight more minutes then. Eat. I'll talk. But not about my childhood. You know enough. I assume Annie filled in the gory stuff. She likes to tell that story."

And so Mae tried to eat as much as she could as fast as she could, while Francis talked about a movie he'd seen the night before in the campus theater. Apparently the director had been there to present it and had answered questions afterward.

"The movie was about a woman who kills her husband and kids, and during the Q&A we find out this director's involved in this protracted custody battle with her own ex-husband. So we were all looking around, thinking, Is this lady working out some issues on-screen, or . . ."

Mae laughed, and then, remembering Francis's own horrible childhood, she caught herself.

"It's fine," he said, knowing immediately why she'd paused. "I don't want you to think you have to tiptoe around me. It's been a long time, and if I didn't feel comfortable in this territory, I wouldn't be working on ChildTrack."

"Well, still. I'm sorry. I'm bad at knowing what to say. But so the project is going well? How close are you to—"

"You're still so off-balance! I like that," Francis said.

"You like a woman who's off-balance."

"Especially in my presence. I want you on your toes, off-balance, intimidated, handcuffed and willing to prostrate yourself at my command."

Mae wanted to laugh, but found she couldn't.

Francis was staring at his plate. "Shit. Every time my brain parks the car neatly in the driveway, my mouth drives through the back of the garage. I'm sorry. I swear I'm working on this."

"It's fine. Tell me about . . ."

"ChildTrack." He looked up. "You really want to know?"

"I do."

"Because once you get me started, it'll make your Monday deluge look like a tinkle."

"We have five and a half minutes left."

"Okay, remember when they tried to do the implants in Denmark?"

Mae shook her head. She had some vague recollection of a terrible child abduction and murder—

Francis checked his watch, as if knowing that explaining Denmark would steal a minute from him. He sighed and started in: "So a couple years ago, the government of Denmark tried a program where they inserted chips in kids' wrists. It's easy, takes two seconds, it's medically sound, and instantly it works. Every parent knows where their kid is at all times. They limited it to under-fourteens, and at first, everyone's fine. The court challenges are dropped because there are so few objections, the polling is through the roof. The parents love it. I mean, *love* it. These are kids, and we'd do anything to keep them safe, right?"

Mae nodded, but suddenly remembered that this story ended horribly.

"But then seven kids go missing one day. The cops, the parents, think, Hey, no problem. We know where the kids are. They follow the chips, but when they get to the chips, all seven tracking to some parking lot, they find them all in a paper bag, all bloody. Just the chips."

"Now I remember." Mae felt sick.

"They find the bodies a week later, and by then the public is in a panic. Everyone's irrational. They think the chips *caused* the kidnapping, the murders, that somehow the chips provoked whoever did this, made the task more tempting."

"That was so horrible. That was the end of the chips."

"Yeah, but the reasoning was illogical. Especially here. We have, what, twelve thousand abductions a year? How many murders? The problem there was how shallow the chips were placed. Anyone can just cut it out of someone's wrist if they wanted to. Too easy. But the tests we're doing here—did you meet Sabine?"

"I did."

"Well, she's on the team. She won't tell you that, because she's doing some related stuff she can't talk about. But for this, she figured out a way to put a chip in the bone. And that makes all the difference."

"Oh shit. What bone?"

"Doesn't matter, I don't think. You're making a face."

Mae corrected her face, tried to look neutral.

"Sure, it's insane. I mean, some people freak out about chips in our heads, our bodies, but this thing is about as technologically advanced as a walkie-talkie. It doesn't do anything but tell you where something is. And they're everywhere already. Every other product you buy has one of these chips. You buy a stereo, it has a chip. You buy a car, it's got a bunch of chips. Some companies put chips in food packaging, to make sure it's fresh when it gets to market. It's just a simple tracker. And if you embed it in bone, it stays there, and can't be seen with the naked eye—not like the wrist ones."

Mae put down her burrito. "Really in the bone?"

"Mae, think about a world where there could never again be a significant crime against a child. None possible. The second a kid's not where he's supposed to be, a massive alert goes off, and the kid can be tracked down immediately. *Everyone* can track her. All authorities know instantly she's missing, but they know exactly where she is. They can call the mom and say 'Hey, she just went to the mall,' or they can track down some molester in seconds. The only hope an abductor would have is to take a kid, run into the woods with her, do something and run off before the world descends upon him. But he would have about a minute and a half to do it."

"Or if they could jam the transmission from the chip."

"Sure, but who has that expertise? How many electronic-genius pedophiles are there? Very few, I'm guessing. So immediately you take all child abduction, rape, murder, and you reduce it by 99 percent. And the price is that the kids have a chip in their ankle. You want a living kid with a chip in his ankle, a kid who you know will grow up safe, a kid who can again run down to the park, ride his bike to school, all that?"

"You're about to say *or.*"

"Right, or do you want a dead kid? Or years of worry every time your kid walks to the bus stop? I mean, we've polled parents worldwide, and after they get over the initial squeamishness, we get an 88 percent approval. Once they get it in their head that this is possible, we have them yelling at us, 'Why don't we already have this? When's it coming?' I mean, this will begin a new golden age for young people. An age without worry. Shit. Now you're late. Look."

He pointed to the clock. 1:02.

Mae ran.

The afternoon was relentless, and her score barely reached 93. By the end of the day, she was exhausted, and she turned to her second screen to find a message from Dan. *Got a second? Gina from CircleSocial was hoping to grab a few minutes with you.*

She wrote him back: *How about in fifteen? I have a handful of follow-ups to do, and haven't peed since noon.* This was the truth. She hadn't left her chair in three hours, and she also wanted to see if she could get the score above 93. She was sure this, her low aggregate, was why Dan wanted her to meet with Gina.

Dan wrote only, *Thank you Mae,* words that she turned over in her mind as she made her way to the bathroom. Was he thanking her for being available in fifteen minutes, or thanking her, grimly, for an unwanted level of hygienic intimacy?

Mae was almost at the bathroom door when she saw a man, in skinny green jeans and a snug long-sleeved shirt, standing in the hallway, under a tall narrow window, staring at his phone. Bathed in a blue-white light, he seemed to be waiting for instructions from his screen.

Mae went inside.

When she was finished, she opened the door to find the man in the same place, now looking out the window.

"You look lost," Mae said.

"Nah. Just figuring out something before, you know, heading upstairs. You work over here?"

"I do. I'm new. In CE."

"CE?"

"Customer Experience."

"Oh right. We used to just call it Customer Service."

"So I take it you're not new?"

"Me? No, no. I've been here a little while. Not so much in this building." He smiled and looked out the window, and with his face turned away, Mae took him in. His eyes were dark, his face oval, and his hair was grey, almost white, but he couldn't have been older than thirty. He was thin, sinewy, and his skinny jeans and tight long-sleeve jersey gave his silhouette the quick thick-thin brushstrokes of calligraphy.

He turned back to her, blinking, scoffing at himself and his poor manners. "Sorry. I'm Kalden."

"Kalden?"

"It's Tibetan," he said. "It means golden something. My parents always wanted to go to Tibet but never got closer than Hong Kong. And your name?"

"Mae," she said, and they shook hands. His handshake was sturdy but perfunctory. He'd been taught how to shake hands, Mae guessed, but had never seen the point.

"So you're not lost," Mae said, realizing she was expected back at her desk; she'd already been late once today.

Kalden sensed it. "Oh. You have to go. Can I walk you there? Just to see where you work?"

"Um," Mae said, now feeling very unsettled. "Sure." If she

hadn't known better, and couldn't see the ID cord around his neck, she would have assumed Kalden, with his pointed but unfocused curiosity, was either someone who'd wandered off the street, or some kind of corporate spy. But she didn't know anything. She'd been at the Circle a week. This could be some sort of test. Or just an eccentric fellow Circler.

Mae led him back to her desk.

"It's very clean," he said.

"I know. I just started, remember."

"And I know some of the Wise Men like the Circle desks very tidy. You ever see those guys around here?"

"Who? The Wise Men?" Mae scoffed. "Not here. Not yet at least."

"Yeah, I guess not," Kalden said and crouched, his head at the level of Mae's shoulder. "Can I see what you do?"

"For my work?"

"Yeah. Can I watch? I mean, not if it makes you uncomfortable."

Mae paused. Everything and everyone else she'd experienced at the Circle hewed to a logical model, a rhythm, but Kalden was the anomaly. His rhythm was different, atonal and strange, but not unpleasant. His face was so open, his eyes liquid, gentle, unassuming, and he spoke so softly that any possibility of threat seemed remote.

"Sure. I guess," she said. "It's not so exciting, though."

"Maybe, maybe not."

And so he watched Mae answer requests. When she turned to him after every seemingly mundane part of her job, the screen danced brightly in his eyes, his face rapt—like he'd never seen anything more interesting in his life. At other moments, though, he seemed removed, seeing something she couldn't. He'd look at the screen but his eyes were seeing something deep within.

She continued, and he continued to ask occasional questions. "Now who was that?" "How often does that happen?" "Why did you respond in that way?"

He was close to her, far too close if he was a normal person with everyday ideas of personal space, but it was abundantly clear he was not this kind of person, a normal kind of person. As he watched the screen, and sometimes Mae's fingers on the keyboard, his chin got ever-closer to her shoulder, his breath light but audible, his smell, a simple one of soap and banana shampoo, coming to her on the winds of his tiny exhalations. The whole experience was so odd that Mae laughed nervously every few seconds, not knowing what else to do. And then it was done. He cleared his throat and stood up.

"Well, I better head out," he said. "I'll just slip away. Don't want to interrupt your pace here. I'll see you around campus I'm sure."

And he was gone.

Before Mae could unpack any of what just happened, a new face was beside her.

"Hi. I'm Gina. Dan said I'd be here?"

Mae nodded, though she didn't remember anything about this. She looked at Gina, a woman a few years older than herself, hoping to remember something about her or this meeting. Gina's eyes, black and heavy with eyeliner and moon-blue mascara, smiled at her, though Mae felt no warmth emanating from these eyes, or from Gina at all.

"Dan said this would be a good moment to set up all your socials. You got time?"

"Sure," Mae said, though she had no time at all.

"I take it last week was too busy for you to set up your company social account? And I don't think you've imported your old profile?"

Mae cursed herself. "I'm sorry. I've been pretty overwhelmed so far."

Gina frowned.

Mae backtracked, masking her miscalculation with a laugh. "No, in a good way! But I haven't had time yet to do extracurricular stuff."

Gina tilted her head and cleared her throat theatrically. "That's so interesting you put it that way," she said, smiling, though she didn't seem happy. "We actually see your profile, and the activity on it, as integral to your participation here. This is how your coworkers, even those on the other side of campus, know who you are. *Communication* is certainly not extracurricular, right?"

Now Mae was embarrassed. "Right," she said. "Of course."

"If you visit a coworker's page and write something on the wall, that's a *positive* thing. That's an act of *community*. An act of *reaching out*. And of course I don't have to tell you that this company exists because of the social media you consider '*extracurricular*.' My understanding was that you used our social media tools before coming here?"

Mae was unsure what she could say to appease Gina. She'd been so busy at work, and didn't want to seem distracted, so she'd delayed re-activating her social profile.

"I'm sorry," Mae managed. "I didn't mean to imply that it

was extracurricular. I actually think it's central. I was just getting acclimated here at work and wanted to focus on learning my new responsibilities."

But Gina had hit a groove and would not be stopped until she'd finished her thought. "You realize that *community* and *communication* come from the same root word, *communis,* Latin for common, public, shared by all or many?"

Mae's heart was hammering. "I'm very sorry, Gina. I fought to get a job here. I do know all this. I'm here because I believe in everything you said. I was just a bit crazed last week and didn't get a chance to set it up."

"Okay. But just know, from now on, that being social, and being a presence on your profile and all related accounts—this is part of why you're here. We consider your online presence to be integral to your work here. It's all connected."

"I know. Again, I'm sorry to have misstated my feelings."

"Good. Okay, let's start by setting this up." Gina reached over Mae's divider and retrieved another screen, bigger than her second screen, which she quickly arranged and connected to Mae's computer.

"Okay. So your second screen will continue to be the way you'll stay in touch with your team. That will be exclusively for CE business. Your third screen is for your social participation, in the company Circle and your wider Circle. Does that make sense?"

"It does."

Mae watched Gina activate the screen, and felt a thrill. She'd never had such an elaborate arrangement before. Three screens for someone so low on the ladder! Only at the Circle.

"Okay, first I want to go back to your second screen," Gina said. "I don't think you've activated CircleSearch. Let's do that." An elaborate, three-dimensional map of the campus appeared. "This is pretty simple, and just allows you to find anyone on campus in case you need a face-to-face."

Gina pointed to a pulsing red dot.

"Here's you. You're red hot! I'm kidding." As if recognizing that might have been considered inappropriate, Gina quickly moved on. "Didn't you say you knew Annie? Let's type in her name." A blue dot appeared in the Old West. "She's in her office, surprise surprise. Annie is a machine."

Mae smiled. "She is."

"I'm so jealous you know her so well," Gina said, smiling but briefly and unconvincingly. "And over here you'll see a cool new app, which sort of gives us a history of the building every day. You can see when each staffer checked in every day, when they left the building. This gives us a really nice sense of the life of the company. This part you don't have to update yourself, of course. If you go to the pool, your ID automatically updates that on the feed. And outside of the movement, any additional commentary would be up to you, and of course would be encouraged."

"Commentary?" Mae asked.

"You know, like what you thought of lunch, a new feature at the gym, anything. Just basic ratings and likes and comments. Nothing out of the ordinary, and of course all input helps us do a better job at serving the Circle community. Now that commentary is done right here," she said, and revealed that every building and room could be clicked on, and within, she could add any comments about anything or anyone.

"So that's your second screen. It's about your coworkers, your team, and it's about finding people in the physical space. Now it's on to the really fun stuff. Screen three. This is where your main social and Zing feeds appear. I heard you weren't a Zing user?"

Mae admitted she hadn't been, but wanted to be.

"Great," Gina said. "So now you have a Zing account. I made up a name for you: MaeDay. Like the war holiday. Isn't that cool?"

Mae wasn't so sure about the name, and couldn't remember a holiday by that name.

"And I connected your Zing account with the total Circle community, so you just got 10,041 new followers! Pretty cool. In terms of your own zinging, we'd expect about ten or so a day, but that's sort of a minimum. I'm sure you'll have more to say than that. Oh, and over here's your playlist. If you listen to music while you work, the feed automatically sends that playlist out to everyone else, and it goes into the collective playlist, which ranks the most-played songs in any given day, week, month. It has the top one hundred songs campuswide, but you can also slice it a thousand ways—top-played hip-hop, indie, country, anything. You'll get recommendations based on what you play, and what others with similar taste play—it's all cross-pollinating while you're working. Make sense?"

Mae nodded.

"Now, next to the Zing feed, you'll see the window for your primary social feed. You'll also see that we split it into two parts, the InnerCircle social feed, and your external social, that's your OuterCircle. Isn't that cute? You can merge them, but we find it helpful to see the two distinct feeds. But of course the OuterCircle is still in the Circle, right? Everything is. Make sense so far?"

Mae said it did.

"I can't believe you've been here a week without being on the main social feed. You're about to have your world rocked." Gina tapped Mae's screen and Mae's InnerCircle stream became a torrent of messages pouring down the monitor.

"See, you're getting all last week's stuff, too. That's why there's so many. Wow, you really missed a lot."

Mae followed the counter on the bottom of the screen, calculating all the messages sent to her from everyone else at the Circle. The counter paused at 1,200. Then 4,400. The numbers scrambled higher, stopping periodically but finally settling at 8,276.

"That was last week's messages? Eight thousand?"

"You can catch up," Gina said brightly. "Maybe even tonight. Now, let's open up your regular social account. We call it Outer-Circle, but it's the same profile, same feed as you've had for years. Mind if I open it up?"

Mae didn't mind. She watched as her social profile, the one she'd first set up years ago, now appeared on her third screen, next to the InnerCircle feed. A cascade of messages and photos, a few hundred, filled the monitor.

"Okay, looks like you have some catching up to do here, too," Gina said. "A feast! Have fun."

"Thank you," Mae said. She tried to sound as excited as she could. She needed Gina to like her.

"Oh wait. One more thing. I should explain message hierarchy. Shit. I almost forgot message hierarchy. Dan would kill me. Okay, so you know that your first-screen CE responsibilities are paramount. We have to serve our customers with our full attention and our full hearts. So that's understood."

"It is."

"On your second screen, you might get messages from Dan and Jared, or Annie, or anyone directly supervising your work. Those messages inform the minute-to-minute quality of your service. So that would be your second priority. Clear?"

"Clear."

"The third screen is your social, Inner- and OuterCircle. But these messages aren't, like, superfluous. They're just as important as any other messages, but are prioritized third. And sometimes they're urgent. Keep an eye on the InnerCircle feed in particular, because that's where you'll hear about staff meetings, mandatory gatherings, and any breaking news. If there's a Circle notice that's really pressing, that'll be marked in orange. Something extremely urgent will prompt a message on your phone, too. You keep that in view?" Mae nodded at her phone, resting just below the screens on her desk. "Good," Gina said. "So those are the priorities, with your fourth priority your own OuterCircle participation. Which is just as important as anything else, because we value your work-life balance, you know, the calibration between your online life here at the company and outside it. I hope that's clear. Is it?"

"It is."

"Good. So I think you're all set. Any questions?"

Mae said she was fine.

Gina's head tilted skeptically, indicating she knew that Mae actually had many questions still, but didn't want to ask them for fear of looking uninformed. Gina stood up, smiled, took a step back, but then stopped. "Crap. Forgot one more thing." She crouched next to Mae, typed for a few seconds, and a number appeared on the third screen, looking much like her aggregate CE score. It said: MAE HOLLAND: 10,328.

"This is your Participation Rank, PartiRank for short. Some people here call it the Popularity Rank, but it's not really that. It's just an algorithm-generated number that takes into account all your activity in the InnerCircle. Does that make sense?"

"I think so."

"It takes into account zings, exterior followers of your intra-company zings, comments on your zings, your comments on others' zings, your comments on other Circlers' profiles, your photos posted, attendance at Circle events, comments and photos posted about those events—basically it collects and celebrates all you do here. The most active Circlers are ranked highest of course. As you can see, your rank is low now, but that's because you're new and we just activated your social feed. But every time you post or comment or attend anything, that gets factored in, and you'll see your rank change accordingly. That's where the fun comes in. You post, you rise in the rankings. A bunch of people like your post, and you really shoot up. It moves all day. Cool?"

"Very," Mae said.

"We started you with a little boost—otherwise you'd be 10,411. And again, it's just for fun. You're not judged by your rank or anything. Some Circlers take it very seriously, of course, and we love it when people want to participate, but the rank is really just a fun way to see how your participation manifests itself vis-à-vis the overall Circle community. Okay?"

"Okay."

"Okay then. You know how to get hold of me."

And with that, Gina turned and left.

Mae opened the intra-company stream and began. She was determined to get through all the Inner and Outer feeds that night.
There were company-wide notices about each day's menus, each
day's weather, each day's words of the wise—last week's apho-
risms were from MLK, Gandhi, Salk, Mother Teresa and Steve
Jobs. There were notices about each day's campus visits: a pet
adoption agency, a state senator, a Congressman from Tennessee,
the director of Médecins Sans Frontières. Mae found out, with
a sting of remorse, that she'd missed, that very morning, a visit
from Muhammad Yunus, winner of the Nobel Prize. She plowed
through the messages, every one, looking for anything she would
have reasonably been expected to answer personally. There were
surveys, at least fifty of them, gauging the Circlers' opinions on
various company policies, on optimal dates for upcoming gatherings, interest groups, celebrations and holiday breaks. There were
dozens of clubs soliciting members and notifying all of meetings:
there were cat-owner groups—at least ten—a few rabbit groups,
six reptile groups, four of them adamantly snake-exclusive. Most
of all, there were groups for dog-owners. She counted twenty-two,
but was sure that wasn't all of them. One of the groups dedicated
to the owners of very small dogs, Lucky Lapdogs, wanted to know
how many people would join a weekend club for walks and hikes
and support; Mae ignored this one. Then, realizing that ignoring
it would only prompt a second, more urgent, message, she typed
a message, explaining that she didn't have a dog. She was asked
to sign a petition for more vegan options at lunch; she did. There
were nine messages from various work-groups within the com-

pany, asking her to join their subCircles for more specific updates and information sharing. For now she joined the ones dedicated to crochet, soccer, and Hitchcock.

There seemed to be a hundred parents' groups—first-time parents, divorced parents, parents of autistic children, parents of Guatemalan adoptees, Ethiopian adoptees, Russian adoptees. There were seven improv comedy groups, nine swim teams—there had been an inter-staff meet last Wednesday, hundreds of swimmers participating, and a hundred messages were about the contest, who won, some glitch with the results and how a mediator would be on campus to settle any lingering questions or grievances. There were visits, ten a day at least, from companies presenting innovative new products to the Circle. New fuel-efficient cars. New fair-trade sneakers. New locally sourced tennis rackets. There were meetings of every conceivable department—R&D, search, social, outreach, professional networking, philanthropic, ad sales, and with a plummeting of her stomach, Mae saw that she'd missed a meeting, deemed "pretty much mandatory" for all newbies. That had been last Thursday. Why hadn't anyone told her? *Well, stupid,* she answered herself. *They did tell you. Right here.*

"Shit," she said.

By ten p.m., she'd made her way through all the intra-company messages and alerts, and now turned to her own Outer-Circle account. She hadn't visited in six days, and found 118 new notices from that day alone. She decided to plow through, newest to oldest. Most recently, one of her friends from college had posted a message about having the stomach flu, and a long thread followed, with friends making suggestions about remedies, some offering sympathy, some posting photos meant to cheer her up. Mae liked two of the photos, liked three of the comments, posted her own well wishes, and sent a link to a song, "Puking Sally," that she'd found. That prompted a new thread, 54 notices, about the song and the band that wrote it. One of the friends on the thread said he knew the bassist in the band, and then looped him into the conversation. The bassist, Damien Ghilotti, was in New Zealand, was a studio engineer now, but was happy to know that "Puking Sally" was still resonating with the flu-ridden. His post thrilled all involved, and another 129 notices appeared, everyone thrilled to hear from the actual bassist from the band, and by the end of the thread, Damien Ghilotti was invited to play a wedding, if he wanted, or visit Boulder, or Bath, or Gainesville, or St. Charles, Illinois, any time he happened to be passing through, and he would have a place to stay and a home-cooked meal. Upon the mention of St. Charles, someone asked if anyone from there had heard about Tim Jenkins, who was fighting in Afghanistan; they'd seen some mention of a kid from Illinois being shot to death by an Afghan insurgent posing as a police officer. Sixty messages later the respondents had determined that it was a different Tim Jenkins, this one from Rantoul, Illinois, not St. Charles. There was relief all around, but soon the thread had been overtaken by a multi-participant debate about the efficacy of that war, U.S. foreign policy in general, whether or not we won in Vietnam or Grenada or even WWI, and the ability of the Afghans to self-govern, and the opium trade financing the insurgents, and the possibility of legalization of any and all illicit drugs in America and Europe. Someone mentioned the usefulness of marijuana in alleviating glaucoma, and someone else mentioned it was helpful for those

104

with MS, too, and then there was a frenetic exchange between three family members of MS patients, and Mae, feeling some darkness opening its wings within her, signed off.

Mae could no longer keep her eyes open. Though she'd only made it through three days of her social backlog, she shut down and made for the parking lot.

Tuesday morning's chute was lighter than Monday's, but the activity on her third screen kept her in her chair for the day's first three hours. Before the third screen, there had always been a lull, maybe ten or twelve seconds, between when she'd answered a query and when she knew whether or not the answer had been satisfying; she'd used the time to memorize the boilerplates and do a few follow-ups, every so often to check her phone. But now that became more challenging. The third-screen feed dropped forty new InnerCircle messages every few minutes, fifteen or so OuterCircle posts and zings, and Mae used every available moment of downtime to quickly scroll through, make sure there was nothing that demanded her immediate attention, and then come back to her main screen.

By the end of the morning, the flow was manageable, even exhilarating. The company had so much going on, so much humanity and good feeling, and was pioneering on all fronts, that she knew she was being improved just by being in the Circlers' proximity. It was like a well-curated organic grocery store: you knew, by shopping there, that you were healthier; you couldn't make a bad choice, because everything had been vetted already. Likewise, everyone at the Circle there had been chosen, and thus the gene pool was extraordinary, the brainpower phenomenal. It was a place where everyone endeavored, constantly and passionately, to improve themselves, each other, share their knowledge, disseminate it to the world.

By lunchtime, though, she was wiped out, and very much looking forward to sitting, with her cerebral cortex removed, for an hour, on the lawn, with Annie, who had insisted on it.

At 11:50, though, a second-screen message from Dan appeared: *You got a few mins?*

She told Annie she might be late, and when she arrived to Dan's office, he was leaning against the doorjamb. He smiled sympathetically at Mae, but with a raised eyebrow, as if there was something about Mae that was perplexing him, something he couldn't put his finger on. He extended his arm into the office, and she slipped past him. He closed the door.

"Sit down, Mae. You know Alistair, I assume?"

She hadn't seen the man sitting in the corner, but now that she saw him, she knew she didn't know him. He was tall, in his late twenties, with a careful swirl of sandy brown hair. He was positioned diagonally against a rounded chair, his thin frame resting stiffly, like a two-by-four. He didn't stand to meet her, so Mae extended her hand to him.

"Nice to meet you," she said.

Alistair sighed with great resignation and extended his hand as if he were about to touch something washed ashore and rotting.

Mae's mouth went dry. There was something very wrong.

Dan sat down. "Now, I hope we can make this right as soon as possible," he said. "Would you like to start, Mae?"

The two men looked at her. Dan's eyes were steady, while Alistair's look was hurt but expectant. Mae had no idea what to say, no idea what was happening. As the silence festered and grew, Alistair blinked furiously, holding back tears.

"I can't believe this," he managed to say.

Dan turned to him. "Alistair, c'mon. We know you're hurting, but let's keep it in perspective." Dan turned to Mae. "I'll point out the obvious. Mae, we're talking about Alistair's Portugal brunch."

Dan let the words linger, expecting Mae to jump in, but Mae had no idea what those words meant: *Alistair's Portugal brunch?* Could she say she had no idea what that meant? She knew she couldn't. She'd been late to the feed. This must have something to do with that.

"I'm sorry," she said. She knew she would have to tread water until she could figure out what all this was about.

"That's a good start," Dan said. "Right, Alistair?"

Alistair shrugged.

Mae continued fumbling. What did she know? There had been a brunch, that much was certain. And clearly she had not been there. The brunch was planned by Alistair, and now he was hurt. All this was reasonable to assume.

"I wish I could have been there," she ventured, and immediately saw slight signs of confirmation in their faces. She was onto something. "But I wasn't sure if . . ." Now she took a leap. "I wasn't sure if I was welcome, being so new here."

Their faces softened. Mae smiled, knowing she'd hit the right note. Dan shook his head, happy to have his assumption—that Mae was not an inherently bad person—confirmed. He got up from his chair, came around his desk and leaned against it.

"Mae, have we not made you feel welcome?" he asked.

"No, you have! You really have. But I'm not a member of Alistair's team, and I wasn't quite sure what the rules were about, you know, members of my team attending the brunches of more seasoned members of other teams."

Dan nodded. "See, Alistair? I told you it was easily explained." Now Alistair was sitting upright, as if ready to engage again.

"Well of course you're welcome," he said, patting her knee playfully. "Even if you're a little ob*liv*ious."

"Now Alistair . . ."

"I'm sorry," he said, and took a deep breath. "I've got it under control now. I'm very happy."

There were a few more statements of apology and laughs about understandings and misunderstandings, and communications and flow and mistakes and the order of the universe, and finally it was time to let it go. They stood.

"Let's hug it out," Dan said. And they did, forming a tight scrum of newfound communion.

By the time Mae was back at her desk, a message was waiting for her.

Thanks again for coming to meet Alistair and me today. I think that was very productive and helpful. HR knows about the situation, and to close it out they always like to get a statement together. So I typed this up. If it sounds good, just sign it on-screen and send it back.

Glitch No. 5616ARN/MRH/RK2
Day: Monday, June 11
Participants: Mae Holland, Alistair Knight
Story: Alistair of the Renaissance, Team Nine, held a brunch for all staffers who had demonstrated an interest in

Portugal. He sent out three notices about the event, none of which Mae, of the Renaissance, Team Six, answered. Alistair became concerned that there was no RSVP or communication of any kind from Mae. When the brunch occurred, Mae did not attend, and Alistair understandably was distressed about why she would not respond to repeated invitations, and then fail to attend. This was non-participation in a classic sense.

Today a meeting was held between Dan, Alistair and Mae, where Mae explained that she was not sure that she was welcome at such an event, given it was being hosted by a member of a different team, and she was in her second week of life at the company. She feels very bad about causing worry and emotional distress to Alistair— not to mention threatening the delicate ecology of the Renaissance. Now all is worked out and Alistair and Mae are great friends and feel rejuvenated. All agree a fresh start is warranted and welcome.

There was a line below the statement where Mae was to sign, and she used her fingernail to sign her name on the screen. She submitted it, and instantly received a thank-you from Dan.

That was great, he wrote. *Alistair is obviously a little sensitive, but that's only because he's such a fiercely committed Circler. Just like you, right? Thank you for being so cooperative. You were great. Onward!*

Mae was late, and hoped Annie would still be waiting. The day was clear and warm, and Mae found Annie on the lawn, typing on her tablet with a granola bar dangling from her mouth. She squinted up at Mae. "Hey. You're tardy."

"Sorry."

"How are you?"

Mae made a face.

"I know, I know. I followed the whole thing," Annie said, chewing extravagantly.

"Stop eating like that. Close your mouth. You did?"

"I was just listening while I worked. They asked me to. And I've heard much worse. Everyone has a few of those early on. Eat fast, by the way. I want to show you something."

In quick succession, two waves passed over Mae. First, profound unease that Annie had been listening without her knowledge, followed by a wave of relief, knowing her friend had been with her, even if remotely, and could confirm that Mae would survive.

"Did *you*?" she asked.

"Did I what?"

"Ever get called on the carpet like that? I'm still shaking."

"Of course. Once a month maybe. I still do. Chew fast."

Mae ate as quickly as she could, watching a game of croquet being played on the lawn. The players seemed to have made up their own rules. Mae finished her lunch.

"Good, get up," Annie said, and they made their way toward TomorrowTown. "What? Your face still has a question protruding from it."

"Did *you* go to that Portugal brunch?"

Annie scoffed. "Me? No, why? I wasn't invited."

"But why was *I*? I didn't sign up for it. I'm not some Portugal freak."

"It's on your profile, isn't it? Didn't you go there once?"

"Sure, but I never mentioned it on my profile. I've been to Lisbon, but that's it. That was five years ago."

They approached the TomorrowTown building, fronted by a wall of ironwork that looked vaguely Turkish. Annie waved her pass over a wall-mounted pad and the door opened.

"Did you take pictures?" Annie asked.

"In Lisbon? Sure."

"And they were on your laptop?"

Mae had to think a second. "I guess so."

"Then that's probably it. If they were on your laptop, now they're in the cloud, and the cloud gets scanned for information like that. You don't have to run around signing up for Portugal interest clubs or anything. When Alistair wanted to do his brunch, he probably just asked for a search of everyone on campus who had visited the country, took pictures or mentioned it in an email or whatever. So then he automatically gets a list, and sends his invitation out. It saves about a hundred hours of nonsense. Over here."

They stopped in front of a long hallway. Annie's eyes were alight with mischief. "Okay. You want to see something surreal?"

"I'm still weirded out."

"Don't be. Get in here."

Annie opened a door to a beautiful room, some cross between a buffet and a museum and a trade show.

"How crazy is this?"

The room looked vaguely familiar. Mae had seen something like this on TV.

"It's like one of those gift bag places for celebrities, right?"

Mae scanned the room. There were products spread all over

dozens of tables and platforms. But here, instead of jewelry and pumps there were sneakers and toothbrushes and a dozen types of chips and drinks and energy bars.

Mae laughed. "I'm guessing this is free?"

"For you, for very important people like you and me, yes."

"Jesus Christ. All of this?"

"Yup, this is the free sample room. It's always full, and this stuff needs to get used one way or the other. We invite rotating groups in—sometimes it's programmers, sometimes CE people like you. Different group every day."

"And you just take whatever you want?"

"Well, you have to zap your ID on anything you're taking so they know who's taken what. Otherwise some idiot takes home the whole room."

"I haven't seen any of this stuff yet."

"In stores? No, none of this stuff is in stores yet. These are prototypes and test runs."

"These are actual Levi's?"

Mae was holding a pair of beautiful jeans, and she was sure they did not yet exist in the world.

"They might be a few months till market, maybe a year. You want those? You can ask for a different size."

"And I can wear them?"

"As opposed to what, wiping your ass with them? Yeah, they want you to wear them. You're an influential person working at the Circle! You're a style leader, early adopter, all that."

"These are actually my size."

"Good. Take two. You have a bag?"

Annie retrieved a cloth bag with the Circle logo on it and gave it to Mae, who was hovering over a display of new phone covers and accessories. She picked up a beautiful phone shell that was sturdy as stone, but with a chamois-smooth surface.

"Crap," Mae said. "I didn't bring my phone."

"What? Where is it?" Annie asked, astounded.

"I guess at my desk."

"Mae, you are incredible. You're so focused and together, but then you have these weird spacy lapses. You came to lunch without your phone?"

"Sorry."

"No. It's what I love about you. You're like part human, part rainbow. What? Don't get upset."

"I'm just getting a lot of input today."

"You're not still worried, are you?"

"You think it's okay, that meeting with Dan and Alistair?"

"It's definitely okay."

"He's just that sensitive?"

Annie rolled her eyes. "Alistair? Beyond all reason. But he writes great code. The guy is a machine. It'd take a year to find and train someone to do what he does. So we have to deal with the crazy. There are just some nuts here. Needy nuts. And there are those, like Dan, who enable the nuts. But don't worry. I don't think you'll overlap much—with Alistair at least." Annie checked the time. She had to go.

"You stay till that bag is full," she said. "I'll see you later."

Mae stayed, and filled her bag with jeans, and food, and shoes, and a few new covers for her phone, a sports bra. She left the room, feeling like a shoplifter, but encountered no one on the way out. When she got back to her desk, there were eleven messages from Annie.

She read the first: *Hey Mae, realizing I shouldn't have gone off on Dan and Alistair that way. Wasn't very nice. Not Circly at all. Pretend I didn't say it.*

The second: *You get my last msg?*

The third: *Starting to freak out a little. Why aren't you answering me?*

Fourth: *Just texted you, called you. Are you dead? Shit. Forgot you forgot your phone. You suck.*

Fifth: *If you were offended by what I said about Dan don't go all silent-treatment. I said sorry. Write back.*

Sixth: *Are you getting these messages? It's v. important. Call me!*

Seventh: *If you're telling Dan what I said you're a bitch. Since when do we tattle on each other?*

Eighth: *Realizing you might just be in a meeting. True?*

Ninth: *It's been 25 mins. What is UP?*

Tenth: *Just checked and see that you're back at your desk. Call me this instant or we're through. I thought we were friends.*

Eleventh: *Hello?*

Mae called her.

"What the hell, spaz?"

"Where *were* you?"

"I saw you twenty minutes ago. I finished in the sample room, used the bathroom, and now I'm here."

"Did you tell on me?"

"Did I what?"

"Did you tell on me?"

114

"Annie, what the fuck?"

"Just tell me."

"No, I didn't tell on you. To who?"

"What did you say to him?"

"Who?"

"Dan."

"I haven't even seen him."

"You didn't send a message to him?"

"No. Annie, shit."

"Promise?"

"Yes."

Annie sighed. "Okay. Fuck. Sorry. I sent him a message, and called him, and hadn't heard back. And then I didn't hear back from you, and my brain just put all this together in a weird way."

"Annie, shit."

"Sorry."

"I think you're overstressed."

"No, I'm fine."

"Let me get you some drinks tonight."

"Thanks, no."

"Please?"

"I can't. We have too many things going on here this week. Just trying to deal with this clusterfuck in Washington."

"Washington? What about it?"

"It's such a long story. I can't say, actually."

"But you're the one that has to handle it? All of Washington?"

"They give me some of the government-hassle stuff because, I don't know, because they think my dimples help. Maybe they do. I don't know. I just wish there were five of me."

"You sound terrible, Annie. Take a night off."

"No, no. I'll be fine. I just have to answer these queries from some subcommittee. It'll be fine. But I better go. Love you."

And she hung up.

Mae called Francis. "Annie won't go out with me. Will you? Tonight?"

"Out-out? There's a band here tonight. You know the Creamers? They're playing in the Colony. It's a benefit."

Mae said yes, that sounded good, but when the time came, she didn't want to see a band called the Creamers play in the Colony. She cajoled Francis into her car, and they left for San Francisco.

"You know where we're going?" he asked.

"I don't. What are you doing?"

He was typing furiously into his phone. "I'm just telling everyone I'm not coming."

"Finished?"

"Yes." He dropped his phone.

"Good. Let's drink first."

And so they parked downtown and found a restaurant that looked so terrible, with faded and unappetizing pictures of the food taped haphazardly to the windows, that they figured it might be cheap. They were right, and they ate curry and drank Singha and sat in bamboo chairs that squealed and strained to stay erect. Somewhere toward the end of her first beer, Mae decided that she would have a second, quickly, and that shortly after dinner she would kiss Francis on the street.

They finished dinner and she did.

"Thank you," he said.

"Did you just thank me?"

"You just saved me so much inner turmoil. I've never made the first move in my life. But usually it takes a woman weeks to figure out she'll have to take the initiative."

Again Mae had the feeling of being clubbed with information that complicated her feelings about Francis, who seemed so sweet one moment and so strange and unfiltered the next.

Still, because she was riding at the crest of a Singha wave, she led him by the hand back to her car, where they kissed more, while parked on a very busy intersection. A homeless man was watching them, as an anthropologist would, from the sidewalk, miming the taking of notes.

"Let's go," she said, and they left the car, and wandered through the city, finding a Japanese souvenir shop open, and, next to it, also open, a gallery full of photorealistic paintings of gigantic human haunches.

"Big pictures of big asses," Francis noted, as they found a bench, in an alley-turned-piazza, the streetlamps above giving it the look of blue moonlight. "That was real art. I couldn't believe they hadn't sold anything yet."

Mae kissed him again. She was in a kissing mood, and knowing that Francis wouldn't make any aggressive moves, she felt at ease, kissing him more, knowing it would be only kissing tonight. She threw herself into the kissing, making it mean lust, and friendship, and the possibility of love, and kissed him while thinking of his face, wondering if his eyes were open, if he cared about the passersby who clucked or who hooted but still passed by.

* * *

In the days that followed, Mae knew that it could be true, that the sun could be her halo, that the leaves could exist to marvel at her every step, to urge her on, to congratulate her on this Francis, what the two of them had done. They had celebrated their shimmering youth, their freedom, their wet mouths, and had done so in public, fueled by the knowledge that whatever hardships they had faced or would face, they were working at the center of the world and trying mightily to improve it. They had reason to feel good. Mae wondered if she was in love. No, she knew she was not in love, but she was, she felt, at least halfway. That week, she and Francis ate lunch together often, even if briefly, and after they ate, they found a place to lean against each other and kiss. Once it was under a fire exit behind the Paleozoic. Once it was in the Roman Empire, behind the paddle courts. She loved his taste, always clean, simple like lemon water, and how he would remove his glasses, look briefly lost, then would close his eyes and look almost beautiful, his face as smooth and uncomplicated as a child's. Having him near brought a new crackle to the days. Everything was astounding. Eating was astounding, under the bright sun, the heat of his shirt, his hands on her ankle. Walking was astounding. Sitting in the Enlightenment was astounding, as they were now doing, awaiting Dream Friday in the Great Hall.

"Pay attention," Francis said. "I really think you'll like this."

Francis wouldn't tell Mae what the subject of that Friday's innovation talk was. The speaker, Gus Khazeni, had apparently been part of Francis's child safety project before he spun off, four months ago, to head up a new unit. Today would be his first airing of his findings and new plan.

Mae and Francis sat near the front, at Gus's request. He wanted to see some friendly faces as he spoke, for the first time, in the Great Hall, Francis said. Mae turned to scan the crowd, seeing Dan a few rows back, and Renata and Sabine, sitting together, concentrating on a tablet laid between them.

Eamon Bailey stepped onto the stage to warm applause.

"Well, we really have a treat for you today," he said. "Most of you know our local treasure and jack-of-all-trades, Gus Khazeni. And most of you know he had an inspiration a while back that we urged him to follow. Today he'll do a bit of a presentation, and I think you'll really like it." And with that, he ceded the stage to Gus, who had the odd combination of preternaturally good looks and a timid, mouselike demeanor. Or at least it seemed that way, as he pittered across the stage like he was tip-toeing.

"Okay, if you're like me, you're single and pathetic and forever a disappointment to your Persian mother and father and grandparents, who see you as a failure for not having a mate and children by now because you're pathetic."

Laughs from the audience.

"Did I use the word *pathetic* twice?" More laughter. "If my family was here, it would have been many more times.

"Okay," Gus continued, "but let's say you want to please your family, and maybe yourself, too, by finding a mate. Anyone interested in finding a mate here?"

A few hands rose up.

"Oh c'mon. You liars. I happen to know that 67 percent of this company is unmarried. So I'm talking to you. The other 33 percent can go to hell."

Mae laughed out loud. Gus's delivery was perfect. She leaned over to Francis. "I love this guy."

He continued: "Now maybe you tried other dating sites. And let's say you're matched up, and that's all good, and you're headed out for a rendezvous. All good, the family's happy, they briefly entertain the idea that you're not a worthless use of their shared DNA.

"Now, the second you ask someone out, you're screwed, right? Actually, you're not screwed. You're celibate, but you want to change that. So you spend the rest of the week stressing over where to take them—food, concert, wax museum? Some kind of dungeon? You have no idea. The wrong choice and you're an idiot. You know that you have a wide variety of tastes, things you like, and they probably do, too, but that first choice is too important. You need help to send the right message—the message being that you're sensitive, intuitive, decisive, you have good taste and you're perfect."

The crowd was laughing; they hadn't stopped laughing. The screen behind Gus now showed a grid of icons, with information listed clearly below each. Mae could make out what seemed to be symbols for a restaurant, for movies, music, shopping, outdoor activities, beaches.

"Okay," Gus continued, "so check this out and remember it's just a beta version. This is called LuvLuv. Okay, maybe that name sucks. Actually, I know it sucks and we're working on it. But this is how it works. When you've found someone, and you have their name, you made contact, you have a date planned—this is when LuvLuv comes in. Maybe you've already memorized their dating-site page, their personal page, all their feeds. But this Luv-Luv gives you an entirely different set of information. So you feed in your date's name. That's the start. Then LuvLuv scans the web and uses some high-powered and very surgical search machinery to ensure that you don't make an ass out of yourself and that you might find love and produce grandchildren for your baba, who thinks you might be sterile."

"You're awesome, Gus!" a woman's voice yelled from the audience.

"Thank you! Will you go out with me?" he said, and waited for an answer. When the woman went quiet, he said, "See, this is why I need help. Now, to test this software, I think we require an actual person who wants to find out more about an actual potential romantic interest. Can I have a volunteer?"

Gus looked out to the audience, theatrically peering around with his hand shielding his eyes.

"No one? Oh wait. I see a hand up."

To Mae's shock and horror, Gus was looking her way. More specifically, he was looking at Francis, whose hand was raised. And before she could say anything to him, Francis was out of his seat and headed up to the stage.

"Give this brave volunteer a round of applause!" Gus said, and Francis jogged up the steps and was enveloped in the warm spotlight, next to Gus. He had not looked back to Mae since he'd left her side.

"Now what is your name, sir?"

"Francis Garaventa."

Mae thought she'd puke. What was happening? This isn't real, she said to herself. Was he really going to talk about her onstage? No, she assured herself. He's just helping a friend, and they'll do their demonstration using fake names.

"Now Francis," Gus continued, "am I to assume you have someone you'd like to date?"

"Yes, Gus, that is correct."

Mae, dizzy and terrified, nonetheless couldn't help noticing that onstage, Francis was transformed, just as Gus had been. He was playing along, showing his teeth, acting shy but doing so with great confidence.

"Is that person a real person?" Gus asked.

"Of course," Francis said. "I no longer date imaginary people." The crowd laughed heartily, and Mae's stomach dropped to her shoes. *Oh shit,* she thought. *Oh shit.*

"And her name?"

"Her name is Mae Holland," Francis said, and for the first time, looked down to her. Her face was in her hands, her eyes peeking from under her trembling fingers. With an almost imperceptible tilt of his head, he seemed to register that Mae wasn't entirely comfortable with the proceedings thus far, but just as soon as he acknowledged her, he turned back to Gus, grinning like a game-show host.

"Okay," Gus said, typing the name into his tablet, "Mae Holland." In the search box, her name appeared in three-foot letters on the screen.

"So Francis wants to go out with Mae, and he doesn't want to make an ass out of himself. What's one of the first things he needs to know. Anyone?"

"Allergies!" someone yelled.

"Okay, allergies. I can search for that."

He clicked on an icon of a cat sneezing, and immediately a stanza appeared below.

Likely gluten allergy
Definite horse allergy
Mother has nut allergy
No other likely allergies

"Okay. I can click on any one of these listings and find out more. Let's try the gluten one." Gus clicked on the first line, revealing a more complex and dense scroll of links and text blocks. "Now as you can see, LuvLuv has searched everything Mae's ever posted. It's collated this information and analyzed it for relevance. Maybe Mae's mentioned gluten. Maybe she's bought or reviewed gluten-free products. This would indicate she's likely gluten-allergic."

Mae wanted to leave the auditorium, but knew it would make more of a scene than staying.

"Now let's look at the horse one," Gus said, and clicked on the next listing. "Here we can make a more definite assertion, given it's found three instances of messages posted that directly say, for example, *I'm allergic to horses.*"

"So does that help you?" Gus asked.

"It does," Francis said. "I was about to take her to some stables to eat leavened bread." He mugged to the audience. "Now I know!"

The audience laughed, and Gus nodded, as if to say, *Aren't we a pair?* "Okay," Gus continued, "now notice that the mentions of the horse allergy were way back in 2010, from Facebook of all places. For all of you who thought it was silly of us to pay what we did for Facebook's archives, take heed! Okay, no allergies. But check this out, right nearby. This is what I had in mind next—food. Did you think you might take her out to eat, Francis?"

Francis answered gamely. "Yes I did, Gus." Mae didn't recognize this man onstage. Where had Francis gone? She wanted to kill this version of him.

"Okay, this is where things usually get ugly and stupid. There's nothing worse than the back-and-forth: 'Where do you want to eat?' 'Oh, anything's fine.' 'No, really. What's your preference?' 'Doesn't matter to me. What's yours?' No more of that bull . . . shite. LuvLuv breaks it down for you. Any time she's posted, any time she's liked or disliked a restaurant, any time she's *mentioned* food—it all gets ranked and sorted and I end up with a list like this."

He clicked on the food icon, which revealed a number of subset lists, with rankings of type of food, names of restaurants, restaurants by city and by neighborhood. The lists were uncanny in their accuracy. They even featured the place she and Francis had eaten earlier that week.

"Now I click on the place I like, and if she paid through TruYou, I know what she ordered last time she ate there. Click here and see the specials for those restaurants on Friday, when our date will happen. Here's the average wait for a table that day. Uncertainty eliminated."

Gus went on and on throughout the presentation, into Mae's preferences for films, for outdoor spaces to walk on and jog through, to favorite sports, favorite vistas. It was accurate, most of it, and while Gus and Francis hammed it up onstage, and the audience grew ever-more impressed with the software, Mae had first hidden behind her hands, then sunk to the lowest-possible place in her seat, and finally, when she felt that any moment she'd be asked to get onstage to confirm the great power of this new tool, she slipped out of her seat, across the aisle, out the auditorium's side door and into the flat white light of an overcast afternoon.

"I'm sorry."

Mae couldn't look at him.

"Mae. Sorry. I don't understand why you're so mad."

She did not want him near her. She was back at her desk, and he'd followed her there, standing over her like some carrion bird. She didn't glance at him, because besides loathing him and finding his face weak and his eyes shifty, besides being sure she'd never need to see that wretched face again, she had work to do. The afternoon chute had been opened and the flow was heavy. "We can talk later," she said to him, but she had no intention of talking to him again, that day or any day. There was relief in that certainty.

Eventually he left, at least his corporeal self left, but he appeared in minutes, on her third screen, pleading for forgiveness. He told her he knew he shouldn't have sprung it on her, but that Gus had insisted on it being a surprise. He sent forty or fifty messages throughout the afternoon, apologizing, telling her what a big hit she was, how it would have been even better if she'd gotten onstage, because people were clapping for her. He assured her that everything that had been on-screen was publicly available, none of it embarrassing, all of it culled from things she'd posted herself, after all.

And Mae knew all this to be true. She wasn't angry at the revelation of her allergies. Or her favorite foods. She had openly offered this information for many years, and she felt that offering her preferences, and reading about others', was one of the things she loved about her life online.

So what had so mortified her during Gus's presentation? She couldn't put her finger on it. Was it only the surprise of it? Was it the pinpoint accuracy of the algorithms? Maybe. But then again, it wasn't entirely accurate, so was *that* the problem? Having a matrix of preferences presented as your essence, as the whole you? Maybe that was it. It was some kind of mirror, but it was incomplete, distorted. And if Francis wanted any or all of that information, why couldn't he just *ask* her? Her third screen, though, all afternoon was filled with congratulatory messages.

You're awesome, Mae.

Good job, newbie.

No horseback rides for you. Maybe a llama?

She pushed through the afternoon and didn't notice her blinking phone till after five. She'd missed three messages from her mother. When she listened to them, they all said the same thing: "Come home."

As she drove over the hills and through the tunnel, heading east, she called her mom and got the details. Her father had had a seizure, had gone to the hospital, was asked to spend the night for observation. Mae was told to drive directly there, but when she arrived, he was gone. She called her mother.

"Where is he?"

"Home. Sorry. We just got here. I didn't think you'd get out here so soon. He's fine."

So Mae drove home, and when she arrived, breathless and angry and scared, she saw Mercer's Toyota pickup in the driveway, and this sent her into a mental bramble. She didn't want him here. It complicated an already gory scene.

She opened the door and saw not her parents, but Mercer's giant shapeless form. He was standing in the foyer. Every time she saw him again after time apart she was jarred by how big he was, how lumpy. His hair was longer now, adding to his mass. His head blocked all light.

"Heard your car," he said. He had a pear in his hand.

"Why are you here?" she asked.

"They called me to help," he said.

"Dad?" She rushed past Mercer and into the living room. There, her father was resting, lengthwise, on the couch, watching baseball on the television.

He didn't turn his head, but looked her way. "Hey hon. Heard you out there."

Mae sat on the coffee table and held his hand. "You okay?"

"I am. Just a scare, really. It started strong but petered out." Almost imperceptibly, he was inching his head forward, to see around her.

"Are you trying to watch the game?"

"Ninth inning," he said.

Mae moved out of the way. Her mother entered the room. "We called Mercer to help get your father into the car."

"I didn't want the ambulance," her father said, still watching the game.

"So was it a seizure?" Mae asked.

"They're not sure," Mercer said from the kitchen.

"Can I hear the answer from my own parents?" Mae called out.

"Mercer was a lifesaver," her father said.

"Why didn't you call me to say it wasn't so serious?" Mae asked.

"It *was* serious," her mother said. "That's when I called."

"But now he's watching baseball."

"It's not as serious now," her mother said, "but for a while there, we really didn't know what was happening. So we called Mercer."

"He saved my life."

"I don't think Mercer saved your life, Dad."

"I don't mean that I was dying. But you know how I hate the whole circus with the EMTs and the sirens, and the neighbors knowing. We just called Mercer, he got here in five minutes, helped get me to the car, into the hospital, and that was that. It made all the difference."

Mae fumed. She'd driven two hours in a red panic to find her father relaxing on the couch, watching baseball. She'd driven two hours to find her ex in her home, anointed the hero of the family. And what was she? She was somehow negligent. She was superfluous. It reminded her of so many of the things she didn't like about Mercer. He liked to be considered kind, but he made sure everyone knew it, and that drove Mae mad, always having to hear about his kindness, his straight-upness, his reliability, his bound-less empathy. But with her he'd been diffident, moody, unavail-able too many times she needed him.

"You want some chicken? Mercer brought some," her mother said, and Mae decided that was a good cue to use her bathroom for a few minutes or ten.

"I'm gonna clean up," she said, and went upstairs.

Later, after they'd all eaten, and recounted the day, explaining how her father's vision had diminished to an alarming state, and the numbness in his hands had worsened—symptoms the doctors said were normal and treatable, or at least addressable—and after her parents had gone to bed, Mae and Mercer sat in the backyard, the heat still coming off the grass, the trees, the rain-washed grey fences that surrounded them.

"Thanks for helping," she said.

"It was easy. Vinnie's lighter than he used to be."

Mae didn't like the sound of that. She didn't want her father to be lighter, easily carried. She changed the subject.

"How's business?"

"Really good. Really good. I actually had to take on an appren-tice last week. Isn't that cool? I have an apprentice. And your job? Great?"

Mae was taken aback. Mercer was rarely so ebullient.

"It *is* great," she said.

"Good. Good to hear. I was hoping it'd work out. So you're doing what, programming or something?"

"I'm in CE. Customer Experience. I deal with the advertisers right now. Wait. I saw something about your stuff the other day. I looked you up and there was this comment about someone getting something shipped damaged? They were so pissed. I'm assuming you saw that."

Mercer exhaled theatrically. "I didn't." His face had gone sour.

"Don't worry," she said. "It was just some nutjob."

"And now it's in my head."

"Don't blame me. I just—"

"You just made me aware that there's some kook out there who hates me and wants to hurt my business."

"There were other comments, too, and most of them were nice. There was actually one really funny one." She began scrolling through her phone.

"Mae. Please. I'm asking you not to read it."

"Here it is: 'All those poor deer antlers died for this shit?'"

"Mae, I asked you not to read me that."

"*What?* It was funny!"

"How can I ask you not to do that in a way where you'll respect my wishes?"

This was the Mercer Mae remembered and couldn't stand—prickly, moody, high-handed.

"What are you talking about?"

Mercer took a deep breath, and Mae knew he was about to give a speech. If there was a podium before him, he'd be stepping up to it, removing his papers from his sportcoat pocket. Two years of community college and he thought he was some kind of professor. He'd given her speeches about organically sourced beef, about the early work of King Crimson, and each time it started with this deep breath, a breath that said *Settle in, this will take a while and will blow your mind.*

"Mae, I have to ask you to—"

"I know, you want me to stop reading you customer comments. Fine."

"No, that's not what I was—"

"You *want* me to read them to you?"

"Mae, how about if you just let me finish my sentence? Then you'll know what I'm saying. You guessing the end of every one of my sentences is never helpful, because you're never right."

"But you talk so *slow.*"

"I talk normally. You've just gotten impatient."

"Okay. Go."

"But now you're hyperventilating."

"I guess I'm just so easily bored by this."

"By talking."

"By talking in slow motion."

"Can I start now? It'll take three minutes. Can you give me three minutes, Mae?"

"Fine."

"Three minutes where you won't know what I'm about to say, okay? It will be a surprise."

"Okay."

"All right. Mae, we have to change how we interact. Every time I see or hear from you, it's through this filter. You send me links, you quote someone talking about me, you say you saw a picture of me on someone's wall. . . . It's always this third-party assault. Even when I'm talking to you face-to-face you're telling me what some stranger thinks of me. It becomes like we're never alone. Every time I see you, there's a hundred other people in the room. You're always looking at me through a hundred other people's eyes."

"Don't get dramatic about it."

"I just want to talk with you directly. Without you bringing in every other stranger in the world who might have an opinion about me."

"I don't do that."

"You do, Mae. A few months ago, you read something about me, and remember this? When I saw you, you were so standoffish."

"That's because they said you were using endangered species for your work!"

"But I've never done that."

"Well, how am *I* supposed to know that?"

"You can *ask* me! Actually ask *me*. You know how weird that is, that you, my friend and ex-girlfriend, gets her information about me from some random person who's never met me? And then I have to sit across from you and it's like we're looking at each other through this strange fog."

"Fine. Sorry."

"Will you promise me to stop doing this?"

"Stop reading online?"

"I don't care what you read. But when you and I communicate, I want to do it directly. You write to me, I write to you. You ask me questions, and I answer them. You stop getting news about me from third parties."

"But Mercer, you run a business. You need to participate

online. These are your customers, and this is how they express themselves, and how you know if you're succeeding." Mae's mind churned through a half-dozen Circle tools she knew would help his business, but Mercer was an underachiever. An underachiever who somehow managed to be smug about it.

"See, that's not true, Mae. It's not true. I know I'm successful if I sell chandeliers. If people order them, then I make them, and they pay me money for them. If they have something to say afterward, they can call me or write me. I mean, all this stuff you're involved in, it's all gossip. It's people talking about each other behind their backs. That's the vast majority of this social media, all these reviews, all these comments. Your tools have elevated gossip, hearsay and conjecture to the level of valid, mainstream communication. And besides that, it's fucking dorky."

Mae exhaled through her nostrils.

"I love it when you do that," he said. "Does that mean you have no answer? Listen, twenty years ago, it wasn't so cool to have a calculator watch, right? And spending all day inside playing with your calculator watch sent a clear message that you weren't doing so well socially. And judgments like 'like' and 'dislike' and 'smiles' and 'frowns' were limited to junior high. Someone would write a note and it would say, 'Do you like unicorns and stickers?' and you'd say, 'Yeah, I like unicorns and stickers! Smile!' That kind of thing. But now it's not just junior high kids who do it, it's everyone, and it seems to me sometimes I've entered some inverted zone, some mirror world where the dorkiest shit in the world is completely dominant. The world has dorkified itself."

"Mercer, is it important to you to be cool?"

"Do I look like it is?" He passed a hand over his expanding

stomach, his torn fatigues. "Clearly I'm no master of cool. But I remember when you'd see John Wayne or Steve McQueen and you'd say, Wow, those guys are badass. They ride horses and motorcycles and wander the earth righting wrongs."

Mae couldn't help but laugh. She saw the time on her phone. "It's been more than three minutes."

Mercer plowed on. "Now the movie stars beg people to follow their Zing feeds. They send pleading messages asking everyone to smile at them. And holy fuck, the mailing lists! Everyone's a junk mailer. You know how I spend an hour every day? Thinking of ways to unsubscribe to mailing lists without hurting anyone's feelings. There's this new neediness—it pervades everything." He sighed as if he'd made some very important points. "It's just a very different planet."

"It's different in a good way," Mae said. "There are a thousand ways it's better, and I can list them. But I can't help it if you're not social. I mean, your social needs are so minimal—"

"It's not that I'm not social. I'm social enough. But the tools you guys create actually *manufacture* unnaturally extreme social needs. No one needs the level of contact you're purveying. It improves nothing. It's not nourishing. It's like snack food. You know how they engineer this food? They scientifically determine precisely how much salt and fat they need to include to keep you eating. You're not hungry, you don't need the food, it does nothing for you, but you keep eating these empty calories. This is what you're pushing. Same thing. Endless empty calories, but the digital-social equivalent. And you calibrate it so it's equally addictive."

"Oh Jesus."

"You know how you finish a bag of chips and you hate yourself? You know you've done nothing good for yourself. That's the same feeling, and you know it is, after some digital binge. You feel wasted and hollow and diminished."

"I never feel diminished." Mae thought of the petition she'd signed that day, to demand more job opportunities for immigrants living in the suburbs of Paris. It was energizing and would have impact. But Mercer didn't know about this, or anything Mae did, anything the Circle did, and she was too sick of him to explain it all.

"And it's eliminated my ability to just talk to you." He was still talking. "I mean, I can't send you emails, because you immediately forward them to someone else. I can't send you a photo, because you post it on your own profile. And meanwhile, your company is scanning all of our messages for information they can monetize. Don't you think this is insane?"

Mae looked at his fat face. He was thickening everywhere. He seemed to be developing jowls. Could a man of twenty-five already have jowls? No wonder snack food was on his mind.

"Thanks for helping my dad," she said, and went inside and waited for him to leave. It took him a few minutes to do so—he insisted on finishing his beer—but soon enough he did, and Mae turned out the downstairs lights, went to her old room and dropped herself into her bed. She checked her messages, found a few dozen that needed her attention, and then, because it was only nine o'clock and her parents were already asleep, she logged on to her Circle account and handled a few dozen queries, feeling, with every fulfilled request, that she was cleaning the Mercer off of herself. By midnight she felt reborn.

*   *   *

On Saturday Mae woke in her old bed, and after breakfast, she sat with her father, the two of them watching women's professional basketball, something he'd taken to doing with great enthusiasm. They wasted the rest of the day playing cards, and running errands, and together cooked a chicken-sauté dish her parents had learned at a cooking class they'd taken at the Y.

On Sunday morning, the routine was the same: Mae slept in, feeling leaden and feeling good about it, and wandered into the TV room, where her father was again watching some WNBA game. This time he was wearing a thick white robe a friend of his had pilfered from a Los Angeles hotel.

Her mother was outside, using duct tape to repair a plastic garbage can that raccoons had damaged while trying to extract its contents. Mae was feeling dull-witted, her body reluctant to do anything but recline. She had been, she realized, on constant alert for a full week, and hadn't slept more than five hours on any given night. Simply sitting in her parents' dim living room, watching this basketball game, which meant nothing to her, all those ponytails and braids leaping, all that squeaking of sneakers, was restorative and sublime.

"You think you can help me up, Sweet Pea?" her father asked. His fists were deep in the couch, but he couldn't lift himself. The cushions were too deep.

Mae got up and reached for his hand but when she did, she heard a faint liquid sound.

"Mother-bastard," he said, and began to sit down again. Then he adjusted his trajectory, and leaned on his side, as if he'd just remembered there was something fragile he couldn't sit on.

"Can you get your mother?" he asked, his teeth clenched, his eyes closed.

"What's wrong?" Mae asked.

He opened his eyes, and there was an unfamiliar fury in them. "Please just get your mother."

"I'm right here. Let me help," she said. She reached for his hand again. He swatted her away.

"Get. Your. Mother."

And then the smell hit her. He'd soiled himself.

He exhaled loudly, composing himself. Now with a softer voice he said, "Please. Please dear. Get Mom."

Mae ran to the front door. She found her mother by the garage and told her what had happened. Mae's mother did not rush inside. Instead, she held Mae's hands in her own.

"I think you better head back now," she said. "He won't want you to see this."

"I can help," Mae said.

"Please, honey. You have to grant him some dignity."

"Bonnie!" His voice boomed from inside the house.

Mae's mother grabbed her hand. "Mae, sweetie, just get your stuff and we'll see you in a few weeks, okay?"

Mae drove back to the coast, her body shaking with rage. They had no right to do that, to summon her home and then cast her out. She didn't *want* to smell his shit! She would help, yes, any time she was asked, but not if they treated her that way. And Mercer! He was scolding her in her own house. Jesus Christ. The three of them. Mae had driven two hours there, and now was driving two back, and what had she gotten for all this work? Just frustration. At night, lectures from fat men, and during the day, shooed away by her own parents.

By the time she got back to the coast, it was 4:14. She had time, she thought. Did the place close at five or six? She couldn't remember. She swerved off the highway and toward the marina. When she got to the beach, the gate to the kayak-storage areas was open, but there was no one in sight. Mae looked around, between the rows of kayaks and paddles and life preservers. "Hello?" she said.

"Hello!" a voice said. "Over here. In the trailer."

Behind the rows of equipment, there was a trailer, on cinderblocks, and through the open door, Mae could see a man's feet on a desk, a phone cord stretching from a desk unit to an unseen face. She walked up the steps, and in the darkened trailer she saw a man, in his thirties, balding, holding his index finger up to her. Mae checked her phone for the time every few minutes, seeing the minutes slip away: 4:20, 4:21, 4:23. When he was off the phone, he smiled.

"Thanks for your patience. How can I help?"

"Is Marion around?"

"No. I'm her son. Walt." He stood and shook Mae's hand. He was tall, thin, sunburned.

"Nice to meet you. Am I too late?"

"Too late for what? Dinner?" he said, thinking he'd made a joke.

"To rent a kayak."

"Oh. Well, what time is it? I haven't checked in a while."

She didn't have to check. "4:26," she said.

He cleared his throat and smiled. "4:26, eh? Well, we usually close at five, but seeing as you're so good with time, I bet I can trust you to bring it back at 5:22. You think that's fair? That's when I have to leave to pick up my daughter."

"Thank you," Mae said.

"Let's get you set up," he said. "We just digitized our system. You said you have an account?"

Mae gave him her name, and he typed it into a new tablet, but nothing registered. After three tries, he realized his wifi wasn't working. "Maybe I can check you in on my phone," he said, taking it from his pocket.

"Can we do it when I come back?" Mae asked, and he agreed, thinking it would give him time to bring the network back up. He set Mae up with a life preserver and kayak, and when she was out on the water, she checked her phone again. 4:32. She had almost an hour. On the bay, an hour was always plenty. An hour was a day.

She paddled out, and this day saw no harbor seals in the marina, though she dawdled purposely to try to draw them out. She made her way over to the old half-sunken pier where they sometimes sunned themselves, but found none. There were no harbor seals, no sea lions, the pier was empty, a sole filthy pelican sitting atop a post.

She paddled beyond the tidy yachts, beyond the mystery ships and into the open bay. Once there, she rested, feeling the water beneath her, smooth and undulating like gelatin, fathoms deep. As she sat, unmoving, a pair of heads appeared twenty yards in front of her. They were harbor seals, and were looking at each other, as if deciding whether they should look at Mae, in unison. Which they presently did.

They stared at each other, the two seals and Mae, no one blinking, until, as if realizing how uninteresting Mae was, just some figure unmoving, one seal leaned into a wave and disappeared, and the second seal quickly followed.

Ahead, halfway into the bay, she saw something new, a man-made shape she hadn't noticed before, and decided that would be her task that day, to make her way to the shape and investigate. She paddled closer, and saw that the shape was actually two vessels, an ancient fishing boat tethered to a small barge. On the barge there was an elaborate but jerry-rigged sort of shelter. If this existed anywhere on land, especially around here, it would be dismantled immediately. It looked like pictures she'd seen of Hooverville or some makeshift refugee settlement.

Mae was sitting, squinting at the mess of it, when, from under a blue tarpaulin, a woman emerged.

"Oh hey," the woman said. "You came out of nowhere." She was about sixty, with long white hair, full and frayed, pulled into a ponytail. She took a few steps forward and Mae saw that she was younger than she'd assumed, maybe early fifties, her hair streaked with blond.

"Hi," Mae said. "Sorry if I'm getting too close. The people in the marina make a point of telling us not to disturb you guys out here."

"Usually, that's the case," the woman said. "But seeing as we're coming out to have our evening cocktail," she said, as she settled into a plastic white chair, "your timing is impeccable." She craned her head back, speaking to the blue tarpaulin. "You gonna hide in there?"

"Getting the drinks, lovebird," a male voice said, his form still invisible, his voice straining to be polite.

The woman turned back to Mae. In the low light her eyes

were bright, a bit wicked. "You seem harmless. You want to come aboard?" She tilted her head, assessing Mae.

Mae paddled closer, and when she did, the male voice emerged from under the tarpaulin and took on human form. He was leathery, a bit older than his companion, and he moved slowly getting out of the boat and onto the barge. He was carrying what appeared to be two thermoses.

"Is she joining us?" the man asked the woman, dropping himself in the matching plastic chair next to hers.

"I asked her to," the woman said.

When Mae was close enough to make out their faces, she could see they were clean, tidy—she'd feared their clothing would confirm what their vessel implied, that they were not just waterborne vagabonds, but dangerous, too.

For a moment, the couple watched as Mae maneuvered her way to their barge, curious about her, but passive, as if this was their living room and she their night's entertainment.

"Well, *help* her," the woman said testily, and the man stood.

The bow of Mae's kayak knocked against the steel edge of the barge and the man quickly tied a rope around it and pulled the kayak so it was parallel. He helped her up and onto the surface, a patchwork of wooden planks.

"Sit here, honey," the woman said, indicating the chair he'd vacated to help her.

Mae sat down, and caught the man giving the woman a wild look.

"Well, get *another* one," the woman said to him. And he disappeared again under the blue tarp.

"I don't usually boss him around so much," she said to Mae,

reaching for one of the thermoses he'd set down. "But he doesn't know how to entertain. You want red or white?"

Mae had no reason to accept either in the middle of the afternoon, when she had the kayak to return, and then the drive home, but she was thirsty, and if the wine was white, it would be so good under the afternoon's low sun, and quickly she decided she wanted some. "White, please," she said.

A small red stool appeared from the folds of the tarpaulin, followed by the man, making a show of looking put-out.

"Just sit and have a drink," the woman said to him, and into paper coffee cups, she poured Mae's white and red for herself and her companion. The man sat, they all raised their glasses, and the wine, which Mae knew was not good, tasted extraordinary.

The man was assessing Mae. "So you're some kind of adventurer, I take it. Extreme sports and such." He drained his cup and reached for the thermos. Mae expected his mate to look at him disapprovingly, as her mother would have, but the woman's eyes were closed, facing the setting sun.

Mae shook her head. "No. Not really at all."

"We don't see that many kayakers out here," he said, refilling his cup. "They tend to stay closer to shore."

"I think she's a nice girl," the woman said, her eyes still closed. "Look at her clothes. She's almost preppy. But she's no drone. She's a nice girl with occasional bursts of curiosity."

Now the man took the role of apologist. "Two sips of wine and she thinks she's some fortune-teller."

"It's okay," Mae said, though she didn't know how she felt about the woman's diagnosis. As she looked at the man, and then at the woman, the woman's eyes opened.

"There's a pod of grey whales heading up here tomorrow," she said, and turned her eyes toward the Golden Gate. She narrowed them, as if completing a mental promise with the ocean that, when the whales arrived, they would be well treated. Then she closed her eyes again. Entertaining Mae seemed to be left to the man for now.

"So how's the bay feel today?" he asked.

"Good," Mae said. "It's so calm."

"Calmest it's been this week," he agreed, and for a while no one spoke, as if the three of them were honoring the water's tranquility with a moment of silence. And in the silence, Mae thought about how Annie, or her parents, would react to seeing her out here, drinking wine in the afternoon on a barge. With strangers who lived on a barge. Mercer, she knew, would approve.

"You see any harbor seals?" the man finally asked.

Mae knew nothing about these people. They hadn't offered their names and hadn't asked Mae for hers.

Far beyond, a foghorn sounded.

"Just a few today, closer to shore," Mae said.

"What'd they look like?" the man asked, and when Mae described them, their grey glassine heads, the man glanced to the woman. "Stevie and Kevin."

The woman nodded in recognition.

"I think the others are further out today, hunting. Stevie and Kevin don't leave this part of the bay too often. They come here all the time to say hello."

Mae wanted to ask these people if they lived here, or, if not, what exactly they were doing out here, on this barge, attached to that fishing boat, neither of which seemed functional in any way.

Were they here for good? How did they get here in the first place? But asking any of these questions seemed impossible when they hadn't asked her name.

"Were you here when that burned?" the man asked, pointing to a large uninhabited island in the middle of the bay. It rose, mute and black, behind them. Mae shook her head.

"It burned for two days. We had just gotten here. At night, the heat—you could feel it even here. We swam every night in this godforsaken water, just to stay cool. We thought the world was ending."

Now the woman's eyes opened and she focused on Mae. "Have you swum in this bay?"

"A few times," Mae said. "It's brutal. But I used to swim in Lake Tahoe growing up. That's at least as cold as this."

Mae finished her wine, and felt briefly aglow. She squinted into the sun, turned away, and saw a man in the distance, on a silver sailboat, raising a tricolored flag.

"How old are you?" the woman asked. "You look about eleven."

"Twenty-four," Mae said.

"My god. You don't have a mark on you. Were we ever twenty-four, my love?" She turned to the man, who was using a ballpoint pen to scratch the arch of his foot. He shrugged, and the woman let the matter drop.

"Beautiful out here," Mae said.

"We agree," the woman said. "The beauty is loud and constant. The sunrise this morning, it was so good. And tonight's a full moon. It's been rising full orange, turning silver as it climbs.

The water will be soaked in gold, then platinum. You should stay."

"I have to return that," Mae said, indicating the kayak. She looked at her phone. "In about eight minutes."

She stood up, and the man stood and took her cup, setting his own cup inside hers. "You think you can get back across the bay in eight minutes?"

"I'll try," Mae said, and stood.

The woman let out a loud tsk. "I can't believe she's leaving already. I liked her."

"She's not dead, dear. She's still with us," the man said. He helped Mae into the kayak and untied it. "Be polite."

Mae dipped her hand into the bay and wet the back of her neck.

"Fly away, traitor," the woman said.

The man rolled his eyes. "Sorry."

"It's okay. Thanks for the wine," Mae said. "I'll come back again."

"That'd be swell," the woman said, though she seemed finished with Mae. It was as if, for a moment, she thought Mae was one kind of person, but now, knowing she was another, she could part with her, she could give her back to the world.

Mae paddled toward the shore, her head feeling very light, the wine putting a crooked smile on her face. And only then did she realize how long she'd been free of thoughts of her parents, of Mercer, of the pressures at work. The wind picked up, now heading west, and she paddled with it recklessly, spray everywhere, soaking her legs and face and shoulders. She felt so strong, her muscles growing bolder with every splash of cold water. She loved it all, seeing the free-range boats get closer, the caged yachts appear and take on names and, finally, the beach take shape with Walt waiting at the waterline.

On Monday, when she got to work and logged on, there were a hundred or so second-screen messages.

From Annie: *We missed you Friday night!*

Jared: *You missed a great bash.*

Dan: *Bummed you weren't at the Sunday Celebr!*

Mae searched her calendar and realized there had been a party on Friday, open to everyone in the Renaissance. Sunday had been a barbecue for newbies—the newbies that had arrived in the two weeks she'd been at the Circle.

Busy day, Dan wrote. *See me asap.*

He was standing in the corner of his office, facing the wall. She knocked lightly and, without turning, he raised his index finger, asking for a moment. Mae watched him, assuming he was on a call, and stood patiently, silently, until she realized he was using his retinals and wanted a blank background. She'd been seeing Circlers occasionally doing this—facing walls, so the images on their retinal displays could be seen more clearly. Now finished, he swirled to Mae, flashing a friendly and quick-dissolving smile.

"You weren't able to come yesterday?"

"Sorry. I was with my folks. My dad—"

"Great event. I think you were the only newb absent. But we can talk about it later. For now I need to ask you a favor. We've had to bring on a lot of new help, given how fast things are

146

expanding now, so I wondered if you could help me with some of the new arrivals."

"Of course."

"I think it'll be a cinch for you. Let me show you. We'll head back to your desk. Renata?"

Renata followed them, carrying a small monitor, about the size of a notebook. She installed it at Mae's desk and left.

"Okay. So ideally you'll be doing what Jared used to do with you, remember? Whenever there's a stumper and it needs to be bounced up to a more seasoned person, you'll be there. You're the veteran now. Does that make sense?"

"It does."

"Now the other thing is that I want the newbies to be able to ask you questions as they work. The easiest way will be on this screen." He pointed to the small screen that had been placed under her main monitor. "You see something appear here you know it's from someone in your pod, okay?" He turned on the new screen and typed out a question, "Mae, help me!" on his tablet, and the words appeared on this new, fourth, screen. "Does that seem easy enough?"

"It does."

"Good. So the newbies will be here after Jared trains them. He's doing it en masse as we speak. There will be twelve new people here by about eleven a.m., okay?"

Dan thanked her and left.

The load was heavy until eleven, but her rating was 98. There were a handful of sub-100s, and two lower-90s that she followed up on, and in most cases the customers corrected their rating to a 100.

At eleven she looked up to see Jared leading a group into the room, all of them seeming very young, all of them stepping carefully, as if afraid to wake some unseen infant. Jared positioned each of them at a desk and the room, which had been utterly empty for weeks, was nearly full in a matter of minutes.

Jared stood on a chair. "Okay everyone!" he said. "This is by far our quickest on-boarding process. And our quickest training session. And our most maniacally fast first day. But I know you all can handle it. And I especially know you can handle it because I'll be here all day to help, and Mae will be here, too. Mae, can you stand up?"

Mae stood. But it was obvious that few of the newbies in the room could see her. "How about standing on your chair?" Jared asked, and Mae did so, straightening her skirt, feeling very silly and visible and hoping she would not fall.

"The two of us will be here all day to answer questions and take stumpers. If you have a stumper just forward it, and it'll be routed to whichever of us has the lightest load. If you have a question, same thing. Send it through the channel I showed you in the orientation, and it'll go to one of us. Between me and Mae, you'll be covered. Everyone feel good?" No one moved or said a word. "Good. I'll open the chute again and we'll go till twelve thirty today. Lunch will be shorter today to account for the training and all, but we'll make it up to you on Friday. Everyone ready?" No one seemed ready. "Go!"

And Jared jumped down, and Mae climbed down, arranged herself again and was immediately thirty queries behind. She started on her first, and within a minute she had a question on her fourth screen, the one for newbies.

Customer wants their entire payment record from last year. Available? And where?

Mae directed the newbie to the right folder, then returned to the query in front of her. She continued this way, being pulled away from her own work every few minutes by a newbie question, until twelve thirty, when she saw Jared again, standing again on a chair.

"Whoa. Whoa," he said. "That's lunch. Intense. Intense. Right? But we did it. Our overall average is at 93, which is normally not so good, but okay considering the new systems and increased flow. Congratulations. Get some food, some fuel, and see you at one p.m. Mae, see me when you can."

He jumped down again, and was at Mae's desk before she could get to his. His expression was one of friendly concern.

"You haven't gone to the clinic."

"Me?"

"Is that true?"

"I guess so."

"You were supposed to have gone your first week."

"Oh."

"They're waiting. Can you go today?"

"Sure. Now?"

"No, no. We're too swamped right now, as you can see. How about at four? I can handle the last shift. And by the afternoon all of these newbies will be better honed. Did you have fun so far today?"

"Sure."

"Stressed?"

"Well, it adds a new layer to things."

"It does. It does. And there will be more layers, I want to assure you. I know someone like you would get bored of just the regular Customer Experience stuff, so next week we'll hook you up with a different aspect of the job. I think you'll love it." He glanced at his bracelet and saw the time. "Oh crap. You should go eat. I'm literally taking food out of your mouth. Go. You have twenty-two minutes."

Mae found a pre-made sandwich in the closest kitchen and ate at her desk. She scrolled through the third-screen social feed, looking for anything urgent or needing a reply. She found and responded to thirty-one messages, feeling satisfied that she'd given careful attention to all those that required it.

The afternoon was a runaway train, with the questions from the newbies constant, contrary to the assurances of Jared, who was in and out throughout the afternoon, leaving the room a dozen times, talking on his phone with great intensity. Mae dealt with the doubled flow and by 3:48 had a personal score of 96; the pod's average was 94. Not bad, she thought, considering the addition of twelve new people, and having to help them, for much of three hours, singlehandedly. When four o'clock came around, she knew she was expected at the clinic, and hoped Jared had remembered. She stood, found him looking her way, and he gave her a thumbs-up. She left.

The clinic's lobby was really not a lobby at all. It looked more like a cafe, with Circlers talking in pairs, a wall of beautifully arrayed health foods, and health drinks, and a salad bar featuring vegetables grown on campus, and a wall-mounted scroll featuring a recipe for paleo soup.

Mae didn't know who to approach. There were five people in the room, four of them working on tablets, one fully retinal, standing in the corner. There was nothing like the standard window through which a medical administrative's face would have greeted her.

"Mae?"

She followed the voice to the face of a woman with short black hair, dimples in both cheeks, smiling at her.

"You ready now?"

Mae was led down a blue hallway and into a room that looked more like a designer kitchen than an examination room. The dimpled woman left her there, showing her to an overstuffed chair.

Mae sat in it, then stood, drawn by the cabinets lining the walls. She could see horizontal lines, as fine as thread, delineating where one drawer ended and the next began, but there were no knobs or handles. She ran her hand across the surface, barely registering the hairline gaps. Above the cabinets was a steel strip, and engraved in it were the words: TO HEAL WE MUST KNOW. TO KNOW WE MUST SHARE.

The door opened and Mae startled.

"Hi Mae," a face said as it floated, gorgeous and smiling, toward her. "I'm Dr. Villalobos."

Mae shook the doctor's hand, mouth agape. The woman was too glamorous for this, for this room, for Mae. She was no more than forty, with a black ponytail and luminous skin. Elegant reading glasses hung from her neck, briefly followed the line of her cream-colored jacket, and rested on her ample chest. She was wearing two-inch heels.

"I'm so glad to see you today, Mae."

Mae didn't know what to say. She arrived at "Thanks for having me," and immediately felt like an idiot.

"No, thank *you* for coming," the doctor said. "We have everyone come in, usually in their first week, so we were getting worried about you. Is there any reason you delayed this long?"

"No, no. Just busy."

Mae scanned the doctor for physical flaws, finally finding a mole on her neck, a single, tiny hair protruding from it.

"Too busy for your health! Don't say that." The doctor had her back turned to Mae, preparing some kind of drink. She turned and smiled. "So this is really just an introductory exam, a basic checkup we give to all new staff members here at the Circle, okay? And first of all, we're a prevention-emphasis clinic. In the interest of keeping our Circlers healthy of mind and body, we provide wraparound wellness services. Does that square with what you've been told?"

"It does. I have a friend who's worked here for a couple years. She says the care is incredible."

"Well that's nice to hear. Who's your friend?"

"Annie Allerton?"

"Oh, that's right. That was in your intake. Who doesn't love Annie? Tell her hello. But I guess I can do that myself. She's in my rotation, so I see her every other week. She told you the checkups are biweekly?"

"So that's—"

The doctor smiled. "Every two weeks. That's the wellness component. If you come here only when there's a problem, you never get ahead of things. The biweekly checkups involve diet consultations, and we monitor any variances in your overall health. This is key for early detection, for calibrating any meds you might be on, for seeing any problems a few miles away, as opposed to after they've run you over. Sound good?"

Mae thought of her dad, how late they'd realized his symptoms were MS. "It does," she said.

"And all the data we generate here is available to you online. Everything we do and talk about, and of course all your past records. You signed the form when you started that allowed us to bring in all your other doctors' information, so finally you'll have it all in one place, and it's accessible to you, to us, and we can make decisions, see patterns, see potential issues, given our access to the complete picture. You want to see it?" the doctor asked, and then activated a screen on the wall. Mae's entire medical history appeared before her in lists and images and icons. Dr. Villalobos touched the wallscreen, opening folders and moving images, revealing the results of every medical visit she'd ever had—back to her first checkup before starting kindergarten.

"How's that knee?" the doctor asked. She'd found the MRI Mae had done a few years ago. Mae had opted not to get ACL surgery; her previous insurance didn't cover it.

"It's functional," Mae said.

"Well, if you want to take care of it, let me know. We do that here at the clinic. It would take an afternoon and of course would be free. The Circle likes its employees to have operational knees." The doctor turned from the screen to smile at Mae, practiced but convincing.

"Piecing together some of the stuff when you were very young was a challenge, but from here on out, we'll have near-complete information. Every two weeks we'll do blood work, cognitive tests, reflexes, a quick eye exam, and a rotating retinue of more exotic tests, like MRIs and such."

Mae couldn't figure it out. "But how is this affordable for you guys? I mean, the cost of an MRI alone—"

"Well, prevention is cheap. Especially compared to finding some Stage-4 lump when we could have found it at Stage 1. And the cost differential is profound. Because Circlers are generally young and healthy, our health care costs are a fraction of those at a similar-sized company—one without the same kind of foresight."

Mae had the feeling, which she was used to by now at the Circle, that they alone were able to think about—or were simply alone in being able to *enact*—reforms that seemed beyond debate in their necessity and urgency.

"So when was your last checkup?"

"Maybe college?"

"Okay, wow. Let's start with your vital signs, all the basics. Have you seen one of these?" The doctor held out a silver bracelet, about three inches wide. Mae had seen health monitors on Jared and Dan, but theirs were made of rubber, and fit loosely. This one was thinner and lighter.

"I think so. It measures your heart rate?"

"Right. Most of the longtime Circlers have some version of it, but they've been complaining about it being too loose, like some kind of bangle. So we've modified it so it stays in place. You want to try it on?"

Mae did. The doctor fit it onto her left wrist, and clicked it closed. It was snug. "It's warm," Mae said.

"It'll feel warm for a few days, then you and the bracelet will get used to each other. But it has to touch the skin, of course, to measure what we'd like to measure—which is everything. You did want the full program, right?"

"I think so."

"In your intake, you said you wanted the complete recommended array of measurements. Is that still true?"

"It is."

"Okay. Can you drink this?" The doctor handed Mae the dense green liquid she'd been preparing. "It's a smoothie."

Mae drank it down. It was viscous and cold.

"Okay, you just ingested the sensor that will connect to your wrist monitor. It was in that glass." The doctor punched Mae's shoulder playfully. "I love doing that."

"I already swallowed it?" Mae said.

"It's the best way. If I put it in your hand, you'd hem and haw. But the sensor is so small, and it's organic of course, so you drink it, you don't notice, and it's over."

"So the sensor is already in me?"

"It is. And now," the doctor said, tapping Mae's wrist monitor, "now it's active. It'll collect data on your heart rate, blood pressure, cholesterol, heat flux, caloric intake, sleep duration, sleep quality, digestive efficiency, on and on. A nice thing for the Circlers, especially those like you who might have occasionally stressful jobs, is that it measures galvanic skin response, which allows you to know when you're amped or anxious. When we see non-normative rates of stress in a Circler or a department, we can make adjustments to workload, for example. It measures the pH level of your sweat, so you can tell when you need to hydrate with alkaline water. It detects your posture, so you know when you need to reposition yourself. Blood and tissue oxygen, your red blood cell count, and things like step count. As you know, doctors recommend about ten thousand steps a day, and this will show you how close you're getting. Actually, let's have you walk around the room."

Mae saw the number 10,000 on her wrist, and with each step she took, it dropped—9999, 9998, 9997.

"We're asking all newbies to wear these second-gen models, and in a few months we'll have all Circlers coordinated. The idea is that with complete information, we can give better care. Incomplete information creates gaps in our knowledge, and medically speaking, gaps in our knowledge create mistakes and omissions."

"I know," Mae said. "That was the problem in college for me. You self-reported your health data, and so it was all over the place. Three kids died of meningitis before they realized how it was spreading."

Dr. Villalobos's expression darkened. "You know, that kind of thing is just unnecessary now. First of all, you can't expect college kids to self-report. It should all be done for them, so they can concentrate on their studies. STDs alone, Hep C—imagine if the data was just there. Then appropriate action could be taken. No guesswork. Have you heard of that experiment up in Iceland?"

"I think so." Mae said, but was only half-sure.

"Well, because Iceland has this incredibly homogenous population, most of the residents have roots many centuries back on the island. Anyone can trace their ancestry very easily back a thousand years. So they started mapping the genomes of Icelanders, every single person, and were able to trace all kinds of diseases to their origins. They've gotten so much valuable data from that pool of people. There's nothing like a fixed and relatively homogenous group, exposed to the same factors—and a group you can study over time. The fixed group, the complete information, both were key in maximizing the takeaway. So the hope is to do something like that here. If we can track all you newbies, and eventually all 10,000-plus Circlers, we can both see problems far before they become serious, and we can collect data about the population as a whole. Most of you newbies are around the same age, and in generally good health, even the engineers," she said, smiling at what was evidently a joke she often told. "So when there are deviations, we'd like to know about them, and see if there are trends we can learn from. Does that make sense?"

Mae was distracted by the bracelet.

"Mae?"

"Yes. That sounds great."

The bracelet was beautiful, a pulsing marquee of lights and charts and numbers. Mae's pulse was represented by a delicately rendered rose, opening and closing. There was an EKG, shooting right like blue lightning and then starting over. Her temperature was rendered large, in green, 98.6, reminding her of that day's aggregate, 97, which she needed to improve. "And what do these do?" she asked. There were a series of buttons and prompts, arranged in a row below the data.

"Well, you can have the bracelet measure about a hundred other things. If you run, it'll measure how far. It tracks your standing heart rate versus active. It'll measure BMI, caloric intake. . . . See, you're getting it."

Mae was busy experimenting. It was one of the more elegant objects she'd ever seen. There were dozens of layers to the information, every data point allowing her to ask more, to go deeper.

When she tapped the digits of her current temperature, it could show the average temperature for the previous twenty-four hours, the high and the low, the median.

"And of course," Dr. Villalobos said, "all that data is stored in the cloud, and in your tablet, anywhere you want it. It's always accessible, and is constantly updated. So if you fall, hit your head, you're in the ambulance, the EMTs can access everything about your history in seconds."

"And this is free?"

"Of course it's free. It's part of your health plan."

"It's so pretty," Mae said.

"Yeah, everyone loves it. So I should ask the rest of the standard questions. When was your last period?"

Mae tried to remember. "About ten days ago."

"Are you sexually active?"

"Not at the moment."

"But in general?"

"Generally, sure."

"Are you taking birth control pills?"

"Yes."

"Okay. You can move that prescription over here. Talk to Tanya on your way out, and she'll give you some condoms for the things the pill can't prevent. Any other medications?"

"Nope."

"Antidepressants?"

"Nope."

"Would you say you're generally happy?"

"I am."

158

"Any allergies?"

"Yes."

"Oh right. I have those here. Horses, too bad. Any family history of illness?"

"Like, at my age?"

"Any age. Your parents? Their health is good?"

Something about how the doctor asked the question, how she so clearly expected the answer to be yes, her stylus hovering above her tablet, knocked the wind out of Mae, and she couldn't speak.

"Oh honey," she said, and bringing her arm around Mae's shoulder and tilting her close. She smelled faintly floral. "There there," she said, and Mae began to cry, her shoulders heaving, her nose and eyes flooding. She knew she was getting the doctor's cotton coat wet, but it felt like release, and forgiveness, and Mae found herself telling Dr. Villalobos about her father's symptoms, his fatigue, his accident over the weekend.

"Oh Mae," the doctor said, stroking her hair. "Mae. Mae."

Mae couldn't stop. She told Dr. Villalobos about his soul-flaying insurance situation, how her mother was expecting to spend the rest of her life caring for him, fighting for every treatment, hours on the phone every day with those people—

"Mae," the doctor finally said, "have you asked HR about adding your parents to the company plan?"

Mae looked up at her. "What?"

"There are a handful of Circlers who have family members like that on the insurance plan. I would imagine it's a possibility in your situation."

Mae had never heard of such a thing.

"You should ask HR," the doctor said. "Or actually, maybe you should just ask Annie."

"Why didn't you tell me sooner?" Annie said that night. They were in Annie's office, a large white room with floor-to-ceiling windows and a pair of low couches. "I didn't know your parents had this insurance nightmare."

Mae was looking at a wall of framed photos, each of them featuring a tree or shrub grown into a pornographic shape. "Last time I was here you had only six or seven, right?"

"I know. Word got out that I was some passionate collector, so now someone gives me one every day. And they're getting filthier all the time. See the one on top?" Annie pointed to a photo of an enormous phallic cactus.

A copper-skinned face appeared in the doorway, her body hidden around the corner. "You need me?"

"Of course I need you, Vickie," Annie said. "Don't go."

"I was thinking of heading to the Sahara kickoff thing."

"Vickie. Don't leave me," Annie said, deadpan. "I love you and don't want us to be apart." Vickie smiled, but seemed to be wondering when Annie would end this bit and let her go.

"Fine," Annie said. "I should go, too. But I can't. So go."

Vickie's face disappeared.

"Do I know her?" Mae asked.

"She's on my team," Annie said. "There are ten of us now but Vickie's my go-to. You hear about this Sahara thing?"

"I think so." Mae had read an InnerCircle notice about it, some plan to count the grains of sand in the Sahara.

"Sorry, we were talking about your dad," Annie said. "I can't understand why you wouldn't tell me."

Mae told her the truth, which was that she didn't see any scenario where her father's health would overlap with the Circle. There was no company in the country that covered an employee's parents or siblings.

"Sure, but you know what we say here," Annie said. "Anything that makes our Circlers' lives better . . ." She seemed to be waiting for Mae to finish the sentence. Mae had no idea. ". . . instantly becomes possible. You should know that!"

"Sorry."

"That was in your intake orientation. Mae! Okay, I'll get on this." Annie was typing something into her phone. "Probably later tonight. I'm running into a meeting now, though."

"It's six o'clock." She checked her wrist. "No. Six thirty."

"This is early! I'll be here till twelve. Or maybe all night. We've got some very fun stuff happening." Her face was aglow, alive to possibility. "Dealing with some juicy Russian tax stuff. Those guys do not fuck around."

"You sleeping in the dorms?"

"Nah. I'll probably just push these two couches together. Oh shit. I better go. Love you."

Annie squeezed Mae and walked out of the room.

Mae was alone in Annie's office, stunned. Was it possible that her father would soon have real coverage? That the cruel paradox of her parents' lives—that their constant battles with insurance companies actually diminished her father's health and prevented her mother from working, eliminating her ability to earn money to pay for his care—would end?

Mae's phone buzzed. It was Annie.

"And don't worry. You know I'm a ninja with stuff like this. It'll be done." And she hung up.

Mae looked out Annie's window to San Vincenzo, most of it built or renovated in the last few years—restaurants to serve Circlers, hotels to serve visitors to the Circle, shops hoping to entice Circlers and their visitors, schools to serve children of the Circle. The Circle had taken over fifty buildings in the vicinity, transforming blighted warehouses into climbing gyms, schools, server farms, each structure bold, unprecedented, well beyond LEED.

Mae's phone went off again and again it was Annie.

"Okay, good news sooner than expected. I checked and it's not a big deal. We have about a dozen other parents on the plan, and even some siblings. I twisted a few arms and they say they can get your dad on."

Mae looked at her phone. It had been four minutes since she'd first mentioned all this to Annie.

"Oh shit. You're serious?"

"You want your mom on the plan, too? Of course you do. She's healthier, so that's easy. We'll put both of them on."

"When?"

"I guess immediately."

"I can't believe this."

"C'mon, give me some credit," Annie said, breathless. She was walking briskly, somewhere. "This is easy."

"So should I tell my parents?"

"What, you want *me* to tell them?"

"No, no. I'm just making sure it's definite."

"It is. It's really not the biggest deal in the world. We have

162

eleven thousand people on the plan. We get to dictate terms, right?"

"Thank you Annie."

"Someone from HR will call you tomorrow. You guys can work out the details. Gotta go again. Now I'm really late."

And she hung up again.

Mae called her parents, telling her mom first, then her dad, and there was some whooping, and there were tears, more praise for Annie as the savior of the family, and some very embarrassing talk about how Mae had become a real adult, how her parents were ashamed and humbled to be leaning on her, leaning so heavily on their young daughter this way, it's just this messed-up system we're all stuck in, they said. But thank you, they said, we're so proud of you. And when she was alone on the phone with her mother, her mother said, "Mae, you've saved not just your father's life but my life, too, I swear to god you have, my sweet Maebelline."

At seven Mae found she couldn't stand it any longer. She couldn't sit still. She had to get up and celebrate in some way. She checked the campus that night. She'd missed the Sahara kickoff and already regretted it. There was a poetry slam, in costume, and she ranked that one first and even RSVP'd to it. But then she saw the cooking class in which they were going to roast and eat an entire goat. She ranked that second. At nine there was an appearance by some activist wanting the Circle's help in her campaign against vaginal mutilation in Malawi. If she tried, Mae could get to at least a few of these events, but just when she was arranging some sort of itinerary, she saw something that obliterated all else: the Funky Arse Whole Circus would be on campus, on the lawn next to the Iron Age, at seven. She'd heard of them, and their reviews and ratings were stellar, and the thought of a circus, that night, most matched her euphoria.

She tried Annie, but she couldn't make it; she would be in her meeting till eleven at least. But CircleSearch indicated a bunch of people she knew, including Renata and Alistair and Jared, would be there—the latter two already were—so she finished up and flew.

The light was fading, threaded in gold, when she turned the corner of the Three Kingdoms and saw a man standing, two stories tall, blowing fire. Beyond him, a woman in a glittering headdress was throwing and catching a neon baton. Mae had found the circus.

There were about two hundred people forming a loose fence around the performers, who worked in open air, with minimal props and what seemed to be a decidedly limited budget. The Circlers ringing the performance emitted an array of lights, some from their wrist monitors, some from their phones, out and aglow, capturing the proceedings. While Mae looked for Jared and Renata, and cautiously kept an eye out for Alistair, she watched the circus swirl in front of her. There seemed to be no definite beginning to the show—it was already under way when she'd arrived—and no discernible structure to any of it. There were ten or so members of the circus, all of them visible at all times, all of them wearing threadbare costumes that reveled in their antique humility. A smallish man did wild acrobatics while wearing a terrifying elephant mask. A mostly naked woman, her face obscured under a flamingo head, danced in circles, her movements alternating between ballet and a stumbling drunk.

Just beyond her, Mae saw Alistair, who waved to her, and then began texting. Moments later she checked her phone and saw that Alistair was putting on another, now bigger and better, event for all Portugal enthusiasts, next week. *It will be thunderous,* he texted. *Films, music, poetry, storytelling and joy!* She texted that she'd be there and could hardly wait. Across the lawn, past the flamingo, Mae saw him reading her message, watched as he raised his eyes to her, waving.

She went back to watching the circus. The performers seemed to be not just affecting the air of poverty but to be living it—everything about them seemed old, and smelled of age and decay. Around them the Circlers captured the performance on their screens, wanting to remember the very strangeness of this band of homeless-seeming revelers, to document how incongruous it was here at the Circle, amid the carefully considered paths and gardens, amid the people who worked there, who showered regularly, tried to stay at least reasonably fashionable, and who washed their clothes.

Mae, making her way through the crowd, found Josiah and Denise, who were delighted to see her, but both seemed scandalized by the circus, the tone and tenor of which, they thought, had gone too far; Josiah had already reviewed it unfavorably. Mae left them, happy they'd seen her, had registered her attendance, and went looking for a beverage. She saw a row of booths in the distance and was making her way to them when one of the performers, a shirtless man with a handlebar mustache, raced over to her, carrying three swords. He seemed unsteady, and in the moments before he reached her, Mae grasped that though he wanted to seem under control, that this was part of his act, he was actually going to run into her with his arms full of blades. She froze, and he was inches away from her, when she felt her shoulders being grabbed and thrown. She fell to her knees, her back to the man with the swords.

"You okay?" a different man asked. She looked up to see he was standing where she'd been.

"I think so," she said.

And then he turned back to the wiry sword-man. "What the fuck, clown?"

Was it Kalden?

The sword juggler was looking to Mae, to assure himself that she was okay, and when he saw that she was, he turned his attention to the man in front of him.

It was Kalden. Now Mae was sure. He had Kalden's calligraphic shape. He was wearing a plain white V-neck undershirt and grey pants, as skinny as the jeans she'd first seen on him. He had not struck Mae as someone quick to fight, and yet he was standing, chest out and hands awake, as the circus performer assessed him, eyes steady, as if choosing between staying in character, in this circus, following through with the show and getting paid, and paid well, by this enormous and prosperous and influential company, or tangling with this guy in front of two hundred people.

Finally he chose to smile, theatrically twirl his mustache by both ends, and turn.

"Sorry that happened," Kalden said, helping her up. "You sure you're okay?"

Mae said she was. The mustache man hadn't touched her, had only scared her, and even then, only for a moment.

She stared at his face, which in the suddenly blue light was like some Brancusi sculpture—smooth, perfectly oval. His eyebrows were Roman arches, his nose like some small sea creature's delicate snout.

"Those assholes shouldn't be here in the first place," he said. "A bunch of court jesters here to entertain royalty. I don't see the point," he said, now looking around him, standing on his tiptoes. "Can we leave here?"

They found the food and drinks table en route and took tapas and sausages and cups of red wine to a row of lemon trees behind the Viking Age.

"You don't remember my name," Mae said.

"No. But I know you, and I wanted to see you. That's why I was near when the mustache came at you."

"Mae."

"Right. I'm Kalden."

"I know. I remember names."

"And I try to. I'm always trying. So are Josiah and Denise your friends?" he asked.

"I don't know. Sure. I mean, they did my orientation and, you know, I've talked to them since. Why?"

"No reason."

"What do you do here, anyway?"

"And Dan? You hang out with Dan?"

"Dan's my boss. You won't tell me what you do, will you?"

"You want a lemon?" he asked, and stood. He kept his eyes on Mae as he reached his hand into the tree and retrieved a large one.

There was a masculine grace to the gesture, how he stretched, fluidly upward, slower than might be expected, that made her think of a diver. Without looking at the lemon, he handed it to her.

"It's green," she said.

He squinted at it. "Oh. I thought that would work. I went for the biggest one I could find. It should have been yellow. Here, stand up."

He gave her his hand, helped her up, and positioned her just away from the boughs of the tree. Then he threw his arms around the trunk and shook it until lemons rained down. Five or six hit Mae.

"Jesus. Sorry," he said. "I'm an idiot."

"No. It was good," she said. "They were heavy, and two hit me in the head. I loved it."

He touched her then, shaping his hand around her head. "Anything especially bad?"

She said she was fine.

"You always hurt the ones you love," he said, his face a dark shape above her. As if realizing what he'd said, he cleared his throat. "Anyway. That's what my parents said. And they loved me very much."

In the morning, Mae called Annie, who was on her way to the airport, heading to Mexico to untangle some regulatory snafu.

"I met someone intriguing," Mae said.

"Good. I wasn't crazy about the other one. Gallipoli."

"Garaventa."

"Francis. He's a nervous little mouse. And this new one?

What do we know about him?" Mae could sense Annie speeding the conversation along.

Mae tried to describe him, but realized she knew almost nothing. "He's thin. Brown eyes, tallish?"

"That's it? Brown eyes and tallish?"

"Oh wait," Mae said, laughing at herself. "He had grey hair. He *has* grey hair."

"Wait. What?"

"He was young, but with grey hair."

"Okay. Mae. It's okay if you're a grandpa chaser—"

"No, no. I'm sure he was young."

"You say he's under thirty, but with grey hair?"

"I swear."

"I don't know anyone here like that."

"You know all ten thousand people?"

"Maybe he's got some temporary contract. You didn't get his last name?"

"I tried, but he was very coy."

"Huh. That's not so Circly, is it? And he had grey hair?"

"Almost white."

"Like a swimmer would? When they use that shampoo?"

"No. This wasn't silver. It was just grey. Like an old man would have."

"And you're sure he *wasn't* some old man? Like some old man you found on the street?"

"No."

"Were you roaming the streets, Mae? Are you into that particular smell of an older man? A much older man? It's musty. Like a wet cardboard box. You like that?"

"Please."

Annie was entertaining herself, and so continued: "I guess there's comfort there, knowing he can cash in his 401(k). And he must be so grateful for any affection at all. . . . Oh shit. I'm at the airport. I'll call you back."

Annie didn't call back, but texted from the plane and later from Mexico City, sending Mae pictures of various old men she saw on the street. *Is this him? This one? That one? Ése? Ése?*

Mae was left to wonder about all of this. How did she not know Kalden's last name? She did a preliminary search in the company directory, and found no Kaldens. She tried Kaldan, Kaldin, Khalden. Nothing. Maybe she'd misspelled or misheard it? She could have done a more surgical search if she'd known what department he was in, what part of campus he might occupy, but she knew nothing.

Still, she could think of little else. His white V-neck, his sad eyes that tried not to seem sad, his skinny grey pants that might have been stylish or horrible, she couldn't decide in the dark, the way he held her at the end of the night, when they'd walked to where the helicopters landed, hoping to see one, and then, seeing none, they walked back to the lemon grove, and there he said he would have to go, and could she walk to the shuttle from there. He pointed to the row of them, not two hundred yards off, and she smiled and said she could handle it. Then he'd brought her to him, so suddenly, too suddenly for her to know if he planned a kiss or grope or what. What he did was a flattening of her shape against his, with his right arm crossing her back, his hand atop her shoulder, and his left hand far lower, bolder, resting on her sacrum, his fingers fanning down.

Then he pulled away and smiled.

"You sure you're okay?"

"I am."

"You're not scared?"

She laughed. "No. I'm not scared."

"Okay. Good night."

And he turned and walked in a new direction, not toward the shuttles or the helicopters or the circus, but through a narrow shadowed path, alone.

All week she thought of his retreating form, and his strong hands reaching, and she looked at the big green lemon he'd picked, which she'd retrieved and thought, wrongly, would have ripened on her desk if given the time. It stayed green.

But she couldn't get hold of him. She put out a few all-company zings, looking for a Kalden, careful not to look desperate. But she got no response.

She knew Annie could figure it out, but Annie was now in Peru. The company was in some moderately hot water over their plans in the Amazon—something involving drones to count and photograph every remaining tree. Between meetings with members of various environmental and regulatory officials, Annie finally called back. "Let me do a facial rec on him. Send me a photo."

But Mae had no photos of him.

"You're kidding. Nothing?"

"It was dark. It was a circus."

"You said that. So he gave you a green lemon and no photos. Are you sure he wasn't just visiting?"

"But I met him before, remember? Near the bathroom? And then he came back to my desk and watched me work."

"Wow, Mae. This guy sounds like a winner. Green lemons and heavy breathing over your shoulder while you answer customer queries. If I were being the slightest bit paranoid, I'd think he was an infiltrator of some kind, or a low-grade molester." Annie had to hang up, but then, an hour later, texted. *You have to keep me posted on this guy. Getting increasingly unsettled. We've had some weird stalker people over the years. Last year we had a guy, some kind of blogger, who attended a party and stayed on campus for two weeks, skulking around and sleeping in storage rooms. He turned out to be relatively harmless, but you can see how some Unidentified Freaky Man would be cause for concern.*

But Mae wasn't concerned. She trusted Kalden, and couldn't believe he had any nefarious intentions. His face had an openness, an unmistakable lack of guile—Mae couldn't quite explain it to Annie, but she had no doubts about him. She knew, though, that he was not reliable as a communicator, but she knew, also, she was sure of it, that he would contact her again. And though being unable to reach anyone else in her life would have been grating, exasperating, having him out there, at least for a few days, unreachable but presumably somewhere on campus, provided a jolt of welcome frisson to her hours. The week's workload was heavy, but while thinking of Kalden, every query was some glorious aria. The customers sang to her and she sang back. She loved them all. She loved Risa Thomason in Twin Falls, Idaho. She loved Mack Moore in Gary, Indiana. She loved the newbies around her. She loved Jared's occasionally worried visage appearing in his doorway, asking her to see how they could keep their aggregate over 98. And she loved that she had been able to ignore Francis and his constant contacting of her. His mini videos. His audio greeting cards. His playlists, all of them songs of apology and woe. He was a memory now, obliterated by Kalden and his elegant silhouette, his strong searching hands. She loved how she could, alone, in the bathroom, simulate the effect of those hands, could, with her own hand, approximate the pressure he applied to her. But where was he? What had been intriguing on Monday and Tuesday was approaching annoying by Wednesday and exasperating by Thursday. His invisibility began to feel intentional and even aggressive. He'd promised to be in touch, hadn't he? Maybe he hadn't, she thought. What *had* he said? She searched her memory and realized, with a kind of panic, that all he'd said, at the end of the night, was "Good night." But Annie would be coming back on Friday, and together, with even an hour together, they could find him, know his name, lock him in.

And finally, on Friday morning, Annie returned, and they made plans to meet just before the Dream Friday. There was supposed to be a presentation about the future of CircleMoney—a way to send all online purchases through the Circle and, eventually, obviate the need for paper currency at all—but then the presentation was cancelled. All staffers were asked to watch a press conference being held in Washington.

Mae hurried down to the lobby of the Renaissance, where a few hundred Circlers were watching the wallscreen. A woman in a blueberry-colored suit stood behind a podium festooned with microphones, surrounded by aides and a pair of American flags. Below her the ticker: SENATOR WILLIAMSON SEEKING TO BREAK UP THE CIRCLE. It was too loud at first to hear anything, but a series of hissing shushes and volume increases made her voice audible. The senator was in the middle of reading a written statement.

"We are here today to insist that the Senate's Antitrust Task Force begin an investigation into whether or not the Circle acts as a monopoly. We believe that the Justice Department will see the Circle for what it is, a monopoly in its purest sense, and move to break it up, just as they did with Standard Oil, AT&T and every other demonstrated monopoly in our history. The dominance of the Circle stifles competition and is dangerous to our way of free-market capitalism."

After she was finished, the screen went back to its usual purpose, to celebrate the thoughts of the Circle staff, and amid the throngs that day were many thoughts. The consensus was that this senator was known for her occasionally outside-the-mainstream positions—she had been against the wars in Iraq and Afghanistan—and thus she would not get much traction with this antitrust crusade. The Circle was a company popular on both sides of the aisle, known for its pragmatic positions on virtually every political issue, for its generous donations, and thus this left-of-center senator wouldn't get much support from her liberal colleagues—much less among the Republican ranks.

Mae didn't know enough about antitrust laws to have an off-the-cuff opinion. Was there really no competition out there? The Circle had 90 percent of the search market. Eighty-eight percent of the free-mail market, 92 percent of text servicing. That was, in her perspective, a simple testament to their making and delivering the best product. It seemed insane to punish the company for its efficiency, for its attention to detail. For succeeding.

"There you are," Mae said, seeing Annie coming toward her. "How was Mexico? And Peru?"

"That idiot," Annie scoffed, narrowing her eyes at the screen where the senator had recently appeared.

"So you're not concerned about this?"

"You mean, like she's going to actually get somewhere with this? No. But personally, she's in a world of shit."

"What do you mean? How do you know this?"

Annie looked at Mae, then turned to face the back of the room. Tom Stenton stood, chatting with a few Circlers, his arms crossed, a posture that in someone else might convey concern or even anger. But more than anything, he seemed amused.

"Let's go," Annie said, and they walked across campus, hoping to get lunch from a taco truck hired to feed Circlers that day. "How's your gentleman caller? Don't tell me he died during sex."

"I still haven't seen him since last week."

"No contact at all?" Annie asked. "What a shit."

"I think he's just from some other era."

"Some other era? And grey hair? Mae, you know that moment in *The Shining* when Nicholson is having some kind of sexy encounter with the woman in the bathroom? And then the lady turns out to be some elderly undead corpse?"

Mae had no idea what Annie was talking about.

"Actually—" Annie said, and her eyes lost focus.

"What?"

"You know, with this Williamson investigation thing, it worries me to have some shadowy guy skulking around campus. Can you tell me the next time you see him?"

Mae looked at Annie, and saw, for the first time she could remember, something like real worry.

At four thirty Dan sent a message: *Great day so far! Meet at five?*

Mae arrived at Dan's door. He stood, guided her to a chair, and closed the door. He sat behind his desk and tapped the glass of his tablet.

"97. 98. 98. 98. Wonderful aggregates this week."

"Thank you," Mae said.

"Really spectacular. Especially considering the increased work-load with the newbs. Has that been difficult?"

"Maybe the first couple days, but now they're all trained and don't need me as much. They're all excellent, so if anything, it's slightly easier, having more people on the job."

"Good. Good to hear." Now Dan looked up, and probed into her eyes. "Mae, have you had a good experience so far here at the Circle?"

"Absolutely," she said.

His face brightened. "Good. Good. That's very good news. I asked you to come in just to, well, to square that with your social behavior here, and the message it's sending. And I think I might have failed to communicate everything about this job properly. So I blame myself if I haven't done that well enough."

"No. No. I know you did a good job. I'm sure you did."

"Well, thank you, Mae. I appreciate that. But what we need to talk about is the, well . . . Let me put it another way. You know

176

this isn't what you might call a clock-in, clock-out type of company. Does that make sense?"

"Oh, I know. I wouldn't . . . Did I imply that I thought . . ."

"No, no. You didn't imply anything. We just haven't seen you around so much after five o'clock, so we wondered if you were, you know, anxious to leave."

"No, no. Do you need me to stay later?"

Dan winced. "No, it's not that. You handle your workload just fine. But we missed you at the Old West party last Thursday night, which was a pretty crucial team-building event, centered around a product we're all very proud of. You missed at least two newbie events, and at the circus, it looked like you couldn't wait to leave. I think you were out of there in twenty minutes. And those things would be understandable if your Participation Rank wasn't so low. Do you know what it is?"

Mae guessed it was in the 8,000-range. "I think so."

"You think so," Dan said, checked his screen. "It's 9,101. Does that sound right?" It had dropped in the last hour, since she'd last checked.

Dan clucked and nodded, as if trying to figure out how a certain spot had appeared on his shirt. "So it's been sort of adding up and, well, we started worrying that we were somehow driving you away."

"No, no! It's nothing like that."

"Okay, let's focus on Thursday at five fifteen. We had a gathering in the Old West, where your friend Annie works. It was a semi-mandatory welcome party for a group of potential partners. You were off-campus, which really confuses me. It's as if you were fleeing."

Mae's mind raced. Why hadn't she gone? Where was she? She didn't know about this event. It was across campus, in the Old West—how had she missed a semi-mandatory event? The notice must have been buried deep in her third screen.

"God, I'm sorry," she said, remembering now. "At five I left campus to get some aloe at this health shop in San Vincenzo. My dad asked for this particular kind of—"

"Mae," Dan interrupted, his tone condescending, "the company store has aloe. Our store's better stocked than some corner store, and with superior products. Ours is carefully curated."

"I'm sorry. I didn't know the company store had something like aloe."

"You went to our store and couldn't find it?"

"No, no. I didn't go to the store. I went straight to the other store. But I'm so glad to know that—"

"Let me stop you there, because you said something interesting. You said you didn't go to our store first?"

"No. Sorry. I just assumed something like that wouldn't be there, so—"

"Now listen. Mae, I should admit that I know you didn't go to the store. That's one of the things I wanted to talk to you about. You haven't been in the store, not once. You—a former college athlete—haven't been to the gym, and you've barely explored the campus. I think you've used about 1 percent of our facilities."

"I'm sorry. It's just been a whirlwind so far, I guess."

"And Friday night? There was a major event then, too."

"I'm sorry. I wanted to go to the party, but I had to run home. My dad had a seizure and it ended up being minor but I didn't know that until I got home."

Dan looked at his glass desk and, with a tissue, tried to remove a smudge. Satisfied, he looked up.

"That's very understandable. To spend time with your parents, believe me, I think that is very, very cool. I just want to emphasize the *community* aspect of this job. We see this workplace as a *community,* and every person who works here is *part* of that community. And to make it all work it requires a certain level of participation. It's like, if we were a kindergarten class, and one girl has a party, and only half the class shows up, how does the birthday girl feel?"

"Not good. I know that. But I was at the circus event and that was great. *So* great."

"It *was* great, wasn't it? And it was great to see you there. But we have no record of you being there. No photos, no zings, no reviews, notices, bumps. Why not?"

"I don't know. I guess I was caught up in the—"

Dan sighed loudly. "You do know that we like to hear from people, right? That Circlers' opinions are valued?"

"Of course."

"And that the Circle is predicated, to a large extent, on the input and participation of people like yourself?"

"I know."

"Listen. It totally makes sense you'd want to spend time with your parents. They're your parents! It's totally honorable of you. Like I said: very, very cool. I'm just saying *we* like you a lot, too, and want to know you better. To that end, I wonder if you'd be willing to stay a few extra minutes, to talk to Josiah and Denise. I think you remember them from your orientation? They'd love to just extend the conversation we're having, and go a bit deeper. Does that sound good?"

"Sure."

"You don't have to rush home or . . . ?"

"No. I'm all yours."

"Good. Good. I like to hear that. Here they are now."

Mae turned to see Denise and Josiah, both waving, on the other side of Dan's glass door.

"Mae, how are you?" Denise said, as they walked to the conference room. "I can't believe it's been three weeks since we gave you your first tour! We'll be in here."

Josiah opened the door to a conference room Mae had passed many times. The room was oval, the walls glass.

"Let's have you sit here," Denise said, indicating a high-backed leather chair. She and Josiah sat across from her, arranging their tablets and adjusting their seats, as if settling in for a task that might take hours, and would almost surely be unpleasant. Mae tried to smile.

"As you know," Denise said, putting a strand of her dark hair behind her ear, "we're from HR, and this is just a regular check-in we do with new community members here. We do them somewhere in the company every day, and we're especially glad to see you again. You're such an enigma."

"I am?"

"You are. It's been years since I can remember someone joining who was so, you know, shrouded in mystery."

Mae wasn't sure how to answer this. She didn't feel shrouded in mystery.

"So I thought maybe we would start by talking a little about you, and after we get to know more about you, we can talk about ways that you might feel comfortable joining in a bit more in terms of the community. Does that sound good?"

Mae nodded. "Of course." She looked to Josiah, who hadn't said a word yet, but who was working furiously on his tablet, typing and swiping.

"Good. I thought we would start by saying that we really like you," Denise said.

Josiah finally spoke, his blue eyes bright. "We *do*," he said. "We really do. You are a super-cool member of the team. Everyone thinks so."

"Thank you," Mae said, feeling sure that she was being fired. She'd gone too far in asking for her parents to be added to the insurance plan. How could she have done that so soon after being hired?

"And that your work here has been exemplary," Denise continued. "Your ratings have been averaging 97, and that's excellent, especially for your first month. Do you feel satisfied with your performance?"

Mae guessed at the right answer. "I do."

Denised nodded. "Good. But as you know, it's not all about work here. Or rather, it's not all about ratings and approvals and such. You're not just some cog in a machine."

Josiah was shaking his head vigorously, no. "We consider you a full, knowable human being of unlimited potential. And a crucial member of the community."

"Thank you," Mae said, now less sure she was being let go.

Denise's smile was pained. "But as you know, you've had a blip or two when it comes to meshing with the community here. We have of course read the report from the incident with Alistair and his Portugal brunch. We found your explanation totally understandable, and we're encouraged that you seem to have recognized the issues at play there. But then there's your absence at most of the weekend and evening events, all of which are of course totally optional. Is there anything else you want to add to our understanding of all this? Maybe with the Alistair situation?"

"Just that I really felt bad that I might have inadvertently caused Alistair any distress."

Denise and Josiah smiled.

"Good, good," Denise said. "So the fact that you understand makes me confused, in terms of squaring that with a few of your actions *since* that discussion. Let's start with this past weekend. We know you left campus at 5:42 p.m. on Friday, and you got back here 8:46 a.m. on Monday."

"Was there work on the weekend?" Mae searched her memory. "Did I miss something?"

"No, no, no. There wasn't, you know, mandatory work here on the weekend. That's not to say that there weren't thousands of people here Saturday and Sunday, enjoying the campus, participating in a hundred different activities."

"I know, I know. But I was home. My dad was sick, and I went back to help out."

"I'm sorry to hear that," Josiah said. "Was this related to his MS?"

"It was."

Josiah made a sympathetic face, and Denise leaned forward. "But see, here's where it gets especially confusing. We don't know anything about this episode. Did you reach out to any Circlers during this crisis? You know that there are four groups on campus for staffers dealing with MS? Two of them are for children of MS sufferers. Have you sought out one of these groups?"

"No, not yet. I've meant to."

"Okay," Denise said. "Let's table that thought for a second, because that's instructive, the fact that you were aware of the groups, but didn't seek them out. Surely you acknowledge the benefit of sharing information about this disease?"

"I do."

"And that sharing with other young people whose parents suffer from the disease—do you see the benefit in this?"

"Absolutely."

"For example, when you heard your dad had a seizure, you drove, what, a hundred miles or so, and never once during that drive did you try to glean any information from the InnerCirclers, or from the larger OuterCircle. Do you see that as an opportunity wasted?"

"Now I do, absolutely. I was just upset, and worried, and I was driving like a maniac. I wasn't very present."

Denise raised a finger. "Ah, *present*. That is a wonderful word. I'm glad you used it. Do you consider yourself usually present?"

"I try to be."

Josiah smiled and tapped a flurry into his tablet.

"But the opposite of present would be what?" Denise asked.

"Absent?"

"Yes. Absent. Let's put a pin in that thought, too. Let's go back to your dad, and this weekend. Did he recover okay?"

"He did. It was a false alarm, really."

"Good. I'm so glad to hear about that. But it's curious that you didn't share this with anyone else. Did you post anything anywhere about this episode? A zing, a comment anywhere?"

"No, I didn't," Mae said.

"Hm. Okay," Denise said, taking a breath. "Do you think someone else might have benefited from your experience? That is, maybe the next person who might drive two or three hours home might benefit from knowing what you found out about the episode, that it was just a minor pseudo-seizure?"

"Absolutely. I could see that being helpful."

"Good. So what *do* you think the action plan should be?"

"I think I'll join the MS club," Mae said, "and I should post something about what happened. I know it'll be beneficial."

Denise smiled. "Fantastic. Now let's talk about the rest of the weekend. On Friday, you find out that your dad's okay. But the rest of the weekend, you basically go blank. It's like you disappeared!" Her eyes grew wide. "This is when someone like you, with a low Participation Rank, might be able to improve that, if she wanted to. But yours actually dropped—two thousand points. Not to get all number-geeky, but you were at 8,625 on Friday and by late Sunday you were at 10,288."

"I didn't know it was that bad," Mae said, hating herself, this self who couldn't seem to get out of her own way. "I guess I was just recovering from the stress of my dad's episode."

"Can you talk about what you did on Saturday?"

"It's embarrassing," Mae said. "Nothing."

"Nothing meaning what?"

"Well, most of the day I stayed at my parents' house and just watched TV."

Josiah brightened. "Anything good?"

"Just some women's basketball."

"There's nothing wrong with women's basketball!" Josiah gushed. "I *love* women's basketball. Have you followed my WNBA zings?"

"No, do you have a Zing feed about the WNBA?"

Josiah nodded, looking hurt, even bewildered.

Denise stepped in. "Again, it's just curious that you didn't choose to share it with anyone. Did you join any of the discussions about the sport? Josiah, how many participants are there in our global WNBA discussion group?"

Josiah, still visibly shaken knowing that Mae hadn't been reading his WNBA feed, managed to find the number on his tablet and muttered, "143,891."

"And how many zingers out there focus on the WNBA?"

Josiah quickly found the number. "12,992."

"And you're not part of either, Mae. Why do you think that is?"

"I guess I just didn't think my interest in the WNBA rose to the level where it warranted joining a discussion group, or, you know, following anything. I'm not that passionate about it."

Denise squinted at Mae. "That's an interesting choice of words: *Passion*. You've heard of PPT? Passion, Participation and Transparency?"

Mae had seen the letters PPT around campus and had not, until that moment, connected the letters to these three words. She felt like a fool.

Denise put her palms on the desk, as if she might get up. "Mae, you know this is a technology company, correct?"

"Of course."

"And that we consider ourselves on the forefront of social media."

"Yes."

"And you know the term *transparency*, correct?"

"I do. Absolutely."

Josiah looked at Denise, hoping to calm her. She put her hands in her lap. Josiah took over. He smiled and swiped his tablet, turning a new page.

"Okay. Let's go to Sunday. Tell us about Sunday."

"I just drove back."

"That's it?"

"I kayaked?"

Josiah and Denise registered dual looks of surprise.

"You kayaked?" Josiah said. "Where?"

"Just in the bay."

"With who?"

"No one. Just alone."

Denise and Josiah looked hurt.

"*I* kayak," Josiah said, and then typed something in his tablet, pressing very hard.

"How often do you kayak?" Denise asked Mae.

"Maybe once every few weeks?"

Josiah was looking intently at his tablet. "Mae, I'm looking at your profile, I'm finding nothing about you and kayaking. No smiles, no ratings, no posts, nothing. And now you're telling me you kayak once *every few weeks*?"

"Well, maybe it's less than that?"

Mae laughed, but Denise and Josiah did not. Josiah continued to stare at his screen, while Denise's eyes probed into Mae.

"When you go kayaking, what do you see?"

"I don't know. All kinds of things."

"Seals?"

"Sure."

"Sea lions?

"Usually."

"Waterbirds? Pelicans?"

"Sure."

Denise tapped at her tablet. "Okay, I'm doing a search now of your name for visual documentation of any of these trips you've taken. I'm not finding anything."

"Oh, I've never brought a camera."

"But how do you identify all these birds?"

"I have this little guide. It's just a thing my ex-boyfriend gave me. It's a little foldable guide to local wildlife."

"So it's just a pamphlet or something?"

"Yeah, I mean, it's waterproof and—"

Josiah exhaled loudly.

"I'm sorry," Mae said.

Josiah rolled his eyes. "No, I mean, this is a tangent, but my problem with paper is that all communication dies with it. It holds no possibility of continuity. You look at your paper brochure, and that's where it ends. It ends with *you*. Like you're the only one who matters. But think if you'd been *doc*umenting. If you'd been using a tool that would help confirm the identity of whatever birds you saw, then anyone can benefit—naturalists, students, historians, the Coast Guard. Everyone can know, then, what birds were on the bay on that day. It's just maddening, thinking of how much knowledge is lost every day through this kind of shortsightedness. And I don't want to call it selfish but—"

"No. It was. I know it was," Mae said.

Josiah softened. "But documentation aside, I'm just fascinated why you wouldn't mention anything about kayaking anywhere. I mean, it's a *part* of you. An *integral* part."

Mae let out an involuntary scoff. "I don't think it's all that integral. Or interesting, really."

Josiah looked up, his eyes fiery. "But it is!"

"Lots of people kayak," Mae said.

"That's exactly it!" Josiah said, quickly turning red. "Wouldn't you like to meet *other* people who kayak?" Josiah tapped at his screen. "There are 2,331 people near you who also like to kayak. Including *me*."

Mae smiled. "That's a lot."

"More or less than you expected?" Denise asked.

"More, I guess," Mae said.

Josiah and Denise smiled.

"So should we sign you up to hear more about the people near you who like to kayak? There are so many tools . . ." Josiah seemed to be opening a page where he could sign her up.

"Oh, I don't know," Mae said.

Their faces plummeted.

Josiah seemed angry again. "Why not? Do you think your passions are unimportant?"

"That's not quite it. I just . . ."

Josiah leaned forward. "How do you think other Circlers feel, knowing that you're so close to them physically, that you're ostensibly part of a community here, but you don't want them to know your hobbies and interests. How do you think they feel?"

"I don't know. I don't think they'd feel anything."

"But they do!" Josiah said. "The point is that you're not *engaged* with the people around you!"

"It's just kayaking!" Mae said, laughing again, trying to bring the discussion back to a place of levity.

Josiah was at work on his tablet. "*Just* kayaking? Do you realize that kayaking is a three-billion-dollar industry? And you say it's 'just kayaking'! Mae, don't you see that it's all connected? You play your part. You have to *part*-icipate."

Denise was looking at Mae intensely. "Mae, I have to ask a delicate question."

"Okay," Mae said.

"Do you think . . . Well, do you think this might be an issue of self-esteem?"

"Excuse me?"

"Are you reluctant to express yourself because you fear your opinions aren't valid?"

Mae had never thought about it quite this way, but it made a certain sense. Was she too shy about expressing herself? "I don't know, actually," she said.

Denise narrowed her eyes. "Mae, I'm no psychologist, but if I were, I might have a question about your sense of self-worth. We've studied some models for this kind of behavior. Not to say this kind of attitude is antisocial, but it's certainly *sub*-social, and certainly far from transparent. And we see that this behavior sometimes stems from a low sense of self-worth—a point of view that says, 'Oh, what I have to say isn't so important.' Do you feel that describes your point of view?"

Mae was too off-balance to see herself clearly. "Maybe," she said, buying time, knowing she shouldn't be too pliant. "But sometimes I'm sure that what I say is important. And when I have something significant to add, I definitely feel empowered to do it."

"But notice you said 'sometimes I'm sure,' " Josiah said, wagging a finger. "The 'sometimes' is interesting to me. Or concerning, I should say. Because I think you're not finding that 'sometime' frequently enough." He sat back, as if resting after the hard work of solving her was complete.

"Mae," Denise said, "we'd love if you could participate in a special program. Does that sound appealing?"

Mae knew nothing about it, but knew, because she was in trouble, and had already consumed so much of their time, she should say yes, so she smiled and said, "Absolutely."

"Good. As soon as we can, we'll hook you up. You'll meet Pete Ramirez, and he'll explain it. I think it might make you feel sure not just *some*times, but *always*. Does that sound better?"

After the interview, at her desk, Mae scolded herself. What kind of person was she? More than anything, she was ashamed. She'd been doing the bare minimum. She disgusted herself and felt for Annie. Surely Annie had been hearing about her deadbeat friend Mae, who took this gift, this coveted job at the Circle—a company that had insured her parents! had saved them from familial catastrophe!—and had been skating through. *Goddamnit, Mae, give a shit!* she thought. *Be a person of some value to the world.*

She wrote to Annie, apologizing, saying she would do better, that she was embarrassed, that she didn't want to abuse this privilege, this gift, and telling her that there was no need to write back, that she would simply do better, a thousand times better, immediately and from then on. Annie texted back, told her not to worry, that it was just a slap on the wrist, a correction, a common thing for newbies.

Mae looked at the time. It was six o'clock. She had plenty of hours to improve, there and then, so she embarked on a flurry of activity, sending four zings and thirty-two comments and eighty-eight smiles. In an hour, her PartiRank rose to 7,288. Breaking 7,000 was more difficult, but by eight o'clock, after joining and posting in eleven discussion groups, sending another twelve zings, one of them rated in the top 5,000 globally for that hour, and signing up for sixty-seven more feeds, she'd done it. She was at 6,872, and turned to her InnerCircle social feed. She was a few hundred posts behind, and she made her way through, replying to seventy or so messages, RSVPing to eleven events on campus, signing nine petitions, and providing comments and constructive criticism on four products currently in beta. By 10:16 her rank was 5,342, and again, the plateau—this time at 5,000—was hard to overcome. She wrote a series of zings about a new Circle service, allowing account holders to know whenever their name was mentioned in any messages sent from anyone else, and one of the zings, her seventh on the subject, caught fire and was rezinged 2,904 times, and this brought her PartiRank up to 3,887.

She felt a profound sense of accomplishment and possibility that was accompanied, in short order, by a near-complete sense of exhaustion. It was almost midnight and she needed sleep. It was too late to go all the way home, so she checked the dorm availability, reserved one, got her access code, walked across campus and into HomeTown.

When she closed the door to her room, she felt like a fool for not taking advantage of the dorms sooner. The room was immaculate, awash in silver fixtures and blond woods, the floors warm from radiant heat, the sheets and pillowcases so white and crisp they crackled when touched. The mattress, explained a card next to the bed, was organic, made not with springs or foam but instead a new fiber that Mae found was both firmer and more pliant—superior to any bed she'd ever known. She pulled the blanket, cloud-white and full of down, around her.

But she couldn't sleep. Now, thinking about how much better she could do, she logged on again, this time on her tablet, and pledged to work till two in the morning. She was determined to break 3,000. And she did so, though it was 3:19 a.m. when it happened. Finally, not quite exhausted but knowing she needed rest, she tucked herself in and turned off the lights.

In the morning, Mae looked through the closets and dressers, knowing that the dorms were stocked with an array of clothes, all new, available to be borrowed or kept. She chose a cotton T-shirt and a pair of capri pants, both pristine. On the sink there were new bottles of moisturizer and mouthwash, both organic and local, and she sampled each. She showered, dressed and was back at her desk by 8:20.

And immediately the fruits of her labors were evident. There was a river of congratulatory messages on her third screen, from Dan, Jared, Josiah, Denise, five or so messages from each of them, and at least a dozen from Annie, who seemed so proud and excited she might burst. Word spread through the InnerCircle, and Mae was sent 7,716 smiles by noon. Everyone had known she could do it. Everyone saw great things for her at the Circle, everyone was certain she would graduate from CE in no time, as soon as September, because rarely had anyone risen so quickly through the PartiRank and with such laser-like focus.

Mae's new feeling of competence and confidence carried her through the week, and given how close she was to the top 2,000, she stayed at her desk late through the weekend and early the next week, determined to crack through, sleeping in the same dorm room every night. She knew the upper 2,000, nicknamed T2K, was a group of Circlers almost maniacal in their social activity and elite in their corresponding followers. The members of the T2K had been more or less locked in place, with few additions or movements within their ranks, for almost eighteen months.

But Mae knew she needed to try. By Thursday night, she'd gotten to 2,219, and knew she was among a group of similar strivers who were, like her, working feverishly to rise. She worked for an hour and saw herself climb only two spots, to 2,217. This would be difficult, she knew, but the challenge was delicious. And every time she'd risen to a new thousand, she received so many accolades, and felt she was repaying Annie in particular, that it drove her on.

By ten o'clock, just when she was tiring, and when she'd gotten as high as 2,188, she had the revelation that she was young, and she was strong, and if she worked through the night, one night without sleep, she could crack the T2K while everyone else was unconscious. She fortified herself with an energy drink and gummy worms, and when the caffeine and sugar kicked in, she felt invincible. The third screen's InnerCircle wasn't enough. She turned on her OuterCircle feed, and was handling that without difficulty. She pushed forward, signing up for a few hundred more Zing feeds, starting with a comment on each. She was soon at 2,012, and now she was really getting resistance. She posted 33 comments on a product-test site and rose to 2,009. She looked at her left wrist to see how her body was responding, and thrilled at the sight of her pulse-rate increasing. She was in command of all this and needed more. The total number of stats she was tracking was only 41. There was her aggregate customer service score, which was at 97. There was her last score, which was 99. There was the average of her pod, which was at 96. There was the number of queries handled that day thus far, 221, and the number of queries handled by that time yesterday, 219, and the number handled by her on average, 220, and by the pod's other members: 198. On her second screen, there were the number of messages sent by other staffers that day, 1,192, and the number of those messages that she'd read, 239, and the number to which she'd responded, 88. There was the number of recent invitations to Circle company events, 41, and the number she'd responded to, 28. There was the number of overall visitors to the Circle's sites that day, 3.2 billion, and the number of pageviews, 88.7 billion. There was the number of friends in Mae's OuterCircle,

762, and outstanding requests by those wanting to be her friend, 27. There was the number of zingers she was following, 10,343, and the number following her, 18,198. There was the number of unread zings, 887. There was the number of zingers suggested to her, 12,862. There was the number of songs in her digital library, 6,877, number of artists represented, 921, and based on her tastes, the number of artists recommended to her: 3,408. There was the number of images in her library, 33,002, and number of images recommended to her, 100,038. There was the temperature inside the building, 70, and the temperature outside, 71. There was the number of staffers on campus that day, 10,981, and number of visitors to campus that day, 248. Mae had news alerts set for 45 names and subjects, and each time any one of them was mentioned by any of the news feeds she favored, she received a notice. That day there were 187. She could see how many people had viewed her profile that day, 210, and how much time on average they spent: 1.3 minutes. If she wanted, of course, she could go deeper, and see precisely what each person had viewed. Her health stats added a few dozen more numbers, each of them giving her a sense of great calm and control. She knew her heart rate and knew it was right. She knew her step count, almost 8,200 that day, and knew that she could get to 10,000 with ease. She knew she was properly hydrated and that her caloric intake that day was within accepted norms for someone of her body-mass index. It occurred to her, in a moment of sudden clarity, that what had always caused her anxiety, or stress, or worry, was not any one force, nothing independent and external—it wasn't danger to herself or the constant calamity of other people and their problems. It was internal: it was subjective: it was *not knowing*.

It wasn't that she had an argument with a friend or was called on the carpet by Josiah and Denise: it was not knowing what it meant, not knowing their plans, not knowing the consequences, the future. If she knew these, there would be calm. She knew, with some degree of certainty, where her parents were: home, as always. She could see, with her CircleSearch, where Annie was: in her office, probably still working, too. But where was Kalden? It had been two weeks since she'd seen or heard from him. She texted Annie.

You awake?

Always.

Still haven't heard from Kalden.

The old man? Maybe he died. He had a good long life.

You really think he was just some interloper?

I think you dodged a bullet. I'm glad he hasn't come back. I was worried about the espionage possibilities.

He wasn't a spy.

Then he was just old. Maybe some Circler's grandfather came to visit and got lost? It's just as well. You were too young to be a widow.

Mae thought of his hands. His hands had ruined her. All she wanted at that moment was his hands upon her again. His hand on her sacrum, pulling her close. Could her desires be so simple? And where in the hell had he gone? He had no right to disappear like this. She checked CircleSearch again; she'd looked for him a hundred times this way, with no success. But she had a right to know where he was. To at least know where he was, who he was. This was the unnecessary, and antiquated, burden of uncertainty. She could know, instantly, the temperature in Jakarta, but she couldn't find one man on a campus like this?

Where is that man who touched you a certain way? If she could eliminate this kind of uncertainty—when and by whom would you be touched a certain way again—you would eliminate most of the stressors of the world, and maybe, too, the wave of despair that was gathering in Mae's chest. She'd been feeling this, this black rip, this loud tear, within her, a few times a week. It didn't usually last long, but when she closed her eyes she saw a tiny tear in what seemed to be black cloth, and through this tiny tear she heard the screams of millions of invisible souls. It was a very strange thing, she realized, and it wasn't anything she'd mentioned to anyone. She might have described it to Annie, but didn't want to worry her so soon into her time at the Circle. But what was this feeling? Who was screaming through the tear in the cloth? She'd found the best way to get past it was to redouble her focus, to stay busy, to give more. She had a brief, silly thought that she might find Kalden on LuvLuv. She checked, and felt stupid when her doubts were confirmed. The tear was opening up inside her, a blackness overtaking her. She closed her eyes and heard underwater screams. Mae cursed the not-knowing, and knew she needed someone who could be known. Who could be located.

The knock on the door was low and tentative.

"It's open," Mae said.

Francis pushed his face into the room and held the door.

"You sure?" he said.

"I invited you," Mae said.

He slipped in and closed the door, as if narrowly escaping

from a pursuer in the hallway. He looked around the room. "Like what you've done with the place."

Mae laughed.

"Let's go to mine instead," he said.

She thought of protesting but wanted to see what his room looked like. All the dorm rooms varied in subtle ways, and now, because they'd become so popular and practical that many Circlers were living in them more or less permanently, they could be customized by their occupants. When they arrived, she saw that his room was a mirror of her own, though with a few Francis touches, most notably a papier-mâché mask he'd made as a child. Yellow and with enormous bespectacled eyes, it looked out from over the bed. He saw her staring at it.

"What?" he said.

"That's odd, don't you think? A mask over the bed?"

"I don't see it when I sleep," he said. "You want something to drink?" He looked in the fridge, finding juices and a new kind of sake in a round glass container tinted pink.

"That looks good," she said. "I don't have that in my room. Mine's in a more standard bottle. Maybe a different brand."

Francis mixed drinks for them both, overfilling each glass.

"I have a few shots every night," he said. "It's the only way to slow my head down so I can crash. You have that problem?"

"It takes me an hour to get to sleep," Mae said.

"Well," Francis said, "this reduces that come-down from an hour to fifteen minutes."

He handed her the glass. Mae looked into it, thinking it very sad at first, the sake every night, then knew she would try it herself, tomorrow.

He was looking at something between her stomach and her elbow.

"What?"

"I can never get over your waist," he said.

"Excuse me?" Mae said, thinking it was not worth it, it couldn't be worth it, to be with this man who said things like this.

"No, no!" he said, "I mean it's so extraordinary. The line of it, how it bends in like some kind of bow."

And then his hands were tracing the contour of her waist, drawing a long C in the air. "I love that you have hips and shoulders. And with that waist." He smiled, staring straight into Mae, as if he had no idea of the strange directness of what he'd said, or didn't care.

"I guess thank you," she said.

"That's really a compliment," he said. "It's like these curves were created for someone to put their hands there." He mimed the resting of his own palms upon her waist.

She stood, took a sip of her drink, and wondered if she should flee. But it was a compliment. He'd given her an inappropriate, clumsy, but very direct compliment that she knew she would never forget and that had already set her heart to a new and erratic pounding.

"You want to watch something?" Francis asked.

Mae shrugged, still struck dumb.

Francis scrolled through the options. They had access to virtually every movie and television show extant, and spent five minutes noting different things they could see, then thinking of something else that was like it but better.

"Have you heard this new stuff by Hans Willis?" Francis asked.

Mae had decided to stay, and had decided that she felt good about herself around Francis. That she had power here, and she liked that power. "No. Who's he?"

"He's one of the musicians-in-residence? He recorded a whole concert last week."

"Is it out?"

"No, but if it gets good ratings from Circlers they might try to release it. Let me see if I can find it."

He played it, a delicate piano piece, sounding like the beginning of rain. Mae got up to turn off the lights, allowing the grey luminescence of the monitor to remain, casting Francis in a ghostly light.

She noticed a thick leathery book and picked it up. "What's this? I don't have one of these in my room."

"Oh that's mine. It's an album. Just pictures."

"Like family pictures?" Mae asked, and then remembered his complicated history. "Sorry. I know that's probably not the best way to put it."

"It's okay," he said. "They're sort of family pictures. My siblings are in some of them. But they're mostly just me and the foster families. You want to look?"

"You keep it here at the Circle?"

He took it from Mae and sat on the bed. "No. It's usually at home, but I brought it in. You want to look at it? It's mostly depressing."

Francis had already opened the album. Mae sat next to him, and watched as he turned the pages. She saw glimpses of Francis in modest living rooms, amber-lit, and in kitchens, the occasional amusement park. Always the parents were blurry or cropped from the frames. He arrived at a photo of himself sitting on a skateboard, looking out through enormous glasses.

"Those must have been the mother's," he said. "Look at the frames." He drew his finger over the round lenses. "That's a woman's style, right?"

"I think so," Mae said, staring at Francis's younger face. He had the same open expression, the same prominent nose, the same full lower lip. She felt her eyes filling.

"I can't remember those frames," he said, "I don't know where they came from. All I can think is that my regular glasses had broken and these were hers, and she was letting me wear them."

"You look cute," Mae said, but she wanted to cry and cry.

Francis was squinting at the photo, as if hoping to glean some answers from it if he looked long enough.

"Where was this?" Mae asked.

"No idea," he said.

"You don't know where you lived?"

"No clue. Even having pictures is pretty rare. Not all the foster families would give you photos, but when they did, they made sure not to show anything that could help you find them. No exteriors of the houses, no addresses or street signs or landmarks."

"You're serious?"

Francis looked at her. "That's the foster care way."

"Why? So you couldn't come back or what?"

"It was just a rule. Yeah, so you couldn't come back. If they had you a year, that was the deal, and they didn't want you landing back on their doorstep again—especially when you got older.

Some of the kids had some serious tendencies, so the families had to worry about when they got older and could track them down."

"I had no idea."

"Yeah. It's a weird system but it makes sense." He drank the rest of his sake and got up to adjust the stereo.

"Can I look?" Mae asked.

Francis shrugged. Mae paged through it, looking for any identifying imagery. But in dozens of photos, she saw no addresses, no homes. All the photos were interiors, or anonymous backyards.

"I bet some of them would want to hear from you," she said.

Francis was done with the stereo, and a new song was playing, an old soul song she couldn't name. He sat down next to her.

"Maybe. But that's not the agreement."

"So you haven't tried to contact them? I mean, with facial recognition—"

"I don't know. I haven't decided. I mean, that's why I brought it here. I'm scanning the pictures tomorrow just to see. Maybe we get a few matches. But I'm not planning to do much beyond that. Just fill in a few gaps."

"You have a right to know at least some basics."

Mae was leafing through the pages, and landed on a picture of a young Francis, no more than five, with two girls, nine or ten, flanking him. Mae knew these were his sisters, the two who had been killed, and she wanted to look at them, though she didn't know why. She didn't want to coerce Francis into talking about them, and knew she shouldn't say anything, that she should allow him to initiate any discussion of them, and if he didn't, soon, she should turn the page.

He said nothing, so she turned the page, feeling a surge of

feeling for him. She'd been too tough on him before. He was here, he liked her, he wanted her with him, and he was the saddest person she'd ever known. She could change that.

"Your pulse is going nuts," he said.

Mae looked down at her bracelet, and saw that her heart rate was at 134.

"Let me see yours," she said.

He rolled up his sleeve. She grabbed his wrist and turned it. His was at 128.

"You're not so calm yourself," she said, and left her hand resting across his lap.

"Leave your hand there and watch it get faster," he said, and together, they did. It was astonishing. It quickly rose to 134. She thrilled at her power, the proof of it, right before her and measurable. He was at 136.

"Want me to try something?" she said.

"I do," he whispered, his breath labored.

She reached down into the folds of his pants and found his penis pressing up against his belt buckle. She rubbed its tip with her index finger, and together they watched the numbers rise to 152.

"You're so easy to excite," she said. "Imagine if something were really happening."

His eyes were closed. "Right," he finally said, his breath labored.

"You're enjoying this?" she asked.

"Mm-hm," he managed.

Mae thrilled at her power over him. Watching Francis, his hands on the bed, his penis straining against his pants, she thought of something she could say. It was corny, and she would never say it if she thought anyone would ever know she'd said it, but it made her smile, and she knew it would send Francis, this shy boy, over the edge.

"What *else* does that measure?" she asked, and lunged.

His eyes went wild, and he struggled with his pants, trying to remove them. But just as he pulled them to his thighs, a sound came from his mouth, something like "Oh god" or "I gotta," just before he doubled over, his head jerking left and right until he crumpled on the bed, his head to the wall. She backed away, looking at him, his shirt hiked up, his crotch exposed. She could think only of a campfire, one small log, all of it doused in milk.

"Sorry," he said.

"No. I liked that," she said.

"That was about as sudden it's ever happened with me." He was still breathing heavily. And then some rogue synapse within her connected this scene to her father, to seeing him on the couch, helpless over his body, and she wanted badly to be somewhere else.

"I should go," she said.

"Really? Why?" he said.

"It's after one, I should sleep."

"Okay," he said, in a way that she found unappealing. He seemed to want her gone as much as she wanted to be gone.

He stood and retrieved his phone, which had been propped upright on the cabinet, facing them.

"What, were you filming us?" she joked.

"Maybe," he said, his tone making clear that he had.

"Wait. Seriously?"

Mae reached for the phone.

"Don't," he said. "It's mine." He shoved it into his pocket.

"It's *yours*? What we just did is *yours*?"

"It's just as much mine as yours. And I was the one having you know, a climax. And why do you care? You weren't naked or anything."

"Francis. I can't believe this. Delete that. Now."

"Did you say 'delete'?" he said, jokingly, but the meaning was clear: *We don't delete at the Circle.* "I have to have a way to see it myself."

"Then *everyone* can see it."

"I won't advertise it or anything."

"Francis. Please."

"C'mon, Mae. You have to understand how much this means to me. I'm not some stud. This is a rare occasion for me, to have something like this happen. Can't I keep a memento of the experience?"

"You can't worry," Annie said.

They were in the Great Room of the Enlightenment. In a rare occurrence, Stenton was to give the Ideas talk, with the promise of a special guest.

"But I *am* worrying," Mae said. She'd been unable to concentrate in the week since her encounter with Francis. The video hadn't been viewed by anyone else, but if it was on his phone, it was in the Circle cloud, and accessible to anyone. More than anything, she was disappointed in herself. She'd let the same man do the same thing to her, twice.

"Don't ask me again to delete it," Annie said, waving to a few senior Circlers in the crowd, members of the Gang of 40.

"Please delete it."

"You know I can't. We don't delete here, Mae. Bailey would freak. He'd weep. It hurts him personally when anyone even considers the deleting of any information. It's like killing babies, he says. You know that."

"But this baby's giving a handjob. No one wants that baby. We need to delete that baby."

"No one will ever see it. You know that. Ninety-nine percent of the stuff in the cloud is never seen by anyone. If it even gets one view, we can talk again. Okay?" Annie put her hand on Mae's. "Now watch this. You don't know how rare it is to have Stenton doing the address. This must be big, and it must involve some kind of government thing. That's his niche."

"You don't know what he's about to say?"

"I have some idea," she said.

Stenton took the stage without an introduction. The audience applauded, but in a way that was markedly different from the way they had for Bailey. Bailey was their talented uncle who had saved every one of their lives personally. Stenton was their boss, for whom they had to act professionally and clap professionally. In a flawless black suit, no tie, he walked to the center of the stage, and without introducing himself or saying hello, he began.

"As you know," he said, "transparency is something we advocate here at the Circle. We look to a guy like Stewart as an inspiration—a man who's willing to open up his life to further our collective knowledge. He's been filming, recording, every moment of his life now for five years, and it's been an invaluable asset to the Circle, and soon, I bet, to all of humankind. Stewart?"

Stenton looked out to the audience, and found Stewart, the Transparent Man, standing with what looked like a small telephoto lens around his neck. He was bald, about sixty, bending slightly, as if from the weight of the device resting on his chest. He got a warm round of applause before sitting down.

"Meanwhile," Stenton said, "there's another area of public life where we want and expect transparency, and that's democracy. We're lucky to have been born and raised in a democracy, but one that is always undergoing improvements. When I was a kid, to combat back-room political deals, for example, citizens insisted upon Sunshine Laws. These laws give citizens access to meetings, to transcripts. They could attend public hearings and petition for documents. And yet still, so long after the founding of this democracy, every day, our elected leaders still find themselves embroiled in some scandal or another, usually involving them doing something they shouldn't be doing. Something secretive, illegal, against the will and best interests of the republic. No wonder public trust for Congress is at 11 percent."

There was a wave of murmuring from the audience. Stenton fed off it. "Congressional approval is actually at 11 percent! And as you know, a certain senator was just revealed to be involved in some very unsavory business."

The crowd laughed, cheered, tittered.

Mae leaned to Annie. "Wait, what senator?"

"Williamson. You didn't hear? She got busted for all kinds of weird stuff. She's under investigation for a half-dozen things, all kinds of ethical violations. They found everything on her computer, a hundred weird searches, downloads—some very creepy stuff."

Mae thought, unwillingly, of Francis. She turned her attention back to Stenton.

"Your occupation could be dropping human feces on the heads of senior citizens," he said, "and your job approval would be higher than 11 percent. So what can be done? What can be done to restore the people's trust in their elected leaders? I am happy to say that there's a woman who is taking all this very seriously, and she's doing something to address the issue. Let me introduce Olivia Santos, representative from District 14."

A stout woman of about fifty, wearing a red suit and a yellow floral scarf, strode from the wings, both arms waving high over her head. From the scattered and polite applause, it was clear that few in the Great Hall knew who she was.

Stenton gave her a stiff hug, and as she stood beside him, her hands clasped in front of her, he continued. "For those who need a civics refresher, Congresswoman Santos represents this very district. It's okay if you didn't know her. Now you do." He turned to her. "How are you today, Congresswoman?"

"I'm fine, Tom, very fine. Very happy to be here."

Stenton offered his version of a warm smile to her, and then turned back to the audience.

"Congresswoman Santos is here to announce what I must say is a very important development in the history of government. And that is a move toward the ultimate transparency that we've all sought from our elected leaders since the birth of representative democracy. Congresswoman?"

Stenton stepped back and sat behind her on a high stool. Representative Santos moved to the front of the stage, hands now entwined behind her, and swept her eyes over the room.

"That's right, Tom. I'm as concerned as you are about the need for citizens to know what their elected leaders are doing. I mean, it is your right, is it not? It's your right to know how they spend their days. Who they're meeting with. Who they're talking to. What they're doing on the taxpayer's dime. Until now, it's been an ad hoc system of accountability. Senators and representatives, mayors and councilpersons, have occasionally released their schedules, and have allowed citizens varying degrees of access. But still we wonder, Why are they meeting with that former-senator-turned-lobbyist? And how did that congressman get that $150,000 the FBI found hidden in his fridge? How did that other senator arrange and carry out trysts with a series of women while his wife was undergoing cancer treatment? I mean, the array of misdeeds carried out while these officials were being paid by you, the citizenry, is not only deplorable, not only unacceptable, but also unnecessary."

There was a smattering of applause. Santos smiled, nodded and continued.

"We've all wanted and expected transparency from our elected leaders, but the technology wasn't there to make it fully possible. But now it is. As Stewart has demonstrated, it's very easy to provide the world at large full access to your day, to see what you see, hear what you hear and what you say. Thank you for your courage, Stewart."

The audience applauded again for Stewart with new vigor, some of them guessing what Santos was about to announce.

"So I intend to follow Stewart on his path of illumination. And along the way, I intend to show how democracy can and should be: entirely open, entirely transparent. Starting today, I will be wearing the same device that Stewart wears. My every meeting, movement, my every word, will be available to all my constituents and to the world."

Stenton got off his stool and made his way to Santos. He looked out to the assembled Circlers. "Can we give Congress-woman Santos a round of applause?"

But the audience was already clapping. There were whoops and whistles, and Santos beamed. While they roared, a techni-cian emerged from the wings and hung a necklace around Santos's head—a smaller version of the camera Stewart had been wear-ing. Santos held the lens to her lips and kissed it. The audience cheered. After a minute, Stenton raised his hands, and the crowd quieted. He turned to Santos.

"So you're saying that every conversation, every meeting, every part of your day will be broadcast?"

"Yes. It will all be available on my Circle page. Every moment till I sleep." The audienced applauded again, and Stenton indulged them, then again asked for quiet.

"And what if those who want to meet with you don't want a given meeting to be broadcast?"

"Well, then they will not meet with me," she said. "You're either transparent or you're not. You're either accountable or you're not. What would anyone have to say to me that couldn't be said in public? What part of representing the people should not be known by the very people I'm representing?"

The applause was drowning her out.

"Indeed," Stenton said.

"Thank you! Thank you!" Santos said, bowing, putting her palms together in a posture of prayer. The applause continued for minutes. Finally, Stenton gestured for calm once more.

"So when are you starting this new program?" he asked.

"No time like the present," she said. She pushed a button on the device around her neck, and there it was, the view from her camera, projected on the giant screen behind her. The audience saw itself, with great clarity, and roared with approval.

"It begins now for me, Tom," she said, "And I hope it begins soon for the rest of the elected leaders in this country—and for those in every one of the world's democracies."

She bowed, she put her hands together again, and then began to walk off the stage. As she was nearing the curtains at stage left, she stopped. "There's no reason for me to go that way—too dark. I'm going this way," she said, and the lights in the auditorium came on as she stepped down to the floor, into the bright light, the room's thousand faces suddenly visible and cheering. She walked straight up the aisle, all the hands reaching to her, grinning faces telling her thank you, thank you, go forth and make us proud.

That night, in the Colony, there was a reception for Congresswoman Santos, and she continued to be swarmed with new admirers. Mae briefly entertained the notion of trying to get close enough to shake her hand, but the crowd around her was five deep, all night, so instead Mae ate from the buffet, some kind of shredded pork that had been made on campus, and waited for

Annie. She'd said she would try to make it down, but was on a deadline, preparing something for a hearing at the EU. "They're whining about taxes again," she said.

Mae wandered the room, which had been decorated in a vaguely desert theme, with scatterings of cacti and sandstone in front of walls of digital sunsets. She saw and said hello to Dan and Jared, and a few of the newbies she'd been training. She looked for Francis, hoping he wouldn't be there, but then remembered, with great relief, that he was at a conference in Las Vegas—a gathering of law enforcement agencies he was introducing to ChildTrack. As she wandered, a wallscreen sunset faded to make way for the face of Ty. His face was unshaven, and there were bags under his eyes, and though he was clearly and thoroughly tired, he was smiling broadly. He was wearing his customary oversized black hoodie, and took a moment to clean his glasses on his sleeve before looking out at the room, left and right, as if he could see them all from wherever he was. Maybe he could. The room quickly hushed.

"Hey everyone. Sorry I can't be there with you all. I've been working on some very interesting new projects that are keeping me away from incredible social activities like the one you're enjoying. But I did want to congratulate you all on this phenomenal new development. I think it's a crucial new step for the Circle and will mean a great deal to our overall awesomeness." For a second he seemed to be looking at whoever was operating the camera, as if confirming he'd said enough. Then his eyes returned to look into the room. "Thank you all for your hard work on it, and let the party truly begin!".

His face disappeared, and the wallscreen again displayed the digital sunset. Mae chatted with some of the newbies in her pod, some of whom hadn't seen any live addresses from Ty before, and were close to euphoric. Mae took a picture, zinged it and added a few words: *Exciting stuff!*

Mae picked up her second glass of wine, deciding how she could do so without taking the napkin under it, which would serve no purpose and end up in her pocket, when she saw Kalden. He was in a shadowy stairwell, sitting on the steps. She meandered her way over to him, and when he saw her, his face brightened.

"Oh hi," he said.

"Oh hi?"

"Sorry," he said, and leaned into her, intending a hug.

She recoiled. "Where have you been?"

"Been?"

"You disappeared for two weeks," Mae said.

"It hasn't been that long, has it? And I've been around. I looked for you one day but you looked busy."

"You came to CE?"

"I did, but I didn't want to bother you."

"And you couldn't leave a message somehow?"

"I didn't know your last name," he said, smiling, as if he knew far more than he was letting on. "Why didn't you contact *me*?"

"I didn't know your last name, either. And there's no Kalden listed anywhere."

"Really? How were you spelling it?"

Mae began to enumerate the permutations she'd tried, when he interrupted.

"Listen, it doesn't matter. We both screwed up. And now we're here."

Mae stepped back to take him in, thinking maybe, somewhere on him, she would find some clue as to whether or not he was real—a real Circler, a real person. Again he was wearing a snug longsleeve shirt, this one with narrow horizontal stripes in greens and reds and browns, and again he had maneuvered his way into very narrow black pants that gave his legs the look of an inverted V.

"You do work here, right?" she asked.

"Of course. How else could I get in? Security is pretty good here. Especially on a day like today, with our luminous guest." He nodded to the congresswoman, who was signing her name on someone's tablet.

"You look like you're ready to leave," Mae said.

"Do I?" Kalden said. "No, no. I'm just comfortable back here. I like to sit during these things. And I guess I like to have the option of fleeing." He threw his thumb over his shoulder, indicating the stairs behind him.

"I'm just glad my supervisors saw me here," Mae said. "That was my first priority. Do you have to be seen here by a supervisor or anything?"

"Supervisor?" For a moment, Kalden looked at her as if she'd just said something in a familiar and yet incomprehensible language. "Oh yeah," he said, nodding. "They saw me here. I took care of that."

"Have you told me what you do here yet?"

"Ah, I don't know. Have I? Look at that guy."

"What guy?"

"Oh, never mind," Kalden said, seeming to have already forgotten whom he was looking at. "So you're in PR?"

"No. Customer Experience."

214

Kalden tilted his head. "Oh. Oh. I knew that," he said, unconvincingly. "You've been there a while?"

Mae had to laugh. The man was not all there. His mind seemed barely tethered to his body, much less the earth.

"I'm sorry," he said, his face turning to her, now looking impossibly sincere and clear-eyed. "But I *want* to remember these things about you. I was actually hoping I'd see you here."

"How long have you worked here again?" she asked.

"Me? Um." He scratched the back of his head. "Wow. I don't know. A while now."

"One month? A year? Six years?" she asked, thinking he really was some kind of savant.

"Six?" he said, "That would be the beginning. You think I look old enough to have been here six years? I don't want to look that old. Is it the grey hair?"

Mae had no idea what to say. Of course it was the grey hair. "Should we get a refreshment?" she asked.

"No, you go ahead," he said.

"Afraid to leave your hideout?"

"No, just feeling less social."

She made her way to a table where a few hundred glasses of wine had been poured and were waiting.

"Mae, right?"

She turned to find the two women, Dayna and Hillary, who were building a submersible for Stenton. Mae remembered meeting them on her first day, and since then had been getting their updates on her second screen at least three times a day. They were weeks away from finishing the craft; Stenton planned to take it to the Marianas Trench.

"I've been following your progress," Mae said. "Incredible. You're building it here?"

Mae glanced over her shoulder to make sure Kalden hadn't made a quick exit.

"With the Project 9 guys, yeah," Hillary said, waving a hand at some other, unknown part of the campus. "Safer to build it here, to keep the patented stuff secure."

"This is the first vessel big enough to really bring back full-sized animal life," Dayna said.

"And you guys get to go?"

Dayna and Hillary laughed. "No," Hillary said. "This thing's built for one man and one man only: Tom Stenton."

Dayna looked askance at Hillary, then back to Mae. "The costs of making it big enough for more people are pretty much prohibitive."

"Right," Hillary said. "That's what I meant."

When Mae returned to Kalden's stairwell, holding two glasses of wine, he was in the same place, but he had somehow gotten himself two glasses of his own.

"Someone came by with a tray," he said, standing up.

They stood briefly, each two-fisted, and Mae could think of nothing but clinking all four glasses together, which they did.

"I ran into the team building the submersible," Mae said. "You know them?"

Kalden rolled his eyes. It was startling. Mae hadn't seen anyone else do that at the Circle.

"What?" Mae said.

"Nothing," he said. "Did you like the speech?" he asked.

"The whole Santos thing? I did. Very exciting." She was

careful with her words. "I think this will be a momentous, uh, moment in the history of demo—" She paused, seeing him smile. "What?" she said.

"Nothing," he said. "You don't have to give me a speech. I heard what Stenton said. You really think this is a good idea?"

"You don't?"

He shrugged and drained half his glass. "That guy just concerns me sometimes." Then, knowing he shouldn't have said that about one of the Wise Men, he changed tacks. "He's just so smart. It's intimidating. You really think I look old? What would you say? Thirty?"

"You don't look that old," Mae said.

"I don't believe you. I know I do."

Mae drank from one of her glasses. They looked around, watching the feed from Santos's camera. It was being projected onto the far wall, and a group of Circlers stood, watching, while Santos mingled a few feet away. One Circler found his own image caught on the congresswoman's camera, and positioned his hand to cover his second, projected, face.

Kalden watched closely, his brow furrowed. "Hm," he said. He tilted his head, like a traveler puzzling out some odd local customs. Then he turned to Mae, and looked at her two glasses and at his own, as if just now realizing the humor in both of them standing two-fisted in a doorway. "I'm gonna get rid of this one," he said, and downed the glass in his left hand. Mae followed suit.

"Sorry," she said, for no reason. She knew she would soon be tipsy, probably too tipsy to hide it; bad decisions would ensue. She tried to think of something intelligent to say while she could.

"So where does all that go?" she asked.

"The stuff from the camera?"

"Yeah, is it stored somewhere here? The cloud?"

"Well, it's in the cloud, sure, but it has to be stored in a physical place, too. The stuff from Stewart's camera . . . Wait. You want to see something?"

He was already halfway down the stairwell, his limbs nimble and spidery.

"I don't know," Mae said.

Kalden looked up, as if he'd had his feelings hurt. "I can show you where Stewart is stored. You want to? I'm not taking you to some dungeon."

Mae looked around the room, scanning for Dan and Jared, but couldn't find them. She'd stayed an hour, and they'd seen her, so she assumed she could leave. She took a few pictures, posted them, and sent a series of zings, detailing and commenting on the proceedings. Then she followed Kalden down the stairs, three flights, to what she assumed was the basement. "I'm really trusting you," she said.

"You should," Kalden said, approaching a large blue door. He passed his fingers over a wall-mounted pad and it opened. "Come."

She followed him down a long hallway, and she had the feeling she was passing from one building to another, through some tunnel far underground. Soon another door appeared, and again Kalden released the lock with his fingerprints. Mae followed, almost giddy, intrigued by his extraordinary access, too tipsy to measure the wisdom of following this calligraphic man through this labyrinth. They rode down what Mae guessed was four floors, exited into another long corridor, and then entered another stairwell, where they again went down. Mae soon found her second glass of wine cumbersome, so she finished it.

"Anywhere I can put this?" she asked. Without a word, Kalden took the glass and left it on the lowest step of the stairway they'd just finished.

Who was this person? He had access to every door he encountered, but he also had an anarchic streak. No one else at the Circle would abandon a glass like that—which amounted to some grand act of pollution—and no one else would take such a journey in the middle of a company party. There was a muffled part of Mae that knew Kalden was likely a troublemaker here, and that what they were doing was probably against some or all rules and regulations.

"I still don't know what you do here," she said.

They were walking through a dimly lit corridor that sloped gently downward and with no apparent end.

He turned. "Not much. I go to meetings. I listen, I provide feedback. It's not very important," he said, walking briskly ahead of her.

"Do you know Annie Allerton?"

"Of course. I love Annie." Now he turned back to her. "Hey, you still have that lemon I gave you?"

"No. It never turned yellow."

"Huh," he said, and his eyes briefly left their focus on her, as if they were needed somewhere else, somewhere deep in his mind, for a brief but crucial calculation.

"Where are we?" Mae asked. "I feel like we're a thousand feet underground."

"Not quite," he said, his eyes returning. "But close. Have you heard of Project 9?"

Project 9, as far as Mae knew, was the all-encompassing name for the secret research being done at the Circle. Anything from space technology—Stenton thought the Circle could design and build a far better reusable spacecraft—to what was rumored to be a plan to embed and make accessible massive amounts of data in human DNA.

"Is that where we're going?" Mae asked.

"No," he said, and opened another door.

They entered a large room, about the size of a basketball court, dimly lit but for a dozen spotlights trained on an enormous red metallic box, the size of a bus. Each side was smooth, polished, the whole thing surrounded by a network of gleaming silver pipes forming an elaborate grid around it.

"It looks like some kind of Donald Judd sculpture," Mae said.

Kalden turned to her, his face alight. "I'm so glad you said that. He was a big inspiration to me. I love that thing he once said: 'Things that exist exist, and everything is on their side.' You ever see his stuff in person?"

Mae was only passingly familiar with the work of Donald Judd—they'd done a few days on him in one of her art history classes—but didn't want to disappoint Kalden. "No, but I love him," she said. "I love his heft."

And with that, something new appeared on Kalden's face, some new respect for, or interest in, Mae, as if at that moment she'd become three-dimensional and permanent.

Then Mae ruined it. "He did this for the company?" she said, nodding at the massive red box.

Kalden laughed, then looked at her, his interest in her not gone, but certainly in retreat. "No, no. He's been dead for decades. This was just inspired by his aesthetic. This is actually a machine. Or inside it is. It's a storage unit."

He looked at Mae, expecting her to complete the thought.

She couldn't.

"This is Stewart," he finally said.

Mae knew nothing about data storage, but had been under the general idea that storing such information could be done in a far smaller space.

"All this for one person?" she asked.

"Well, it's the storage of the raw data, and then the capacity to run all kinds of scenarios through it. Every bit of video is being mapped a hundred different ways. Everything Stewart sees is correlated with the rest of the video we have, and it helps map the world and everything in it. And of course, what you get through Stewart's cameras is exponentially more detailed and layered than any consumer device."

"And why have it here, as opposed to stored in the cloud or in the desert somewhere?"

"Well, some people like to scatter their ashes and some like to have a plot close to home, right?"

Mae wasn't precisely sure what that meant but she didn't feel she could admit that. "And the pipes are for electricity?" she asked.

Kalden opened his mouth, paused, then smiled. "No, that's water. A ton of water's needed to keep the processors cool. So the water runs through the system, cooling the overall apparatus. Millions of gallons every month. You want to see Santos's room?"

He led her through a door to another, identical, room, with another great red box dominating the space. "This was supposed to be for someone else, but when Santos stepped up, it was assigned to her."

Mae had already said too many silly things that night, and was feeling light-headed, so she didn't ask the questions she wanted to ask, such as, How could these things take up so much space? And use so much water? And if even a hundred more people wanted to store their every minute—and surely millions would opt to go transparent, would beg to—how could we do this when each life took up so much space? Where would all these great red boxes go?

"Oh wait, something's about to happen," Kalden said, and he took her hand and led her back into Stewart's room, where the two of them stood, listening to the hum of the machines.

"Has it happened?" Mae asked, thrilling at the feel of his hand, his palm soft and his fingers warm and long.

Kalden raised his eyebrows, telling her to wait.

A loud rush came from overhead, the unmistakable movement of water. Mae looked up, briefly thinking they would be drenched, but realized it was only the water coming through the pipes, heading for Stewart, cooling all he'd done and seen.

"Such a pretty sound, don't you think?" Kalden said, looking to her, his eyes seeming to want to get back to the place where Mae was something more than ephemeral.

"Beautiful," she said. And then, because the wine had her teetering, and because he'd just held her hand, and because something about the rush of water set her free, she took Kalden's face in her hands and kissed his lips.

His hands rose from his sides and held her, tentatively, around the waist, just his fingertips, as if she were a balloon he didn't want to pop. But for a terrible moment, his mouth was inanimate, stunned. Mae thought she'd made a mistake. Then, as if a bundle of signals and directives had finally reached his cerebral cortex, his lips awakened and returned the force of her kiss.

"Hold on," he said after a moment, and pulled away. He nodded toward the red box containing Stewart, and led her by the hand out of the room and into a narrow corridor she hadn't seen before. It was unlit, and as they stepped further, the light from Stewart no longer penetrated.

"Now I'm scared," Mae said.

"Almost there," he said.

And then there was the creaking of a steel door. It opened, and revealed an enormous chamber illuminated by weak blue light. Kalden led her through the doorway and into what seemed to be a great cave, thirty feet high, with a barrel-vaulted ceiling.

"What is this?" she asked.

"It was supposed to be part of the subway," he said. "But they abandoned it. Now it's just empty, a strange combination of man-made tunnel and actual cave. See the stalactites?"

He pointed down the great tunnel, where stalagmites and stalactites gave the tunnel the look of a mouth full of uneven teeth.

"Where does it go?" she asked.

"It connects to the one under the bay," he said. "I've gone about a half mile into it, but then it gets too wet."

Where they stood, they could see black water, a shallow lake on the tunnel floor.

"My guess is that this is where the future Stewarts will go," he said. "Thousands of them, probably smaller. I'm sure they'll get the containers down to people-size soon enough."

They looked into the tunnel together, and Mae pictured it, an endless grid of red steel boxes stretching into the darkness.

He looked back to her. "You can't tell anyone I took you here."

"I won't," Mae said, then knew that to keep this promise she would have to lie to Annie. In the moment, it seemed a small price to pay. She wanted to kiss Kalden again, and she took his face again, down to hers, and opened her mouth to his. She closed her eyes, and pictured the long cave, the blue light above, the dark water below.

And then, in the shadows, away from Stewart, something in Kalden changed, and his hands became more sure of themselves. He held her closer, his hands gaining strength. His mouth moved from hers, across her cheek and onto her neck, pausing there, and climbing to her ear, his breath hot. She tried to keep up, holding his head in her hands, exploring his neck, his back, but he was leading, he had plans. His right hand was on the small of her back, bringing her into him, where she felt him hard and pressing against her stomach.

And then she was lifted. She was in the air, and he was carrying her, and she wrapped her legs around him as he strode purposefully to some point behind her. She opened her eyes, briefly, then closed them, not wanting to know where he was taking her, trusting him, though knowing how wrong this was, trusting him, so far underground, a man she couldn't find, whose full name she didn't know.

Then he was lowering her, and she braced herself to feel the stone of the cave floor, but instead she felt the soft landing of some kind of mattress. Now she opened her eyes. They were in an alcove, a cave within the cave, a few feet off the ground and carved into the wall. It was filled with blankets and pillows, and he eased her down upon them.

"This is where you sleep?" she asked, in her fevered state thinking it almost logical.

"Sometimes," he said, and breathed fire into her ear.

She remembered the condoms she'd been given at Dr. Villalobos's office. "I have something," she said.

"Good," he said, and he took one from her, tearing the wrapper as she pushed his pants down his hips.

In two quick motions he pulled her pants and panties down and tossed them aside. He buried his face in her stomach, his hands holding the back of her thighs, his fingers crawling upward, inward.

"Come back up here," she said.

He did, and he hissed into her ear. "Mae."

She couldn't form words.

"Mae," he said again, as she fell apart all over him.

She woke up in the dorms and first imagined she'd dreamt it, every moment: the underground chambers, the water, the red boxes, that hand on the small of her back and then the bed, the pillows in the cave within the cave—none of it seemed plausible. It was the kind of random assemblage of details that dreams fumbled with, none of it possible in this world.

But as she rose and showered and dressed, she realized that everything had happened the way she remembered. She had kissed this person Kalden, who she knew very little about, and he had led her not only through a series of high-security chambers, but into some dark anteroom, where they'd lost themselves for hours and passed out.

She called Annie. "We consummated."

"Who did? You and the old man?"

"He's not old."

"He didn't have a musty smell? Did he mention his pacemaker or diapers? Don't tell me he died on you."

"He's not even thirty."

"Did you get his last name this time?"

"No, but he gave me a number where I can call him."

"Oh, that's classy. And have you tried it?"

"Not yet."

"Not yet?"

Mae's stomach tightened. Annie exhaled loudly.

"You know I'm worried about him being some kind of spy or stalker. Did you confirm that he's legit?"

"I did. He works at the Circle. He said he knew you, and he had access to lots of places. He's normal. Maybe a little eccentric."

"Access to places? What do you mean?" Annie's tone took on a new edge.

At that moment, Mae knew she would begin lying to Annie. Mae wanted to be with Kalden again, wanted to throw herself around him at that moment, and she didn't want Annie to do anything to jeopardize her access to him, and his broad shoulders, his elegant silhouette.

"I just mean he knew his way around," Mae said. There was a part of her that thought he might indeed be there illegally, that

226

he was some interloper, and, in a sudden revelation, she realized he might be living in that strange underground lair. He might represent some force opposed to the Circle. Maybe he worked for Senator Williamson in some capacity, or some would-be competitor to the Circle. Maybe he was a simple nobody blogger-stalker who wanted to get closer to the machine at the center of the world.

"So you consummated where? In your dorm?"

"Yup," Mae said. It was not so difficult to lie this way.

"And he slept over?"

"No, he had to get home." And, realizing that the longer she spent talking to Annie the more lies she would tell, Mae concocted a reason to hang up. "I'm supposed to get hooked up for the CircleSurvey today," she said. Which was more or less true.

"Call me later. And you have to get his name."

"Okay."

"Mae, I'm not your boss. I don't want to be your supervisor or anything. But the company needs to know who this guy is. Company security's something we have to take seriously. Let's get him nailed down today, okay?" Annie's voice had changed; she sounded like a displeased superior. Mae held her anger and hung up.

Mae called the number Kalden had given her. But when she did, the phone rang without end. There was no voicemail. And again Mae realized she had no way to get in touch with him. Intermittently, throughout the night, she'd thought to ask him his last name, for any other kind of information, but the time was never right, and he hadn't asked for hers, and she assumed that when they left each other, they would exchange information. But then they'd forgotten. She, at least, had forgotten. How had they parted, after all? He walked her to the dorms, and kissed her again, there, under the doorway. Or maybe not. Mae thought again, and remembered he'd done what he did before: he'd pulled her aside, out of the light of the doorway, and he'd kissed her four times, on her forehead, her chin, each cheek, the sign of the cross. Then he spun away from her, disappearing into the shadows near the waterfall, the one where Francis found the wine.

During lunch Mae made her way to the Cultural Revolution, where, at the behest of Jared and Josiah and Denise, she would be outfitted to answer CircleSurveys. She had been assured this was a reward, an honor, and an enjoyable one—to be one of the Circlers asked about her tastes, her preferences, her buying habits and plans, for use by the Circle's clients.

"This is really the right next step for you," Josiah had said.

Denise had nodded. "I think you'll love it."

Pete Ramirez was a blandly handsome man a few years older than Mae, whose office seemed to have no desk, no chairs, no right angles. It was round, and when Mae entered, he was standing, talking on a headset, swinging a baseball bat, and looking out the window. He waved her in and finished his call. He was still holding the bat with his left hand when he shook her hand with his right.

"Mae Holland. So good to have you. I know you're on lunch, so we'll be quick. You'll be out in seven minutes if you forgive my brusqueness, okay?"

"Okay."

"Great. Do you know why you're here?"

"I think so."

"You're here because your opinions are valued. They're so valued that the world needs to know them—your opinions on just about everything. Isn't that flattering?"

Mae smiled. "It is."

"Okay, you see this headset I have on?"

He pointed to the assembly on his head. A hair-thin arm, a microphone at its end, followed his cheekbone.

"I'm going to hook you up with the same sweet setup. Sound good?" Mae smiled, but Pete wasn't waiting for answers. He arranged an identical headset over her hair and adjusted the microphone.

"Can you say something so I can check the levels?"

He had no tablet or screen visible, so Mae assumed he was fully retinal—the first one she'd met.

"Just tell me what you ate for breakfast."

"A banana, granola," she said.

"Great. Let's decide first on a sound. Do you have a preferred one for your notices? Like a chirp or tri-tone or something?"

"Maybe a standard chirp?"

"This is the chirp," he said, and she heard it through her headphones.

"That's fine."

"It should be better than fine. You'll be hearing it a lot. You want to be sure. Try a few more."

They ran through a dozen more options, finally settling on the sound of a tiny bell, distant and with an intriguing reverb, as if it had been rung in some faraway church.

"Great," Pete said. "Now let me explain how it works. The

idea is to take the pulse of a chosen sampling of Circle members. This job is important. You've been chosen because your opinions are crucial to us, and to our clients. The answers you provide will help us in tailoring our services to their needs. Okay?"

Mae began to respond but he was already talking again.

"So every time you hear the bell, you'll nod, and the headset will register your nod, and the question will be heard through your headphone. You'll answer the question in standard English. In many cases you'll be asked a question that's structured to receive one of the standard two answers, *smile* and *frown*. The voice rec is exquisitely attuned to these two answers, so you don't have to worry about mumbling or anything. And of course you shouldn't have trouble with any answer if you enunciate. You want to try one?"

Mae nodded, and at the sound of the bell, she nodded, and a question arrived through the earpiece: "How do you feel about shoes?"

Mae smiled, then said, "Smile."

Pete winked at her. "Easy one."

The voice asked, "How do you feel about dressy shoes?"

Mae said, "Smile."

Pete raised his hand in pause. "Now of course the majority of the questions won't be subject to one of the three standard answers: *smile, frown,* or *meh*. You can answer any question with more detail. The next one will require more. Here goes."

"How often do you buy new shoes?"

Mae answered "Once every two months," and there was the sound of a tiny bell.

"I heard a bell. Is that good?"

"Yeah, sorry," he said. "I just activated the bell, which will mean your answer was heard and recorded, and that the next question is ready. Then you can nod again, which will bring on your next question, or you can wait for the prompt."

"What's the difference again?"

"Well, you have a certain, well, I don't want to say *quota,* but there's a number of questions that would be ideal and expected for you to answer in a given workday. Let's call it five hundred, but it might be more, might be less. You can either get through them at your own pace, by powering through, or by spreading them throughout the workday. Most people can do five hundred in an hour, so it's not too stressful. Or you can wait for the prompts, which will occur if the program thinks you should pick up the pace. Have you ever done one of those online traffic court programs?"

Mae had. There had been two hundred questions, and it was estimated that it should take two hours to complete. She'd done it in twenty-five minutes. "Yes," she said.

"This is just like that. I'm sure you can get through the day's questions in no time. Of course, we can increase the pace if you really get going. Good?"

"Great," she said.

"And then, so if you happen to get busy, after a while, there'll be a second signal, that reminds you to get back to the questions. This signal should be different. You want to choose a second?"

And so they ran through the signals again, and she chose a distant foghorn.

"Or," he said, "there's a random one that some people choose. Listen to this. Actually, hold on a second." He lost his focus on

Mae and talked into his headset. "Demo Mae voice M-A-E." Now he turned to Mae again. "Okay, here it goes."

Mae heard her own voice say her name, in something just above a whisper. It was very intimate and sent a strange swirling wind through her.

"That's your own voice, right?"

Mae was flushed, bewildered—it didn't sound like her at all—but she managed to nod.

"The program does a voice capture from your phone and then we can form any words. Even your own name! So that should be your second signal?"

"Yes," Mae said. She wasn't sure she wanted to hear her own voice saying her own name, repeatedly, but she knew, too, that she wanted to hear it again as soon as possible. It was so odd, just a few inches from normal.

"Good," Pete said. "So we're done. You get back to your desk, and the first bell will come on. Then you run through as many as you can this afternoon—certainly the first five hundred. Good?"

"Good."

"Oh, and when you get back to your desk, you'll see a new screen. Every so often, one of the questions will be accompanied by an image if it's necessary. We keep these to a minimum, though, because we know you need to concentrate."

When Mae got back to her desk, a new screen, her fifth, had been set up just to the right of her newbie-question screen. She had a few minutes before one o'clock, so she tested the system. The first bell rang, and she nodded. A woman's voice, sounding like a newscaster's, asked her, "For vacations, are you inclined toward one of relaxation, like a beach or luxury hotel, or are you inclined toward adventure, like a white-water rafting trip?"

Mae answered "Adventure."

A tiny bell rang, faint and pleasant.

"Thank you. What sort of adventure?" the voice asked.

"White-water rafting," Mae answered.

Another tiny bell. Mae nodded.

"Thank you. For white-water rafting, do you prefer a multi-day trip, with overnight camping, or a day trip?"

Mae looked up to find the room filling with the rest of the pod, returning from lunch. It was 12:58.

"Multi-day," she said.

Another bell. Mae nodded.

"Thank you. How does a trip down the Grand Canyon sound?"

"Smile."

The bell sang faintly. Mae nodded.

"Thank you. Would you be willing to pay 1,200 dollars for a weeklong trip down the Grand Canyon?" the voice asked.

"Meh," Mae said, and looked up to see Jared, standing on his chair.

"The chute is open!" he yelled.

Almost immediately twelve customer queries appeared. Mae answered the first, got a 92, followed up, and it rose to 97. She answered the next two, for an average of 96.

"Mae."

It was a woman's voice. She looked around, thinking it might be Renata. But there was no one near her.

"Mae."

Now she realized it was her own voice, the prompt she'd agreed to. It was louder than she'd expected, louder than the questions or the bell, and yet it was seductive, thrilling. She turned the volume down on the headset, and again the voice came: "Mae."

Now, with it turned down, it wasn't nearly as intriguing, so she returned the volume to the previous level.

"Mae."

It was her voice, she knew, but then somehow it sounded less like her and more like some older, wiser version of herself. Mae had the thought that if she had an older sister, an older sister who had seen more than she had, that sister's voice would sound like this.

"Mae," the voice said again.

The voice seemed to lift Mae off her seat and spin her around. Every time she heard it, her heart sped up.

"Mae."

"Yes," she said finally.

But nothing happened. It was not programmed to answer questions. She hadn't been told how to respond. She tried nodding. "Thank you, Mae," her voice said, and the bell rang.

"Would you be willing to pay 1,200 dollars for a weeklong trip down the Grand Canyon?" the first voice asked again.

"Yes."

The bell rang.

It was all easy enough to assimilate. The first day, she'd gotten through 652 of the survey questions, and congratulatory messages came from Pete Ramirez, Dan and Jared. Feeling strong and wanting to impress them even more, she answered 820 the next day, and 991 the day after that. It was not difficult, and the validation felt good. Pete told her how much the clients were appreciating her input, her candor and her insights. Her aptitude for the program was making it easier to expand it to others in her pod, and by the end of the second week, a dozen others in the room were answering survey questions, too. It took a day or so to get used to, seeing so many people nodding so frequently—and with varying styles, some with sudden birdlike jerks, others more fluidly—but soon it was as normal as the rest of their routines, involving typing and sitting and seeing their work appear on an array of screens. At certain moments, there was the happy visual of a herd of heads nodding in what appeared to be unison, as if there were some common music playing in all of their minds.

The extra layer of the CircleSurveys helped distract Mae from thinking about Kalden, who had yet to contact her, and who had not once answered his phone. She'd stopped calling after two days, and had chosen not to mention him at all to Annie or anyone else. Her thoughts about him followed a similar path as they had after their first encounter, at the circus. First, she found his unavailability intriguing, even novel. But after three days, it seemed willful and adolescent. By the fourth day, she was tired of the game. Anyone who disappeared like that was not a serious person. He wasn't serious about her or how she felt. He had seemed supremely sensitive each time they'd met, but then, when apart, his absence, because it was total—and because total non-communication in a place like the Circle was so difficult, it felt like violence. Even though Kalden was the only man for whom she'd ever had real lust, she was finished. She would rather have someone lesser if that person were available, familiar, locatable.

In the meantime, Mae was improving her CircleSurvey performance. Because their peers' survey numbers were made available, competition was healthy and kept them all on their toes. Mae's average was 1,345 questions each day, second-highest only to a newbie named Sebastian, who sat in the corner and never left his desk for lunch. Given she was still getting the newbies' question-overrun on her fourth screen, Mae felt fine about being second in this one category. Especially given her PartiRank had been in the 1,900s all month, and Sebastian had yet to crack 4,000.

She was trying to push into the 1,800s one Tuesday afternoon, commenting on hundreds of InnerCircle photos and posts, when she saw a figure in the distance, resting against the doorjamb at the far end of the room. It was a man, and he was wearing the same striped shirt Kalden was wearing when she'd last seen him. His arms were crossed, his head tilted, as if he was seeing something he couldn't quite understand or believe. Mae was sure it was Kalden, and forgot to breathe. Before she could conceive of a less eager reaction, she waved, and he waved back, raising his hand just above his waist.

"Mae," the voice said through her headset.

And at that moment, the figure in the doorway spun away and was gone.

"Mae," the voice said again.

She took off the headphones and jogged to the door where she'd seen him, but he was gone. She instinctively went to the bathroom where she'd first met him, but he wasn't there, either.

When she got back to her desk, there was someone in her chair. It was Francis.

"I'm still sorry," he said.

She looked at him. His heavy eyebrows, his boat-keel nose, his tentative smile. Mae sighed and took him in. That smile, she realized, was the smile of someone who was never sure he'd gotten the joke. Still, Mae had, in recent days, thought of Francis, the profound contrast he offered to Kalden. Kalden was a ghost, wanting Mae to chase him, and Francis was so available, so utterly without mystery. In a weak moment or two, Mae had wondered what she might do the next time she saw him. Would she succumb to Francis's ready presence, to the simple fact that he wanted to be near her? The question had been in her head for days, but only now did she know the answer. No. He still disgusted her. His meekness. His neediness. His pleading voice. His thievery.

"Have you deleted the video?" she asked.

"No," he said. "You know I can't." Then he smiled, swiveling in her chair. He thought they were being friendly. "You had an InnerCircle survey question and I answered it. I assume you approve of the Circle sending aid to Yemen?"

She pictured, briefly, burying her fist in his face.

"Please leave," she said.

"Mae. No one's watched the video. It's just a part of the archive. It's one of ten thousand clips that go up every day here at the Circle alone. One of a billion worldwide, every day."

"Well, I don't want it to be one of the billion."

"Mae, you know technically neither one of us owns that video anymore. I couldn't delete it if I tried. It's like news. You don't own the news, even if it happens to you. You don't own history. It's part of the collective record now."

Mae's head was about to explode. "I have to work," she said, managing not to slap him. "Can you leave?"

Now he seemed, for the first time, to grasp that she really loathed him and did not want him near. His face twisted into something like a pout. He looked at his shoes. "You know they approved ChildTrack in Vegas?"

And she felt for him, even if briefly. Francis was a desperate man who'd never had a childhood, had no doubt tried all his life to please those around him, the succession of foster parents who had no intention of keeping him.

"That's great, Francis," she said.

The beginnings of a smile lifted his face. Hoping it might pacify him and allow her to get back to work, she went further. "You're saving a lot of lives."

Now he beamed. "You know, in six months it could be all over. It could be everywhere. Full saturation. Every child track-able, every child safe forever. Stenton told me this himself. Did you know he visited my lab? He's taken a personal interest. And apparently they might change the name to TruYouth. Get it? TruYou, TruYouth?"

"That's so good, Francis," Mae said, her body overtaken by a surge of feeling for him, some mix of empathy and pity and even admiration. "I'll talk to you later."

Developments like Francis's were happening with incredible frequency in those weeks. There was talk of the Circle, and Stenton in particular, taking over the running of San Vincenzo. It made sense, given most of the city's services were funded by, and had been improved by, the company. There was a rumor that Project 9 engineers had figured out a way to replace the random jumble of our nighttime dreaming with organized thinking and real-life problem solving. Another Circle team was close to figuring out how to disassemble tornadoes as soon as they formed. And then there was everyone's favorite project, in the works for months now: the counting of the sands in the Sahara. Did the world need this? The utility of the project was not immediately clear, but the Wise Men had a sense of humor about it. Stenton, who had initiated the endeavor, called it a lark, something they were doing, first of all, to see if it could be done—though there seemed to be no doubt, given the easy algorithms involved—and only secondarily for any scientific benefit. Mae understood it as most Circlers did: as a show of strength, and as a demonstration that with the will and ingenuity and economic wherewithal of the Circle, no earthly question would remain unanswered. And so, throughout the fall, with a bit of theatricality—they dragged out the process longer than necessary, for it only took them three weeks to count—they finally revealed the number of grains of sand in the Sahara, a number that was comically large and did not, immediately, mean much to anyone, beyond the acknowledgment that the Circle did what they said they would do. They got things done, and with spectacular speed and efficiency.

The main development, and one that Bailey himself zinged about every few hours, was the rapid proliferation of other elected leaders, in the U.S. and globally, who had chosen to go clear. It was, to most minds, an inexorable progression. When Santos had first announced her new clarity, there was media coverage, but not the kind of explosion anyone at the Circle had hoped for. But then, as people logged on and began watching, and began realizing that she was deadly serious—that she was allowing viewers to see and hear precisely what went into her day, unfiltered and uncensored—the viewership grew exponentially. Santos posted her schedule each day, and by the second week, when she was meeting with a group of lobbyists wanting to drill in the Alaskan tundra, there were millions watching her. She was candid with these lobbyists, avoiding anything like preaching or pandering. She was so frank, asking the questions she would have asked behind closed doors, that it made for riveting, even inspiring viewing.

By the third week, twenty-one other elected leaders in the U.S. had asked the Circle for their help in going clear. There was a mayor in Sarasota. A senator from Hawaii and, not surprisingly, both senators from California. The entire city council of San Jose. The city manager of Independence, Kansas. And each time one of them made the commitment, the Wise Men zinged about it, and there was a hastily arranged press conference, showing the actual moment when their days went transparent. By the end of the first month, there were thousands of requests from all over the world. Stenton and Bailey were astounded, were flattered, were overwhelmed, they said, but were caught flat-footed. The Circle couldn't meet all the demand. But they endeavored to do so.

Production on the cameras, which were as yet unavailable to consumers, went into overdrive. The manufacturing plant, in China's Guangdong province, added shifts and began construction on a second factory to quadruple their capacity. Every time a camera was installed and a new leader had gone transparent, there was another announcement from Stenton, another celebration, and the viewership grew. By the end of the fifth week, there were 16,188 elected officials, from Lincoln to Lahore, who had gone completely clear, and the waiting list was growing.

The pressure on those who hadn't gone transparent went from polite to oppressive. The question, from pundits and constituents, was obvious and loud: If you aren't transparent, what are you hiding? Though some citizens and commentators objected on grounds of privacy, asserting that government, at virtually every level, had always needed to do some things in private for the sake of security and efficiency, the momentum crushed all such arguments and the progression continued. If you weren't operating in the light of day, what were you doing in the shadows?

And there was a wonderful thing that tended to happen, something that felt like poetic justice: every time someone started shouting about the supposed monopoly of the Circle, or the Circle's unfair monetization of the personal data of its users, or some other paranoid and demonstrably false claim, soon enough it was revealed that that person was a criminal or deviant of the highest order. One was connected to a terror network in Iran. One was a buyer of child porn. Every time, it seemed, they would end up on the news, footage of investigators leaving their homes with computers, on which any number of unspeakable searches had been executed and where reams of illegal and inappropriate materials were stored. And it made sense. Who but a fringe character would try to impede the unimpeachable improvement of the world?

Within weeks, the non-transparent officeholders were treated like pariahs. The clear ones wouldn't meet with them if they wouldn't go on camera, and thus these leaders were left out. Their constituents wondered what they were hiding, and their electoral doom was all but assured. In any coming election cycle, few would dare to run without declaring their transparency—and, it was assumed, this would immediately and permanently improve the quality of candidates. There would never again be a politician without immediate and thorough accountability, because their words and actions would be known and recorded and beyond debate. There would be no more back rooms, no more murky deal-making. There would be only clarity, only light.

It was inevitable that transparency would come to the Circle, too. As clarity among elected officials proliferated, there were rumblings inside and outside the Circle: What about the Circle itself? Yes, Bailey said, in public and to the Circlers, we should also be clear. We should also be open. And so started the Circle's own transparency plan, which began with the installation of a thousand SeeChange cameras on campus. They were placed in common rooms, cafeterias and outdoor spaces first. Then, as the Wise Men assessed any problems they might pose for the protection of intellectual property, they were placed in hallways, work areas, even laboratories. The saturation was not complete—there were still hundreds of more sensitive spaces without access, and the cameras were prohibited from bathrooms and other private rooms, but otherwise the campus, to the eyes of a billion-odd Circle users, was suddenly clear and open, and the Circle devotees, who already felt loyal to the company and enthralled by its mystique, now felt closer, felt part of an open and welcoming world.

There were eight SeeChange cameras in Mae's pod, and within

hours of them going live, she and everyone else in the room were provided another screen, on which they could see a grid of their own and lock into any view on campus. They could see if their favorite table at the Glass Eatery was available. They could see if the health club was jammed. They could see if the kickball game was a serious one or for duffers only. And Mae was surprised by how interesting Circle campus life was to outsiders. Within hours she was hearing from friends from high school and college, who had located her, who now could watch her work. Her middle school gym teacher, who had once thought Mae insufficiently serious about the President's Physical Fitness Test, now seemed impressed. *Good to see you working so hard, Mae!* A guy she dated briefly in college wrote: *Don't you ever leave that desk?*

She began to think a bit harder about the clothes she wore to work. She thought more about where she scratched, when she blew her nose or how. But it was a good kind of thinking, a good kind of calibration. And knowing she was being watched, that the Circle was, overnight, the most-watched workplace in the world, reminded her, more profoundly than ever, just how radically her life had changed in only a few months. She had been, twelve weeks ago, working at the public utility in her hometown, a town no one had heard of. Now she was communicating with clients all over the planet, commanding six screens, training a new group of newbies, and altogether feeling more needed, more valued, and more intellectually stimulated than she ever thought possible.

And, with the tools the Circle made available, Mae felt able to influence global events, to save lives even, halfway across the world. That very morning, a message from a college friend, Tania

Schwartz, came through, pleading for help with an initiative her brother was spearheading. There was a paramilitary group in Guatemala, some resurrection of the terrorizing forces of the eighties, and they had been attacking villages and taking women captive. One woman, Ana María Herrera, had escaped and told of ritual rapes, of teenage girls being made concubines, and the murders of those who would not cooperate. Mae's friend Tania, never an activist in school, said she had been compelled to action by these atrocities, and she was asking everyone she knew to join in an initiative called We Hear You Ana María. *Let's make sure she knows she has friends all over the world who will not accept this,* Tania's message said.

Mae saw a picture of Ana María, sitting in a white room on a folding chair, looking up, expressionless, an unnamed child in her lap. Next to her picture was a smile button that said "I hear you Ana María," which, when clicked on, would add Mae's name to a list of those lending their support to Ana María. Mae clicked the button. *Just as important,* Tania wrote, *is that we send a message to the paramilitaries that we denounce their actions.* Below the picture of Ana María was a blurry photo of a group of men in mismatched military garb, walking through dense jungle. Next to the photo was a frown button that said "We denounce the Central Guatemalan Security Forces." Mae hesitated briefly, knowing the gravity of what she was about to do—to come out against these rapists and murderers—but she needed to make a stand. She pushed the button. An autoresponse thanked her, noting that she was the 24,726th person to send a smile to Ana María and the 19,282nd to send a frown to the paramilitaries. Tania noted that while the smiles were sent directly to Ana María's phone, Tania's brother was still working on a way to get the frowns to the Central Guatemalan Security Forces.

After Tania's petition Mae sat for a moment, feeling very alert, very aware of herself, knowing that not only had she possibly made a group of powerful enemies in Guatemala, but that untold thousands of SeeChange watchers were seeing her doing it. It gave her layers of self-awareness and a distinct sense of the power she could wield in her position. She decided to use the restroom, to throw some cold water on her face and use her legs a bit, and it was in the bathroom that her phone buzzed. The caller ID was blocked.

"Hello?"

"It's me. Kalden."

"Where have you been?"

"It's complicated now. All the cameras."

"You're not a spy, are you?"

"You know I'm not a spy."

"Annie thinks you are."

"I want to see you."

"I'm in the bathroom."

"I know."

"You know?"

"CircleSearch, SeeChange . . . You're not hard to find."

"And where are *you*?"

"I'm coming. Stay there."

"No. No."

"I need to see you. Stay there."

"No. I can see you later. There's a thing in the New Kingdom. Open-mic folk night. A safe, public place."

"No, no. I can't do that."

"You can't come here."

"I can and I will."

And he hung up.

Mae checked her purse. She had a condom. And she stayed. She chose the far stall and waited. She knew that waiting for him was not wise. That it was wrong on many levels. She wouldn't be able to tell Annie about this. Annie would approve of most carnal activity but not here, at work, in a bathroom. This would demonstrate poor judgment, and reflect poorly on Annie. Mae watched the time. Two minutes had passed and still she was in a bathroom stall, waiting for a man she knew only vaguely, and who, she guessed, wanted only to ravish her, repeatedly, in ever-stranger places. So why was she there? Because she wanted this to happen. She wanted him to take her, in the stall, and she wanted to know that she had been taken in the stall, at work, and that only the two of them would ever know. Why was this some glittering thing she needed? She heard the door open, and then the clicking of the lock on the door. A lock she didn't know existed. Then she heard the sound of Kalden's long strides. The footsteps stopped near the stalls, giving way to a dark squeaking, the strain of bolts and steel. She felt a shadow above her and craned her neck to see a figure descending. Kalden had climbed the high stall wall, and had crawled across the grid to get to hers. She felt him slip in behind her. The heat of his body warmed her back, his breath hot on the nape of her neck.

"What are you doing?" she asked.

His mouth opened on her ear, his tongue diving. She gasped and leaned into him. Kalden's hands came around her stomach, traced her waist, traveled quickly to her thighs, holding them firmly. She pushed his hands inward and up, her mind battling, and finally asserting her right to do this. She was twenty-four, and if she did not do this kind of thing now—did not do exactly *this*, exactly *now*—she never would. It was the imperative of youth.

"Mae," he whispered, "stop thinking."

"Okay."

"And close your eyes. Picture what I'm doing to you."

His mouth was on her neck, kissing it, licking it, while his hands were busy with her skirt and panties. He eased both off her hips and to the floor and brought her to him, filling her at once. "Mae," he said, as she pushed herself into him, his hands holding her hips, bringing him so deep she could feel his swollen crown somewhere near her heart. "Mae," he said, as she held the walls on either side of them, as if holding back the rest of the world.

She came, gasping, and he finished, too, shuddering but silent. And immediately they both laughed, quietly, knowing they'd done something reckless and career-threatening and that they needed to leave. He turned her toward him and kissed her mouth, his eyes open, looking astounded and full of mischief. "Bye," he said, and she only waved, feeling his shape rise again behind her, climb the walls and make his way out.

And because he paused at the door to unlock it, and because she thought she might never see him again, Mae found her phone, reached over the stall wall, and took a picture, not knowing whether or not she would catch any semblance of him. When she looked at what she'd captured, it was only his right arm, from the elbow to his fingertips, the rest of him already gone.

Why lie to Annie? Mae asked herself, not knowing the answer, but knowing she would lie to her anyway. After composing herself in the bathroom, Mae had gone back to her desk, and immediately, unable to control herself, had messaged Annie, who was flying somewhere to or over Europe: *Again with grey-hair,* she wrote. Telling Annie at all would precipitate a series of lies, big and small, and Mae found herself, in the minutes between when she sent the message and Annie's inevitable reply, wondering just how much to conceal, and why.

Finally Annie's message came. *Must know everything now. I'm in London with some Parliament lackeys. I think one just pulled out a monocle. Give me distraction.*

While she decided just how much to tell Annie, Mae teased out details. *In a bathroom.*

Annie replied immediately.

The old man? In a bathroom? Did you use the diaper-changing station?

No. In a stall. And he was VIGOROUS.

A voice behind Mae said her name. Mae turned to find Gina and her enormous nervous smile. "You have a second?" Mae attempted to turn away the screen containing the dialogue with Annie, but Gina had already seen it.

"You're talking to Annie?" she said. "You guys really are tight, huh?"

Mae nodded, turned her screen, and all light left Gina's face. "Is this still a good time to explain Conversion Rate and Retail Raw?"

Mae had forgotten, entirely, that Gina was supposed to come to demonstrate a new layer.

"Sure," Mae said.

"Has Annie told you about this stuff already?" Gina said, her face looking very fragile.

"No," Mae said, "she hasn't."

"She didn't tell you about Conversion Rate?"

"No."

"Or Retail Raw?"

"No."

Gina's face brightened. "Oh. Okay. Good. So we'll do it now?" Gina's face searched Mae's, as if looking for the slightest sign of doubt, which Gina would take as reason to collapse entirely.

"Great," Mae said, and Gina brightened again.

"Good. Let's start with the Conversion Rate. This is fairly obvious anyway, but the Circle would not exist, and would not grow, and would not be able to get closer to completing the Circle, if there were not actual purchases being made, actual commerce spurred. We're here to be a gateway to all the world's information, but we are supported by advertisers who hope to reach customers through us, right?"

Gina smiled, her large white teeth briefly overtaking her face. Mae was trying to concentrate, but she was thinking of Annie, in her Parliament meeting, who was no doubt thinking of Mae and Kalden. And when Mae thought of herself and Kalden, she thought of his hands on her waist, pulling her gently down onto him, her eyes closed, her mind enlarging all—

Gina was still talking. "But how to provoke, how to stimulate purchases—that's the conversion rate. You can zing, you could comment on and rate and highlight any product, but can you translate all this into action? Leveraging your credibility to spur action—this is crucial, okay?"

Now Gina was sitting next to Mae, her fingers on her keyboard. She brought up a complex spreadsheet. At that moment, another message from Annie arrived on Mae's second screen. She turned it slightly. *Now I have to be the boss. You got his last name this time?*

Mae saw that Gina was reading the message, too, making no pretense of doing otherwise.

"Go ahead," Gina said. "That looks important."

Mae reached over Gina, to her keyboard, and typed the lie she knew, moments after leaving the bathroom, she would tell Annie. *Yes. I know all.*

Immediately Annie's reply arrived: *And his name is?*

Gina looked at this message. "That must be so crazy, to just get messages from Annie Allerton."

"I guess so," Mae said, and typed *Can't tell.*

Gina read Mae's message and seemed less interested in the content of it than the fact that this back-and-forth was actually happening in front of her. "You guys just message each other like it's no big deal?" she asked.

Mae softened the impact. "Not all day."

"Not all day?" Gina's face came alive with a tentative smile.

Annie burst through. *You're actually not telling me? Tell me now.*

"Sorry," Mae said. "Almost done." She typed *No. You'll hassle him.*

Send me a picture, Annie wrote.

No. But I have one, Mae typed, executing the second lie she knew was necessary. She did have a photo of him, and once she realized she did, and that she could tell Annie this, and be telling the truth without telling all of it, and that this photo, along with the white lie of knowing his actual last name, would allow her to continue with this man, Kalden, who very well might be a danger to the Circle, she knew she would use this second lie with Annie, and it would buy her more time—more time to rise and fall on Kalden, while trying to ascertain exactly who he was and what he wanted from her.

An action shot, she typed. *I did a facial-rec and it all connects.*

Thank god, Annie wrote. *But you're a bitch.*

Gina, who had read the message, was visibly flustered. "Maybe we should do this later?" she said, her forehead suddenly glistening.

"No, sorry," Mae said. "Go on. I'll turn the screen away."

Another message appeared from Annie. While turning the screen away, Mae glanced at it. *Did you hear the fracturing of any bones while sitting on him? Older men have bird bones, and pressure like you're talking about could be fatal.*

"Okay," Gina said, swallowing hard, "for years lesser companies had been tracking, and trying to influence, the connection between online mentions, reviews, comments, ratings and actual purchases. Circle developers have figured out a way to measure the impact of these factors, of your participation, really, and articulate it with the Conversion Rate."

Another message appeared, but Mae ignored it, and Gina forged on, thrilled to have been deemed more important than Annie, even for a moment.

"So every purchase initiated or prompted by a recommendation you make raises your Conversion Rate. If your purchase or recommendation spurs fifty others to take the same action, then your CR is x50. There are Circlers with a conversion rate of x1,200. That means an average of 1,200 people buy whatever they buy. They've accumulated enough credibility that their followers trust their recommendations implicitly, and are deeply thankful for the surety in their shopping. Annie, of course, has one of the highest CRs in the Circle."

Just then, another droplet sounded. Gina blinked as if she'd been slapped, but continued.

"Okay, so your average Conversion Rate so far has been x119. Not bad. But on a scale of 1 to 1,000, there's a lot of room for improvement. Below the Conversion Rate is your Retail Raw, the total gross purchase price of recommended products. So let's say you recommend a certain keychain, and 1,000 people take your recommendation; then those 1,000 keychains, priced at $4 each, bring your Retail Raw to $4,000. It's just the gross retail price of the commerce you've stoked. Fun, right?"

Mae nodded. She loved the notion of actually being able to track the effect of her tastes and endorsements.

Another droplet sounded. Gina seemed to be blinking back tears. She stood up.

"Okay. I feel like I'm invading your lunch and your friendship. So that's the Conversion Rate and Retail Raw. I know you understand it. There'll be a new screen by the end of the day to measure these scores."

Gina tried to smile, but couldn't seem to lift the sides of her mouth enough to seem convincing. "Oh, and the minimum expectation for high-functioning Circlers is a conversion rate of x250, and a weekly Retail Raw of $45,000, both of which are modest goals that most Circlers far exceed. And if you have questions, well," she stopped, her eyes fragile. "I'm sure you can ask Annie."

She turned and left.

A few nights later, on a cloudless Thursday, Mae drove home, her first time since her father's Circle insurance had taken effect. She knew her father had been feeling far better, and she was looking forward to seeing him in person, hoping, ridiculously, for some miraculous change, but knowing she would see only minor improvements. Still, her parents' voices, on the phone and in texts, had been ebullient. "Everything's different now," they'd been saying for weeks, and had been asking to have her come celebrate. And so, looking forward to the imminent gratitude, she drove east and south and when she arrived, her father greeted her at the door, looking far stronger and, more important, more confident, more like a man—the man he once was. He held out his wrist monitor and arranged it parallel to Mae's. "Look at us. We match. You want some vino?"

Inside, the three of them arranged themselves as they always had, along the kitchen counter, and they diced, and breaded, and they talked about the various ways the health of Mae's father had improved. Now he had his choice of doctors. Now he had no limitations on the medicines he could take; they were all covered, and there was no copay. Mae noticed, as they narrated the story of his recent health, that her mother was brighter, more buoyant. She was wearing short-shorts.

"The best thing about it," her father said, "is that now your mother has whole swaths of extra time. It's all so simple. I see the doctor and the Circle takes care of the rest. No middleman. No discussion."

"Is that what I think it is?" Mae said. Over the dining room table, there was a silver chandelier, though upon closer inspection it seemed like one of Mercer's. The silver arms were actually painted antlers. Mae had been only passingly enthusiastic about any of his work—when they were dating, she labored for kind things to say—but this one she genuinely liked.

"It is," her mother said.

"Not bad," Mae said.

"Not bad?" her father said. "It's his best work, and you know it. This thing would go for five grand in one of those San Francisco boutiques. He gave it to us for free."

Mae was impressed. "Why for free?"

"Why for free?" her mother asked. "Because he's our friend. Because he's a nice young man. And wait before you roll your eyes or come back with some witty comment."

Mae did wait, and after she'd passed on a half-dozen unkind things she could say about Mercer and had chosen silence, she found herself feeling generous toward him. Because she no longer needed him, because she was now a crucial and measurable driver of world commerce, and because she had two men at the Circle to choose from—one of them a volcanic, calligraphic enigma who climbed walls to take her from behind—she could afford to be generous toward poor Mercer, his shaggy head and grotesque fatty back.

"It's really nice," Mae said.

"Glad you think so," her mother said. "You can tell him your-self in a few minutes. He's coming for dinner."

"No," Mae said. "Please no."

"Mae," her father said firmly, "he's coming, okay?"

And she knew she couldn't argue. Instead, she poured herself a glass of red wine and, while setting the table, she downed half of it. By the time Mercer knocked and let himself in, her face was half-numb and her thoughts were vague.

"Hey Mae," he said, and gave her a tentative hug.

"Your chandelier thing is really great," she said, and even while saying the words, she saw their effect on him, so she went further. "It's really beautiful."

"Thanks," he said. He looked around to Mae's parents, as if confirming they had heard the same thing. Mae poured herself more wine.

"It really is," Mae continued. "I mean, I know you do good work." And when she said this, Mae made sure not to look at him, knowing his eyes would doubt her. "But this is the best one you've done yet. I'm so happy that you put this much into . . . I'm just happy that my favorite piece of yours is in my parents' dining room."

Mae took out her camera and took a picture.

"What're you doing?" Mercer said, though he seemed pleased that she'd deem it worthy of a photograph.

"I just wanted to take a picture. Look," she said, and showed him.

Now her parents had disappeared, no doubt thinking she wanted time alone with Mercer. They were hilarious and insane.

"It looks good," he said, staring at the photo a bit longer than

Mae had expected. He was not, evidently, above taking pleasure, and pride, in his own work.

"It looks in*cred*ible," she said. The wine had sent her aloft. "That was very nice of you. And I know it means a lot to them, especially now. It adds something very important here." Mae was euphoric, and it wasn't just the wine. It was release. Her family had been released. "This place has been so dark," she said.

And for a brief moment, she and Mercer seemed to find their former footing. Mae, who for years had thought about Mercer with a disappointment bordering on pity, remembered now that he was capable of great work. She knew he was compassionate, and very kind, even though his limited horizons had been exasperating. But now, seeing this—could she call it artwork? It was something like art—and the effect it had on the house, her faith in him was rekindled.

That gave Mae an idea. Under the pretense that she was going to her room to change, she excused herself and hurried upstairs. But instead, sitting on her old bed, in three minutes she'd posted her photo of the chandelier in two dozen design and home design feeds, linking to Mercer's website—which featured just his phone number and a few pictures; he hadn't updated it in years—and his email address. If he wasn't smart enough to get business for himself, she would be happy to do it for him.

When she was finished, Mercer was sitting with her parents at the kitchen table, which was crowded with salad and stir-fried chicken and vegetables. Their eyes followed her down the stairs. "I called up there," her father said.

"We like to eat when it's hot," her mother added.

Mae hadn't heard them. "Sorry. I was just— Wow, this looks good. Dad, don't you think Mercer's chandelier is awesome?"

"I do. And I told you, and him, as much. We've been asking for one of his creations for a year now."

"I just needed the right antlers," Mercer said. "I hadn't gotten any really great ones in a while." He went on to explain his sourcing, how he bought antlers only from trusted collaborators, people he knew hadn't hunted the deer, or if they had, had been instructed to do so by Fish and Game to curb overcrowding.

"That is fascinating," her mother said. "Before I forget, I want to raise a toast . . . What's that?"

Mae's phone had beeped. "Nothing," she said. "But in a second I think I'll have some good news to announce. Go on, Mom."

"I was just saying that I wanted to toast having us—"

Now it was Mercer's phone ringing.

"Sorry," he said, and maneuverered his hand outside his pants, finding the off button.

"Everyone done?" her mother asked.

"Sorry Mrs. Holland," Mercer said. "Go on."

But at that moment, Mae's phone buzzed loudly again, and when Mae looked to its screen, she saw that there were thirty-seven new zings and messages.

"Something you have to attend to?" her father said.

"No, not yet," Mae said, though she was almost too excited to wait. She was proud of Mercer, and soon she'd be able to show him something about the audience he might have outside Longfield. If there were thirty-seven messages in the first few minutes, in twenty minutes there would be a hundred.

Her mother continued. "I was going to thank you, Mae, for all you've done to improve your father's health, and my own sanity. And I wanted to toast Mercer, too, as part of our family, and to thank him for his beautiful work." She paused, as if expecting a buzz to sound any moment. "Well, I'm just glad I got through that. Let's eat. The food's getting cold."

And they began to eat, but after a few minutes, Mae had heard so many dings, and she'd seen her phone screen update so many times, that she couldn't wait.

"Okay, I can't stand it anymore. I posted that photo I took of your chandelier, Mercer, and people love it!" She beamed, and raised her glass. "That's what we should toast."

Mercer didn't look amused. "Wait. You posted them where?"

"That's great, Mercer," her father said, and raised his own glass.

Mercer's glass was not raised. "Where'd you post them, Mae?"

"Everywhere relevant," she said, "and the comments are amazing." She searched her screen. "Just let me read the first one. And I quote: *Wow, that is gorgeous.* That's from a pretty well-known industrial designer in Stockholm. Here's another one: *Very cool. Reminds me of something I saw in Barcelona last year.* That was from a designer in Santa Fe who has her own shop. She gave your thing three out of four stars, and had some suggestions about how you might improve it. I bet you could sell them there if you wanted to. So here's another—"

Mercer had his palms on the table. "Stop. Please."

"Why? You haven't even heard the best part. On DesignMind, you already have 122 smiles. That's an incredible amount to get so quickly. And they have a ranking there, and you're in the top fifty for today. Actually, I know how you could raise that—" At the same time, it occurred to Mae that this kind of activity would surely get her PartiRank into the 1,800s. And if she could get enough of these people to buy the work, it would mean solid Conversion and Retail Raw numbers—

"Mae. Stop. Please stop." Mercer was staring at her, his eyes small and round. "I don't want to get loud here, in your parents' home, but either you stop or I have to walk out."

"Just hold on a sec," she said, and scrolled through her messages, looking for one that she was sure would impress him. She'd seen a message come in from Dubai, and if she found it, she knew, his resistance would fall away.

"Mae," she heard her mother say. "Mae."

But Mae couldn't locate the message. Where was it? While she scrolled, she heard the scraping of a chair. But she was so close to finding it that she didn't look up. When she did, she found Mercer gone and her parents staring at her.

"I think it's nice you want to support Mercer," her mother said, "but I just don't understand why you do this now. We're trying to enjoy a nice dinner."

Mae stared at her mother, absorbing all the disappointment and bewilderment that she could stand, then ran outside and reached Mercer as he was backing out of the driveway.

She got into the passenger seat. "Stop."

His eyes were dull, lifeless. He put the car in park and rested his hands in his lap, exhaling with all the condescension he could muster.

"What the hell is your problem, Mercer?"

"Mae, I asked you to stop, and you didn't."

"Did I hurt your feelings?"

"No. You hurt my brain. You make me think you're batshit crazy. I asked you to stop and you wouldn't."

"I wouldn't stop trying to help you."

"I didn't ask for your help. And I didn't give you permission to post a photo of my work."

"Your *work*." She heard something barbed in her voice that she knew wasn't right or productive.

"You're snide, Mae, and you're mean, and you're callous."

"What? I'm the *opposite* of callous, Mercer. I'm trying to help you because I believe in what you do."

"No you don't. Mae, you're just unable to allow anything to live inside a room. My work exists in one room. It doesn't exist anywhere else. And that's how I intend it."

"So you don't want business?"

Mercer looked through his windshield, then leaned back. "Mae, I've never felt more that there is some cult taking over the world. You know what someone tried to sell me the other day? Actually, I bet it's somehow affiliated with the Circle. Have you heard of Homie? The thing where your phone scans your house for the bar codes of every product—"

"Right. Then it orders new stuff whenever you're getting low. It's brilliant."

"You think this is okay?" Mercer said. "You know how they framed it for me? It's the usual utopian vision. This time they were saying it'll reduce waste. If stores know what their customers want, then they don't overproduce, don't overship, don't have to throw stuff away when it's not bought. I mean, like everything else you guys are pushing, it sounds perfect, sounds progressive, but it carries with it more control, more central tracking of everything we do."

"Mercer, the Circle is a group of people like me. Are you saying that somehow we're all in a room somewhere, watching you, planning world domination?"

"No. First of all, I *know* it's all people like you. And that's what's so scary. *Individually* you don't know what you're doing *collectively*. But secondly, don't presume the benevolence of your leaders. For years there was this happy time when those controlling the major internet conduits were actually decent enough people. Or at least they weren't predatory and vengeful. But I always worried, what if someone was willing to use this power to punish those who challenged them?"

"What are you saying?"

"You think it's just a coincidence that every time some congresswoman or blogger talks about monopoly, they suddenly become ensnared in some terrible sex-porn-witchcraft controversy? For twenty years, the internet was capable of ruining anyone in minutes, but not until your Three Wise Men, or at least one of them, was anyone willing to do it. You're saying this is news to you?"

"You're so paranoid. Your conspiracy theory brain always depressed me, Mercer. You sound so ignorant. And saying that Homie is some scary new thing, I mean, for a hundred years there were milkmen who brought you milk. They knew when you needed it. There were butchers who sold you meat, bakers who would drop off bread—"

"But the milkman wasn't scanning my house! I mean, anything with a UPC code can be scanned. Already, millions of people's phones are scanning their homes and communicating all that information out to the world."

"And so what? You don't want Charmin to know how much of their toilet paper you're using? Is Charmin oppressing you in some significant way?"

"No, Mae, it's different. That would be easier to understand. Here, though, there are no oppressors. No one's forcing you to do this. You willingly tie yourself to these leashes. And you willingly become utterly socially autistic. You no longer pick up on basic human communication clues. You're at a table with three humans, all of whom are looking at you and trying to talk to you, and you're staring at a screen, searching for strangers in Dubai."

"You're not so pure, Mercer. You have an email account. You have a website."

"Here's the thing, and it's painful to say this to you. But you're not very interesting anymore. You sit at a desk twelve hours a day and you have nothing to show for it except for some numbers that won't exist or be remembered in a week. You're leaving no evidence that you lived. There's no proof."

"Fuck you, Mercer."

"And worse, you're not *doing* anything interesting anymore. You're not seeing anything, saying anything. The weird paradox is that you think you're at the center of things, and that makes your opinions more valuable, but you yourself are becoming less vibrant. I bet you haven't done anything offscreen in months. Have you?"

"You're such a fucker, Mercer."

"Do you go outside anymore?"

"You're the interesting one, is that it? The idiot who makes chandeliers out of dead animal parts? You're the wonderboy of all that's fascinating?"

"You know what I think, Mae? I think you think that sitting at your desk, frowning and smiling somehow makes you think you're actually living some fascinating life. You comment on things, and that substitutes for doing them. You look at pictures of Nepal, push a smile button, and you think that's the same as going there. I mean, what would happen if you actually went? Your CircleJerk ratings or whatever-the-fuck would drop below an acceptable level! Mae, do you realize how incredibly boring you've become?"

For many years now, Mercer had been the human she'd loathed more than any other. This was not new. He'd always had the unique ability to send her into apoplexy. His professorial smugness. His antiquarian bullshit. And most of all, his baseline assumption—so wrong—that he knew her. He knew the parts of her he liked and agreed with, and he pretended those were her true self, her essence. He knew nothing.

But with every passing mile, as she drove home, she felt better. Better with every mile between her and that fat fuck. The fact that she'd ever slept with him made her physically sick. Had she been possessed by some weird demon? Her body must have been overtaken, for those three years, by some terrible force that blinded her to his wretchedness. He'd been fat even then, hadn't he? What kind of guy is fat in high school? He's talking to *me* about sitting behind a desk when he's forty pounds overweight? The man was upside down.

She would not talk to him again. She knew this, and there was comfort in that. Relief spread over her like warm water. She would never talk to him, write to him. She would insist that her parents sever any connection to him. She planned to destroy the chandelier, too; it would look like an accident. Maybe stage a break-in. Mae laughed to herself, thinking of exorcizing that fat idiot from her life. That ugly, ever-sweating moose-man would never have a say in her world again.

She saw the sign for Maiden's Voyages and thought nothing of it. She passed the exit and didn't feel a thing. Seconds later, though, she was leaving the highway, and doubling back toward the beach. It was almost ten o'clock, so she knew the shop had been closed for hours. So what was she doing? She wasn't reacting to Mercer's bullshit questions about what she was or wasn't doing outside. She was only seeing if the place was open; she knew it wouldn't be, but maybe Marion was there, and maybe she'd let Mae take one out for half an hour? She lived in the trailer next door, after all. Maybe Mae could catch her walking within the compound, and be able to persuade her to rent her one.

Mae parked and peered through the chain-link fence, seeing no one, only the shuttered rental kiosk, the rows of kayaks and paddleboards. She stood, hoping to see a silhouette within the trailer, but there was none. The light within was dim, rose-colored, the trailer empty.

She walked to the tiny beach and stood, watching the moonlight play on the still surface of the bay. She sat. She didn't want to go home, though there was no point in staying. Her head was full of Mercer, and his giant infant's face, and all the bullshit things he said that night and said every night. That would be, she was certain, the last time she tried to help him in any way. He was in her past, in *the* past, he was an antique, a dull, inanimate object she could leave in an attic.

She stood up, thinking she should go back to work on her PartiRank, when she saw something odd. Against the far side of the fence, outside the enclosure, she saw a large object, leaning precariously. It was either a kayak or paddleboard, and she quickly made her way to it. It was a kayak, she realized, and it was resting on the free side of the fence, a paddle next to it. The positioning of the kayak made little sense; she'd never seen one standing nearly upright before, and was sure that Marion wouldn't have approved. Mae could only think that someone had brought a rental back after closing, and tried to get it as close to the enclosure as possible.

Mae thought at the very least she should bring the kayak to the ground, to reduce the chances that it would fall overnight. She did so, carefully lowering it to the sand, surprised by how light it was.

Then she had a thought. The water was just thirty yards away, and she knew that she could easily drag it to shore. Would it be theft to borrow a kayak that had already been borrowed? She wasn't lifting it over the fence, after all; she was only extending the borrowing that someone else had extended. She would return it in an hour or two, and no one would know the difference.

Mae put the paddle inside and dragged the kayak across the sand for a few feet, testing the feeling of this act. *Was* it theft? Certainly Marion would understand if she knew. Marion was a free spirit, not a rule-bound shrew, and seemed like the type of person who, in Mae's shoes, would do the same thing. She would not like the liability implications, but then again, *were* there such implications? How could Marion be held accountable if the kayak was taken without her knowledge?

Now Mae was at the shore, and the bow of the kayak was wet. And then, feeling the water under the vessel, the way the current seemed to pull the kayak out from her and into the fuller volume of the bay, Mae knew that she would do this. The one complication was that she wouldn't have a life preserver. It was the one thing the borrower managed to heave over the fence. But the water was so calm that Mae saw no possibility of real danger if she stayed close to the shore.

Once she was out on the water, though, feeling the heavy glass under her, the quick progress she was making, she thought she might not stay in the shallows. That this would be the night to make it to Blue Island. Angel Island was easy, people went there all the time, but Blue Island was strange, jagged, never visited. Mae smiled, picturing herself there, and smiled wider, thinking of Mercer, his smug face, surprised, upended. Mercer would be too fat to fit into a kayak, she thought, and too lazy to make it out of the marina. A man, fast approaching thirty, making antler chandeliers and lecturing her—who worked at the Circle!—about life paths. This was a joke. But Mae, who was in the T2K and who was moving quickly up through the ranks, was also brave, capable of taking a kayak in the night into the blackwater bay, to explore an island Mercer would only view through a telescope, sitting on his potato-sack ass, painting animal parts with silver paint.

Hers was not an itinerary rooted in any logic. She had no idea of the currents deeper in the bay, or of the wisdom in getting so close to the tankers that used the nearby shipping lane, especially given she would be in the dark, invisible to them. And by the time she reached, or got close to, the island, the conditions might be too rough for her to go back. But driven by a force within her as strong and reflexive as sleep, she knew she would not stop until she'd made it to Blue Island, or was somehow prevented from doing so. If the wind kept quiet and the water held steady, she would make it there.

As she paddled beyond the sailboats and breakers, she looked south, squinting in search of the barge where the woman and man lived, but the shapes that far away were not clear, and anyway, they were unlikely to have lights on this late. She stayed on course, cutting quickly beyond the anchored yachts and into the round stomach of the bay.

She heard a quick splash behind her, and turned to find the black head of a harbor seal, not fifteen feet away. She waited for him to drop below the surface, but he stayed, staring at her. She turned back and paddled again toward the island, and the seal followed her for a bit, as if also wanting to see what she wanted to see. Mae wondered, briefly, if the seal would follow her all the way, or if he was, perhaps, on his way to the group of rocks near the island, where many times, driving on the bridge overhead, she'd seen seals sunning. But the next time she turned around, the animal was gone.

The water's surface remained calm even as she ventured deeper. Where it usually turned rough, where the water was exposed to ocean winds, it was, this night, utterly placid, and her progress remained swift. In twenty minutes she was halfway to the island, or it appeared that way. The distances were impossible to tell, especially at night, but the island was growing in her vision, and features of the rock she'd never grasped before were now visible. She saw something reflective at the top, the moonlight casting it in bright silver. She saw the remains of what she was sure was a window, resting on the black sand of the shore. Far away, she heard a foghorn, coming from the mouth of the Golden Gate. The fog must be thick there, she thought, even while where she was, only a few miles away, the night was clear, the moon brilliant and nearly whole. Its shimmer on the water was outlandish, so bright she found herself squinting. She wondered about the rocks near the island where she'd seen seals and sea lions. Would they be there, and would they flee before her arrival? A breeze came from the west, a Pacific wind swooping down off the hills, and she sat still for a moment, measuring it. If it picked up, she would have to turn back. She was now closer to the island than the shore, but if the water grew choppy, the danger, alone and without a life preserver, sitting atop a kayak, would be untenable. But as quickly as it had come, the wind disappeared.

A loud murmuring sound brought her attention to the north. A boat, something like a tug, was coming toward her. On the roof of the cabin she saw lights, white and red, and knew it was a patrol of some kind, Coast Guard probably, and they were close enough to see her. If she remained upright, her silhouette would quickly give her away.

She flattened herself against the floor of the kayak, hoping that if they saw the shape she was making, they would assume it was a rock, a log, a seal, or simply a wide black ripple interrupting the bay's silver shimmer. The groan of the boat's engine grew louder, and Mac was sure there would soon be some bright flood upon her, but the boat passed quickly and Mae went unseen.

The last push to the island was so quick Mae questioned her sense of distance. One moment she felt she was halfway there at best, and the next she was racing toward the island's beach as if propelled by heavy tailwinds. She jumped from the bow, the water white-cold and seizing her. She rushed to get the kayak on shore, dragging it up until it was entirely out of the water and onto the sand. Remembering the time when a quickly rising tide nearly took her vessel away, she turned it parallel to the shore and placed large stones on either side.

She stood, breathing heavily, feeling strong, feeling enormous. What a strange thing, she thought, to be here. There was a bridge nearby, and while driving over it she'd seen this island a hundred times and had never seen a soul, human or animal. No one dared or bothered. What was it about her that made her this curious? It occurred to her that this was the only, or at least the best, way to come here. Marion would not have wanted her to go this far, and might have sent a speedboat to find her and bring her back. And the Coast Guard, didn't they routinely dissuade people from coming here? Was it a private island? All of these questions and concerns were irrelevant now, because it was dark, no one could see her, and no one would ever know she was here. But she would know.

She walked the perimeter. The beach collared most of the southern side of the island, then gave way to a sheer cliff. She looked up, seeing no footholds, and below was the frothy shore, so she returned the way she came, finding the hillside rough and rocky, and the shore largely unremarkable. There was a thick stripe of seaweed, with crab shells and flotsam embedded, and she threaded her fingers through it. The moonlight gave the seaweed some of the phosphorescence she'd seen before, adding a rainbow sheen, as if lit from within. For a brief moment, she felt like she was on some body of water on the moon itself, everything cast in a strange inverted palette. What should have been green looked grey, what should have been blue was silver. Everything she was seeing she'd never seen before. And just as she had this thought, out of the corner of her eye, dropping over the Pacific, she saw what she was sure was a shooting star. She'd only seen one before, and couldn't be sure what she saw was the same thing, an arc of light, disappearing behind the black hills. But what else could it be? She sat for a moment on the beach, staring into the same spot where she'd seen it, as if there might be another, or that it might give way to a shower.

But she was, she knew, putting off what she wanted most to do, to climb the short peak of the rock, which now she set herself upon. There was no path, a fact that gave her great pleasure—no one, or almost no one, had ever been where she was—and so she climbed using tufts of grass and roots for handholds, and placed her feet upon the occasional rock outcroppings. She stopped once, having found a large hole, almost round, almost tidy, in the hillside. It had to be an animal's home, but what sort she couldn't be sure. She imagined the burrows of rabbits and foxes, snakes and moles and mice, any of them equally possible and impossible here, and then she continued, up and up. It was not difficult. She was at the peak in minutes, joining a lone pine, not much bigger than herself. She stood next to it, using its rough trunk for balance, and turned around. She saw the tiny white windows of the city far beyond. She watched the progress of a tanker, low-slung and carrying a constellation of red lights into the Pacific.

The beach suddenly seemed so far beneath her, and her stomach somersaulted. She looked east, now getting a better view of the seals' group of rocks, and saw a dozen or so of them lying about, sleeping. She looked up to the bridge above, not the Golden Gate but a lesser one, its liquid white stream of cars, still constant at midnight, and wondered if anyone could see her human silhouette against the silver bay. She remembered what Francis had once said, that he'd never known there was an island beneath the bridge at all. Most of the drivers and their passengers would not be looking down at her, would not have the faintest idea of her existence.

Then, still holding the pine's bony trunk, she noticed, for the first time, a nest, resting in the tree's upper boughs. She didn't dare touch it, knowing she would upset its equilibrium of scents and construction, but she badly wanted to see what was inside. She stood on a stone, trying to get above it, to look down into it, but she couldn't position herself high enough to get any perspective. Could she lift it, bring it down to her to peek in? Just for a second? She could, couldn't she, and then put it right back? No. She knew enough to know she couldn't. If she did, she'd ruin whatever was inside.

She sat down, facing south, where she could see the lights, the bridges, the black empty hills dividing the bay from the Pacific. All this had been underwater some millions of years ago, she'd been told. All these headlands and islands had been so far under they would have barely registered as ridges on the ocean floor. Across the silver bay she saw a pair of birds, egrets or herons, gliding low, heading north, and she sat for a time, her mind drifting toward blank. She thought of the foxes that might be underneath her, the crabs that might be hiding under the stones on the shore, the people in the cars that might be passing overhead, the men and women in the tugs and tankers, arriving to port or leaving, sighing, everyone having seen everything. She guessed at it all, what might live, moving purposefully or drifting aimlessly, in the deep water around her, but she didn't think too much about any of it. It was enough to be aware of the million permutations possible around her, and take comfort in knowing she would not, and really could not, know much at all.

When Mae arrived back at Marion's beach, it looked, at first, just as she'd left it. There were no people visible, and the light within Marion's trailer was as it was before, rose-colored and dim.

Mae jumped to the shore, her feet shushing deep into the wet sand, and she dragged the kayak up the beach. Her legs were sore, and she stopped, dropped the kayak, and stretched. With her hands over her head, she looked toward the parking lot, seeing her car, but now there was another car next to it. And as she was regarding this second car, wondering if Marion was back, Mae was blinded by white light.

"Stay there," an amplified voice roared.

She turned instinctively away.

The amplified voice came again. "Don't move!" it said, now with venom.

Mae froze there, off-balance, worrying briefly about how long she could maintain such a pose, but there was no need. Two shadows descended upon her, grabbed roughly at her arms, and handcuffed her hands behind her.

Mae sat in the back of the squad car, and the officers, calmer now, weighed whether or not what Mae was telling them—that she was a regular renter, had a membership, and was merely late in returning a rental—could be the truth. They had reached Marion on the phone, and she corroborated that Mae was a customer, but when they had asked if Mae had rented that day and was just tardy, Marion had hung up and said she'd be right over.

Twenty minutes later, Marion arrived. She was in the passenger seat of a vintage red pickup truck, the driver a bearded man who appeared bewildered and annoyed. Mae, seeing Marion walk unsteadily to the police car, realized she had been drinking, and possibly the bearded man had, too. He was still in the car, and seemed determined to stay there.

As Marion made her way to the car, Mae caught her eye, and Marion, seeing Mae in the back of a squad car, her arms cuffed behind her, seemed to sober instantly.

"Oh Jesus Christ," she said, rushing to Mae. She turned to the officers. "This is Mae Holland. She rents here all the time. She has the run of the place. How the hell did this happen? What's going on here?"

The officers explained that they'd gotten two separate messages about a probable theft. "We got one call from a citizen who doesn't wish to be identified." And then they turned to Marion. "And the other warning came from one of your own cameras, Ms. Lefebvre."

Mae barely slept. Her adrenaline kept her pacing through the night. How could she be so stupid? She wasn't a thief. What if Marion hadn't saved her? She could have lost everything. Her parents would have been called to bail her out, and her position at the Circle would be lost. Mae had never gotten a speeding ticket, had never been in trouble at any level, and now she was stealing a thousand-dollar kayak.

But it was over, and Marion had even insisted, when they parted, that Mae come back. "I know you'll be embarrassed, but I want you to come back here. I will hound you if you don't." She knew Mae would be so sorry, and full of shame, that she wouldn't want to face Marion again.

Still, when she woke after a few hours of fitful sleep, Mae felt a strange sense of liberation, as if she'd woken up from a nightmare to know it hadn't happened. The slate was blank and she went to work.

She logged on at eight thirty. Her rank was 3,892. She worked through the morning, feeling the extraordinary focus possible for a few hours after a largely sleepless night. Periodically, memories from the night before came to her—the silent silver of the water, the lone pine on the island, the blinding light of the squad car, its plastic smell, the idiotic conversation with Mercer—but these memories were fading, or she was forcing them to fade, when she received a second-screen message from Dan: *Please come to my office asap. Jared will cover for you.*

She rushed there, and when she got to his door, Dan was standing, ready. His face seemed to show some satisfaction that she'd hurried. Dan closed the door and they sat down.

"Mae, do you know what I want to talk about?"

Was this a test to see if she would lie?

"I'm sorry, I don't," she tried.

Dan blinked slowly. "Mae. Last chance."

"Is it about last night?" she said. If he didn't know about the police, she could make something else up, something else that had happened after hours.

"It is. Mae, this is very serious stuff."

He knew. God, he knew. In some recess of her mind Mae realized that the Circle must have some web alert to notify them anytime a staff member was charged or questioned by the police. It only made sense.

"But there were no charges," she protested. "Marion cleared everything up."

"Marion is the owner of the shop?"

"Yes."

"But Mae, you and I know that there was a crime committed, don't we?"

Mae had no idea what to say.

"Mae, I'll spare you. Did you know that a member of the Circle, Gary Katz, had placed a SeeChange camera at that beach?"

Her stomach dropped into her shoe. "No, I didn't."

"And the owner's son, Walt, had set one up, too?"

"No."

"Okay, first of all, that's troubling in and of itself. You go kay-aking sometimes, yes? I see on your profile that you're a kayaker. Josiah and Denise say you had a good talk about this."

"I do go sometimes. It's been a few months."

"But you've never thought to check SeeChange to see about water conditions?"

"No. I should. But every time I go, it's really a spur-of-the-moment thing. The beach is on my way home from my parents' house so—"

"And you were at your parents' house yesterday?" Dan said, in a way that made clear that if she said yes, he would be even angrier.

"I was. Just for dinner."

Dan stood now, and turned from Mae. She could hear his breathing, a series of exasperated bursts.

Mae had the distinct sensation she would be fired any moment. Then she remembered Annie. Could Annie save her? Not this time.

"Okay," Dan said. "So you go home, missing any number of activities here, and when you drive back this way, you stop by the rental shop, after hours. Don't tell me you didn't know they were closed."

"I figured they were, but I just stopped to make sure."

"And when you saw a kayak outside the fence, you just decided to take it."

"Borrow it. I'm a member there."

"Have you seen the footage of this?" Dan asked.

He turned on his wallscreen. Mae saw a clear, moonlight

image of the beach from a wide-angle camera. The logline at the bottom of the screen indicated it had been taken at 10:14 p.m. "Don't you think a camera like this would be useful to you?" Dan asked. "Water conditions at the very least?" He didn't wait for a response. "Let's see you here." He fast-forwarded a few seconds, and Mae saw her shadowy figure appear on the beach. Everything was very clear—her surprise at finding the kayak, her moments of deliberation and doubt, then her quick work of bringing the vessel to the water and paddling out of view.

"Okay," Dan said, "as you can see, it's pretty obvious you knew you were doing something wrong. This is not the behavior of someone with a standing arrangement with Marge or whomever. I mean, I'm happy that you two colluded on your story and that you weren't arrested, because that would have made your working here impossible. Felons don't work at the Circle. But still, all of this makes me frankly sick to my stomach. Lies and aversions. It's just astounding to even have to deal with this."

Again Mae had the distinct feeling, a vibration in the air, that said she was being fired. But if she was being fired, Dan wouldn't have spent this kind of time with her, would he? And would he fire someone Annie, who was far higher on the ladder, had hired? If she were to hear about her termination from anyone, it would be Annie herself. So Mae sat, hoping this was going somewhere else.

"Now, what's missing here?" he asked, pointing to the frozen image of Mae getting into the kayak.

"I don't know."

"You really don't know?"

"Permission to use the kayak?"

"Sure," he said curtly, "but what else?"

Mae shook her head. "I'm sorry. I don't know."

"Don't you usually wear a life preserver?"

"I do, I do. But they were on the other side of the fence."

"And if something happened to you out there, god forbid, how would your parents feel? How would Marge feel?"

"Marion."

"How would she feel, Mae? Overnight, her business is over. Finished. All the people who work for her. They're all out of work. The beach is shut down. Kayaking in the bay, as a business overall, goes through the floor. All because of your carelessness. Forgive me for the bluntness, but because of your selfishness."

"I know," Mae said, feeling the sting of truth. She had been selfish. She hadn't thought of anything but her own desire.

"It's sad, because you've been improving so much. Your Parti-Rank was as high as 1,668. Your Conversion Rate and Retail Raw were in the top quartile. And now this." Dan sighed elaborately. "But as upsetting as this all is, it provides us with a teachable moment. And I mean a teachable moment on a life-changing level. This shameful episode has given you the chance to meet Eamon Bailey himself."

Mae's gasp was audible.

"Yes. He took an interest in this, seeing how much it overlaps with his interests and the overall goals of the Circle. Would you be interested in speaking to Eamon about this?"

"Yes," Mae managed. "Of course."

"Good. He's anxious to meet you. At six this evening, you'll be brought to his office. Please collect your thoughts in the meantime."

Mae's head echoed with self-denunciations. She hated who she was. How could she have done that, risked her job? Embarrassed her best friend? Jeopardized her father's health insurance? She was an imbecile, yes, but was she some sort of schizophrenic, too? What had overtaken her the night before? What sort of person does that? Her mind argued with itself while she worked, feverishly, trying to do something visible to demonstrate her commitment to the company. She handled 140 customer queries, her record so far, while answering 1,129 survey questions, and while keeping the newbies on target. The pod aggregate score was 98, which she took pride in even while knowing there was some luck, and some of Jared's involvement, too—he knew what was happening with Mae and had pledged his help. At five p.m. the chute closed and Mae worked on her PartiRank for forty-five minutes, bringing it from 1,827 to 1,430, a process entailing 344 comments, posts and almost a thousand smiles and frowns. She converted 38 major topics and 44 minor ones, and her Retail Raw was $24,050. She felt sure that this would be noticed and appreciated by Bailey, whose concentration on PartiRank was the most acute of the Three Wise Men.

At five forty-five, a voice called her name. She looked up to see a figure at the door, someone new, a man of about thirty. She met him at the door.

"Mae Holland?"

"Yes."

"I'm Dontae Peterson. I work with Eamon, and he's asked me to bring you up to his office. You ready?"

They took the same route Mae had taken with Annie, and along the way Mae realized that Dontae didn't know Mae had been to Bailey's office before. Annie had never sworn her to secrecy, but the fact that Dontae didn't know indicated that Bailey didn't know, and that she shouldn't reveal this herself.

As they entered the long crimson hallway, Mae was sweating heavily. She could feel rivulets making their way from her armpits to her waist. She couldn't feel her feet.

"Here's a funny portrait of the Three Wise Men," Dontae said as they stopped at the door. "Bailey's niece did it."

Mae pretended to be surprised by it, delighted by its innocence and crude insight.

Dontae took the large gargoyle knocker and rapped the door. It opened, and Bailey's smiling face filled the void.

"Hello!" he said. "Hi Dontae, hi Mae!" He smiled wider, acknowledging his rhyme. "Come in."

He was wearing khakis and a white button-down, looking freshly showered. Mae followed him as he took in the room, scratching the nape of his neck, as if almost embarrassed by how well he'd done here.

"So this is my favorite room. Very few people have seen it. Not like I'm super-secret about it or anything, but time just doesn't allow me to give tours and such. Have you seen anything like this before?"

Mae wanted to say, but couldn't, that she had seen this very room before. "Not remotely," she said.

Something happened in Bailey's face at that moment, some twitch that seemed to bring the left corner of his eye and the left side of his mouth closer together.

"Thank you Dontae," Bailey said.

Dontae smiled and left, closing the heavy door behind him.

"So Mae. Tea?" Bailey was standing before an antique tea set, a silver pot emitting a narrow corkscrew of steam.

"Sure," she said.

"Green? Black?" he asked, smiling. "Grey?"

"Green, thanks. But you don't have to."

Bailey was busy with the preparations. "You've known our beloved Annie a long time?" he asked, pouring carefully.

"I have. Since sophomore year in college. Five years now."

"Five years! That's, what, 30 percent of your life!"

Mae knew he was rounding up a bit, but she emitted a tiny laugh. "I guess so. A long time." He handed her a saucer and cup and gestured for her to sit down. There were two chairs, both leather and overstuffed.

Bailey dropped himself into his chair with a loud sigh, and rested his ankle on his knee. "Well, Annie is very important to us here, and thus you are, too. She talks about you like you could end up being very valuable to this community. Do you believe that's true?"

"That I could be valuable here?"

He nodded, then blew on his tea. He looked over his teacup to her, his eyes steady. She met his gaze, then, briefly overwhelmed, she looked away, only to find his face again, this time in a framed photo on a nearby shelf. It was a formal portrait of Bailey's family in black and white, his three girls standing around their mother and Bailey, who were both sitting. Bailey's son was on his lap, wearing a tracksuit and holding an Iron Man action figure.

"Well, I hope so," Mae said. "I've been trying as hard as I can.

I love the Circle, and can't express how much I appreciate the opportunity I've been given here."

Bailey smiled. "Good, good. So tell me, how are you feeling about what happened last night?" He asked the question as if genuinely curious, as if her answer might go in any number of directions.

Mae was on firm ground now. No obfuscation was necessary. "Terrible," she said. "I barely slept. I'm so ashamed I want to puke." She wouldn't have used the word when talking to Stenton, but she felt Bailey might appreciate the coarseness.

He smiled almost imperceptibly and moved on. "Mae, let me ask you a question. Would you have behaved differently if you'd known about the SeeChange cameras at the marina?"

"Yes."

Bailey nodded empathetically. "Okay. How?"

"I wouldn't have done what I did."

"And why not?"

"Because I would have been caught."

Bailey tilted his head. "Is that all?"

"Well, I wouldn't want anyone seeing me do that. It wasn't right. It's embarrassing."

He put his cup on the table next to him and rested his hands on his lap, his palms in a gentle embrace. "So in general, would you say you behave differently when you know you're being watched?"

"Sure. Of course."

"And when you'll be held accountable."

"Yes."

"And when there will be a historical record. That is, when or if your behavior will be permanently accessible. That a video of your behavior, for example, will exist forever."

"Yes."

"Good. And do you remember my talk from earlier in the summer, about the ultimate goal of SeeChange?"

"I know it would eliminate most crime, if there was full saturation."

Bailey seemed pleased. "Right. Correct. Everyday citizens, like Gary Katz and Walt Lefebvre in this instance, because they took the time to set up their cameras, they help keep us all safe. The crime was minor in this case, and there were no victims, thank god. You're alive. Marion's business, and the kayaking industry generally, lives to see another day. But one night of selfishness from you could have risked it all. The individual act has reverberations that can be nearly endless. Do you agree?"

"I do. I know. It's unconscionable." And here Mae again had the feeling that she was a very short-sighted person, who repeatedly jeopardized all she'd been given by the Circle.

"Mr. Bailey, I can't believe I did this. And I know you're wondering if I fit in here. I just want you to know how much I value my position here and your faith in me. And I want to honor that. I'll do anything to make this up to you. Seriously, I'll take on any extra work, I'll do anything. Just tell me."

Bailey's face broke into a highly amused grin. "Mae, your job isn't in jeopardy. You're here for good. Annie's here for good. Sorry if you believed otherwise, for even a second. We don't want either of you to ever leave."

"That's very good to hear. Thank you," Mae said, though her heart was hammering harder now.

He smiled, nodding, as if happy and relieved to have all that settled. "But this whole episode gives us a very important teachable moment, don't you think?" The question seemed rhetorical, but Mae nodded anyway. "Mae," he said, "when is a secret a good thing?"

Mae took a few seconds on this. "When it can protect someone's feelings."

"For example?"

"Well," she fumbled. "Let's say you know your friend's boyfriend is cheating on her but—"

"But what? You don't tell your friend?"

"Okay. That's not a good example."

"Mae, are you ever happy when a friend keeps a secret from you?"

Mae thought about the many small lies she'd told to Annie recently. Lies that she'd not only *spoken* but *typed,* lies made permanent and undeniable.

"No. But I understand when they have to."

"That's interesting. Can you think of a time when you were happy one of your friends kept something from you?"

Mae could not. "Not at the moment." She felt sick.

"Okay," Bailey said, "for now, we can't think of good secrets between friends. Let's move on to families. In a family, is a secret a good thing? Theoretically, do you ever think, *You know what would be great to keep from my family? A secret.*"

Mae thought of the many things her parents were likely keeping from her—the various indignities her father's illness caused them. "No," she said.

"No secrets within a family?"

"Actually," Mae said. "I don't know. There are definitely things you don't want your parents to know."

"Would your parents *want* to know these things?"

"Maybe."

"So you're depriving your parents of something they want. This is good?"

"No. But maybe better for all."

"Better for you. Better for the keeper of the secret. Some dark secret is better kept from the parents. Is this a secret about some wonderful thing you've done? Perhaps knowing about it would bring just too much joy to your parents?"

Mae laughed. "No. Clearly a secret is something you don't want them to know about because you're ashamed or you want to spare them from knowing you screwed up."

"But we agree they would *like* to know."

"Yes."

"And are they entitled to know?"

"I guess."

"Okay. So can we agree that we're talking about a situation where, in a perfect world, you're not doing anything you'd be ashamed of telling your parents?"

"Sure. But there are other things they might not understand."

"Because they weren't ever sons or daughters themselves?"

"No. But—"

"Mae, do you have any gay relatives or friends?"

"Sure."

"Do you know how different the world was for gays before and after people began coming out?"

"I have an idea of it."

Bailey stood and attended to the tea set. He poured more for himself and for Mae, and sat down again.

"I don't know if you do. I was from the generation that struggled greatly with coming out. My brother is gay, and he was twenty-four before he admitted it to my family. And until then, it nearly killed him. It was a tumor festering inside him, and it was growing every day. But why did he think it would be better kept inside? When he told our parents, they barely blinked. He had created all this drama in his mind—all this mystery and weight around his big secret. And part of the problem, historically, was with other people keeping similar things secret. Coming out was so difficult until millions of other men and women came out. Then it got a lot easier, don't you agree? When millions of men and women came out of the closet, it made homosexuality not some mysterious so-called deviance but a mainstream life path. You follow?"

"Yes. But—"

"And I would argue that any place in the world where gays are still persecuted, you could instantly achieve great progress if all the gays and lesbians came out publicly at once. Then whoever is persecuting them, and all those who tacitly support this persecution, would realize that to persecute them would mean persecuting at least 10 percent of the population—including their sons, daughters, neighbors and friends—even their own parents. It would be instantly untenable. But the persecution of gays or any minority group is made uniquely possible through secrecy."

"Okay. I hadn't thought of it that way."

"That's fine," he said, satisfied, and sipped his tea. He ran his finger over his upper lip, drying it. "So we've explored the damage of secrets within the family and between friends, and the role of secrecy in persecuting large classes of people. Let's keep on our quest to find a use for a policy of secrecy. Should we look into politics? Do you think a president should keep secrets from the people she or he governs?"

"No, but there have to be some things that we can't know. For national security alone."

He smiled, happy, it seemed, that she'd said what he expected her to say. "Really, Mae? Do you recall when a man named Julian Assange leaked several million pages of secret U.S. documents?"

"I read about it."

"Well, first of all, the U.S. government was very upset, as was much of the media. Many people thought this was a serious breach of security and that it presented a clear and present danger to our men and women in uniform here and abroad. But do you remember if any soldiers ever actually were harmed by these documents being released?"

"I don't know."

"None were. Not a one. Same thing happened in the seventies with the Pentagon Papers. Not one soldier got even a splinter due to the release of these documents. The main effect, I remember, of these documents being made public is that we found out that many of our diplomats are gossipy about the leaders of other countries. Millions of documents, and the main takeaway was that U.S. diplomats thought Gadhafi was a kook, with all his female bodyguards and strange eating habits. If anything, the release of the documents just put these diplomats on better behavior. They were more careful about what they said."

"But national defense—"

"What about it? The only time we're in danger is when we don't know the plans or motives of the countries we're supposedly at odds with. Or when they don't know our plans but worry about them, right?"

"Sure."

"But what if they *did* know our plans and we knew theirs? You'd suddenly be free of what they used to call the risk of mutually assured destruction, and instead you'd arrive at mutually assured *trust*. The U.S. has no purely nefarious motives, right? We're not planning to wipe some country off the map. Sometimes, though, we take surreptitious steps to get what we want. But what if everyone was, and had to be, open and upfront?"

"It would be better?"

Bailey smiled broadly. "Good. I agree." He put his cup down and again rested his hands in his lap.

Mae knew she shouldn't press him, but her mouth got ahead of her. "But you can't be saying that everyone should know everything."

Bailey's eyes widened, as if pleased she'd led him to an idea he coveted. "Of course not. But I am saying that everyone should have a *right* to know everything, and should have the *tools* to know anything. There's not enough time to know everything, though I certainly wish there was."

He paused, lost briefly in thought, then returned his focus to Mae. "I understand you weren't very happy about being the subject of Gus's LuvLuv demonstration."

"It just caught me by surprise. He hadn't told me about it beforehand."

"Is that all?"

"Well, it presented a distorted impression of me."

"Was the information he presented incorrect? There were factual mistakes?"

"Well, it wasn't that. It was just . . . piecemeal. And maybe that made it *seem* incorrect. It was taking a few slivers of me and presenting that as the whole me——"

"It seemed incomplete."

"Right."

"Mae, I'm very glad you put it that way. As you know, the Circle is itself trying to become complete. We're trying to close the circle at the Circle." He smiled at his own wordplay. "But you know the overall goals of completion, I assume."

She didn't. "I think so," she said.

"Look at our logo," he said, and pointed to a wallscreen, where, on his cue, the logo appeared. "See how that 'c' in the middle is open? For years it's bothered me, and it's become symbolic of what's left to do here, which is to close it." The "c" on screen closed and became a perfect circle. "See that?" he said. "A circle is the strongest shape in the universe. Nothing can beat it, nothing can improve upon it, nothing can be more perfect. And that's what we want to be: perfect. So any information that eludes us, anything that's not accessible, prevents us from being perfect. You see?"

"I do," Mae said, though she wasn't sure she did.

"This is in line with our goals for how the Circle can help us, individually, feel more complete, and feel that others' impressions of us are complete—are based on complete information. And to prevent us from feeling, as you did, that some distorted view of ourselves is presented to the world. It's like a broken mirror. If we look into a broken mirror, a mirror that's cracked or missing parts, what do we get?"

Now it made sense to Mae. Any assessment, judgment, or picture utilizing incomplete information would always be wrong. "We get a distorted and broken reflection," she said.

"Right," Bailey said. "And if the mirror is whole?"

"We see everything."

"A mirror is truthful, correct?"

"Of course. It's a mirror. It's reality."

"But a mirror can only be truthful when it's complete. And I think for you, the problem with Gus's LuvLuv presentation was that it wasn't complete."

"Okay."

"Okay?"

"Well, that's true," she said. She wasn't sure why she opened her mouth, but the words tumbled out before she could restrain them. "But I still think there are things, even if just a few, that we want to keep to ourselves. I mean, everyone does things alone, or in the bedroom, that they're ashamed of."

"But why should they be ashamed?"

"Maybe not always ashamed. But things they don't want to share. That maybe they don't think people will understand. Or will change the perception of them."

"Okay, with that kind of thing, one of two things will eventually happen. First, we'll realize that whatever behavior we're talking about is so widespread and harmless that it needn't be secret. If we demystify it, if we admit that it's something we all do, then it loses its power to shock. We move toward honesty, and we move away from shame. Or second, and even better, if we all, as a society, decide that this is behavior we'd rather not engage in, the fact that everyone knows, or has the power to know who's doing it, this would prevent the behavior from being engaged in. This is just as you said—you wouldn't have stolen if you knew you were being watched."

"Right."

"Would the guy down the hall view porn at work if he knew he was being watched?"

"No. I guess not."

"So, problem solved, right?"

"Right. I guess."

"Mae, have you ever had a secret that festered within you, and once that secret was out, you felt better?"

"Sure."

"Me too. That's the nature of secrets. They're cancerous when kept within us, but harmless when they're out in the world."

"So you're saying there should be no secrets."

"I have thought on this for years, and I have yet to conjure a scenario where a secret does more good than harm. Secrets are the enablers of antisocial, immoral and destructive behavior. Do you see how this is?"

"I think so. But—"

"You know what my spouse said to me years ago when we got married? She said that whenever we were apart, for instance when I might go on a business trip, I should behave as if there were a camera on me. As if she were watching. Way back when, she was saying this in a purely conceptual way, and she was half-kidding, but the mental picture helped me. If I found myself alone in a room with a woman colleague, I would wonder, *What would*

Karen think of this if she were watching from a closed-circuit camera?
This would gently guide my behavior, and it would prevent me
from even approaching behavior she wouldn't like, and of which
I wouldn't be proud. It kept me honest. You see what I mean?"

"I do," Mae said.

"I mean, the trackability of self-driving cars is solving a lot of
this, of course. Spouses increasingly know where the other has been,
given the car logs where it's been driven. But my point is, what if
we *all* behaved as if we were being watched? It would lead to a more
moral way of life. Who would do something unethical or immoral
or illegal if they were being watched? If their illegal money transfer was being tracked? If their blackmailing phone call was being
recorded? If their stick-up at the gas station was being filmed by a
dozen cameras, and even their retinas identified during the robbery?
If their philandering was being documented in a dozen ways?"

"I don't know. I'm imagining all that would be greatly
reduced."

"Mae, we would finally be compelled to be our best selves.
And I think people would be relieved. There would be this phenomenal global sigh of relief. Finally, finally, we can be good. In
a world where bad choices are no longer an option, we have no
choice *but* to be good. Can you imagine?"

Mae nodded.

"Now, speaking of relief, is there anything you'd like to tell
me before we wrap up?"

"I don't know. So many things, I guess," Mae said. "But you've
been so nice to spend all this time with me, so——"

"Mae, is there something specific that you've kept hidden
from me as we've been together here in this library?"

Mae knew, instantly, that lying was not an option.

"That I've been here before?" she said.

"Have you?"

"Yes."

"But you implied when you entered that you hadn't."

"Annie brought me. She said it was some kind of secret. I don't know. I didn't know what to do. I didn't see either way as being ideal. I get in trouble either way."

Bailey smiled extravagantly. "See, that's not true. Only lies get us in trouble. Only the things we hide. Of *course* I knew you'd been here. Give me some credit! But I was curious that you hid this from me. It made me feel distant from you. A secret between two friends, Mae, is an ocean. It's wide and deep and we lose ourselves in it. And now that I know your secret, do you feel better or worse?"

"Better."

"Relief?"

"Yes, relief."

Mae did feel relief, a surge of it that felt like love. Because she still had her job, and she would not have to go back to Longfield, and because her father would stay strong and her mother unburdened, she wanted to be held by Bailey, to be subsumed by his wisdom and generosity.

"Mae," he said, "I truly believe that if we have no path but the right path, the best path, then that would present a kind of ultimate and all-encompassing relief. We don't have to be tempted by darkness anymore. Forgive me for putting it in moral terms. That's the Midwestern church-goer in me. But I'm a believer in the perfectibility of human beings. I think we can be better. I think we can be perfect or near to it. And when we become our best selves, the possibilities are endless. We can solve any problem. We can cure any disease, end hunger, everything, because we won't be dragged down by all our weaknesses, our petty secrets, our hoarding of information and knowledge. We will finally realize our potential."

Mae had been dizzy from the conversation with Bailey for days, and now it was Friday, and the thought of going onstage at lunch made concentration almost impossible. But she knew she had to work, to set an example for her pod, at the very least, given this would likely be her last full day at CE.

The flow was steady but not overwhelming, and she got through 77 customer queries that morning. Her score was 98 and the pod aggregate was 97. All respectable numbers. Her Parti-Rank was 1,921, another fine figure, and one she felt comfortable taking into the Enlightenment.

At 11:38, she left her desk and walked to the side door of the auditorium, arriving ten minutes before noon. She knocked and the door opened. Mae met the stage manager, an older, almost spectral man named Jules, who brought her into a simple dressing room of white walls and bamboo floors. A brisk woman named Teresa, enormous eyes outlined in blue, sat Mae down, looked over her hair and blushed her face with a feathery brush, and applied a lavalier microphone to her blouse. "No need to touch anything," she said. "It'll be activated once you go out onstage."

It was happening very quickly, but Mae felt this was best. If she had more time she would only get more nervous. So she listened to Jules and Teresa, and in minutes she was in the wings of the stage, listening to a thousand Circlers enter the auditorium, talking and laughing and dropping themselves into their seats with happy thumps. She wondered, briefly, if Kalden was anywhere out there.

"Mae."

She turned to find Eamon Bailey behind her, wearing a sky-blue shirt, smiling warmly at her. "Are you ready?"

"I think so."

"You'll be great," he said. "Don't worry. Just be natural. We're just re-creating the conversation we had last week. Okay?"

"Okay."

And then he was onstage, waving to the crowd, everyone clapping with abandon. There were two burgundy-colored chairs on the stage, facing each other, and Bailey sat down in one and spoke into the darkness.

"Hello, Circlers," he said.

"Hello Eamon!" they roared back.

"Thank you for being here today, on a very special Dream Friday. I thought we'd change it up a bit today and have not a speech, but an interview. As some of you know, we do these from time to time to shed light on members of the Circle and their thoughts, their hopes and in this case, their evolutions."

He sat in one of the chairs and smiled into the wings. "I had a conversation with a young Circler the other day that I wanted to share with you. So I've asked Mae Holland, who some of you might know as one of our newbies in Customer Experience, to join me today. Mae?"

Mae stepped into the light. The feeling was of instant weightlessness, of floating in black space, with two distant but bright suns blinding her. She couldn't see anyone in the audience, and could barely orient herself to the stage. But she managed to direct her body, her legs made of straw, her feet leaden, toward Bailey. She found her chair, and with two hands, feeling numb and blind, lowered herself into it.

"Hello Mae. How are you?"

"Terrified."

The audience laughed.

"Don't be nervous," Bailey said, smiling to the audience and giving her the slightest look of concern.

"Easy for you to say," she said, and there was laughter throughout the room. This laughter felt good and calmed her. She breathed in, and looked in the front row, finding five or six shadowy faces, all smiling. She was, she realized and now felt in her bones, among friends. She was safe. She took a sip of water, felt it cool everything inside her, and put her hands in her lap. She felt ready.

"Mae, in one word how would you describe the awakening you had this past week?"

This part they had rehearsed. She knew Bailey wanted to start with this idea of an awakening. "It was just that, Eamon"—she'd been instructed to call him Eamon—"it was an awakening."

"Oops. I guess I just stole your thunder," he said. The audience laughed. "I should have said, 'What did you have this week?' But tell us, why that word?"

"Well, *awakening* seems right to me . . ." Mae said, and then added ". . . now."

The word *now* appeared a split-second later than it should

have, and Bailey's eye twitched. "Let's talk about this awakening," he said. "It started on Sunday night. Many of the people in the room already know the broad outlines of the events, with SeeChange and all. But give us a summary."

Mae looked at her hands, in what she realized was a theatrical gesture. She had never before looked at her hands to indicate some level of shame.

"I committed a crime, basically," she said. "I borrowed a kayak without the knowledge of the owner, and I paddled to an island in the middle of the bay."

"That was Blue Island, I understand?"

"It was."

"And did you tell anyone you were doing this?"

"No, I didn't."

"Now Mae, did you have the intention of telling anyone about this trip afterward?"

"No."

"And did you document it at all? Pictures, video?"

"No, nothing."

There were some murmurs from the audience. Mae and Eamon had expected a reaction to this revelation, and they both paused to allow the crowd to assimilate this information.

"Did you know you were doing something wrong, in borrowing this kayak without the owner's knowledge?"

"I did."

"But you did it anyway. Why?"

"Because I thought no one would know."

Another low murmur from the audience.

"So this is an interesting point. The very fact that you thought this action would remain secret enabled you to commit this crime, correct?"

"Correct."

"Would you have done it had you known people were watching?"

"Definitely not."

"So in a way, doing all this in darkness, unobserved and unaccountable, it facilitated impulses that you regret?"

"Absolutely. The fact that I thought I was alone, unwatched, enabled me to commit a crime. And I risked my life. I wasn't wearing a life preserver."

Again, a loud murmur rippled through the audience.

"So you not only committed a crime against the owner of this property, but you risked your own life. All because you were being enabled by some, what, some cloak of invisibility?"

The audience rumbled with laughter. Bailey's eyes stayed on Mae, telling her *Things are going well*.

"Right," she said.

"I have a question, Mae. Do you behave better or worse when you're being watched?"

"Better. Without a doubt."

"When you're alone, unwatched, unaccountable, what happens?"

"Well, for one thing, I steal kayaks."

The audience laughed in a sudden bright burst.

"Seriously. I do things I don't want to do. I lie."

"The other day, when we spoke, you had a way of putting it that I thought was very interesting and succinct. Can you tell us all what you said?"

"I said that secrets are lies."

"Secrets are lies. It's very memorable. Can you walk us through your logic with that phrase, Mae?"

"Well, when there's something kept secret, two things happen. One is that it makes crimes possible. We behave worse when we're not accountable. That goes without saying. And second, secrets inspire speculation. When we don't know what's being hidden, we guess, we make up answers."

"Well that's interesting, isn't it?" Bailey turned to the audience. "When we can't reach a loved one, we speculate. We panic. We make up stories about where they are or what's happened to them. And if we're feeling ungenerous, or jealous, we make up lies. Sometimes some very damaging lies. We assume they're doing something nefarious. All because we don't know something."

"It's like when we see two people whispering," Mae said. "We worry, we feel insecure, we make up terrible things they might be saying. We assume it's about us and that it's catastrophic."

"When they're probably asking where the bathroom is." Bailey got a big laugh and enjoyed it.

"Right," Mae said. She knew she was approaching a few phrases she needed to get right. She'd said them in Bailey's library, and she just needed to say them again the way she'd first said them. "For example, if there's a locked door, I start to make up all kinds of stories about what might be behind it. I feel like it's some kind of secret, and it leads to me making up lies. But if all the doors are open, physically and metaphorically, there's only the one truth."

Bailey smiled. She'd nailed it.

"I like that, Mae. When the doors are open, there's only one truth. So let's recap that first statement of Mae's. Can we get that on the screen?"

The words SECRETS ARE LIES appeared on the screen behind Mae. Seeing the words four feet tall gave her a complicated feeling—something between thrill and dread. Bailey was all smiles, shaking his head, admiring the words.

"Okay, we've resolved that had you known that you'd be held accountable for your actions, you wouldn't have committed this crime. Your access to the shadows, in this case illusory shadows, facilitates bad behavior. And when you know you're being watched, you are your better self. Correct?"

"Correct."

"Now let's talk about the second revelation you made after this episode. You mentioned that you didn't document this trip to Blue Island in any way. Why not?"

"Well, first of all, I knew I was doing something illegal."

"Sure. But you've said that you often kayak in the bay, and you'd never documented these trips. You hadn't joined any Circle clubs devoted to kayaking, and you hadn't posted accounts, photos, video or comments. Have you been doing these kayak trips under the auspices of the CIA?"

Mae, and the audience, laughed. "No."

"Then why these secret trips? You haven't told anyone about them before or after, you haven't mentioned them anywhere. No accounts exist of any of these excursions, am I right?"

"You are right."

Mae heard loud clucks spread through the auditorium.

"What did you see on this last trip, Mae? I understand it was quite beautiful."

"It was, Eamon. There was an almost-full moon, and the water was very calm, and I felt like I was paddling through liquid silver."

"Sounds incredible."

"It was."

"Animals? Wildlife?"

"I was followed for a while by a sole harbor seal, and he dipped above and below the surface, as if he was curious, and also urging me on. I'd never been to this island. Very few people have. And once I got to the island, I climbed to the top, and the view from the peak was incredible. I saw the golden lights of the city, and the black foothills toward the Pacific, and even saw a shooting star."

"A shooting star! Lucky you."

"I was very lucky."

"But you didn't take a picture."

"No."

"Not any video."

"No."

"So there's no record of any of this."

"No. Not outside my own memory."

There were audible groans from the audience. Bailey turned to the audience, shaking his head, indulging them.

"Okay," he said, sounding as if he were bracing himself, "now this is where we get into something personal. As you all know, I have a son, Gunner, who was born with CP, cerebral palsy. Though he's living a very full life, and we're trying, always, to improve his opportunities, he *is* confined to a wheelchair. He can't walk. He can't run. He can't go kayaking. So what does he do if he wants to experience something like this? Well, he watches video. He looks at pictures. Much of his experiences of the world come through the experiences of others. And of course so many of you Circlers have been so generous, providing him with video and photos of your own travels. When he experiences the SeeChange view of a Circler climbing Mount Kenya, he feels like he's climbed Mount Kenya. When he sees firsthand video from an America's Cup crew member, Gunner feels, in some way, that he's sailed in the America's Cup, too. These experiences were facilitated by generous humans who have shared what they saw with the world, my son included. And we can only extrapolate how many others there are out there like Gunner. Maybe they're disabled. Maybe they're elderly, homebound. Maybe a thousand things. But the point is that there are millions of people who can't see what you saw, Mae. Does it feel right to have deprived them of seeing what you saw?"

Mae's throat was dry and she tried not to show her emotion. "It doesn't. It feels very wrong." Mae thought of Bailey's son Gunner, and thought of her own father.

"Do you think they have a right to see things like you saw?"

"I do."

"In this short life," Bailey said, "why shouldn't everyone see whatever it is they want to see? Why shouldn't everyone have equal access to the sights of the world? The knowledge of the world? All the experiences available in this world?"

Mae's voice was just above a whisper. "Everyone should."

"But this experience you had, you kept it to yourself. Which is curious, because you do share online. You work at the Circle.

Your PartiRank is in the T2K. So why do you think this particular hobby of yours, these extraordinary explorations, why hide these from the world?"

"I can't quite figure out what I was thinking, to be honest," Mae said.

The crowd murmured. Bailey nodded.

"Okay. We just talked about how we, as humans, hide what we're ashamed of. We do something illegal, or unethical, and we hide it from the world because we know it's wrong. But hiding something glorious, a wonderful trip on the water, the moonlight coming down, a shooting star . . ."

"It was just selfish, Eamon. It was selfish and nothing more. The same way a child doesn't want to share her favorite toy. I understand that secrecy is part of, well, an aberrant behavior system. It comes from a bad place, not a place of light and generosity. And when you deprive your friends, or someone like your son Gunner, of experiences like I had, you're basically stealing from them. You're depriving them of something they have a right to. Knowledge is a basic human right. Equal access to all possible human experiences is a basic human right."

Mae surprised herself with her eloquence, and the audience answered with thunderous applause. Bailey was looking at her like a proud father. When the applause subsided, Bailey spoke softly, as if reluctant to get in her way.

"You had a way of putting it that I'd like you to repeat."

"Well, it's embarrassing, but I said that sharing is caring."

The audience laughed. Bailey smiled warmly.

"I don't think it's embarrassing. This expression has been

around for a while, but it applies here, doesn't it, Mae? Maybe uniquely apropos."

"I think it's simple. If you care about your fellow human beings, you share what you know with them. You share what you see. You give them anything you can. If you care about their plight, their suffering, their curiosity, their right to learn and know anything the world contains, you share with them. You share what you have and what you see and what you know. To me, the logic there is undeniable."

The audience cheered, and while they did so, three new words, SHARING IS CARING, appeared on the screen, below the previous three. Bailey was shaking his head, amazed.

"I love that. Mae, you have a way with words. And there's one more statement you made that I think should cap off what I think everyone here would agree has been a wonderfully enlightening and inspiring talk."

The audience clapped warmly.

"We were talking about what you saw as the impulse to keep things to yourself."

"Well, it's not something I'm proud of, and I don't think it rises above the level of simple selfishness. Now I really understand that. I understand that we're obligated, as humans, to share what we see and know. And that all knowledge must be democratically accessible."

"It's the natural state of information to be free."

"Right."

"We all have a right to know everything we can. We all collectively own the accumulated knowledge of the world."

"Right," Mae said. "So what happens if I deprive anyone or

everyone of something I know? Aren't I stealing from my fellow humans?"

"Indeed," Bailey said, nodding earnestly. Mae looked to the audience, and saw the entire first row, the only faces visible, nodding, too.

"And given your way with words, Mae, I wonder if you can tell us this third and last revelation you made. What did you say?"

"Well, I said, privacy is theft."

Bailey turned to the audience. "Isn't that an interesting way of putting it, guys? 'Privacy is theft.'" The words now appeared on the screen behind him, in great white letters:

PRIVACY IS THEFT

Mae turned to look at the three lines together. She blinked back tears, seeing it all there. Had she really thought of all that herself?

SECRETS ARE LIES
SHARING IS CARING
PRIVACY IS THEFT

Mae's throat was tight, dry. She knew she couldn't speak, so she hoped Bailey wouldn't ask her to. As if sensing how she felt, that she was overcome, he winked at her and turned to the audience.

"Let's thank Mae for her candor, her brilliance and her consummate humanity, can we please?"

The audience was on its feet. Mae's face was on fire. She didn't know if she should sit or stand. She stood briefly, then felt silly, so sat down again, and waved from her lap.

Somewhere in the stampeding applause, Bailey managed to announce the capper to it all—that Mae, in the interest of sharing all she saw and could offer the world, would be going transparent immediately.

BOOK II

IT WAS A BIZARRE creature, ghostlike, vaguely menacing and never still, but no one who stood before it could look away. Mae was hypnotized by it, its slashing form, its fins like blades, its milky skin and wool-grey eyes. It was certainly a shark, it had its distinctive shape, its malevolent stare, but this was a new species, omnivorous and blind. Stenton had brought it back from his trip to the Marianas Trench, in the Circle submersible. The shark was not the only discovery—Stenton had retrieved heretofore unknown jellyfishes, seahorses, manta rays, all of them near-translucent, ethereal in their movements, all on display in a series of enormous aquariums he'd had constructed, nearly overnight, to house them.

Mae's tasks were to show her watchers the beasts, to explain when necessary and to be, through the lens worn around her neck, a window into this new world, and the world, generally, of the Circle. Every morning Mae put on a necklace, much like Stewart's, but lighter, smaller, and with the lens worn over her heart.

There, it presented the steadiest view, and the widest. It saw everything that Mae saw, and often more. The quality of the raw video was such that viewers could zoom, pan, freeze and enhance. The audio was carefully engineered to focus on her immediate conversations, to record but make secondary any ambient sound or background voices. In essence, it meant that any room she was in was scannable by anyone watching; they could focus in on any corner, and, with some effort, isolate and listen to any other conversation.

There was to be a feeding for all of Stenton's discoveries any minute, but the animal she and her watchers were particularly interested in was the shark. She hadn't yet seen it eat, but word was it was insatiable and very quick. Though blind, it found its meals immediately, no matter how big or small, alive or dead, and digested them with alarming speed. One minute a herring or squid would be dropped into the tank with it, and moments later the shark would deposit, on the aquarium floor, all that remained of that animal—a tiny grainy substance that looked like ash. This act was made more fascinating given the shark's translucent skin, which allowed an unfettered view into its digestive process.

She heard a droplet through her earpiece. "Feeding moved back to 1:02," a voice said. It was now 12:51.

Mae looked down the dark hallway, to the three other aquariums, each of them slightly smaller than the one before it. The hall was kept entirely unlit, to best highlight the electric-blue aquariums and the fog-white creatures within.

"Let's move over to the octopus for now," the voice said.

The main audio feed, from Additional Guidance to Mae, was provided via a tiny earpiece, and this allowed the AG team to give her occasional directions—to suggest she drop by the Machine Age, for example, to show her watchers a new, solar-powered consumer drone that could travel unlimited distances, across continents and seas, provided adequate exposure to sun; she'd done that visit earlier this day. This was a good portion of her day, the touring of various departments, the introduction of new products, either Circle-made or Circle-endorsed. It ensured that every day was different, and had, in the six weeks she'd been transparent, exposed Mae to virtually every corner of the campus—from the Age of Sail to the Old Kingdom, where they were, on a lark more than anything, working on a project to attach a camera to every remaining polar bear.

"Let's see the octopus," Mae said to her viewers.

She moved over to a round glass structure sixteen feet high and twelve feet in diameter. Inside, a pale spineless being, the hue of a cloud but veined in blue and green, was feeling around, guessing and flailing, like a near-blind man fumbling for his glasses.

"This is a relative of the telescope octopus," Mae said, "but this one has never been captured alive before."

Its shape seemed to change continuously, balloon-like and bulbous one moment, as if inflating itself, confident and growing, then the next it would be shrinking, spinning, stretching and reaching, unsure of its true form.

"As you can see, its true size is very hard to discern. One second it seems like you could hold it in your hand, and the next it encompasses most of the tank."

The creature's tentacles seemed to want to know everything: the shape of the glass, the topography of the coral below, the feel of the water all around.

"He's almost endearing," Mae said, watching the octopus reach from wall to wall, spreading itself like a net. Something about its curiosity gave it a sentient presence, full of doubt and wanting.

"Stenton found this one first," she said about the octopus, which was now rising from the floor, slowly, flamboyantly. "It came from behind his submersible and shot in front, as if it were asking him to follow. You can see how fast it might have moved." The octopus was now careening around the aquarium, propelling itself in motions like the opening and closing of an umbrella.

Mae checked the time. It was 12:54. She had a few minutes to kill. She kept her lens on the octopus.

She was under no illusion that every minute of every day was equally scintillating to her watchers. In the weeks Mae had been transparent, there had been downtime, a good deal of it, but her task, primarily, was to provide an open window into life at the Circle, the sublime and the banal. "Here we are in the gym," she might say, showing viewers the health club for the first time. "People are running and sweating and devising ways to check each other out without getting caught." Then, an hour later, she might be eating lunch, casually and without commentary, across from other Circlers, all of them behaving, or attempting to, as if no one was watching at all. Most of her fellow Circlers were happy to be on camera, and after a few days all Circlers knew that it was a part of their job at the Circle, and an elemental part of the Circle, period. If they were to be a company espousing transparency, and the global and unending advantages of open access, they needed to be living that ideal, always and everywhere, and especially on campus.

Thankfully, there was enough to illuminate and celebrate within the Circle gates. The fall and winter had brought the inevitable, all of it, with blitzkrieg speed. All over campus there were signs that hinted at imminent Completion. The messages were cryptic, meant to pique curiosity and discussion. *What would Completion mean?* Staffers were asked to contemplate this, submit answers, and write on the idea boards. *Everyone on Earth has a Circle account!* one popular message said. *The Circle solves world hunger,* said another. *The Circle helps me find my ancestors,* said yet another. *No data, human or numerical or emotional or historical, is ever lost again.* That one had been written and signed by Bailey himself. The most popular was *The Circle helps me find myself.*

So many of these developments had been long in the planning stages at the Circle, but the timing had never been quite so right, and the momentum was too strong to be resisted. Now, with 90 percent of Washington transparent, and the remaining 10 percent wilting under the suspicion of their colleagues and constituents, the question beat down on them like an angry sun: What are you hiding? The plan was that most Circlers would be transparent within the year, but for the time being, to work out the bugs and get everyone used to the idea, it was just Mae and Stewart, but his experiment had been largely eclipsed by Mae's. Mae was young, and moved far quicker than Stewart, and had her voice—watchers loved it, comparing it to music, calling it *like woodwind* and *a wonderful acoustic strum*—and Mae was loving it, too, feeling daily the affection of millions flow through her.

It took getting used to, though, starting with the basic working of the equipment. The camera was light, and after a few days, Mae could barely sense the weight of the lens, no heavier than a locket, over her breastbone. They'd tried various ways to keep it on her chest, including velcro attached to her clothing, but nothing was as effective, and simple, as simply hanging it around her neck. The second adjustment, one she found continually fascinating and occasionally jarring, was seeing—through a small frame on her right wrist—what the camera was seeing. She'd all but forgotten about her left-wrist health monitor, but the camera had made essential the use of this, a second, right-wrist bracelet. It was the same size and material as her left, but with a larger screen to accommodate video and a summation of all of her data on her usual screens. With a bracelet on each wrist, each snug and with a brushed-metal finish, she felt like Wonder Woman and knew something of her power—though the idea was too ridiculous to tell anyone about.

On her left wrist, she saw her heartbeat; on her right, she could see what her watchers were seeing—a real-time view from her lens, which allowed her to make any necessary adjustments to the view. It also gave her current watcher numbers, her rankings and ratings, and highlighted the most recent and most popular comments from viewers. At that moment, standing before the octopus, Mae had 441,762 watchers, which was a little above her average, but still less than what she'd hoped for while revealing Stenton's deep-sea discoveries. The other numbers displayed were unsurprising. She was averaging 845,029 unique visitors to her live footage in any given day, and had 2.1 million followers to her Zing feed. She no longer had to worry about staying in the T2K; her visibility, and the immense power of her audience, guaranteed stratospheric Conversion Rates and Retail Raws, and ensured she was always in the top ten.

"Let's see the seahorses," Mae said, and moved to the next aquarium. There, amid a pastel bouquet of coral and flowing fronds of blue seaweed, she saw hundreds, maybe thousands, of tiny beings, no bigger than the fingers of a child, hiding in nooks, clinging to the foliage. "Not particularly friendly fish, these guys. Wait, are they even fish?" she asked, and looked to her wrist, where a watcher had already sent the answer. *Absolutely a fish! Class Actinopterygii. Same as cod and tuna.*

"Thank you, Susanna Win from Greensboro!" Mae said, and rezinged the information to her followers. "Now let's see if we can find the daddy of all these baby seahorses. As you might know, the male seahorse is the one that carries the offspring. The hundreds of babies you see were birthed just after the daddy arrived here. Now where is he?" Mae walked around the aquarium, and soon found him, about the size of her hand, resting at the bottom of the tank, leaning against the glass. "I think he's hiding," Mae said, "but he doesn't seem to know we're on the other side of the glass here, and can see everything."

She checked her wrist and adjusted the angle of her lens a bit, to get the best look at the fragile fish. He was curled with his back to her, looking exhausted and shy. She put her face, and lens, up to the glass, so close to him she could see the tiny clouds in his intelligent eyes, the unlikely freckles on his delicate snout. He was an improbable creature, a terrible swimmer, built like a Chinese lantern and utterly without defense. Her wrist highlighted a zing with exceptionally high ratings. *The croissant of the animal kingdom,* it said, and Mae repeated it aloud. But despite his fragility, somehow he had already reproduced, had given life to a hundred more like himself, while the octopus and the shark had traced the contours of their tanks and eaten. Not that the seahorse seemed to care. He was apart from his progeny, as if having no clue where they came from, and no interest in what happened to them.

Mae checked the time. 1:02. Additional Guidance spoke through her earpiece: "Shark feeding ready."

"Okay," Mae said, glancing at her wrist. "I'm seeing a bunch of requests that we get back to the shark, and it's after one, so I'm thinking we'll do that." She left the seahorse, who turned to her, briefly, as if not wanting to see her go.

Mae made her way back to the first and largest aquarium, which held Stenton's shark. Above the aquarium, she saw a young woman, with curly black hair and cuffed white jeans, standing atop a sleek red ladder.

"Hello," Mae said to her. "I'm Mae."

The woman seemed ready to say "I know that," but then, as if remembering they were on camera, adopted a studied, performative tone. "Hello Mae, I'm Georgia, and I'll be feeding Mr. Stenton's shark now."

And then, though it was blind, and there was no food yet in the tank, the shark seemed to sense a feast was at hand. It began turning like a cyclone, rising ever-closer to the surface. Mae's watchers had already risen by 42,000.

"*Some*one's hungry," Mae said.

The shark, which had seemed only passingly menacing before, now appeared vicious and wholly sentient, the embodiment of the predatory instinct. Georgia was attempting to look confident, competent, but Mae saw fear and trepidation in her eyes. "Ready down there?" she asked, without taking her eyes off the shark making its way toward her.

"We're ready," Mae said.

"Okay, I'm going to feed the shark something new today. As you know, he's been fed all kinds of stuff, from salmon to herring to jellyfish. He's devoured everything with equal enthusiasm. Yesterday we tried a manta, which we didn't expect him to enjoy, but he didn't hesitate, and ate with gusto. So today we're again experimenting with a new food. As you can see," she said, and Mae noticed that the bucket she carried was made of lucite, and inside she saw something blue and brown, with too many legs. She heard it ticking against the bucket walls: a lobster. Mae had never thought of sharks eating lobsters, but she couldn't see why they wouldn't.

"Here we have a regular Maine lobster, which we're not sure if this shark is equipped to eat."

Georgia was perhaps trying to put on a good show, but even Mae was nervous about how long she was holding the lobster over the water. *Drop it,* Mae thought to herself. *Please drop it.*

But Georgia was holding it over the water, presumably for the benefit of Mae and her viewers. The shark, meanwhile, had sensed the lobster, had no doubt mapped its shape with whatever sensors it possessed, and was circling quicker, still obedient but at the end of its patience.

"Some sharks can process the shells of crustaceans like this, some can't," Georgia said, now dangling the lobster such that its claw was lazily touching the surface. *Drop it, please,* Mae thought. *Please drop it now.*

"So I'll just drop this little guy into—"

But before she could finish her sentence the shark had risen up and snatched the lobster from the caretaker's hand. By the time Georgia let out a squeal and grabbed her fingers, as if to count them, the shark was already back in the middle of the tank, the lobster engulfed in its jaws, the crustacean's white flesh spraying from the shark's wide mouth.

"Did he get you?" Mae asked.

Georgia shook her head, holding back tears. "Almost." She rubbed her hand as if it had been burned.

The lobster had been consumed, and Mae saw something gruesome and wonderful: the lobster was being processed, inside the shark, in front of her, with lightning speed and incredible clarity. Mae saw the lobster broken into dozens, then hundreds of pieces, in the shark's mouth, then saw those pieces make their way through the shark's gullet, its stomach, its intestines. In minutes the lobster had been reduced to a grainy, particulate substance. The waste left the shark and fell like snow to the aquarium floor.

"Looks like he's still hungry," Georgia said. She was atop the ladder again, but now with a different lucite container. While Mae had been watching the digestion of the lobster, Georgia had retrieved a second meal.

"Is that what I think it is?" Mae asked.

"This is a Pacific sea turtle," Georgia said, holding up the container that held the reptile. It was about as big as Georgia's torso, painted in a patchwork of green and blue and brown, a beautiful animal unable to move in the tight space. Georgia opened the door at one end of the container, as if inviting the turtle to exit if he so chose. He chose to stay where he was.

"There's little chance our shark has encountered one of these, given the difference in their habitats," Georgia said. "This turtle would have no reason to spend time where Stenton's shark dwells, and the shark surely has never seen the light-dappled areas where the turtles live."

Mae wanted to ask if Georgia were truly about to feed that turtle to the shark. Its eyes had beheld the predator below, and was now, with the slow energy it could harness, pushing its way to the back of the container. Feeding this kindly creature to the shark, no matter the necessity or scientific benefit, would not please many of Mae's watchers. Already zings were coming through her wrist. *Please don't kill that turtle. It looks like my granddad!* There was a second thread, though, that insisted the shark, which was not much bigger than the turtle, would not be able to swallow or digest the reptile, with its impenetrable shell. But just when Mae was about to question the imminent feeding, an AG voice came through Mae's earpiece. "Hold tight. Stenton wants to see this happen."

In the tank, the shark was circling again, looking every bit as lean and ravenous as before. The lobster had been nothing to it, a meaningless snack. Now it rose closer to Georgia, knowing the main course was approaching.

"Here we go," Georgia said, and tilted the container until the turtle began sliding, slowly, toward the neon water, which was swirling beneath him—the shark's turning had created a vortex. When the container was vertical, and the turtle's head had cleared the lucite threshold, the shark could wait no longer. It rose up, grabbed the turtle's head in its jaws, and pulled it under. And like the lobster, the turtle was consumed in seconds, but this time it took a shape-shifting that the crustacean hadn't required. The shark seemed to unhook its jaw, doubling the size of its mouth, enabling it to easily subsume the whole of the turtle in one swallow. Georgia was narrating, saying something about how many sharks, when eating turtles, will turn their stomachs inside out, vomiting the shells after digesting the fleshy parts of the reptile. But Stenton's shark had other methods. The shell seemed to dissolve inside the shark's mouth and stomach like a cracker soaked in saliva. And in less than a minute, the turtle, all of it, had been turned to ash. It exited the shark as had the lobster, in flakes that fell ponderously to the aquarium floor, joining, and indistinguishable from, those that had come before.

Mae was watching this when she saw a figure, nearly a silhouette, on the other side of the glass, beyond the aquarium's far wall. His body was just a shadow, his face invisible, but then, for a moment, the light from above reflected on the circling shark's skin, and revealed the figure's face.

It was Kalden.

Mae hadn't seen him in a month, and since her transparency, hadn't heard any word from him. Annie had been in Amsterdam, then China, then Japan, then back to Geneva, and so hadn't had time to focus on Kalden, but the two of them had traded occasional messages about him. How concerned should they be about this unknown man?

But then he'd disappeared.

Now he was standing, looking at her, unmoving.

She wanted to call out, but then worried. Who was he? Would calling to him, capturing him on camera, create some scene? Would he flee? She was still in shock from the shark's digestion of the turtle, from its dull-eyed wrath, and she found she had no voice, no strength to say Kalden's name. So she stared at him, and he stared at her, and she had the thought that if she could catch him on her camera, perhaps she could show this to Annie, and that might lead to some clarity, some identification. But when Mae looked to her wrist, she saw only the darkest form, his face obscured. Perhaps her lens couldn't see him, was watching from a different angle. As she tracked his shape on her wrist, he backed away and walked off into the shadows.

Meanwhile, Georgia had been nattering about the shark and what they'd witnessed, and Mae hadn't caught any of it. But now she was standing atop her ladder, waving, hoping that Mae was finished, because she had nothing left to feed the animal. The show was over.

"Okay then," Mae said, thankful for the chance to get away and to follow Kalden. She said goodbye and thanks to Georgia, and walked briskly through the dark hallway.

She caught sight of his silhouette leaving through a faraway door, and she picked up her pace, careful not to shake her lens or call out. The door he'd slipped through led to the newsroom, which would be a logical enough place for Mac to be visiting next. "Let's see what's going on in the newsroom," she said, knowing all within would be aware of her approach in the twenty steps it would take her to get there. She also knew that the SeeChange cameras in the hallway, over the doorway, would have caught Kalden, and she'd know sooner or later if it was actually him. Every movement within the Circle was caught on one camera or another, usually three, and reconstructing anyone's movements, after the fact, was only a few minutes' work.

As she approached the newsroom door, Mae thought of Kalden's hands upon her. His hands reaching low, pulling himself into her. She heard the low rumble of his voice. His taste, like some wet fresh fruit. What if she found him? She couldn't take him to the bathroom. Or could she? She would find a way.

She opened the door to the newsroom, a wide space Bailey had modeled on old-time newspaper offices, with a hundred low cubicles, news tickers and clocks everywhere, each desk with a retro analog telephone, a row of white buttons below the numbers, blinking arrhythmically. There were old printers, fax machines, telex devices, letterpresses. The decor, of course, was for show. All the retro machines were nonfunctional. The news gatherers, whose faces were now upon Mae, smiling, saying hello to her and her watchers, were able to do most of their reporting via SeeChange. There were now over a hundred million cameras functional and accessible around the world, making in-person reporting unnecessarily expensive and dangerous, to say nothing of the carbon expenditures.

As Mae walked through the newsroom, the staff waved to her, unsure if this was an official visit. Mae waved back, scanning the room, knowing she appeared distracted. Where was Kalden? There was only one other exit, so Mae rushed through the room, nodding and greeting, until she came to the door on the far end. She opened it, flinching at the bright light of day, and saw him. He was crossing the wide green lawn, passing the new sculpture by that Chinese dissident—she remembered she should highlight it soon, maybe even today—and just then he turned briefly, as if checking to see if Mae was still following. Her eyes met his, provoking a tiny smile before he turned again and walked quickly around the Period of Five Dynasties.

"Where are you headed?" the voice in her ear asked.

"Sorry. No place. I was just. Never mind."

Mae was allowed, of course, to go where she pleased—her meanderings were what so many watchers appreciated most—but the Additional Guidance office still liked to check in from time to time. As she stood in the sunlight, Circlers all around, she heard her phone ring. She checked her wrist; there was no caller identified. She knew it could only be Kalden.

"Hello?" she said.

"We have to meet," he said.

"Excuse me?" she asked.

"Your watchers can't hear me. They only hear you. Right now your engineers are wondering why the incoming audio isn't working. They'll fix it in a few minutes." His voice was tense, shaky. "So listen. Most of what's happening must stop. I'm serious. The Circle is almost complete and Mae, you have to believe me that this will be bad for you, for me, for humanity. When can we meet? If it has to be in the bathroom that's fine with me—"

Mae hung up.

"Sorry about that," said AG through her earpiece. "Somehow the incoming audio wasn't working. We're working on it. Who was it?"

Mae knew she couldn't lie. She wasn't sure if anyone had indeed heard Kalden. "Some lunatic," Mae improvised, proud of herself. "Babbling about the end of the world."

Mae checked her wrist. Already people were wondering what

had happened and how. The most popular zing: *Tech problems at Circle HQ? Next: Santa forgets Christmas?*

"Tell them the truth, as always," AG said.

"Okay, I have no idea what just happened," Mae said aloud. "When I do, I'll let you all know."

But she was shaken. She was still standing, in the sunlight, waving occasionally to Circlers noticing her. She knew her watchers might wonder what was happening next, where she was going. She didn't want to check her wrist, knowing that the comments would be perplexed and even concerned. Off in the distance, she saw what looked like a game of croquet, and alighting on an idea, she made her way to it.

"Now, as you all know," she said when she was close enough to see and wave to the four players, who she realized were two Circlers and a pair of visitors from Russia, "we do not always play here at the Circle. Sometimes we have to work, which this group is demonstrating. I don't want to disturb them, but I can assure you that what they're doing involves problem-solving and complex algorithms and will result in the improving of the products and services we can provide to you. Let's soak this in."

That would give her a few minutes to think. Periodically, she would focus her lens on something like this, a game or demonstration or speech, and this might allow her mind to wander, while the watchers watched. She checked the view on her wrist, and saw that her watchers, 432,028, were within the average, and there were no urgent comments, so she permitted herself three minutes before she had to retake control of the feed. With a wide smile—for she was surely visible on three or four outdoor SeeChanges—she took a breath. This was a new skill she'd acquired, the ability to look, to the outside world, utterly serene and even cheerful, while, in her skull, all was chaos. She wanted to call Annie. But she couldn't call Annie. She wanted Kalden. She wanted to be alone with Kalden. She wanted to be back in that bathroom sitting on him, feeling the crown of him push through. But he was not normal. He was some kind of spy here. Some kind of anarchist, doomsayer. What had he meant when he warned of the completion of the Circle? She didn't even know what Completion meant. No one did. The Wise Men had recently begun to hint about it, though. One day, in new tiles all over campus, cryptic messages had appeared: THINK COMPLETION and COMPLETE THE CIRCLE and THE CIRCLE MUST BE WHOLE, and these slogans had stirred up the desired intrigue. But no one knew what it meant, and the Wise Men weren't telling.

Mae checked the time. She'd been watching the croquet match for ninety seconds. She could only reasonably hold this pose for another minute or two. So what was her responsibility to report this call? Had anyone actually heard what Kalden had said? What if they had? What if this was some kind of test, to see if she'd report a rogue call? Maybe this was part of Completion—a test like this to measure her loyalty, to thwart anyone or anything that would impede Completion? Oh shit, she thought. She wanted to talk to Annie, but she knew she couldn't. She thought of her parents, who would give good counsel, but their house was transparent, too, full of SeeChange cameras—a condition of her father's treatment. Maybe she could go there, meet *them* in the bathroom? No. She hadn't, actually, been in touch with them for a few days. They had warned her they were having some technical difficulties, would be back in touch soon, that they loved her, and then hadn't answered any of her messages for the last forty-eight hours. And in that time, she hadn't checked the cameras in their house. She had to do that. She made a mental note. Maybe she could call them? Make sure they were okay, and then hint, somehow, that she wanted to talk to them about something very unsettling and personal?

No, no. This was all mad. She'd gotten a random call from a man she now knew to be nuts. Oh shit, she thought, hoping no one could guess at the chaos in her mind. She relished being where she was, visible like this, a conduit like this, a guide to her watchers, but this responsibility, this unnecessary intrigue, it crippled her. And when she felt this paralysis, caught between entirely too many possibilities and unknowns, there was only one place she felt right.

At 1:44 Mae entered the Renaissance, felt, above her, the greeting of the slowly turning Calder, and took the elevator to the fourth floor. Just rising through the building calmed her. Walking down the catwalk, the atrium visible below, brought her great peace. This, Customer Experience, was home, where there were no unknowns.

At first, Mae had been surprised when they'd asked her to continue working, at least a few hours a week, at CE. She'd enjoyed her time there, yes, but she assumed transparency would mean she'd leave that far behind. "That's exactly the point," Bailey had explained. "I think Number One, it'll keep you connected with the ground-level work you did here. Number Two, I think your followers and viewers will appreciate you continuing to do this essential work. It'll be a very moving act of humility, don't you think?"

Mae was at once aware of the power she wielded—instantly, she became one of the three most visible Circlers—and determined to wear it lightly. So Mae had found time in each week to return to her old pod, and to her old desk, which they'd left vacant. There had been changes made—there were now nine screens, and the CEs were encouraged to be delving far deeper with their clients, to reciprocate in far-reaching ways—but the work was essentially the same, and Mae found that she appreciated the rhythm of it, the almost meditative quality of doing something she knew in her bones, and she found herself being drawn to CE at times of stress or calamity.

And so, in her third week of transparency, on a sunny Wednesday, she planned on putting in ninety minutes at CE before the rest of the day overtook her. At three she had to give a tour of the Napoleonic Era, where they were modeling the elimination of physical money—the trackability of internet currency would eliminate huge swaths of crime overnight—and at four, she was supposed to highlight the new musicians' residences on campus—twenty-two fully equipped apartments where musicians, especially those who couldn't count on making a living through sales of their music, could live for free and play regularly for the Circlers. That would take her through the afternoon. At five, she was supposed to attend an announcement from the latest politician to go clear. Why they continued to make these proclamations with fanfare—they were now calling them Clarifications—was a mystery to her and many of her watchers. There were tens of thousands of clear elected officials all over the country and world, and the movement was less a novelty and more of an inevitability; most observers predicted full governmental transparency, at least in democracies—and with SeeChange there would soon be no other kind—within eighteen months. After the Clarification, there was an improv comedy battle on campus, a fundraiser for a school in rural Pakistan, a wine tasting, and finally an all-campus barbecue, with music by a Peruvian trance choir.

Mae walked into her old pod room, where her own words—SECRETS ARE LIES; SHARING IS CARING; PRIVACY IS THEFT—had been cast in steel and dominated an entire wall. The place was bursting with newbies, all of whom looked up, alarmed and happy to see her there among them. She waved to them, gave them a theatrical faux-curtsey, saw Jared standing in the doorway to his office, and waved at him, too. Then, determined to do her work without fanfare, Mae sat down, logged on and opened the chute. She answered three queries in rapid succession, with an average of 99. Her fourth client was the first to notice that it was Mae, Transparent Mae, handling her query.

I'm watching you! the client, a media buyer for a sporting-goods importer in New Jersey, wrote. Her name was Janice, and she couldn't get over the fact she could watch Mae typing the answer to her query in real-time, on her screen, right next to where she was receiving Mae's typed answer. *Hall of mirrors!!* she wrote.

After Janice, Mae had a series of clients who did not know it was her answering their queries, and Mae found that this bothered her. One of them, a T-shirt distributor from Orlando named Nanci, asked her to join her professional network, and Mae readily agreed. Jared had told her about a new level of reciprocation encouraged among the CE staff. If you send a survey, be prepared to answer one yourself. And so after she joined the Orlando T-shirt distributor's professional network, she got another message from Nanci. She asked Mae to respond to a short questionnaire about her preferences in casual apparel, and Mae agreed. She linked to the questionnaire, which she realized was not short; it encompassed fully 120 questions. But Mae was happy to answer them, feeling her opinion mattered and was being heard, and this kind of reciprocation would engender loyalty from Nanci and all who Nanci came into contact with. After she answered the survey questions, Nanci sent her a profuse thank-you, and told her she could choose the T-shirt of her choice, and directed Mae to her consumer site. Mae said she would choose at a later time, but Nanci wrote back, telling Mae that she could not wait to see which shirt Mae would choose. Mae checked her clock; she'd been on the Orlando query for eight minutes, far surpassing the new guideline per query, which was 2.5.

Mae knew she would have to power through the next ten or so queries to get back to an acceptable average. She went to Nanci's site, chose a shirt that featured a cartoon dog in a superhero costume, and Nanci told her that it was a great choice. Mae then took the next query, and was in the process of an easy boilerplate conversion, when another message came from Nanci. *Sorry to be Ms. Sensitive, but after I invited you to join my professional network, you didn't ask me to join* your *professional network, and though I know I'm just a nobody in Orlando, I felt like I had to tell you that it made me feel devalued.* Mae told Nanci she had no intentions of making her feel devalued, that things were just busy at the Circle, and that she had spaced on this essential reciprocation, which she quickly remedied. Mae finished her next query, got a 98, and was following up on that one, when she got another message from Nanci. *Did you see my message on the professional network?* Mae looked at all her feeds and saw no message from Nanci. *I posted it on the message board of* your *professional network!* she said. And so Mae went to that page, which she didn't visit often, and saw that Nanci had written, *Hello stranger!* Mae typed *Hello yourself! But you're no stranger!!* and thought for a moment that that would mean the end of their exchange, but she paused on the page, briefly, with a sense that Nanci was not quite finished. And she wasn't. *So glad you wrote back! Thought you might be offended that I called you 'Stranger.' Promise you weren't peeved?* Mae promised Nanci that she was not peeved, answered with an XO, sent her ten subsequent smiles, and went back to her queries, hoping that Nanci was satisfied and happy and that they were cool. She took three more queries, followed up with surveys and saw that her average was at 99. This provoked a flurry of congratulatory zings, watchers happy to see Mae's commitment, still, to the day-to-day tasks at the Circle and essential to the operation of the world. So many of her watchers, they reminded her, were working at desk jobs, too, and because she continued to do this work, voluntarily and with evident joy, they saw her as a role model and inspiration. And this felt good. This felt truly valuable to Mae. The customers made her better. And serving them while transparent made her far better. She expected this. She was apprised by Stewart that when thousands, or even millions, are watching, you perform your best self. You are cheerier, more positive, more polite, more generous, more inquisitive. But he had not told her of the smaller, improving alterations to her behavior.

The first time the camera redirected her actions was when she went to the kitchen for something to eat. The image on her wrist showed the interior of the refrigerator as she scanned for a snack. Normally, she would have grabbed a chilled brownie, but seeing the image of her hand reaching for it, and seeing what everyone else would be seeing, she pulled back. She closed the fridge, and from the bowl on the counter, she selected a packet of almonds, and left the kitchen. Later that day, a headache appeared—caused, she thought, by eating less chocolate than usual. She reached into her bag, where she kept a few single-serving aspirin packets, but again, on her screen, she saw what everyone was seeing. She saw a hand searching her bag, clawing, and instantly she felt desperate and wretched, like some kind of pill-popping addict.

She did without. Every day she'd done without things she didn't want to want. Things she didn't need. She'd given up soda, energy drinks, processed foods. At Circle social events, she nursed one drink only, and tried each time to leave it unfinished. Anything immoderate would provoke a flurry of zings of concern, so she stayed within the bounds of moderation. And she found it freeing. She was liberated from bad behavior. She was liberated from doing things she didn't want to be doing, eating and drinking things that did her no good. Since she'd gone transparent, she'd become more noble. People called her a role model. Mothers said their daughters looked up to her, and this gave her more of a feeling of responsibility, and that feeling of responsibility—to the Circlers, to their clients and partners, to the youth who saw inspiration in her—kept her grounded and fueled her days.

She was reminded of the Circle's own survey questions, and

she put on her survey headset and got started. To her watchers she was expressing her opinions constantly, yes, and felt far more influential than before, but something about the tidy rhythm and call-and-response nature of the surveys felt missing. She took another customer query, and then nodded. The distant bell rang. She nodded.

"Thank you. Are you happy with the state of airport security?"

"Smile," Mae said.

"Thank you. Would you welcome change in airport security procedures?"

"Yes."

"Thank you."

"Does the state of airport security dissuade you from flying more often?"

"Yes."

"Thank you."

The questions continued, and she was able to get through ninety-four of them before she allowed herself to lapse. Soon the voice arrived, unchanged.

"Mae."

She ignored it on purpose.

"Mae."

Her name, spoken by her voice, continued to hold its power over her. And she hadn't discovered why.

"Mae."

It sounded, this time, like some purer version of herself.

"Mae."

She looked down to her bracelet, seeing a number of zings asking if she was okay. She knew she had to respond, lest her watchers think she'd lost her mind. This was one of the many small adjustments she had to get used to—now there were thousands out there seeing what she saw, having access to her health data, hearing her voice, seeing her face—she was always visible through one or another of the campus SeeChange cameras, in addition to the one on her monitor—and so when anything deviated from her normal buoyancy, people noticed.

"Mae."

She wanted to hear it again, so she said nothing.

"Mae."

It was a young woman's voice, a young woman's voice that sounded bright and fierce and capable of anything.

"Mae."

It was a better, more indomitable version of herself.

"Mae."

She felt stronger every time she heard it.

She stayed at CE until five, when she showed her watchers the newest Clarification, the governor of Arizona, and enjoyed the surprise transparency of the governor's entire staff— something that many officials were doing, to ensure to their constituents that deals were not being done, in darkness, outside the light of the clear leader. At the Clarifying event, Mae met up with Renata and Denise and Josiah—these Circlers who had once wielded some power over her and now were her acolytes—and afterward, they all had dinner in the Glass Eatery. There was little reason to leave campus for meals given that Bailey, hoping to engender more discussions and brain-sharing and socialization among Circlers, had instituted a new policy, whereby all food would be not only free, as it always had been, but prepared daily by a different notable chef. The chefs were happy for the exposure—thousands of Circlers smiling, zinging, posting photos—and the program was instantly and wildly popular and the cafeterias were overflowing with people and, presumably, ideas.

Among the bustle that night, Mae ate, feeling unsteady, Kalden's words and cryptic messages still rattling in her head. She was glad, then, for the distractions of the night. The improv comedy battle was appropriately terrible and funny despite its wall-to-wall incompetence, the Pakistan fundraiser was thoroughly inspiring—the event was able to amass 2.3 million smiles for the school—and finally there was the barbecue, where Mae allowed herself a second glass of wine before settling into her dorm.

The room had been hers for six weeks now. It no longer made sense to drive back to her apartment, which was expensive and, last time she'd been there, after being gone for eight days, had mice. So she gave it up, and became one of the hundred Settlers, Circlers who had moved onto campus permanently. The advantages were obvious and the waiting list was now 1,209 names long. There was room on campus now for 288 Circlers, and the company had just bought a nearby building, a former factory, planning to convert it into 500 more rooms. Mae's had been upgraded and now had fully smart appliances, wallscreens and shades, everything centrally monitored. The room was cleaned daily and the refrigerator stocked with both her standard items—tracked via Homie—and products in beta. She could have anything she wanted so long as she provided feedback to the manufacturers.

She washed her face and brushed her teeth and settled into the cloud-white bed. Transparency was optional after ten p.m., and she usually went dark after her teeth-brushing, which she found people interested in generally, and, she believed, might promote good dental health among her younger watchers. At 10:11 p.m., she said good night to her watchers—there were only 98,027 at that point, a few thousand of whom reciprocated her goodnight wishes—lifted the lens over her head and placed it in its case. She was allowed to turn off the SeeChange cameras in the room, but she found she rarely did. She knew that the footage she might gather, herself, for instance about movements during sleep, could be valuable someday, so she left the cameras on. It had taken a few weeks to get used to sleeping with her wrist monitors—she'd scratched her face one night, and cracked her right screen another—but Circle engineers had improved the design, replacing the rigid screens with more flexible, unbreakable ones, and now she felt incomplete without them.

She sat up in bed, knowing that it usually took her an hour or so to make her way to sleep. She turned on the wallscreen, planning to check on her parents. But their SeeChange cameras were all dark. She sent them a zing, expecting no answer and getting none. She sent a message to Annie but got no response. She paged through her Zing feed, reading a few funny ones, and, because she'd lost six pounds since going transparent, she spent twenty minutes looking for a new skirt and T-shirt, and somewhere in the eighth site she visited, she felt the tear opening up in her again. For no good reason, she checked to see if Mercer's site was still down, and found it was. She looked for any recent mention of him online or news of his whereabouts, and found none. The tear was growing within her, opening quickly, a fathomless blackness spreading under her. In her fridge she had some of the sake Francis had introduced her to, so she got up, poured herself far too much, and drank it down. She went to the SeeChange portal and watched feeds from beaches in Sri Lanka and Brazil, feeling calmer, feeling warmer, and then remembered that a few thousand college kids, calling themselves ChangeSeers, had spread themselves all over the planet, installing cameras in the most remote regions. So for a time she watched the view from a camera in a Namibian desert village, a pair of women preparing a meal, their children playing in the background, but after a few minutes watching, she found the tear opening wider, the underwater screams getting louder, an unbearable hiss. She looked again for Kalden, spelling his name in new and irrational ways, scanning, for forty-five minutes, the company directory by face, finding no one like him at all. She turned off the SeeChange cameras, poured more sake, drank it down and got into bed and, thinking of Kalden and his hands, his thin legs, his long fingers, she circled her nipples with her left hand while, with her right, she moved her underwear to the side and simulated the movements of a tongue, of his tongue. It had no effect. But the sake was draining her mind of worry, and finally, at just before twelve, she found something like sleep.

"Okay, everyone," Mae said. The morning was bright and she was feeling chipper enough to try out a phrase she hoped might catch on Circle-wide or beyond. "This is a day like every other day, in that it is unlike any other day!" After she said it, Mae checked her wrist, but saw little sign it had struck a nerve. She was momentarily deflated, but the day itself, the unlimited promise it offered, buoyed her. It was 9:34 a.m., the sun was again bright and warm, and the campus was busy and abuzz. If the Circlers needed any confirmation that they were in the middle of everything that mattered, the day had already brought it. Starting at 8:31, a series of helicopters had shaken the campus, bringing leaders from all the major health insurance companies, world health agencies, the Centers for Disease Control, and every significant pharmaceutical company. Finally, it was rumored, there would be complete information-sharing among all of these previously disconnected and even adversarial entities, and when they were coordinated, and once all the health data they'd collected was shared, most of this made possible through the Circle and more important, TruYou, viruses could be stopped at their sources, diseases would be tracked to their roots. All morning Mae had watched these executives and doctors and officials stride happily through the grounds, heading for the just-built Hippocampus. There, they'd have a day of meetings—private this time, with public forums promised in the future—and, later, there would be a concert from some aging singer-songwriter only Bailey cared for, who had come in the night before, for dinner with the Wise Men.

Most important for Mae, though, was that one of the many morning helicopters contained Annie, who was finally coming home. She'd been gone for almost a month in Europe and China and Japan, ironing out some regulatory wrinkles, meeting with some of the transparent leaders there, the results of which seemed good, judging from the number of smiles Annie had posted on her Zing feed at the trip's conclusion. But more meaningful conversation between Mae and Annie had been difficult. Annie had congratulated her on her transparency, on her *ascension,* as Annie put it, but then had become very busy. Too busy to write notes of consequence, too busy to have phone calls she could be proud of, she'd said. They'd exchanged brief messages every day, but Annie's schedule had been, in her words, *madcap,* and the time difference meant they were rarely in sync and able to exchange anything profound.

Annie had promised to arrive in the morning, direct from Beijing, and Mae was having trouble concentrating while waiting. She'd been watching the helicopters land, squinting high on the rooftops, looking for Annie's yellow head, to no avail. And now she had to spend an hour at the Protagorean Pavilion, a task she knew was important and normally would find fascinating but today felt like an unbreachable wall between herself and her closest friend.

On a granite panel outside the Protagorean Pavilion the building's namesake was quoted loosely: *Humans are the measure of all things.* "More important for our purposes," Mae said, opening the door, "is that now, with the tools available, *humans* can *measure* all things. Isn't that right Terry?"

In front of her stood a tall Korean-American man, Terry Min. "Hello Mae, hello Mae's watchers and followers."

"You cut your hair some new way," Mae said.

With Annie coming back, Mae was feeling loopy, goofy, and Terry was temporarily derailed. He hadn't counted on ad-libs. "Uh, yeah," he said, running his fingers through it.

"It's angular," Mae said.

"Right. It is more angular. Should we go inside?"

"We should."

The designers of the building had taken pains to use organic shapes, to soften the rigid math of the engineers' daily work. The atrium was encased in silver and seemed to undulate, as if they stood at the bottom of an enormous corrugated tube.

"What will we be seeing today, Terry?"

"I thought we'd start with a tour, and then go a bit deeper with some stuff we're doing for the educational sector."

Mae followed Terry through the building, which was more of an engineer's lair than the parts of campus she'd become accustomed to visiting. The trick with her audience was to balance the mundane with the more glamorous parts of the Circle; both were necessary to reveal, and certainly thousands of viewers were more interested in the boiler rooms than the penthouses, but the calibration had to be precise.

They passed Josef and his teeth, and then said hello to various developers and engineers, each of whom turned to explain their work as best they could. Mae checked the time and saw there was a new notice from Dr. Villalobos. She asked Mae to come visit as soon as she could. *Nothing urgent,* she said. *But it should be today.* As they made their way through the building, Mae typed back to the doctor, saying she'd see her in thirty minutes. "Should we see the education project now?"

"I think that's a great idea," Terry said.

They walked through a curving hallway and into a great open space, with at least a hundred Circlers working without division. It looked a bit like a midcentury stock market.

"As your viewers might know," Terry said, "the Department of Education has given us a nice grant—"

"Wasn't it three billion dollars?" Mae asked.

"Well, who's counting?" Terry said, abundantly satisfied with the number and what it demonstrated, which was that Washington knew the Circle could measure anything, including student achievement, better than they ever hope to. "But the point is that they asked us to design and implement a more effective wraparound data assessment system for the nation's students. Oh wait, this is cool," Terry said.

They stopped in front of a woman and a small child. He looked about three, and was playing with a very shiny silver watch attached to his wrist.

"Hi Marie," Terry said to the woman. "This is Mae, as you probably know."

"I *do* know Mae," Marie said in the slightest French accent, "and Michel here does, too. Say hello, Michel."

Michel chose to wave.

"Say something to Michel, Mae," Terry said.

"How are you, Michel?" Mae said.

"Okay, now show her," Terry said, nudging Michel's shoulder.

On its tiny display, the watch on Michel's wrist had registered the four words Mae had just said. Below these numbers was a counter, with the number 29,266 displayed.

"Studies show that kids need to hear at least 30,000 words a day," Marie explained. "So the watch does a very simple thing by recognizing, categorizing and, most crucially, counting those words. This is primarily for kids at home, and before school age. Once they're there, we're assuming all this is tracked in the classroom."

"That's a good segue," Terry said. They thanked Marie and Michel, and made their way down the hall to a large room decorated like a classroom but rebooted, with dozens of screens, ergonomic chairs, collaborative workspaces.

"Oh, here's Jackie," Terry said.

Jackie, a sleek woman in her midthirties, emerged and shook Mae's hand. She was wearing a sleeveless dress, highlighting her broad shoulders and mannequin arms. She had a small cast on her right wrist.

"Hi Mae, I'm so glad you could visit today." Her voice was polished, professional, but with something flirtatious in it. She stood in front of the camera, her hands clasped before her.

"So Jackie," Terry said, clearly enjoying being near her. "Can you tell us a bit about what you're doing here?"

Mae saw an alert on her wrist, and interrupted. "Maybe first tell us where you came from. Before heading up this project. That's an interesting story."

"Well, thank you for saying that, Mae. I don't know how interesting it is, but before joining the Circle, I was in private equity, and before that I was part of a group that started—"

"You were a swimmer," Mae prompted. "You were in the Olympics!"

"Oh, that," Jackie said, throwing a hand in front of her smiling mouth.

"You won a bronze medal in 2000?"

"I did." Jackie's sudden shyness was endearing. Mae checked to confirm, and saw the accumulation of a few thousand smiles.

"And you had said internally that your experience as a world-class swimmer informed your plan here?"

341

"Yes it did, Mae," Jackie said, now seeming to grasp where Mae was going with the dialogue. "There are so many things we could talk about here in the Protagorean Pavilion, but one interesting one for your viewers is what we're calling YouthRank. Come over here for a second. Let's look at the big board." She led Mae over to a wallscreen, about twenty feet square. "We've been testing a system in Iowa for the last few months, and now that you're here, it seems a good time to demonstrate it. Maybe one of your viewers, if they're currently in high school in Iowa, would like to send you their name and school?"

"You heard the woman," Mae said. "Anyone out there watching from Iowa and currently in high school?"

Mae checked her wrist, where eleven zings came through. She showed them to Jackie, who nodded.

"Okay," Mae said. "So you just need her name?"

"Name and school," Jackie said.

Mae read one of the zings. "I have here Jennifer Batsuuri, who says she attends Achievement Academy in Cedar Rapids."

"Okay," Jackie said, turning back to the wallscreen. "Let's bring up Jennifer Batsuuri from Achievement Academy."

The name appeared on the screen, with a school photo accompanying it. The photo revealed her to be an Indian-American girl of about sixteen, with braces and wearing a green and tan uniform. Beside her photo, two numerical counters were spinning, the numbers rising until they slowed and stopped, the upper figure at 1,396, the one below it at 179,827.

"Well, well. Congratulations, Jennifer!" Jackie said, her eyes to the screen. She turned to Mae. "It seems we have a real achiever here from Achievement Academy. She's ranked 1,396 out of 179,827 high school students in Iowa."

Mae checked the time. She needed to speed Jackie's demonstration up. "And this is calculated—"

"Jennifer's score is the result of comparing her test results, her class rank, her school's relative academic strength and a number of other factors."

"How's that look to you, Jennifer?" Mae asked. She checked her wrist, but Jennifer's feed was silent.

There was a brief awkward moment where Mae and Jackie expected Jennifer to return, expressing her joy, but she did not come back. Mae knew it was time to move on.

"And can this be compared against all the other students in the country, and maybe even the world?" she asked.

"That's the idea," Jackie said. "Just as within the Circle we know our Participation Rank, for example, soon we'll be able to know at any given moment where our sons or daughters stand against the rest of American students, and then against the world's students."

"That sounds very helpful," Mae said. "And would eliminate a lot of the doubt and stress out there."

"Well, think of what this would do for a parent's understanding of their child's chances for college admission. There are about twelve thousand spots for Ivy League freshmen every year. If your child is in the top twelve thousand nationally, then you can imagine they'd have a good chance at one of those spots."

"And it'll be updated how often?"

"Oh, daily. Once we get full participation from all schools and districts, we'll be able to keep daily rankings, with every test, every pop quiz incorporated instantly. And of course these can be broken up between public and private, regional, and the rankings can be merged, weighted and analyzed to see trends among various other factors—socioeconomic, race, ethnicity, everything."

AG dinged in Mae's ear. "Ask about how it intersects with TruYouth."

"Jackie, I understand this overlaps in an interesting way with TruYouth, formerly known as ChildTrack." Mae got the sentence out just before a wave of nausea and sweat overtook her. She didn't want to see Francis. Maybe it wouldn't be Francis? There were other Circlers on the project. She checked her wrist, thinking she might be able to quickly find him with CircleSearch. But then there he was, striding toward her.

"Here's Francis Garaventa," Jackie said, oblivious to Mae's distress, "who can talk about the intersection between Youth-Rank and TruYouth, which I must say is at once revolutionary and necessary."

As Francis walked toward them, his hands coyly behind his back, Mae and Jackie both watched him, Mae feeling sweat pool in her armpits and also sensing that Jackie had a more than professional feeling for him. This was a different Francis. He was still shy, still slight, but his smile was confident, as if he'd been recently praised and expected more.

"Hi Francis," Jackie said, shaking his hand with her unbroken one, and turning her shoulder flirtatiously. It was not apparent to the camera, or to Francis, but to Mae it was as subtle as a gong.

"Hello Jackie, hello Mae," he said, "can I bring you into my lair?" He smiled, and without waiting for a response, turned and led them into the next room. Mae hadn't seen his office, and felt conflicted about sharing it with her watchers. It was a dark room with dozens of screens arranged on the wall into a seamless grid.

"So as your watchers might know, we've been pioneering a program to make kids safer. In the states where we've been testing the program, there's been an almost 90 percent drop in all crime, and a 100 percent drop in child abductions. Nationwide, we've had only three abductions, total, and all were rectified within minutes, given our ability to track the location of the participating children."

"It's been just *incred*ible," Jackie said, shaking her head, her voice low and soaked in something like lust.

Francis smiled at her, oblivious or pretending to be. Mae's wrist was alive with thousands of smiles and hundreds of comments. Parents in states without TruYouth were considering moving. Francis was being compared to Moses.

"And meanwhile," Jackie said, "the crew here at the Protagorean Pavilion has been working to coordinate all student measurements—to make sure that all homework, reading, attendance and test scores are all kept in one unified database. They're almost there. We're inches away from the moment when, by the time a student is ready for college, we have complete knowledge of everything that student has learned. Every word they read, every word they looked up, every sentence they highlighted, every equation they wrote, every answer and correction. The guesswork of knowing where all students stand and what they know will be over."

Mae's wrist was still scrolling madly. *Where was this 20 yrs ago?* a watcher wrote. *My kids would have gone to Yale.*

Now Francis stepped in. The idea that he and Jackie had been rehearsing this made Mae ill. "Now the exciting, and blazingly simple part," he said, smiling at Jackie with professional respect, "is that we can store all this information in the nearly microscopic chip, which is now used purely for safety reasons. But what if it provides both locational tracking and educational tracking? What if it's all in one place?"

"It's a no-brainer," Jackie said.

"Well, I hope parents will see it that way. For participating families, they'll have constant and real-time access to everything—location, scores, attendance, everything. And it won't be in some handheld device, which the kid might lose. It'll be in the cloud, and in the child him- or herself, never to be lost."

"Perfection," Jackie said.

"Well, I hope so," Francis said, looking at his shoes, hiding in what Mae knew to be a fog of false modesty. "And as you all know," he said, turning to Mae, speaking to her watchers, "we here at the Circle have been talking about Completion a lot, and though even us Circlers don't know yet just what Completion means, I have a feeling it's something like this. Connecting services and programs that are just inches apart. We track kids for safety, we track kids for educational data. Now we're just connecting these two threads, and when we do, we can finally know the whole child. It's simple, and, dare I say, it's complete."

Mae was standing outside, in the center of the western part of campus, knowing she was stalling until Annie returned. It was 1:44, far later than she thought it would be before her arrival, and now she worried about missing her. Mae had an appointment with

Dr. Villalobos at two o'clock, and that might take a while, given the doctor had warned her that there was something relatively serious—but not health-serious, she'd made clear—to talk about. But crowding out thoughts of Annie and the doctor was Francis, who was suddenly, bizarrely, attractive to her again.

Mae knew the easy trick that had been played upon her. He was thin, and without any muscle tone, his eyes were weak, and he had a pronounced problem with premature ejaculation, yet simply because she'd seen the lust in Jackie's eyes, Mae found herself wanting to be alone with him again. She wanted to bring him into her room that night. The thought was demented. She needed to clear her mind. It seemed like an appropriate time to explain and reveal the new sculpture.

"Okay, we have to see this," Mae said. "This was done by a renowned Chinese artist who's been in frequent trouble with the authorities there." At that moment, though, Mae couldn't remember the artist's name. "While we're on the subject, I want to thank all the watchers who sent frowns to the government there, both for their persecution of this artist, and for their restrictions on internet freedoms. We've sent over 180 million frowns from the U.S. alone, and you can bet that has an effect on the regime."

Mae still couldn't retrieve the artist's name and felt the omission was about to be noticed. Then it came through her wrist. *Say the man's name!* And they provided it.

She directed her lens toward the sculpture, and a few Circlers, standing between her and the piece, stepped out of the way. "No, no, it's good," Mae said. "You guys help show the scale of it. Stay there," she said, and they stepped back toward the object, which dwarfed them.

The sculpture was fourteen feet high, made of a thin and perfectly translucent form of plexiglass. Though most of the artist's previous work had been conceptual, this was representational, unmistakable: a massive hand, as big as a car, was reaching out from, or through, a large rectangle, which most took to imply some sort of computer screen.

The title of the piece was *Reaching Through for the Good of Humankind,* and had been noted, immediately upon its introduction, for its earnestness, anomalous to the artist's typical work, which had a darkly sardonic tone, usually at the expense of rising China and its attendant sense of self-worth.

"This sculpture is really hitting the Circlers at their core," Mae said. "I've been hearing about people weeping before it. As you can see, people like to take photos." Mae had seen Circlers posing before the giant hand, as if it were reaching for them, about to take them, elevate them. Mae decided to interview the two people who were standing near the sculpture's outstretched fingers.

"And you are?"

"Gino. I work in the Machine Age."

"And what does this sculpture mean to you?"

"Well, I'm not an art expert, but I think it's pretty obvious. He's trying to say that we need more ways to reach through the screen, right?"

Mae was nodding, because this was the clear meaning for everyone on campus, but she felt it might as well be said, on camera, for anyone less adept at art interpretation. Efforts to contact the artist after its installation had been unsuccessful. Bailey, who had commissioned the work, said he had no hand—"you know me and puns," he said—in its theme or execution. But he was thrilled with the result, and dearly wanted the artist to come to the campus to talk about the sculpture, but the artist had said he was unable to come in person, or even to teleconference. He'd rather let the sculpture speak for itself, he said. Mae turned to the woman with him.

"Who are you?"

"Rinku. Also from the Machine Age."

"Do you agree with Gino?"

"I do. I mean, this feels very soulful to me. Like, in how we need to find more ways to connect. The screen here is a barrier, and the hand is transcending it . . ."

Mae was nodding, thinking she needed to wrap this up, when she saw, through the translucent wrist of the giant hand, someone who looked like Annie. It was a young woman, blond, about Annie's height and build, and she was walking briskly across the quad. Rinku was still talking, having warmed up.

"I mean, how can the Circle find a way to make the connection between us and our users stronger? To me it's incredible that this artist, so far away and from such a different world, expressed what was on the minds of all of us here at the Circle? How to do better, do more, reach further, you know? How do we throw our hands through the screen to get closer to the world and everyone in it?"

Mae was watching the Annie-like figure walk toward the Industrial Revolution. When the door opened, and Annie, or Annie's twin, stepped within, Mae smiled at Rinku, thanked her and Gino and checked the time.

It was 1:49. She had to be with Dr. Villalobos in eleven minutes.

"Annie!"

The figure continued to walk. Mae was torn between really yelling, which typically upset the viewers, or running after Annie, which would cause the camera to shake violently—which also upset the viewers. She settled on a kind of speed walking while holding the camera against her chest. Annie turned another corner and then was gone. Mae heard the click of a door, the door to a stairway, and rushed to it. If she didn't know better, she would have thought Annie was avoiding her.

When Mae entered the stairway, she looked up, saw Annie's distinctive hand and yelled up. "Annie!"

Now the figure stopped. It was Annie. She turned, slowly made her way down the steps and, when she saw Mae, she smiled a practiced, exhausted smile. They hugged, Mae knowing any embrace always provided for her viewers a semi-comical, and occasionally mildly erotic, moment, as the other hugger's body swooped toward and eventually subsumed the camera's lens.

Annie pulled back, looked down at the camera, stuck out her tongue and looked up at Mae.

"Everyone," Mae said, "this is Annie. You've heard about her—Gang of 40 member, world-strider, beautiful colossus and my close personal friend. Say hi, Annie."

"Hi," Annie said.

"So how was the trip?" Mae asked.

Annie smiled, though Mae could tell, through the briefest of grimaces, that Annie was not enjoying this. But she conjured a happy mask and put it on. "It was great," she said.

"Anything you'd like to share? How did things go with everyone in Geneva?"

Annie's smile wilted.

"Oh, you know we shouldn't talk about much of that stuff, given so much of it is—"

Mae nodded, assuring Annie she knew. "I'm sorry. I was just talking about Geneva as a location. Nice?"

"Sure," Annie said. "Just great. I saw the Von Trapps, and they've gotten some new clothes. Also made of drapes."

Mae glanced at her wrist. She had nine minutes until she had to see Dr. Villalobos.

"Anything else you'd like to talk about?" she asked.

"What else?" Annie said. "Well let me think . . ."

Annie tilted her head, as if surprised, and mildly annoyed, that this faux-visit was still continuing. But then something came over her, as if finally settling into what was happening—that she was stuck on camera and had to assume her mantle as company spokesperson.

"Okay, there's another very cool program that we've been hinting at for a while, a system called PastPerfect. And in Germany I was working out some last hurdles to help it happen. We're currently looking for the right volunteer here within the Circle to try it out, but when we find the right person, it'll mean the start of a very new era for the Circle, and, not to be overly dramatic about it, for humankind."

"Not dramatic at all!" Mae said. "Can you say anything more about it?"

"Sure, Mae. Thank you for asking," Annie said, looking briefly at her shoes before raising her eyes back to Mae, with a professional smile. "I can say that the basic idea is to take the power of the Circle community and to map not just the present but the past, too. We're right now digitizing every photo, every newsreel, every amateur video in every archive in this country and Europe—I mean, we're doing our best at least. The task is herculean, but once we have a critical mass, and with facial recognition advances, we can, we hope, identify pretty much everyone in every photo and every video. You want to find every picture of your great-grandparents, we can make the archive searchable, and you can—we expect, we bet—then gain a greater understanding of them. Maybe you catch them in a crowd at the 1912 World's Fair. Maybe you find video of your parents at a baseball game in 1974. The hope, in the end, is to fill in your memory and the historical record. And with the help of DNA and far better genealogical software, within the year we're hoping that anyone can quickly access every available piece of information about their family lineage, all images, all video and film, with one search request."

"And I imagine that when everyone else joins in, the Circle participants that is, the gaps will quickly be filled." Mae smiled, her eyes telling Annie she was doing great.

"That's right, Mae," Annie said, her voice stabbing at the space between them, "like any project online, most of the completion will be done by the digital community. We're gathering our own millions of photos and videos, but the rest of the world will provide billions more. We expect that with even partial participation, we'll be able to fill in most historical holes easily. If you're looking for all the residents of a certain building in Poland, circa 1913, and you're missing one, it won't take long to triangulate that last person by cross-referencing from all the other data we'll get."

"Very exciting."

"Yes, it is," Annie said, and flashed the whites of her eyes, urging Mae to wrap all this up.

"But you don't have the guinea pig yet?" Mae asked.

"Not yet. For the first person, we're looking for someone whose family goes back pretty far in the United States. Just because we know we'll have more complete access to records here than in some other countries."

"And this is part of the Circle's plan to complete everything this year? It's still on schedule?"

"It is. PastPerfect is just about ready to use now. And with all the other aspects of Completion, it looks like the beginning of next year. Eight months and we'll be done. But you never know: the way things are going, with the help of so many Circlers out there, we could finish ahead of time."

Mae smiled, nodded, and she and Annie shared a long, strained moment, when Annie's eyes again asked how long they needed to go on with this semiperformative dialogue.

Outside, the sun broke through the clouds, and the light through the window shone down on Annie's face. Mae saw, then, for the first time, how old she looked. Her face was drawn, her skin pale. Annie was not yet twenty-seven but there were bags under her eyes. In this light, she seemed to have aged five years in the last two months.

Annie took Mae's hand, and dug her fingernails into her palm just enough to get her attention. "I actually have to use the bathroom. Come with?"

"Sure. I have to go, too."

Though Mae's transparency was complete, in that she could

not turn off the visual or audio feeds at any time, there were a few exceptions, insisted upon by Bailey. One was during bathroom usage, or at least time spent on the toilet. The video feed was to remain on, because, Bailey insisted, the camera would be trained on the back of the stall door, so it hardly mattered. But the audio would be turned off, sparing Mae, and the audience, the sounds.

Mae entered the stall, Annie entered the one next to her, and Mae deactivated her audio. The rule was that she had up to three minutes of silence; more than that would provoke concern from viewers and Circlers alike.

"So how are you?" Mae asked. She couldn't see Annie, but her toes, looking crooked and in need of a pedicure attention, were visible under the door.

"Great. Great. You?"

"Good."

"Well, you *should* be good," Annie said. "You are killing it!"

"You think?"

"C'mon. False modesty won't work here. You should be psyched."

"Okay. I am."

"I mean, you're like a meteor here. It's insane. People are coming to *me* trying to get to *you*. It's just . . . so crazy."

Something had crept into Annie's voice that Mae recognized as envy, or its close cousin. Mae ran through a string of possibilities of what she could say in response. Nothing was right. *I couldn't have done it without you* would not work; it sounded both self-aggrandizing and condescending. In the end, she chose to change the subject.

"Sorry about asking stupid questions back there," Mae said.

"It's okay. But you put me on the spot."

"I know. I just—I saw you and wanted to spend time with you. And I didn't know what else to ask about. So are you really okay? You look wiped out."

"Thank you, Mae. You know how much I like to be told seconds after I appear in front of your millions that I look terrible. Thank you. You're sweet."

"I'm just worried. Have you been sleeping?"

"I don't know. Maybe I'm off-schedule. I'm jet-lagged."

"Is there anything I can do? Let me take you out to eat."

"Take me out to eat? With your camera and me looking so terrible? That sounds fantastic, but no."

"Let me do something for you."

"No, no. I just need to get caught up."

"Anything interesting?"

"Oh you know, the usual."

"The regulatory stuff went well? They were really putting a lot on you out there. I worried."

A chill swept through Annie's voice. "Well, you had no reason to worry. I've been doing this for a while now."

"I didn't mean I was worried in that way."

"Well, don't worry in *any* way."

"I know you can handle it."

"Thank *you*! Mae, your confidence in me will be the wind beneath my wings."

Mae chose to ignore the sarcasm. "So when do I get to see you?"

"Soon. We'll make something happen."

"Tonight? Please?"

"Not tonight. I'm just gonna crash and get fresh for tomorrow. I have a bunch of stuff. There's all the new work on Completion, and . . ."

"Completing the Circle?"

There was a long pause, during which Mae was sure that Annie was relishing this piece of news, unknown to Mae.

"Yeah. Bailey didn't tell you?" Annie said. A certain exasperating music had entered her voice.

"I don't know," Mae said, her heart burning. "Maybe he did."

"Well, they're feeling very close now. I was out there removing some of the last barriers. The Wise Men think we're down to the last few hurdles."

"Oh. I think I might have heard that," Mae said, hearing herself, hearing how petty she sounded. But she *was* jealous. Of course she was. Why would she have access to information that Annie did? She knew she had no right to it, but still, she wanted it, and felt she was closer to it than this, than hearing about it from Annie, who had been halfway around the world for three weeks. The omission threw her back to some ignominious spot at the Circle, some plebeian place of being a spokeswoman, a public shill.

"So you're sure I can't do anything for you? Maybe some kind of mudpack to help with the puffiness under your eyes?" Mae hated herself for saying it, but it felt so good in that moment, like an itch scratched hard.

Annie cleared her throat. "You're so kind," she said. "But I should get going."

"You sure?"

"Mae. I don't want this to sound rude, but the best thing for me right now is to get back to my desk so I can get back to work."

"Okay."

"I'm not saying that in a rude way. I actually just need to get caught up."

"No, I know. I get it. That's fine. I'll see you tomorrow anyway. At the Concept Kingdom meeting."

"What?"

"There's a Concept King—"

"No. I know what it is. You're going?"

"I am. Bailey thought I should go."

"And broadcast it?"

"Of course. Is that a problem?"

"No. No," Annie said, clearly stalling, processing. "I'm just surprised. Those meetings are full of sensitive intellectual property. Maybe he's planning to have you attend the beginning or something. I can't imagine . . ."

Annie's toilet flushed, and Mae saw that she'd stood up.

"You leaving?"

"Yeah. I'm really so late I want to puke now."

"Okay. Don't puke."

Annie hurried to the door and was gone.

Mae had four minutes to get to Dr. Villalobos. She stood, turned her audio back on, and left the bathroom.

Then she walked back in, silenced her audio, sat down in the same stall, and gave herself a minute to get herself together. Let people think she was constipated. She didn't care. She was sure Annie was crying by now, wherever she was. Mae was sobbing, and was cursing Annie, cursing every blond inch of her, her smug sense of entitlement. So what that she'd been at the Circle longer. They were peers now, but Annie couldn't accept it. Mae would have to make sure she did.

It was 2:02 when she arrived.

"Hello Mae," Dr. Villalobos said, greeting her in the clinic lobby. "I see your heart rate is normal, and I imagine with your jog over here, all your viewers are getting some interesting data, too. Come in."

In retrospect, it shouldn't have been a surprise that Dr. Villalobos had become a viewers' favorite, too. With her extravagant curves, her sultry eyes and harmonica voice, she was volcanic on-screen. She was the doctor everyone, especially straight men, wished they'd had. Though TruYou had made lewd comments almost impossible for anyone wanting to keep their job or spouse, Dr. Villalobos brought out a genteel, but no less demonstrative, brand of appreciation. *So good to see the good doctor!* one man wrote as Mae entered the office. *Let the examination begin,* said another, braver, soul. And Dr. Villalobos, while putting on a show of brisk professionalism, seemed to enjoy it, too. Today she was wearing a zippered blouse that displayed an amount of her ample chest that at a proper distance was appropriate but, seen through Mae's close camera, was somehow obscene.

"So your vitals have been looking good," she said to Mae.

Mae was sitting on the examination table, the doctor standing before her. Looking at her wrist, Mae checked the image her viewers were getting, and she knew the men would be pleased.

As if realizing the picture might be getting too provocative, Dr. Villalobos turned to the wallscreen. On it, a few hundred data points were displayed.

"Your step count could be better," she said. "You're averaging only 5,300, when you should be at 10,000. Someone your age, especially, should be even higher than that."

"I know," Mae said. "It's just been busy lately."

"Okay. But let's bring those steps up. As a promise to me? Now, because we're talking to all your watchers now, I'd like to tout the overall program your own data feeds into, Mae. It's called the Complete Health Data program, or CHAD for short. Chad was an ex of mine, and Chad, if you're out there, I didn't name it for you."

Mae's wrist went wild with messages. *Chad, you fool.*

"Through CHAD, we get real-time data on everyone at the Circle. Mae, you and the newbies were the first to get the new wristbands, but since then, we've equipped everyone else at the Circle. And this has enabled us to get perfect and complete data on the eleven thousand people here. Can you imagine? The first boon has been that when the flu arrived on campus last week, we knew in minutes who brought it. We sent her home and no one else was infected. If only we could prevent people from bringing germs *onto* campus, right? If they never left, getting dirty out there, then we'd be all set. But let me get off my soapbox and focus on you, Mae."

"As long as the news is good," Mae said, and tried to smile. But she was uneasy and wanted to move all this along.

"Well, I think it's good," the doctor said. "This comes from a watcher in Scotland. He'd been tracking your vitals, and cross-referencing with your DNA markers, he realized that the way you're eating, particularly nitrates, is elevating your propensity for cancer."

"Jesus. Really? Is that the bad news I'm here for?"

"No, no! Don't worry. It's easily solved. You don't have cancer and probably won't get it. But you know you have a marker for gastrointestinal cancer, just an increased risk, and this researcher in Glasgow, who'd been following you and your vitals, saw that you're eating salami and other meats with nitrates that might be tipping you toward cellular mutation."

"You keep scaring me."

"Oh god, I'm sorry! I don't mean to. But thank god he was watching. I mean, we're watching, too, and we're getting better at watching all the time. But the beauty of having so many friends out there, as you do, is that one of them, five thousand miles away, has helped you avert a growing risk."

"So no more nitrates."

"Right. Let's skip the nitrates. I've zinged you a list of foods that contain them, and your watchers can see, too. They should always be eaten in moderation, but should be avoided altogether if there's any history of or risk of cancer. I hope you'll be sure to convey this to your parents, in case they haven't been checking their own Zing feed."

"Oh, I'm sure they have," Mae said.

"Okay, and this is the not-so-good news. It's not about you or your health. It's your parents. They're fine, but I want to show you something." The doctor brought up the SeeChange camera feeds in Mae's parents' house, set up a month into her father's treatment. The medical team at the Circle was taking a strong interest in her father's case, and wanted as much data as it could get. "You see anything wrong?"

Mae scanned the screen. Where a grid of sixteen images should have been visible, twelve were blank. "There are only four working," she said.

"Correct," said the doctor.

Mae watched the four feeds for signs of her parents. She saw none. "Has tech been there to check?"

"No need. We saw them do it. For each one, they reached up and put some kind of cover over them. Maybe just some sticker or fabric. Did you know about this?"

"I didn't. I'm so sorry. They shouldn't have done this."

Instinctively, Mae checked her current viewership: 1,298,001. It always spiked during the visits to Dr. Villalobos. Now all these people knew. Mae felt her face flush.

"Have you heard from your folks recently?" Dr. Villalobos asked. "Our records say you haven't. But maybe—"

"Not in the last few days," Mae said. In fact, she hadn't been in touch for over a week. She'd tried to call them, to no avail. She'd zinged and received no response.

"Would you be willing to go visit?" the doctor asked. "As you know, good medical care is hard to provide when we're in the dark."

Mae was driving home, having left work at five—something she hadn't done in weeks—and was thinking of her parents, what kind of madness had overtaken them, and she was worried that somehow Mercer's own madness had infected them. How dare they disconnect cameras! After all she'd done to help, after all the Circle had done to bend all rules to come to their aid! And what would Annie say?

Damn her, Mae thought as she made her way home, the air growing warmer as the distance grew between her and the Pacific. Mae had set up her lens on the car dash, inserting it into a special mount created for her time in the car. *That fucking debutante.* This was bad timing. Annie would likely find some way to turn all this to her advantage. Just when her envy of Mae—and it was that, it was so abundantly obvious—was growing, she could cut Mae down to size again. Mae and her nothing town, her parking-garage parents who couldn't keep their screens operational, who couldn't keep themselves healthy. Who took a monumental gift, premium health care, for free, and abused it. Mae knew what Annie was thinking in her little entitled blond head: *You just can't help some people.*

Annie's family line went back to the *Mayflower,* her ancestors having settled this country, and their ancestors having owned some vast swath of England. Their blood was blue all the way back, it seemed, to the invention of the wheel. In fact, if anyone's bloodline *had* invented the wheel, it would have been Annie's. It would make absolute and perfect sense and would surprise no one.

Mae had discovered all this one Thanksgiving at Annie's house, with twenty-odd relatives there, all with their thin noses, their pink skin, their weak eyes hidden behind forty lenses, when she became aware, during an appropriately self-effacing conversation—for Annie's family was equally unwilling to talk too much or care too much about their lineage—that some distant relative of theirs had been at the very first Thanksgiving.

"Oh god, who cares?" Annie's mother had said, when Mae had pressed for more details. "Some random guy got on a boat. He probably owed money all over the Old Country."

And they had proceeded with dinner. Afterward, Annie had, at Mae's insistence, shown her some documents, ancient yellowed papers detailing their family history, a beautiful black portfolio of genealogies, scholarly articles, pictures of grave old men with extravagant sideburns standing near rough-hewn cabins.

In other visits to Annie's house, her family was equally generous, unassuming and careless with their name. But when Annie's sister was married, and the extended family arrived, Mae saw a different side. She was seated at a table of single men and women, most of them Annie's cousins, and next to Annie's aunt. She was a wiry woman in her forties, her features similar to Annie's but arranged with lesser results. She was recently divorced, having left a man "beneath my station," she said with pretend haughtiness.

"And you know Annie from . . . ?" She'd first turned to Mae fully twenty minutes into dinner.

"College. We were roommates."

"I thought her roommate was Pakistani."

"That was freshman year."

"And you saved the day. Where are you from?"

"Middle of the state. Central Valley. A small town no one's heard of. Sort of near Fresno."

Mae drove on, remembering all this, some of it injecting fresh pain into her, something still wet and raw.

"Wow, Fresno!" the aunt had said, pretending to smile. "I haven't heard that word in a long time, thank god." She'd taken a swallow from her gin and tonic and squinted out at the wedding party. "The important thing is that you got out. I know good colleges look for people like you. That's probably why I didn't get in where I wanted to. Don't let anyone tell you Exeter helps. So many quota spots to fill with people from Pakistan and Fresno, right?"

The first time she'd gone home transparent had been revelatory and had burnished Mae's faith in humanity. She'd had a simple evening with her parents, making and eating dinner and while doing so, they'd discussed the differences in her father's treatment before and after they became insured through the Circle. Viewers could see both the triumphs of his treatment—her father seemed vibrant and moved with ease through the house—but they also saw the toll the disease was taking on him. He fell awkwardly while trying to make his way upstairs, and afterward there was a flood of messages from concerned viewers, followed by thousands of smiles from all over the world. People suggesting new drug combinations, new physical therapy regimens, new doctors, experimental treatments, Eastern medicine, Jesus. Hundreds of churches put him in their weekly prayers. Mae's parents felt confident in their doctors, and most viewers could see that her father's care was exceptional, so what was more important and plentiful than the medical comments were those simply cheering him and the family on. Mae cried reading the messages; it was a flood of love. People sharing their own stories, so many living with MS themselves. Others spoke of their own struggles—living with osteoporosis, with Bell's palsy, with Crohn's disease. Mae had been forwarding the messages to her parents, but after a few days decided to make their own email and mailing address public, so her parents could be emboldened and inspired by the outpouring themselves, every day.

This, the second time she'd gone home, would, she knew, be even better. After she addressed the issue with the cameras, which she expected was some sort of misunderstanding, she planned to give all those who had reached out the chance to see her parents again, and to give her parents a chance to thank all those who had sent them smiles and help.

She found the two of them in the kitchen, chopping vegetables.

"How are you guys?" she said, while forcing them into a three-way embrace. They both smelled of onions.

"You're sure affectionate tonight, Mae!" her father said.

"Ha ha," Mae said, and tried to indicate, with a rolling back of her eyelids, that they should not imply that she was ever less affectionate.

As if remembering that they were on camera, and that their daughter was now a more visible and important person, her parents adjusted their behavior. They made lasagna, with Mae adding a few ingredients Additional Guidance had asked her to bring and display to watchers. When dinner was ready, and Mae had given adequate camera time to the products, they all sat down.

"So there's a slight concern from the health folks that some of your cameras aren't working," Mae said, keeping it light.

"Really?" her father said, smiling. "Maybe we should check the batteries?" He winked at her mother.

"You guys," Mae said, knowing she had to make this statement very clear, knowing this was a pivotal moment, for their own health and the overall health data–gathering system the Circle was trying to make possible. "How can anyone provide you with good health care when you don't allow them to see how you're doing? It's like going to see a doctor and not allowing her to take your pulse."

"That's a very good point," her father said. "I think we should eat."

"We'll get them fixed right away," her mother said, and that began what was a very strange night, during which Mae's parents agreed readily with all of Mae's arguments about transparency, nodded their heads vigorously when she talked about the necessity for everyone to be on board, the corollary to vaccines, how they only worked with full participation. They agreed heartily with it all, complimenting Mae repeatedly on her powers of persuasion and logic. It was odd; they were being far too cooperative.

They sat down to eat, and Mae did something she'd never done before, and which she hoped her parents wouldn't ruin by acting like it was unusual: she gave a toast.

"Here's a toast to you two," she said. "And while we're at it, a toast to all the thousands of people who reached out to you guys after the last time I was here."

Her parents smiled stiffly and raised their glasses. They ate for a few moments, and when her mother had carefully chewed and swallowed her first bite, she smiled and looked directly into the lens—which Mae had told her repeatedly not to do.

"Well, we sure did get a *lot* of messages," her mother said.

Mae's father joined in. "Your mom's been sorting through

them, and we've been making a little dent in the pile every day. But it's a lot of work, I have to say."

Her mother rested her hand on Mae's arm. "Not that we don't appreciate it, because we do. We surely do. I just want to go on record as asking everyone's forgiveness for our tardiness in answering all the messages."

"We've gotten thousands," her father noted, poking at his salad.

Her mother smiled stiffly. "And again, we appreciate the outpouring. But even if we spent one minute on each response, that's a thousand minutes. Think of it: sixteen hours just for some basic response to the messages! Oh jeez, now I sound ungrateful."

Mae was glad her mother said this, because they did sound ungrateful. They were complaining about people caring about them. And just when Mae thought her mother would reverse herself, would encourage more good wishes, her father spoke and made it worse. Like her mother, he spoke directly into the lens.

"But we do ask you, from now on, to just send your best wishes through the air. Or if you pray, just pray for us. No need to put it into a message. Just"—and he closed his eyes and squeezed them tight—"send your good wishes, your good vibes, our way. No need to email or zing or anything. Just good thoughts. Send 'em through the air. That's all we ask."

"I think you just mean to say," Mae said, trying to hold her temper, "that it'll just take you a little while to answer all of the messages. But you'll get to them all eventually."

Her father didn't hesitate. "Well, I can't say that, Mae. I don't want to promise that. It's actually very stressful. And we've already had many people get angry when they don't hear back from us in a given amount of time. They send one message, then they send ten more in the same day. 'Did I say something wrong?' 'Sorry.' 'I was only trying to help.' 'Up yours.' They have these neurotic conversations with themselves. So I don't want to imply the kind of immediate message turnaround that most of your friends seem to require."

"Dad. Stop. You sound terrible."

Her mother leaned forward. "Mae, your dad's just trying to say that our lives are already pretty fraught, and we have our hands full just working, paying bills and taking care of the health stuff. If we have sixteen hours' more work to do, then that puts us in an untenable position. Can you see where we're coming from? I say that, again, with all due respect and gratitude to everyone who has wished us well."

After dinner, her parents wanted to watch a movie, and they did so, *Basic Instinct,* at her father's insistence. He'd seen it more than any other film, always citing the nods to Hitchcock, the many witty homages—though he'd never made clear his love of Hitchcock in the first place. Mae had long suspected that the movie, with its constant and varied sexual tensions, made him randy.

As her parents watched the film, Mae tried to make the time more interesting by sending a series of zings about it, tracking and commenting on the number of moments offensive to the LGBT community. She was getting a great response, but then saw the time, 9:30, and figured she should get on the road and back to the Circle.

"Well, I'm gonna head out," she said.

Mae thought she caught something in her father's eye, some quick look to her mother that might have said *at last*, but she could have been mistaken. She put on her coat and her mother met her at the door, an envelope in her hand.

"Mercer asked us to give this to you."

Mae took it, a simple business-sized envelope. It wasn't even addressed to her. No name, nothing.

She kissed her mother's cheek, left the house, the air outside still warm. She pulled out and drove toward the highway. But the letter was on her lap, and her curiosity overtook her. She pulled over and opened it.

> Dear Mae,
> Yes, you can and should read this on camera. I expected that you would, so I'm writing this letter not only to you, but to your "audience." Hello, audience.

She could almost hear his introductory intake of breath, his settling in before an important speech.

> I can't see you anymore, Mae. Not that we had such a constant or perfect friendship anyway, but I can't be your friend and also part of your experiment. I'll be sad to lose you, as you have been important in my life. But we've taken very different evolutionary paths and very soon we'll be too far apart to communicate.
> If you saw your parents, and your mom gave you this note, then you saw the effect all your stuff has had on them. I wrote this note after seeing them, both of them strung

out, exhausted by the deluge you unleashed on them. It's too much, Mae. And it's not right. I helped them cover some of the cameras. I even bought the fabric. I was happy to do it. They don't want to be smiled upon, or frowned upon, or zinged. They want to be alone. And not watched. Surveillance shouldn't be the tradeoff for any goddamn service we get.

If things continue this way, there will be two societies—or at least I hope there will be two—the one you're helping create, and an alternative to it. You and your ilk will live, willingly, joyfully, under constant surveillance, watching each other always, commenting on each other, voting and liking and disliking each other, smiling and frowning, and otherwise doing nothing much else.

Already there were comments pouring through her wrist. *Mae, were you ever so young and dumb? How did you end up dating a zero like this?* That was the most popular, soon superseded by *Just looked up his picture. Does he have some Sasquatch somewhere in the family tree?*

She continued reading the letter:

I will always wish all good things for you, Mae. I also hope, though I realize how unlikely it is, that somewhere down the line, when the triumphalism of you and your peers—the unrestrained Manifest Destiny of it all—goes too far and collapses into itself, that you'll regain your sense of perspective, and your humanity. Hell, what am I saying? It's already gone too far. What I should say is that I await the day when some vocal minority finally rises up to *say* it's gone too far, and that this tool, which is far more insidious than any human invention that's come before it, must be checked, regulated, turned back, and that, most of all, we need options for opting out. We are living in a tyrannical state now, where we are not allowed to—

Mae checked how many pages were left. Four more double-sided sheets, likely containing more of the same directionless blather. She threw the pile on the passenger seat. Poor Mercer. He'd always been a blowhard, and he never knew his audience. And though she knew he was using her parents against her, something was bothering her. Were they really that annoyed? She was only a block away, so she got out and walked back home. If they were truly upset, well, she would and could address it.

When she walked in, she didn't see them in the two most likely places, the living room and the kitchen, and peeked around the corner into the dining room. They were nowhere. The only sign of them at all was a pot of water boiling on the stove. She tried not to panic, but that pot of boiling water, and the otherwise eerie quiet of the house, arranged itself in a crooked way in her mind, and very suddenly she was thinking of robberies, or suicide pacts, or kidnappings.

She ran up the stairs, taking them three at a time, and when she reached the top and turned left quickly, into their bedroom, she saw them, their eyes turned to her, round and terrified. Her father was sitting on the bed, and her mother was kneeling on the floor, his penis in her hand. A small container of moisturizer rested against his leg. In an instant they all knew the ramifications.

Mae turned away, directing the camera toward a dresser. No one said a word. Mae could think only of retreating to the bathroom, where she pointed the camera at the wall and turned off the audio. She rewound her spool to see what had been caught on camera. She hoped the lens swinging from her neck had somehow missed the offending image.

But it had not. If anything, the angle of the camera revealed the act more clearly than she'd witnessed it. She turned the playback off. She called AG.

"Is there anything we can do?" she asked.

Within minutes she was on the phone with Bailey himself. She was glad to get him, because she knew that if anyone would agree with her on this, it would be Bailey, a man of unerring moral compass. He didn't want a sex act like that broadcast around the world, did he? Well, that had already been done, but surely they could erase a few seconds, so the image wouldn't be searchable, wouldn't be made permanent?

"Mae, c'mon," he said. "You know we can't do that. What would transparency be if we could delete anything we felt was embarrassing in some way? You know we don't delete." His voice was empathetic and fatherly, and Mae knew she would abide by whatever he said. He knew best, could see miles further than Mae or anyone else, and this was evident in his preternatural calm. "For this experiment, Mae, and the Circle as a whole, to work, it has to be absolute. It has to be pure and complete. And I know this episode will be painful for a few days, but trust me, very soon nothing like this will be the least bit interesting to anyone. When everything is known, everything acceptable will be accepted. So for the time being, we need to be strong. You need to be a role model here. You need to stay the course."

Mae drove back to the Circle, determined that when she got back to campus, she would stay there. She'd had enough of the chaos of her family, of Mercer, her wretched hometown. She hadn't even asked her parents about the SeeChange cameras, had she? Home was madness. On campus, all was familiar. On campus there was no friction. She didn't need to explain herself, or the future of the world, to the Circlers, who implicitly understood her and the planet and the way it had to be and soon would be.

Increasingly, she found it difficult to be off-campus anyway. There were homeless people, and there were the attendant and assaulting smells, and there were machines that didn't work, and floors and seats that had not been cleaned, and there was, everywhere, the chaos of an orderless world. The Circle was helping to improve it, she knew, and so many of these things were being addressed—homelessness could be helped or fixed, she knew, once the gamificaton of shelter allotment and public housing in general was complete; they were working on this in the Nara Period—but in the meantime, it was increasingly troubling to be amid the madness outside the gates of the Circle. Walking through San Francisco, or Oakland, or San Jose, or any city, really, seemed more and more like a Third World experience, with unnecessary filth, and unnecessary strife and unnecessary errors and inefficiencies—on any city block, a thousand problems correctible through simple enough algorithms and the application of available technology and willing members of the digital community. She left her camera on.

She made the drive in less than two hours and it was only midnight when she arrived. She was wired from the trip, from her nerves on constant alert, and needed relaxation, and distraction. She went to CE, knowing there she could be useful and that there, her efforts would be appreciated, immediately and demonstrably. She entered the building, looking briefly up at the slow-turning Calder, and rose through the elevator, breezed across the catwalk and to her old station.

At her desk, she saw a pair of messages from her parents. They were still awake, and they were despondent. They were outraged. Mae tried to send them the positive zings she'd seen, messages that celebrated that an older couple, dealing with MS no less, could still be sexually active. But they weren't interested.

Please stop, they asked. *Please, no more.*

And they, like Mercer, insisted that she cease to contact them unless privately. She tried to explain to them that they were on the wrong side of history. But they weren't listening. Mae knew that eventually she'd convince them, that it was only a matter of time, for them and for everyone—even Mercer. He and her parents had been late to get PCs, late to buy a cell phone, late to everything. It was comical and it was sad, and it served no purpose, to put off the undeniable present, the unavoidable future.

So she would wait. In the meantime, she opened the chute. There were few people with pressing needs at that hour, but there were always unanswered queries waiting for business hours to start, so she figured she could chip away at the load before the newbies came in. Maybe she'd finish them all, stun everyone, let them come in with a clean slate, an empty chute.

There were 188 latent queries. She'd do what she could do. A customer in Twin Falls wanted a rundown of all the other businesses visited by customers who had visited his. Mae found the information easily and sent it to him, and instantly she felt calmer. The next two were easy, boilerplate answers. She sent surveys and got 100s on both. One of them sent her a survey in return; she answered it and was done in ninety seconds. The next few queries were more complicated but she kept her rating at 100. The sixth was more complicated still, but she answered it, got a 98, followed up and brought it to a 100. The client, a heating/air-conditioning advertiser from Melbourne, Australia, asked if he could add her to his professional network and she readily agreed. That's when he realized she was Mae.

THE Mae? he typed. His name was Edward.

Can't deny it, she answered.

I'm honored, Edward typed. *What time is it there? We're just finishing our workday here.* She said it was late. He asked if he could add her to his mailing list, and again she readily agreed. What followed was a quick deluge of news and information about the insurance world of Melbourne. He offered to make her an honorary member of the MHAPB, the Melbourne Heating and Air-Conditioning Providers Guild, formerly the Melbourne Heating and Air-Conditioning Providers Brotherhood, and she said she would be flattered. He added her to the friends on his personal Circle profile, and asked that she reciprocate. She did.

Gotta get back to work now, she wrote, *say hello to all in Melbourne!* She felt, already, all of the madness of her parents, of Mercer, evaporating like mist. She took the next query, which came from a pet grooming chain based in Atlanta. She got a 99, followed up, got back a 100, and sent six other surveys, five of which the client answered. She took another query, this one from Bangalore, and was in the middle of amending the boilerplate to the query when another message came through from Edward. *Did you see my daughter's request?* he asked. Mae checked her screens, looking for some request from Edward's daughter. Eventually he clarified that his daughter had a different last name, and was in school in New Mexico. She was raising awareness of the plight of bison in the state, and was asking Mae to sign a petition and mention the campaign in whatever forums she could. Mae said she would try, and quickly sent a zing about it. *Thank you!* Edward wrote, followed, a few minutes later, by a thank-you from his daughter, Helena. *I can't believe Mae Holland signed my petition! Thanks!* she wrote. Mae answered three more queries, her rating dipping to 98, and though she sent multiple follow-ups to these three, she got no satisfaction. She knew she'd have to get twenty-two or so 100s to average the 98 up to 100 overall; she checked the clock. It was 12:44. She had plenty of time. Another message came from Helena, asking about jobs at the Circle. Mae offered her usual advice, and sent her the email address of the HR department. *Can you put in a good word for me?* Helena asked. Mae said she would do as much as she could, given they had never met. *But you know me pretty well by now!* Helena said, and then directed her to her own profile page. She encouraged Mae to read her essays about wildlife preservation, and the essay she used to get into college, which she said was still relevant. Mae said she would try to read them when she could. Wildlife and New Mexico brought Mercer to mind. That self-righteous waste. Where was that man who made love to her on the edge of the Grand Canyon? They had both been so comfortably lost then, when he picked her up from college and they drove through the Southeast with no schedule, no itinerary, never with any idea of where they'd stay that night. They passed through New Mexico in a blizzard and then to Arizona where they parked, and found a cliff overlooking the canyon, with no fences, and there under a noonday sun he undressed her, a four-thousand-foot drop behind her. He held her and she had no doubts because he was strong then. He was young then, he had vision then. Now he was old and acted older. She looked up the profile page she'd set up for him, and found it blank. She made an inquiry to tech and found he'd been trying to take it down. She sent him a zing and got no answer. She looked up his business page but it had been taken down, too; there was only a message saying he was now running an analog-only business. Another message came through from Helena: *What did you think?* Mae told her she hadn't had time to read anything yet, and the next message was from Edward, Helena's father: *It sure would mean a lot if you were to recommend Helena for a job there at the Circle. No pressure but we're counting on you!* Mae told them, again, that she'd do her best. A notice came through her second screen about a Circle campaign to eradicate smallpox in West Africa. She signed her name, sent a smile, pledged fifty dollars, and sent a zing about it. She saw immediately that Helena and Edward rezinged the message. *We're doing our part!* Edward wrote. *Quid pro quo?* It was 1:11 when the blackness swept through her. Her mouth tasted acidic. She closed her eyes and saw the tear, now filled with light. She opened her eyes again. She took a swallow of water but it only seemed to heighten her panic. She checked her watchers; there were only 23,010, but she didn't want to show them her eyes, fearing they would betray her anxiety. She closed them again, which she felt would seem natural enough for a minute, after so many hours in front of the screen. *Just resting the eyes,* she typed and sent. But when she closed them again, she saw the tear, clearer now, louder now. What was the sound she was hearing? It was a scream muffled by fathomless waters, that high-pitched scream of a million drowned voices. She opened her eyes. She called her parents. No answer. She wrote to them, nothing. She called Annie. No answer. She wrote to her, nothing. She looked her up in the CircleSearch but she wasn't on campus. She went to Annie's profile page, scrolled through a few hundred photos, most of them from her Europe-China trip, and, feeling her eyes burn, she closed them again. And again she saw the rip, the light trying to get through, the underwater screams. She opened her eyes. Another message came through from Edward. *Mae? You out there? Sure would be nice to know if you can help out. Do write back.* Could Mercer really disappear like this? She was determined to find him. She searched for him, for messages he might have sent to others. Nothing. She called him, but his number had been disconnected. Such an aggressive move, to change your number and leave no new one. What had she seen in him? His disgusting fat back, those terrible patches of hair on his shoulders. Jesus, where was he? There was something very wrong when you couldn't find someone you were trying to find. It was 1:32. *Mae? Edward again. Can you reassure Helena that you'll look at her site sometime soon? She's a bit upset now. Just any word of encouragement would be helpful. I know you're a good person and wouldn't intentionally mess with her head, you*

know, promising to help and then ignoring her. Cheers! Edward. Mae
went to Helena's site, read one of the essays, congratulated her,
told her it was brilliant, and sent out a zing telling everyone that
Helena from Melbourne/New Mexico was a voice to be reckoned
with, and that they should support her work in any way they
could. But the rip was still open inside Mae, and she needed to
close it. Not knowing what else to do, she activated CircleSurveys, and nodded to begin.

"Are you a regular user of conditioner?"

"Yes," she said.

"Thank you. What do you think about organic hair products?"
Already she felt calmer.

"Smile."

"Thank you. What do you think about nonorganic hair products?"

"Frown," Mae said. The rhythm felt right.

"Thank you. If your favored haircare product isn't available
at your usual store or online site, would you substitute it for a
similar brand?"

"No."

"Thank you."

The steady completion of tasks felt right. Mae checked her
bracelet, which showed hundreds of new smiles. There was something refreshing, the comments were asserting, about seeing a
Circle semi-celebrity like herself contributing to the data pool
like this. She was hearing, also, from customers she'd helped in
her CE days. Customers from Columbus, Johannesburg and Bris-
bane all said hello and congratulations. The owner of a marketing
firm in Ontario thanked her, via zing, for her good example, for

her goodwill, and Mae briefly corresponded, asking how business was up and over there.

She answered three more queries, and was able to get all three customers to fill out extended surveys. The pod rating was 95, which she hoped she could personally help bring up. She was feeling very good, and needed.

"Mae."

The sound of her name, spoken by her processed voice, was jarring. She felt like she hadn't heard this voice in months, but it hadn't lost its power. She knew she should nod, but she wanted to hear it again, so she waited.

"Mae."

It felt like home.

Mae knew, intellectually, that the only reason she was in Francis's room was that everyone else in her life had, for the time being, abandoned her. After ninety minutes at CE, she checked the CircleSearch to see where Francis was, and saw he was in one of the dorms. Then she saw he was awake and online. Minutes later he'd invited her over, so grateful and so happy, he said, to be hearing from her. *I'm sorry,* he wrote, *and I'll say that again when you get to my door.* She turned off her camera and went to him.

The door opened.

"I'm so sorry," he said.

"Stop," Mae said. She stepped in and closed the door.

"You want anything?" he asked. "Water? There's this new vodka, too, that was here when I got back tonight. We can try it."

"No thanks," she said, and sat on a credenza against the wall. Francis had set up his portables there.

"Oh wait. Don't sit there," he said.

She stood up. "I didn't sit on your devices."

"No, it's not that," he said. "It's the credenza. They told me it's fragile," he said, smiling. "Sure you don't want a drink or anything?"

"No. I'm really tired. I just didn't want to be alone."

"Listen," he said. "I know I should have asked your permission first. I know this. But I hope you can understand where I was coming from. I couldn't believe I was with you. And there was some part of me that assumed it would be the only time. I wanted to remember it."

Mae knew the power she had over him, and that power gave her a distinct thrill. She sat on the bed. "So did you find them?" she asked.

"How do you mean?"

"Last I saw you, you were planning to scan those photos, the ones from your album."

"Oh yeah. I guess I haven't talked to you since then. I did scan them. The whole thing was easy."

"So you found who they were?"

"Most of them had Circle accounts so I could just face-rec them. I mean, it took about seven minutes. There were a few I had to use the feds' database for. We don't have total access yet, but we can see DMV photos. That's most of the adults in the country."

"And did you contact them?"

"Not yet."

"But you know where they're all from?"

"Yeah, yeah. Once I knew their names, I could find all their addresses. Some had moved a few times, but I could cross-reference with the years I might have been with them. I actually did this whole timeline of when I might have been at each place. Most of them were in Kentucky. A few in Missouri. One was in Tennessee."

"So that's it?"

"Well, I don't know. A couple are dead, so . . . I don't know. I might just drive by some of these houses. Just to fill in some gaps. I don't know. Oh," he said, turning over, brightening, "I did have a couple revelations. I mean, most of the stuff was standard memories of these people. But there was one family who had an older girl, she was about fifteen when I was twelve. I didn't remember much, but I know she was my first serious sexual fantasy."

Those words, *sexual fantasy,* had an immediate effect on Mae. In the past, whenever they'd been uttered, with or by any man, it led to the discussion of fantasies, and some degree of enacting one or another fantasy. Which she and Francis did, even if briefly. His fantasy was to leave the room and knock on the door, pretending to be a lost teenager knocking on the door of a beautiful suburban house. Her job was to be a lonely housewife and invite him in, scantily clad and desperate for company.

And so he knocked, and she greeted him at the door, and he told her he was lost, and she told him he should get out of those old clothes, that he could put on some of her husband's. Francis liked that so much that things accelerated quickly, and in seconds he was undressed and she was on top of him. He lay beneath her for a minute or two, letting Mae rise and fall, looking up at her with the wonderment of a boy at the zoo. Then his eyes closed, and he went into paroxysms, emitting a brief squeal before grunting his arrival.

Now, as Francis brushed his teeth, Mae, exhausted and feeling not love but something close to contentment, arranged herself under the thick comforter and faced the wall. The clock said 3:11.

Francis emerged from the bathroom.

"I have a second fantasy," he said, pulling the blanket over him and bringing his face close to Mae's neck.

"I'm inches from sleep," she muttered.

"No, nothing strenuous. No activity required. This is just a verbal thing."

"Okay."

"I want you to rate me," he said.

"What?"

"Just a rating. Like you do at CE."

"Like from 1 to 100?"

"Exactly."

"Rate what? Your performance?"

"Yes."

"C'mon. I don't want to do that."

"It's just for fun."

"Francis. Please. I don't want to. It takes the enjoyment out of it for me."

Francis sat up with a loud sigh. "Well, *not* knowing takes the enjoyment out of it for me."

"Not knowing what?"

"How I did."

"How you *did*? You did fine."

Francis made a loud sound of disgust.

She turned over. "What's the matter?"

"Fine?" he said. "I'm *fine*?"

"Oh god. You're great. You're perfect. When I say fine, I just mean that you couldn't do better."

"Okay," he said, moving closer to her. "Then why didn't you say that before?"

"I thought I did."

"You think 'fine' is the same as 'perfect' and 'couldn't do better'?"

"No. I know it's not. I'm just tired. I should have been more precise."

A self-satisfied smile overtook Francis's face. "You know you just proved my point."

"What point?"

"We just argued about all this, about the words you used and what they meant. We didn't understand their meaning the same way, and we went around and around about it. But if you had just used a number I would have understood right away." He kissed her shoulder.

"Okay. I get it," she said, and closed her eyes.

"Well?" he said.

She opened her eyes to Francis's pleading mouth.

"Well what?"

"You're still not going to give me a number?"

"You really want a number?"

"Mae! Of course I do."

"Okay, a hundred."

She turned to the wall again.

"That's the number?"

"It is. You get a perfect 100."

Mae felt like she could hear him grinning.

"Thank you," he said, and kissed the back of her head. "Night."

The room was grand, on the top floor of the Victorian Era, with its epic views, its glass ceiling. Mae entered and was greeted by most of the Gang of 40, the group of innovators who routinely assessed and greenlighted new Circle ventures.

"Hello Mae!" said a voice, and she found its source, Eamon Bailey, arriving and taking his place at the other end of the long room. Wearing a zippered sweatshirt, his sleeves rolled above his elbows, he entered theatrically and waved to her and, she knew, to all those who might be watching. She expected the audience to be large, given she and the Circle had been zinging about it for days. She checked her bracelet and the current viewership was 1,982,992. Incredible, she thought, and it would climb. She sat in the middle of the table, better to grant the viewers access not just to Bailey but to most of the Gang, their comments and reactions.

After she'd sat, and after it was too late to move, Mae realized she didn't know where Annie was. She scanned the forty faces in front of her, on the table's opposite side, and didn't see her. She craned her neck around, careful to keep the camera trained on Bailey, and finally caught sight of Annie, by the door, behind two rows of Circlers, those standing by the door, in case they needed to leave unnoticed. Mae knew Annie had seen her, but she made no acknowledgment.

"Okay," Bailey said, smiling broadly at the room, "I think we should just dig in, given we're all present"—and here his eyes stopped, ever so briefly, on Mae and the camera around her neck. It was important, Mae had been told, that the entire event seem natural, and that it appear that Mae, and the audience, were being invited into a very regular sort of event.

"Hi gang," Bailey said. "Pun intended." The forty men and women smiled. "Okay. A few months ago we all met Olivia Santos, a very courageous and visionary legislator who is bringing transparency to a new—and I daresay *ultimate*—level. And you might have seen that as of today, over twenty thousand other leaders and legislators around the world have followed her lead and have taken the pledge to make their lives as public servants completely transparent. We've been very encouraged by this."

Mae checked the view on her wrist. Her camera was trained on Bailey and the screen behind him. Comments were already coming in, thanking her and the Circle for this kind of access. One watcher compared it to watching the Manhattan Project. Another mentioned Edison's Menlo Park lab, circa 1879.

Bailey continued: "Now this new era of transparency dovetails with some other ideas I have about democracy, and the role that technology can play in making it complete. And I use the word *complete* on purpose, because our work toward transparency might actually achieve a fully accountable government. As you've seen, the governor of Arizona has had her entire staff go transparent, which is the next step. In a few cases, even with a clear elected official, we've seen some corruption behind the scenes. The transparent elected have been used as figureheads, shielding the backroom from view. But that will change soon, I believe.

The officials, and their entire offices with nothing to hide, will go transparent within the year, at least in this country, and Tom and I have seen to it that they get a steep discount on the necessary hardware and server capacity to make it happen."

The 40 clapped heartily.

"But that's only half the battle. That's the *elected* half of things. But what about the other half—*our* half as citizens? The half where we're all supposed to participate?"

Behind Bailey, a picture of an empty polling place appeared, in a desolate high school gym somewhere. It dissolved into an array of numbers.

"Here are the numbers of participants in the last elections. As you can see, at the national level, we're at around 58 percent of those eligible to vote. Incredible, isn't it? And then you go down the line, to state and local elections, and the percentages drop off a cliff: 32 percent for state elections, 22 percent for counties, 17 percent for most small-town elections. How illogical is that, that the closer government is to home, the less we care about it? It's absurd, don't you think?"

Mae checked her watchers; there were over two million. She was adding about a thousand viewers a second.

"Okay," Bailey continued, "so we know there are a bunch of ways that technology, much of it originating here, has helped make it easier to vote. We're building on a history of trying to increase access and ease. Back in my day there was the motor voter bill. That helped. Then some states allowed you to register or update your registration online. Fine. But how did it impact voter turnout? Not enough. But here's where it gets interesting. Here's how many people voted in the last national election."

The screen behind him read "140 million."

"Here's how many were eligible to vote."

The screen read "244 million."

"Meanwhile, there's us. Here's how many Americans are registered with the Circle."

The screen read "241 million."

"That's some startling math, right? A hundred million more people are registered with us than voted for the president. What does that tell you?"

"We're awesome!" an older man, with a gray ponytail and a frayed T-shirt, yelled from the second row. Laughter opened up the room.

"Well sure," Bailey said, "but besides that? It tells you that the Circle has a knack for getting people to participate. And there are a lot of people in Washington who agree. There are people in DC who see us as the solution to making this a fully participatory democracy."

Behind Bailey, the familiar image of Uncle Sam pointing appeared. Then another image, of Bailey wearing the same outfit, in the same pose, appeared next to Uncle Sam. The room guffawed.

"So now we get to the meat of today's session, and that is: What if your Circle profile *automatically* registered you to vote?"

Bailey swept his eyes across the room, hesitating again at Mae and her watchers. She checked her wrist. *Goosebumps,* one viewer wrote.

"With TruYou, to set up a profile, you have to be a real person, with a real address, complete personal info, a real Social Security number, a real and verifiable date of birth. In other words, all the information the government traditionally wants when you register to vote. In fact, as you all know, we have far *more* information. So why wouldn't this be enough information to allow you to register? Or better yet, why wouldn't the government—our government or any government—just *consider you registered* once you set up a TruYou profile?"

The forty heads in the room nodded, some out of acknowledgment of a sensible idea, some clearly having thought of this before, that it was a notion long discussed.

Mae checked her bracelet. The viewer numbers were climbing quicker, ten thousand a second, and were now over 2,400,000. She had 1,248 messages. Most had come through in the last ninety seconds. Bailey glanced down at his own tablet, no doubt seeing the same numbers she was seeing. Smiling, he continued: "There's no reason. And a lot of legislators agree with me. Congresswoman Santos does, for one. And I have verbal commitments from 181 other members of Congress and 32 senators. They've all agreed to push legislation to make your TruYou profile your automatic path to registration. Not bad, right?"

There was a brief round of applause.

"Now think," Bailey said, his voice a whisper of hope and wonder, "think if we can get closer to full participation in all elections. There would be no more grumbling from the sidelines from people who had neglected to participate. There would be no more candidates who had been elected by a fringe, wedge group. As we know here at the Circle, with full participation comes full knowledge. We know what Circlers want because we ask, and because they know their answers are necessary to get a full and accurate picture of the desires of the whole Circle community. So if we observe the same model nationally, electorally, then we can get very close, I think, to 100 percent participation. One hundred percent democracy."

Applause rippled through the room. Bailey smiled broadly, and Stenton stood; it was, for him at least, apparently the end of the presentation. But an idea had been forming within Mae's mind, and she raised her hand, tentatively.

"Yes Mae," Bailey said, his face still locked into a broad grin of triumph.

"Well, I wonder if we couldn't take this one step further. I mean . . . Well, actually, I don't think it—"

"No, no. Go on, Mae. You started well. I like the words *one step further*. That's how this company was built."

Mae looked around the room, the faces a mix of encouraging and concerned. Then she alighted on Annie's face, and because it was stern, and dissatisfied, and seemed to be expecting, or wanting, Mae to fail, to embarrass herself, Mae gathered herself, took a breath and forged ahead.

"Okay, well, you were saying we could get close to 100 percent participation. And I wonder why we couldn't just work backwards from that goal, using all the steps you outlined. All the tools we already have."

Mae looked around the room, ready to quit at the first pair of skeptical eyes, but she saw only curiosity, the slow collective nodding of a group practiced in pre-emptive validation.

"Go on," Bailey said.

"I'm just going to connect some dots," Mae said. "Well, first of all, we all agree that we'd like 100 percent participation, and that everyone would agree that 100 percent participation is the ideal."

"Yes," Bailey said. "It's certainly the idealist's ideal."

"And we currently have 83 percent of the voting-age Americans registered on the Circle?"

"Yes."

"And it seems that we're on our way to voters being able to register, and maybe even to actually vote, through the Circle."

Bailey's head was bobbing side to side, some indication of mild doubt, but he was smiling, his eyes encouraging. "A small leap, but okay. Go on."

"So why not *require* every voting-age citizen to have a Circle account?"

There was some shuffling in the room, some intake of breath, mostly from the older Circlers.

"Let her finish," someone, a new voice, said. Mae looked around to find Stenton near the door. His armed were crossed, his eyes staring at the floor. He looked, briefly, up to Mae, and nodded brusquely. She regained her direction.

"Okay, I know the initial reaction will be resistance. I mean, how can we *require* anyone to use our services? But we have to remember that there are all kinds of things that are mandatory for citizens of this country—and these things are mandatory in most industrialized countries. Do you have to send your kids to school? Yes. That's mandatory. It's a law. Kids have to go to school, or you have to arrange some kind of home schooling. But it's mandatory. It's also mandatory that you register for the draft, right? That you get rid of your garbage in an acceptable way; you can't drop it on the street. You have to have a license if you want to drive, and when you do, you have to wear a seat belt."

Stenton joined in again. "We require people to pay taxes. And to pay into Social Security. To serve on juries."

"Right," Mae said, "and to pee indoors, not on the streets. I mean, we have ten thousand laws. We require so many legitimate things of citizens of the United States. So why can't we require them to vote? They do in dozens of countries."

"It's been proposed here," one of the older Circlers said.

"Not by us," Stenton countered.

"And that's my point," Mae said, nodding to Stenton. "The technology has never been there before. I mean, at any other moment in history, it would have been prohibitively expensive to track down everyone and register them to vote, and then to make sure they actually did. You'd have to go door to door. Drive people to polls. All these unfeasible things. Even in the countries where it's mandatory, it's not really enforced. But now it's within reach. I mean, you cross-reference any voting rolls with the names in our TruYou database, and you'd find half the missing voters right there and then. You register them automatically, and then when election day comes around, you make sure they vote."

"How do we do that?" a female voice said. Mae realized it was Annie's. It wasn't a direct challenge, but the tone wasn't friendly, either.

"Oh jeez," Bailey said, "a hundred ways. That's an easy part. You remind them ten times that day. Maybe their accounts don't work that day till they vote. That's what I'd favor anyway. 'Hello Annie!' it could say. 'Take five minutes to vote.' Whatever it is. We do that for our own surveys. You know that, Annie." And when he said her name, he shaded it with disappointment and warning, discouraging her from opening her mouth again. He brightened and turned back to Mae. "And the stragglers?" he asked.

Mae smiled at him. She had an answer. She looked at her bracelet. There were now 7,202,821 people watching. When had that happened?

"Well, everyone has to pay taxes, right? How many people do it online now? Last year, maybe 80 percent. What if we all stopped duplicating services and made it all part of one unified system? You use your Circle account to pay taxes, to register to vote, to pay your parking tickets, to do anything. I mean, we would save each user hundreds of hours of inconvenience, and collectively, the country would save billions."

"*Hundreds* of billions," Stenton amended.

"Right," Mae said. "Our interfaces are infinitely easier to use than, say, the patchwork of DMV sites around the country. What if you could renew your license through us? What if every government service could be facilitated through our network? People would leap at the chance. Instead of visiting a hundred different sites for a hundred different government services, it could all be done through the Circle."

Annie opened her mouth again. Mae knew it was a mistake. "But why wouldn't the government," Annie asked, "just build a similar wraparound service? Why do they need us?"

Mae couldn't decide if she was asking this rhetorically or if she truly felt this was a valid point. In any case, much of the room was now snickering. The government building a system, from scratch, to rival the Circle? Mae looked to Bailey and to

Stenton. Stenton smiled, raised his chin and decided to take this one himself.

"Well, Annie, a government project to build a similar platform from the ground up would be ludicrous, and costly, and, well, impossible. We already have the infrastructure, and 83 percent of the electorate. Does that make sense to you?"

Annie nodded, her eyes showing fear and regret and maybe even some quickly fading defiance. Stenton's tone was dismissive, and Mae hoped he would soften when he continued.

"Now more than ever," he said, but now more condescending than before, "Washington is trying to save money, and is disinclined to build vast new bureaucracies from scratch. Right now it costs the government about ten dollars to facilitate every vote. Two hundred million people vote, and it costs the feds two billion to run the presidential election every four years. Just to process the votes for that one election, that one day. You factor in every state and local election, we're talking hundreds of billions every year in unnecessary costs associated with simple vote processing. I mean, they're still doing it on paper in some states. If we provide these services for free, we're saving the government billions of dollars, and, more important, the results would be known simultaneously. Do you see the truth in that?"

Annie nodded grimly, and Stenton looked to her, as if assessing her anew. He turned to Mae, urging her to continue.

"And if it's mandatory to have a TruYou account to pay taxes or receive any government service," she said, "then we're very close to having 100 percent of the citizenry. And then we can take the temperature of everyone at any time. A small town wants everyone to vote on a local ordinance. TruYou knows everyone's address, so only residents of that town can vote. And when they do, the results are known in minutes. A state wants to see how everyone feels about a new tax. Same thing—instant and clear and verifiable data."

"It would eliminate the guesswork," Stenton said, now standing at the head of the table. "Eliminate lobbyists. Eliminate polls. It might even eliminate Congress. If we can know the will of the people at any time, without filter, without misinterpretation or bastardization, wouldn't it eliminate much of Washington?"

The night was cold and the winds were lacerating but Mae didn't notice. Everything felt good, clean and right. To have the validation of the Wise Men, to have perhaps pivoted the entire company in a new direction, to have, perhaps, *perhaps,* ensured a new level of participatory democracy—could it be that the Circle, with her new idea, might really *perfect* democracy? Could she have conceived of the solution to a thousand-year-old problem?

There had been some concern, just after the meeting, about a private company taking over a very public act like voting. But the logic of it, the savings inherent, was winning the day. What if the schools had two hundred billion? What if the health care system had two hundred billion? Any number of the country's ills would be addressed or solved with that kind of savings—savings not just every four years, but some semblance of them every year. To eliminate all costly elections, replaced by instantaneous ones, all of them nearly cost-free?

This was the promise of the Circle. This was the unique position of the Circle. This is what people were zinging. She read the zings as she rode with Francis, in a train under the bay, the two of them grinning, out of their minds. They were being recognized. People were stepping in front of Mae to get onto her video feed, and she didn't care, hardly noticed, because the news coming through her right bracelet was too good to take her eyes off.

She checked her left arm, briefly; her pulse was elevated, her heart rate at 130. But she was loving it. When they arrived downtown, they took the stairs three at a time and arrived above ground, suddenly lit in gold, on Market Street, the Bay Bridge blinking beyond.

"Holy shit, it's Mae!" Who had said that? Mae found, hurrying toward them, a teenaged pair, hoodies and headphones. "Rock on, Mae," the other one said, their eyes approving, starstruck, before the two of them, clearly not wanting to seem stalky, hurried down the stairs.

"That was fun," Francis said, watching them descend.

Mae walked toward the water. She thought of Mercer and saw him as a shadow, quickly disappearing. She hadn't heard from him, or Annie, since the talk, and she didn't care. Her parents hadn't said a word, and might not have seen her performance, and she found herself unconcerned. She cared only about this moment, this night, the sky clear and starless.

"I can't believe how poised you were," Francis said, and he kissed her—a dry, professional kiss on the lips.

"Was I okay?" she asked, knowing how ridiculous it sounded, this kind of doubt in the wake of such an obvious success, but wanting once more to hear that she had done a good job.

"You were perfect," he said. "A 100."

Quickly, as they walked toward the water, she scrolled through the most popular recent comments. There seemed to be one particular zing with heat, something about how all this could or would lead to totalitarianism. Her stomach sank.

"C'mon. You can't listen to a lunatic like that," Francis said. "What does she know? Some crank somewhere with a tinfoil hat." Mae smiled, not knowing what the tinfoil hat reference meant, but knowing she'd heard her father say it, and it made her smile to think of him saying it.

"Let's get a libation," Francis said, and they decided on a glittering brewery on the water fronted by a wide outdoor patio. Even as they approached, Mae saw recognition in the eyes of the array of pretty young people drinking outdoors.

"It's Mae!" one said.

A young man, seeming too young to be drinking at all, aimed his face at Mae's camera. "Hey mom, I'm home studying." A woman of about thirty, who may or may not have been with the too-young man, said, walking out of view, "Hey honey, I'm at a book club with the ladies. Say hi to the kids!"

The night was dizzy and bright and went too fast. Mae barely moved at the bayside bar—she was surrounded, she was handed drinks, she was patted on the back, she was tapped on the shoulder. All night she pivoted, turning a few degrees, like a haywire clock, to greet each new well-wisher. Everyone wanted a picture with her, wanted to ask her when all this would happen. When would we break through all these unnecessary barriers? they asked. Now that the solution seemed clear and easy enough to execute, no one wanted to wait. A woman a bit older than

Mae, slurring and holding a Manhattan, expressed it best, though unwittingly: How, she asked, spilling her drink but with eyes sharp, How do we get the inevitable sooner?

Mae and Francis found themselves at a quieter place down the Embarcadero, where they ordered another round and found themselves joined by a man in his fifties. Uninvited, he sat down with them, holding a large drink in both hands. In seconds he'd told them he was once a divinity student, was living in Ohio and heading for the priesthood, when he discovered computers. He'd dropped it all and moved to Palo Alto, but had felt removed, for twenty years, he said, from the spiritual. Until now.

"I saw your talk today," he said. "You connected it all. You found a way to save all the souls. This is what we were doing in the church—we tried to get them all. How to save them all? This has been the work of missionaries for millennia." He was slurring, but took another long swallow from his drink. "You and yours at the Circle"—and here he drew a circle in the air, horizontally, and Mae thought of a halo—"you're gonna save all the souls. You're gonna get everyone in one place, you're gonna teach them all the same things. There can be one morality, one set of rules. Imagine!" And here he slammed his open palm upon the iron table, rattling his glass. "Now all humans will have the eyes of God. You know this passage? 'All things are naked and opened unto the eyes of God.' Something like that. You know your Bible?" Seeing the blank looks on the faces of Mae and Francis, he scoffed and took a long pull from his drink. "Now we're all God. Every one of us will soon be able to see, and cast judgment upon, every other. We'll see what He sees. We'll articulate His judgment. We'll channel His wrath and deliver His forgiveness.

On a constant and global level. All religion has been waiting for this, when every human is a direct and immediate messenger of God's will. Do you see what I'm saying?" Mae looked at Francis, who was having little success holding back a laugh. He burst first, and she followed, and they cackled, trying to apologize to him, holding their hands up, begging his forgiveness. But he was having none of it. He stepped away from the table, then swirled back to get his drink, and, now complete, he rambled crookedly down the waterfront.

Mae awoke next to Francis. It was seven a.m. They'd passed out in her dorm room shortly after two. She checked her phone, finding 322 new messages. As she was holding it, her eyes bleary, it rang. The caller ID was blocked, and she knew it could only be Kalden. She let it go to voicemail. He called a dozen more times throughout the morning. He called while Francis got up, kissed her and returned to his own room. He called while she was in the shower, while she was dressing. She brushed her hair, adjusted her bracelets and lifted the lens over her head, and he called again. She ignored the call and opened her messages.

There was an array of congratulatory threads, from inside and outside the Circle, the most intriguing of which was spurred by Bailey himself, who alerted Mae that Circle developers had begun to act on her ideas already. They'd been working through the night, in a fever of inspiration, and within a week hoped to prototype a version of Mae's notions, to be used first in the Circle, polished there and later rolled out for use in any nation where Circle membership was strong enough to make it practical.

We're calling it Demoxie, Bailey zinged. *It's democracy with your voice, and your moxie. And it's coming soon.*

That morning Mae was invited to the developers' pod, where she found twenty or so exhausted but inspired engineers and designers, who apparently already had a beta version of Demoxie ready. When Mae entered, cheers erupted, the lights dimmed and a single light shone on a woman with long black hair and a face of barely contained joy.

"Hello Mae, hello Mae's watchers," she said, bowing briefly. "My name is Sharma, and I'm so glad, and so honored, to be with you today. Today we'll be demonstrating the very earliest form of Demoxie. Normally we wouldn't move so quickly, and so, well, transparently, but given the Circle's fervent belief in Demoxie, and our confidence that it will be adopted quickly and globally, we couldn't see any reason to delay."

The wallscreen came to life. The word *Demoxie* appeared, rendered in a spirited font and set inside a blue-and-white striped flag.

"The goal is to make sure that everyone who works at the Circle can weigh in on issues that affect their lives—mostly on campus, but in the larger world, too. So throughout any given day, when the Circle needs to take the company's temperature on any given issue, Circlers will get a pop-up notice, and they'll be asked to answer the question or questions. The expected turnaround will be speedy, and will be essential. And because we care so much about everyone's input, your other messaging systems will freeze temporarily until you answer. Let me show you."

On the screen, below the Demoxie logo, the question *Should we have more veggie options at lunch?* was bookended by buttons on either side, *Yes* and *No*.

Mae nodded. "Very impressive, guys!"

"Thank you," Sharma said. "Now, if you'll indulge us. You have to answer, too." And she invited Mae to touch either Yes or No on the screen.

"Oh," Mae said. She walked up to the screen and pushed Yes. The engineers cheered, the developers cheered. On the screen, a happy face appeared, with the words *You are heard!* arcing above. The question disappeared, replaced by the words *Demoxie result: 75% of respondents want more veggie options. More veggie options will be provided.*

Sharma was beaming. "See? That's a simulated result, of course. We don't have everyone on Demoxie yet, but you get the gist. The question appears, everyone stops briefly what they're doing, responds, and instantly, the Circle can take appropriate action knowing the full and complete will of the people. Incredible, right?"

"It is," Mae said.

"Imagine this rolled out nationwide. Worldwide!"

"It's beyond my capability to imagine."

"But you came up with this!" Sharma said.

Mae didn't know what to say. Had she invented this? She wasn't sure. She'd connected a few dots: the efficiency and utility of the CircleSurveys, the constant Circle goal of total saturation, the universal hope for real and unfiltered—and, most crucially, complete—democracy. Now it was in the hands of the developers, hundreds of them at the Circle, the best in the world. Mae told them this, that she was just one person who connected a few ideas that stood inches apart, and Sharma, and her team, beamed, and shook her hand, and they all agreed that what had already been done was setting the Circle, and possibly all of humanity, on a significant new path.

Mae left the Renaissance and was greeted, just outside the door, by a group of young Circlers, all of whom wanted to tell her—all of them on their tiptoes, bursting—that they had never voted before, that they had been utterly uninterested in politics, had felt disconnected entirely from their government, feeling they had no real voice. They told her that by the time their vote, or their name on some petition, was filtered through their local government, and then their state officials, and finally their representatives in Washington, it felt like sending a message in a bottle across a vast and troubled sea. But now, the young Circlers said, they felt involved. If Demoxie worked, they said, then laughed—when Demoxie is implemented, of *course* it will work, they said—and when it does, you'll finally have a fully engaged populace, and when you do, the country and the world will hear from the youth, and their inherent idealism and progressivism will upend the planet. This is what Mae heard all day, as she wandered through the campus. She could barely get from one building to another without being accosted. *We're on the verge of actual change,* they said. *Change at the speed that our hearts demand.*

But throughout the morning, the calls from the blocked number continued. She knew it was Kalden, and she knew she wanted no part of him. Talking to him, much less seeing him, would be a significant step back now. By noon, Sharma and her team

402

announced that they were ready for the first actual all-campus Demoxie tryout. At 12:45 everyone would receive five questions, and the results would not only be tabulated immediately, but, the Wise Men promised, the will of the people would be enacted within the day.

Mae was standing in the center of the campus, amid a few hundred Circlers eating lunch, all of them buzzing about the imminent Demoxie demonstration, and she thought of that painting of the Constitutional Convention, all those men in powdered wigs and waistcoats, standing stiffly, all of them wealthy white men who were only passably interested in representing their fellow humans. They were purveyors of an innately flawed kind of democracy, where only the wealthy were elected, where their voices were heard loudest, where they passed their seats in Congress to whatever similarly entitled person they deemed appropriate. There had been some incremental improvements in the system since then, maybe, but Demoxie would explode it all. Demoxie was purer, was the only chance at direct democracy the world had ever known.

It was twelve thirty, and because Mae was feeling strong, and feeling so confident, she finally succumbed and answered her phone, knowing it would be Kalden.

"Hello?" she said.

"Mae," he said, his voice terse, "this is Kalden. Don't say my name. I've rigged it so the incoming audio isn't working."

"No."

"Mae. Please. This is life or death."

Kalden held a power over her that shamed her. It made her feel weak and pliable. In every other facet of her life she was in

403

control, but his voice alone disassembled her, and opened her to an array of bad decisions. A minute later she was in the stall, her audio was off and her phone rang again.

"I'm sure someone is tracing this," she said.

"No one is. I bought us time."

"Kalden, what do you want?"

"You can't do this. Your mandatory thing, and the positive reaction it's gotten—this is the last step toward closing the Circle, and that can't happen."

"What are you talking about? This is the whole point. If you've been here so long, you know more than anyone that that's been the goal of the Circle since the beginning. I mean, it's a circle, stupid. It has to close. It has to be complete."

"Mae, all along, for me at least, this kind of thing was the fear, not the goal. Once it's mandatory to have an account, and once all government services are channeled through the Circle, you'll have helped create the world's first tyrannical monopoly. Does it seem like a good idea to you that a private company would control the flow of all information? That participation, at their beck and call, is mandatory?"

"You know what Ty said, right?"

Mae heard a loud sigh. "Maybe. What did he say?"

"He said the soul of the Circle is democratic. That until everyone has equal access, and that access is free, no one is free. It's on at least a few tiles around campus."

"Mae. Fine. The Circle's good. And whoever invented TruYou is some kind of evil genius. But now it has to be reined in. Or broken up."

"Why do you care? If you don't like it, why don't you leave?

I know you're some spy for some other company. Or Williamson. Some loony anarchist politician."

"Mae, this is it. You know this affects everyone. When were you last able to meaningfully contact your parents? Obviously things are messed up, and you're in a unique position to influence very crucial historic events here. This is it. This is the moment where history pivots. Imagine if you could have been there before Hitler became chancellor. Before Stalin annexed Eastern Europe. We're on the verge of having another very hungry, very evil empire on our hands, Mae. Do you understand?"

"Do you know how crazy you sound?"

"Mae, I know you're doing that big plankton meeting in a couple days. The one where the kids pitch their ideas, hoping the Circle buys them and devours them."

"So?"

"The audience will be big. We need to reach the young, and the plankton pitching is when your watchers will be young and vast. It's perfect. The Wise Men will be there. I need you to take that opportunity to warn everyone. I need you to say, 'Let's think about what closing the Circle means.' "

"You mean completing?"

"Same thing. What it means for personal liberties, for the freedom to move, do whatever one wants to do, to be free."

"You're a lunatic. I can't believe I——" Mae meant to finish that sentence with "slept with you" but now, even the thought of it seemed sick.

"Mae, no entity should have the power those guys have."

"I'm hanging up."

"Mae. Think about it. They'll write songs about you."

She hung up.

By the time she made it to the Great Hall, it was raucous with a few thousand Circlers. The rest of the campus had been asked to stay at their workspaces, to demonstrate to the world how Demoxie would work across the whole company, with Circlers voting from their desks, from their tablets and phones and even retinally. On the screen in the Great Room, a vast grid of SeeChange cameras showed Circlers at the ready in every corner of every building. Sharma had explained, in one of a series of zings, that once the Demoxie questions were sent, each Circler's ability to do anything else—any zing, any keystroke—would be suspended until they voted. *Democracy is mandatory here!* she said, and added, much to Mae's delight, *Sharing is caring.* Mae planned to vote on her wrist, and had promised her watchers that she would take into account their input, too, if they were quick enough. The voting, Sharma suggested, shouldn't take longer than sixty seconds.

And then the Demoxie logo appeared on the screen, and the first question arrived below it.

1. Should the Circle offer more veggie options at lunch?

The crowd in the Great Hall laughed. Sharma's team had chosen to start with the question they'd been testing. Mae checked her wrist, seeing that a few hundred watchers had sent smiles, and so she chose that option and pushed "send." She looked up to the screen, watching Circlers vote, and within eleven seconds the whole campus had done so, and the results were tabulated. Eighty-eight percent of the campus wanted more veggie options at lunch.

A zing came through from Bailey: *It shall be done.*

The Great Hall shook with applause.

The next question appeared: *2. Should Take Your Daughter to Work Day happen twice a year, instead of just once?*

The answer was known within 12 seconds. Forty-five percent said yes. Bailey zinged: *Looks like once is enough for now.*

The demonstration so far was a clear success, and Mae was basking in the congratulations of Circlers in the room, and on her wrist, and from watchers worldwide. The third question appeared, and the room broke up with laughter.

3. John or Paul or . . . Ringo?

The answer, which took 16 seconds, provoked a riot of surprised cheers: Ringo had won, with 64 percent of the vote. John and Paul were nearly tied, at 20 and 16.

The fourth question was preceded by a sober instruction: *Imagine the White House wanted the unfiltered opinion of its constituents. And imagine you had the direct and immediate ability to influence U.S. foreign policy. Take your time on this one. There might come a day—there should come a day—when all Americans are heard in such matters.*

The instructions disappeared, and the question arrived:

4. Intelligence agencies have located terrorist mastermind Mohammed Khalil al-Hamed in a lightly populated area of rural Pakistan. Should we send a drone to kill him, considering the likelihood of moderate collateral damage?

Mae caught her breath. She knew this was a demonstration only, but the power felt real. And it felt right. Why wouldn't the wisdom of three hundred million Americans be taken into account when making a decision that affected them all? Mae paused, thinking, weighing the pros and cons. The Circlers in the room seemed to be taking the responsibility as seriously as Mae. How many lives would be saved by killing al-Hamed? It could be thousands, and the world would be rid of an evil man. The risk seemed worth it. She voted yes. The full tally arrived after one minute, eleven seconds: 71 percent of Circlers favored a drone strike. A hush fell over the room.

Then the last question appeared:

5. *Is Mae Holland awesome or what?*

Mae laughed, and the room laughed, and Mae blushed, thinking this was all a bit much. She decided she couldn't vote on this one, given how absurd it would be to cast a vote either way, and she simply watched her wrist, which, she soon realized, had been frozen. Soon the question on her wristscreen was blinking urgently. *All Circlers must vote,* the screen said, and she remembered that the survey couldn't be complete until every Circler had registered their opinion. Because she felt silly calling herself awesome, she pushed "frown," guessing it would be the only one, and would get a laugh.

But when the votes were tallied, seconds later, she was not the only one to have sent a frown. The vote was 97 percent to 3, smiles to frowns, indicating that overwhelmingly, her fellow Circlers found her awesome. When the numbers appeared, the Great Room erupted in whoops, and she was patted on the back as everyone filed out, feeling the experiment a monumental success. And Mae felt this way, too. She knew Demoxie was working, and its potential unlimited. And she knew she should feel good about 97 percent of the campus finding her awesome. But as she left the hall, and made her way across campus, she could only think of the 3 percent who did not find her awesome. She did the math. If there were now 12,318 Circlers—they'd just subsumed a Philadelphia startup specializing in the gamification of affordable housing—and every one of them had voted, that meant that 369 people had frowned at her, thought she was something other than awesome. No, 368. She'd frowned at herself, assuming she'd be the only one.

She felt numb. She felt naked. She walked through the health club, glancing at the bodies sweating, stepping on and off machines, and she wondered who among them had frowned at her. Three hundred and sixty-eight people loathed her. She was devastated. She left the health club and looked for a quiet place to collect her thoughts. She made her way to the rooftop near her old pod, where Dan had first told her of the Circle's commitment to community. It was a half-mile walk from where she was, and she wasn't sure she could make it. She was being stabbed. She had been stabbed. Who were these people? What had she done to them? They didn't know her. Or did they? And what kind of community members would send a frown to someone like Mae, who was working tirelessly with them, *for* them, in full view?

She was trying to hold it together. She smiled when she passed fellow Circlers. She accepted their congratulations and gratitude, each time wondering which of them was two-faced, which of them had pushed that frown button, each push of that button the pull of a trigger. That was it, she realized. She felt full of holes, as if every one of them had shot her, from behind, cowards filling her with holes. She could barely stand.

And then, just before reaching her old building, she saw Annie. They hadn't had a natural interaction in months, but immediately something in Annie's face spoke of light and happiness. "Hey!" she said, catapulting herself forward to take Mae in a wraparound hug.

Mae's eyes were suddenly wet, and she wiped them, feeling silly and elated and confused. All her conflicted thoughts of Annie were, for a moment, washed away.

"You're doing well?" she asked.

"I am. I am. So many good things happening," Annie said. "Did you hear about the PastPerfect project?"

Mae sensed something in Annie's voice then, an indication that Annie was talking, primarily, to the audience around Mae's neck. Mae went along.

"Well, you told me the gist before. What's new with PastPerfect, Annie?"

While looking at Annie, and appearing interested in what Annie was saying, Mae's mind was elsewhere: Had Annie frowned at her? Maybe just to knock her down a notch? And how would *Annie* fare in a Demoxie poll? Could she beat 97 percent? Could anyone?

"Oh gosh, so many things, Mae. As you know, PastPerfect has been in the works for many years. It's what you might call a passion project of Eamon Bailey. What if, he thought, we used the power of the web, and of the Circle and its billions of members, to try to fill in the gaps in personal history, and history generally?"

Mae, seeing her friend trying so hard, could do nothing but try to match her glossy enthusiasm.

"Whoa, that sounds incredible. Last we talked, they were looking for a pioneer to be the first to have their ancestry mapped. Did they find that person?"

"Well, they did, Mae, I'm glad you asked. They found that person, and that person is me."

"Oh, right. So they really didn't choose yet?"

"No, really," Annie said, her voice lowering, and suddenly sounding more like the actual Annie. Then she brightened again, rising an octave. "It's me!"

Mae had become practiced in waiting before speaking—transparency had taught her to measure every word—and now, instead of saying, *I expected it to be some newbie, someone without a whole lot of experience. Or at the very least a striver, someone trying to make some PartiRank leaps, or curry favor with the Wise Men. But you?* she realized that Annie was, or felt she was, in a position where she needed a boost, an edge. And thus she'd volunteered.

"You volunteered?"

"I did. I did," Annie said, looking at Mae but utterly through her. "The more I heard about it, the more I wanted to be the first. As you know, but your watchers might not, my family came here on the *Mayflower*"—and here she rolled her eyes—"and though we have some high-water marks in our family history, there's so much I don't know."

Mae was speechless. Annie had gone haywire. "And everyone's on board with this? Your parents?"

"They're so excited. I guess they've always been proud of our heritage, and the ability to share it with people, and along the way find out a bit about the history of the country, well, it appealed to them. Speaking of parents, how are yours?"

My god, this was strange, Mae thought. There were so many layers to all this, and while her mind was counting them, mapping them and naming them, her face and mouth had to carry on this conversation.

"They're fine," Mae said, even though she knew, and Annie knew, that Mae hadn't been in touch with them in weeks. They had sent word, through a cousin, of their health, which was fine, but they had left their home, "fleeing" was the only word they used in their brief message, telling Mae not to worry about anything.

Mae wrapped up the conversation with Annie and walked slowly, foggy-headed, back through campus, knowing Annie was satisfied in how she'd communicated her news, and trumped and thoroughly confused Mae, all in one brief encounter. Annie had been appointed the center of PastPerfect and Mae hadn't been told, and was made to look idiotic. Certainly that would have been Annie's goal. And why *Annie*? It didn't make sense to go to Annie, when it would have been easier to have Mae do it; Mae was already transparent.

Mae realized that Annie had asked for this. Begged the Wise Men for this. Her proximity to them had made it possible. And so Mae was not as close as she'd imagined; Annie still held some particular status. Again Annie's lineage, her head start, the varied and ancient advantages she enjoyed, were keeping Mae second. Always second, like she was some kind of little sister who never had a chance of succeeding an older, always older sibling. Mae was trying to remain calm, but messages were coming through her wrist that made clear her viewers were seeing her frustration, her distraction.

She needed to breathe. She needed to think. But there was too much in her head. There was Annie's ludicrous gamesmanship. There was this ridiculous PastPerfect thing, which should have gone to Mae. Was it because Mae's parents had slipped off the path? And where *were* her parents, anyway? Why were they sabotaging everything Mae was working for? But what was she working for, anyway, if 368 Circlers didn't approve of her? Three hundred and sixty-eight people who apparently actively hated her, enough to push a button at her—to send their loathing directly to her, knowing she would know, immediately, their sentiments. And what about this cellular mutation some Scottish scientist was worried about? A cancerous mutation that might be happening inside Mae, provoked by mistakes in her diet? Had that really happened? And shit, Mae thought, her throat tightening, did she really send a frown to a group of heavily armed paramilitaries in Guatemala? What if they had contacts here? Certainly there were plenty of Guatemalans in California, and certainly they would be more than happy to have a trophy like Mae, to punish her for her opprobrium. Fuck, she thought. Fuck. There was a pain in her, a pain that was spreading its black wings inside her. And it was coming, primarily, from the 368 people who apparently hated her so much they wanted her gone. It was one thing to send a frown to Central America, but to send one just across campus? Who would do that? Why was there so much animosity in the world? And then it occurred to her, in a brief and blasphemous flash: she didn't *want* to know how they felt. The flash opened up into something larger, an even more blasphemous notion that her brain contained too much. That the volume of information, of data, of judgments, of measurements, was too much, and there were too many people, and too many desires of too many people, and too many opinions of too many people, and too much pain from too many people, and having all of it constantly collated, collected, added and aggregated, and presented to her as if that all made it tidier and more manageable—it was too much. But no. No, it was not, her better brain corrected. No. You're hurt by these 368 people. This was the truth. She was hurt by them, by the 368 votes to kill her. Every one of them preferred her dead. If only she didn't know about this. If only she could return to life before this 3 percent, when she could walk through campus, waving, smiling, chatting idly, eating, sharing human contact, without knowing what was deep in the hearts of the 3 percent. To frown at her, to stick their fingers at that button, to shoot her that way, it was a kind of murder. Mae's wrist was flashing with dozens of messages of concern. With help from the campus SeeChange cameras, watchers were noticing her standing, stock-still, her face contorted into some raging, wretched mask.

She needed to do something. She went back to CE, waved to Jared and the rest and logged herself into the chute.

In minutes she had helped with a query from a small jewelry maker in Prague, had checked out the maker's website, had found the work intriguing and wonderful and had said so, aloud and in a zing, which produced an astronomical Conversion Rate and a Retail Raw, in ten minutes, of 52,098 euros. She helped a sustainably sourced furniture wholesaler in North Carolina, Design for Life, and after answering their query, they wanted her to fill out a customer survey, which was especially important given her age and income bracket—they needed more information about the preferences of customers in her demographic. She did that, and also commented on a series of photos her contact at Design for

Life, Sherilee Fronteau, had sent her of her son at his first T-ball practice. When Mae commented on those photos, she received a message from Sherilee thanking Mae, and insisting that she come to Chapel Hill sometime, to see Tyler in person and eat some genuine barbecue. Mae agreed she would, feeling very good to have this new friend on the opposite coast, and moved on to her second message, from a client, Jerry Ulrich, in Grand Rapids, Michigan, who ran a refrigerated truck company. He wanted Mae to forward a message to everyone on her list about the company's services, that they were trying very hard to increase their presence in California, and any help would be appreciated. Mae zinged him that she would tell everyone she knew, starting with the 14,611,002 followers she had, and he sent word back that he was thrilled to have been so introduced, and that he welcomed business or comments from all 14,611,002 people—1,556 of whom instantly greeted Jerry and said they, too, would spread the word. Then, as he was enjoying the flood of messages, he asked Mae how his niece, who was graduating from Eastern Michigan University in the spring, might go about getting a job at the Circle; it was her dream to work there, and should she move out west to be closer, or should she hope to get an interview based on her résumé alone? Mae directed him to the HR department, and gave him some hints of her own. She added the niece to her contact list, and made a note to keep track of her progress, if she indeed applied for work there. One customer, Hector Casilla of Orlando, Florida, told Mae about his interest in birding, sent her some of his photos, which Mae praised and added to her own photo cloud. Hector asked her to rate them, for this might get him noticed in the photo-sharing group he was trying to join. She did so, and he was ecstatic. Within minutes, Hector said, someone in his photo-sharing group had been deeply impressed that an actual Circler was aware of his work, so Hector thanked Mae again. He sent her an invitation to a group exhibition he was part of that winter, in Miami Beach, and Mae said if she found herself down that way in January, she would certainly attend, and Hector, perhaps misconstruing the level of her interest, connected her with his cousin, Natalia, who owned a bed and breakfast only forty minutes from Miami, and who could absolutely get Mae a deal if she chose to come out—her friends, too, were welcome. Natalia then sent a message, with the B&B's rates, which, she noted, were flexible if she wanted to stay during the week. Natalia followed up a moment later with a long message, full of links to articles and images of the Miami area, elucidating the many activities possible in winter—sport fishing, jet-skiing, dancing. Mae worked on, feeling the familiar tear, the growing blackness, but working through it, killing it, until she finally noticed the time: 10:32.

She'd been in CE for more than four hours. She walked to the dorms, feeling far better, feeling calm, and found Francis in bed, working on his tablet, pasting his face into his favorite movies. "Check this out," he said, and showed her a sequence from an action movie where, instead of Bruce Willis, the protagonist now seemed to be Francis Garaventa. The software was near-perfect, Francis said, and could be operated by any child. The Circle had just purchased it from a three-person startup out of Copenhagen.

"I guess you'll see more new stuff tomorrow," Francis said, and Mae remembered the meeting with the plankton pitchers. "It'll be fun. Sometimes the ideas are even good. And speaking of good ideas . . ." And then Francis pulled her down to him, and kissed her, and pulled her hips into him, and for a moment she thought they were about to have something like a real sexual experience, but just when she was taking off her shirt, she saw Francis clench his eyes and jerk forward, and she knew he was already done. After changing and brushing his teeth, he asked Mae to rate him, and she gave him a 100.

Mae opened her eyes. It was 4:17 a.m. Francis was turned away from her, sleeping soundlessly. She closed her eyes, but could think only of the 368 people who—it seemed self-evident now—would rather she'd never been born. She had to get back into the CE chute. She sat up.

"What's the matter?" Francis said.

She turned to find him staring at her.

"Nothing. Just this Demoxie vote thing."

"You can't worry about that. It's a few hundred people."

He reached for Mae's back, and, attempting to comfort her from the other side of the bed, achieved more of a wiping motion across her waist.

"But who?" Mae said. "Now I have to walk around campus not knowing who wants me dead."

Francis sat up. "So why don't you check?"

"Check what?"

"Who frowned at you. Where do you think you are? The eighteenth century? This is the Circle. You can find out who frowned at you."

"It's transparent?"

Instantly Mae felt silly even asking.

"You want me to look?" Francis said, and in seconds he was on his tablet, scrolling. "Here's the list. It's public—that's the whole thing with Demoxie." His eyes narrowed as he read the list. "Oh, that one's no surprise."

"What?" Mae said, her heart jumping. "Who?"

"Mr. Portugal."

"Alistair?"

Mae's head was on fire.

"Fucker," Francis said. "Whatever. Fuck him. You want the whole list?" Francis turned the tablet to her, but before she knew what she was doing, she was backing away, her eyes clenched. She stood in the corner of the room, covering her face with her arms.

"Whoa," Francis said. "It's not some rabid animal. They're just names on a list."

"Stop," Mae said.

"Most of these people probably didn't even mean it. And some of these people I *know* actually like you."

"Stop. Stop."

"Okay, okay. You want me to clear the screen?"

"Please."

Francis complied.

Mae went into the bathroom and closed the door.

"Mae?" Francis was on the other side.

She turned on the shower and took off her clothes.

"Can I come in?"

Under the pounding water, Mae felt calmer. She reached the wall and turned on the light. She smiled, thinking her reaction to the list was foolish. Of *course* the votes were public. With actual democracy, a purer kind of democracy, people would be unafraid to cast their votes, and, more important, unafraid to be held accountable for those votes. It was up to her, now, to know who those who frowned at her were, and to win them over. Maybe not immediately. She needed time before she'd be ready, but she would know—she needed to know, it was her responsibility to know—and once she knew, the work to correct the 368 would be simple and honest. She was nodding, and smiled realizing she was alone in the shower, nodding. But she couldn't help it. The elegance of it all, the ideological purity of the Circle, of real transparency, gave her peace, a warming feeling of logic and order.

The group was a gorgeous rainbow coalition of youth, dreadlocks and freckles, eyes of blue and green and brown. They were all sitting forward, their faces alight. Each had four minutes to present his or her idea to the Circle braintrust, including Bailey and Stenton, who were in the room, talking intently to other members of the Gang of 40, and Ty, who was appearing via video feed. He sat somewhere else, in a blank white room, wearing his oversized hoodie and staring, not bored and not visibly interested, into the camera and into the room. And it was he, as much or more than any other Wise Men or senior Circlers, that the presenters wanted to impress. They were his children, in some sense: all of them motivated by his success, his youth, his ability to see ideas into execution, while remaining himself, perfectly aloof and yet furiously productive. They wanted that, too, and they wanted the money they knew went along with the role.

This was the assembly Kalden had been talking about, where,

he was certain, there would be a maximum viewing audience, and where, he insisted, Mae should tell all her watchers that the Circle could not complete, that Completion would lead to some kind of armageddon. She had not heard from him since that conversation in the bathroom, and she was glad for it. Now she was sure, more than ever, that he was some kind of hacker-spy, someone from a would-be competitor, trying to turn Mae and whomever else against the company, to blow it up from within.

She shook all thoughts of him from her mind. This forum would be good, she knew. Dozens of Circlers had been hired this way: they came to campus as aspirants, presented an idea and that idea was bought on the spot and the aspirant was thereafter employed. Jared had been hired this way, Mae knew, and Gina, too. It was one of the more glamorous ways to arrive at the company: to pitch an idea, have it acquired, be rewarded with employment and stock options and see their idea executed in short order.

Mae explained all of this to her watchers as the room settled. There were about fifty Circlers, the Wise Men, the Gang of 40 and a few assistants in the room, all of them facing a row of aspirants, a few of them still in their teens, each of them sitting, waiting for his or her turn.

"This will be very exciting," Mae said to her watchers. "As you know, this is the first time we've broadcast an Aspirant session." She almost said "plankton" and was happy to have caught the slur before uttering it. She glanced down at her wrist. There were 2.1 million watchers, though she expected that to climb quickly.

The first student, Faisal, looked no more than twenty. His skin glowed like lacquered wood, and his proposal was exceedingly simple: instead of having endless mini-battles over whether or not a given person's spending activity could or could not be tracked, why not make a deal with them? For highly desirable consumers, if they agreed to use CircleMoney for all their purchases, and agreed to make their spending habits and preferences accessible to CirclePartners, then the Circle would give them discounts, points and rebates at the end of each month. It would be like getting frequent flyer miles for using the same credit card.

Mae knew she would personally sign up for such a plan, and assumed that, by extension, so would millions more.

"Very intriguing," Stenton said, and Mae would later learn that when he said "very intriguing" he meant that he would purchase that idea and hire its inventor.

The second notion came from an African-American woman of about twenty-two. Her name was Belinda and her idea, she said, would eliminate racial profiling by police and airport security officers. Mae began nodding; this was what she loved about her generation—the ability to see the social-justice applications to the Circle and address them surgically. Belinda brought up a video feed of a busy urban street with a few hundred people visible and walking to and from the camera, unaware they were being watched.

"Every day, police pull over people for what's known as 'driving while black' or 'driving while brown,' " Belinda said evenly, "And every day, young African-American men are stopped in the street, thrown against a wall, frisked, stripped of their rights and dignity."

And for a moment Mae thought of Mercer, and wished he could be hearing this. Yes, sometimes some of the applications of the internet could be a bit crass and commercial, but for every one commercial application, there were three like this, proactive applications that used the power of the technology to improve humanity.

Belinda continued: "These practices only create more animosity between people of color and the police. See this crowd? It's mostly young men of color, right? A police cruiser goes by an area like this, and they're all suspects, right? Every one of these men might be stopped, searched, disrespected. But it doesn't have to be that way."

Now, on-screen, amid the crowd, three of the men in the picture were glowing orange and red. They continued to walk, to act normally, but now they were bathed in color, as if a spotlight, with colored gels, was singling them out.

"The three men you see in orange and red are repeat offenders. Orange indicates a low-level criminal—a guy convicted of petty thefts, drug possession, nonviolent and largely victimless crimes." There were two men in the frame who had been colored orange. Walking closer to the camera, though, was an innocuous-enough seeming man of about fifty, glowing red from head to toe. "The man signaling red, though, has been convicted of violent crimes. This man has been found guilty of armed robbery, attempted rape, repeated assaults."

Mae turned to find Stenton's face rapt, his mouth slightly open.

Belinda continued. "We're seeing what an officer would see if he were equipped with SeeYou. It's a simple enough system that works through any retinal. He doesn't have to do a thing. He scans any crowd, and he immediately sees all the people with prior convictions. Imagine if you're a cop in New York. Suddenly a city of eight million becomes infinitely more manageable when you know where to focus your energies."

Stenton spoke. "How do they know? Some kind of chip?"

"Maybe," Belinda said. "It could be a chip, if we could get that to happen. Or else, even easier would be to attach a bracelet. They've been using ankle bracelets for decades now. So you modify it so the bracelet can be read by the retinals, and provides the tracking capability. Of course," she said, looking to Mae with a warm smile, "you could also apply Francis's technology, and make it a chip. But that would take some legal doing, I expect."

Stenton leaned back. "Maybe, maybe not."

"Well, obviously that would be ideal," Belinda said. "And it would be permanent. You'd always know who the offenders were, whereas the bracelet is still subject to some tampering and removal. And then there are those who might say it should be removed after a certain period. The violators expunged."

"I hate that notion," Stenton said. "It's the community's right to know who's committed crimes. It just makes sense. This is how they've been handling sex offenders for decades. You commit sexual offenses, you become part of a registry. Your address becomes public, you have to walk the neighborhood, introduce yourself, all that, because people have a right to know who lives in their midst."

Belinda was nodding. "Right, right. Of course. And so, for lack of a better word, you tag the convicts, and from then on, if you're a police officer, instead of driving down the street, shaking down anyone who happens to be black or brown or wearing baggy pants, imagine instead you were using a retinal app that saw career criminals in distinct colors—yellow for low-level offenders, orange for nonviolent but slightly more dangerous offenders and red for the truly violent."

Now Stenton was leaning forward. "Take it a step further. Intelligence agencies can instantly create a web of all of a suspect's contacts, co-conspirators. It takes seconds. I wonder if there could be variations on the color scheme, to take into account those who might be known *associates* of a criminal, even if they haven't personally been arrested or convicted yet. As you know, a lot of mob bosses are never convicted of anything."

Belinda was nodding vigorously. "Yes. Absolutely," she said. "And in those cases, you'd be using a mobile device to tag that person, given you wouldn't have the benefit of a conviction to ensure the mandatory chip or bracelet."

"Right. Right," Stenton said. "There are possibilities there, though. Good things to think about. I'm intrigued."

Belinda glowed, sat down, feigned nonchalance by smiling at Gareth, the next aspirant, who stood up, nervous and blinking. He was a tall man with cantaloupe-colored hair, and now that he had the room's attention, he grinned shyly, crookedly.

"Well, for better or worse, my idea was similar to Belinda's. Once we realized we were working on similar notions, we collaborated a bit. The main commonality is that we're both interested in safety. My plan, I think, would eliminate crime block by block, neighborhood by neighborhood."

He stood before the screen and revealed a rendering of a small neighborhood of four blocks, twenty-five houses. Bright green lines denoted the buildings, allowing viewers to see inside; it reminded Mae of heat-reading visual displays.

"It's based on the neighborhood watch model, where groups of neighbors look out for each other, and report any anomalous behavior. With NeighborWatch—that's my name for this, though it could be changed of course—we leverage the power of SeeChange specifically, and the Circle generally, to make the committing of a crime, any crime, extremely difficult in a fully participating neighborhood."

He pushed a button and now the houses were full of figures, two or three or four in each building, all of them colored blue. They moved around in their digital kitchens, bedrooms and backyards.

"Okay, as you can see, here are the residents of the neighborhood, all going about their business. They're rendered blue here, because they've all registered with NeighborWatch, and their prints, retinas, phones and even body profile have been memorized by the system."

"This is the view any resident can see?" Stenton asked.

"Exactly. This is their home display."

"Impressive," Stenton said. "I'm already intrigued."

"So as you can see, all is well in the neighborhood. Everyone who's there is supposed to be there. But now we see what happens when an unknown person arrives."

A figure, colored red, appeared, and walked up to the door of one of the houses. Gareth turned to the audience and raised his eyebrows.

"The system doesn't know this man, so he's red. Any new person entering the neighborhood would automatically trigger the computer. All the neighbors would receive a notice on their home and mobile devices that a visitor was in the neighborhood. Usually it's no big deal. Someone's friend or uncle is dropping by. But either way, you can see there's a new person, and where he is."

Stenton was sitting back, as if he knew the rest of the story but wanted to help it speed along. "I'm assuming, then, there's a way to neutralize him."

"Yes. The people he's visiting can send a message to the system saying he's with them, IDing him, vouching for him: 'That's Uncle George.' Or they could do that ahead of time. So then he's tagged blue again."

Now Uncle George, the figure on the screen, went from red to blue, and entered the house.

"So all is well in the neighborhood again."

"Unless there's a real intruder," Stenton prodded.

"Right. On the rare occasion when it's truly someone with ill-intent . . ." Now the screen featured a red figure stalking outside the house, peering in the windows. "Well, then the whole neighborhood would know it. They'd know where he was, and could either stay away, call the police, confront him, whatever it is they want to do."

"Very good. Very nice," Stenton said.

Gareth beamed. "Thank you. And Belinda made me think that, you know, any ex-cons living in the neighborhood would register as red or orange in any display. Or some other color, where you'd know they were residents of the neighborhood, but you'd also know they were convicts or whatever."

Stenton nodded. "It's your right to know."

"Absolutely," Gareth said.

"Seems like this solves one of the problems of SeeChange," Stenton said, "which is that even when there are cameras everywhere, not everyone can watch everything. If a crime is committed at three a.m., who's watching camera 982, right?"

"Right," Gareth said. "See, this way the cameras are just part of it. The color-tagging tells you who's anomalous, so you only have to pay attention to that particular anomaly. Of course, the catch is whether or not this violates any privacy laws."

"Well, I don't think that's a problem," Stenton said. "You have a right to know who lives on your street. What's the difference between this and simply introducing yourself to everyone on the street? This is just a more advanced and thorough version of 'good fences make good neighbors.' I would imagine this would eliminate pretty much all crime committed by strangers to any given community."

Mae glanced at her bracelet. She couldn't count them all, but hundreds of watchers were insisting on Belinda's and Gareth's products, now. They asked *Where? When? How much?*

Now Bailey's voice popped through. "The one unanswered question, though, is what if the crime is committed by someone *inside* the neighborhood? Inside the house?"

Belinda and Gareth looked to a well-dressed woman, with very short black hair and stylish glasses. "I guess that's my cue." She stood and straightened her black skirt.

"My name is Finnegan, and my issue was violence against children in the home. I myself was a victim of domestic violence when I was young," she said, taking a second to let that register. "And this crime, among all others, seems like the most difficult thing to prevent, given the perpetrators are ostensibly part of the family, right? But then I realized that all the necessary tools already exist. First, most people already have one or another monitor that can track when their anger rises to a dangerous level. Now, if we couple that tool with standard motion sensors, then we can know immediately when something bad is happening, or is about to happen. Let me give you an example. Here's a motion sensor installed in the kitchen. These are often used in factories and even restaurant kitchens to sense whether the chef or worker is completing a given task in a standard way. I understand the Circle uses these to ensure regularity in many departments."

"We do indeed," Bailey said, provoking some distant laughter from the room where he was sitting.

Stenton explained: "We own the patent for that particular technology. Did you know that?"

Finnegan's face flushed, and she seemed to be deciding whether or not to lie. Could she say she *did* know?

"I was not aware of that," she said, "but I'm very glad to know that now."

Stenton seemed impressed with her composure.

"As you know," she continued, "in workplaces, any irregularity of movement or in the order of operations, and the computer either reminds you of what you might have forgotten, or it logs the mistake for management. So I thought, why not use the same motion sensor technology in the home, especially high-risk homes, to record any behavior outside the norm?"

"Like a smoke detector for humans," Stenton said.

"Right. A smoke detector will go off if it senses even the slightest increase in carbon dioxide. So this is the same idea. I've installed a sensor here in this room, actually, and want to show you how it sees."

On the screen behind her, a figure appeared, the size and shape of Finnegan, though featureless—a blue-shadow version of herself, mirroring her movements.

"Okay, this is me. Now watch my motions. If I walk around, then the sensors see that as within the norm."

Behind her, her form remained blue.

"If I cut some tomatoes," Finnegan said, miming the cutting of imaginary tomatoes, "same thing. It's normal."

The figure behind her, her blue shadow, mimicked her.

"But now see what happens if I do something violent."

Finnegan raised her arms quickly and brought them down in front of her, as if hitting a child beneath her. Immediately, onscreen, her figure turned orange, and a loud alarm went off.

The alarm was a rapid rhythmic screeching. It was, Mae realized, far too loud for a demonstration. She looked to Stenton, whose eyes were round and white.

"Turn it off," he said, barely controlling his rage.

Finnegan hadn't heard him, and was going about her presentation as if this were part of it, an acceptable part of it. "That's the alarm of course and—"

"Turn it off!" Stenton yelled, and this time, Finnegan heard. She flailed on her tablet, looking for the right button.

Stenton was looking at the ceiling. "Where is that sound coming from? How is it so loud?"

The screeching continued. Half the room was holding their ears.

"Turn it off or we walk out of here," Stenton said, standing, his mouth small and furious.

Finally Finnegan found the right button and the alarm went silent.

"That was a mistake," Stenton said. "You don't punish the people you're pitching. Do you understand that?"

Finnegan's eyes were wild, vibrating, filling with tears. "Yes, I do."

"You could have simply said an alarm goes off. No need to have the alarm go off. That's my business lesson for today."

"Thank you sir," she said, her knuckles white and entwined in front of her. "Should I go on?"

"I don't know," Stenton said, still furious.

"Go ahead, Finnegan," Bailey said. "Just make it quick."

"Okay," she said, her voice shaking, "the essence is that the sensors would be installed in every room and would be programmed to know what was within the normal boundaries, and what was anomalous. Something anomalous happens, the alarm goes off, and ideally the alarm alone stops or slows whatever's happening in the room. Meanwhile, the authorities have been notified. You could hook it up so neighbors would be alerted, too, given they'd be the closest and most likely to be able to step in immediately and help."

"Okay. I get it," Stenton said. "Let's move on." Stenton meant *move on to the next presenter,* but Finnegan, showing admirable resolve, continued.

"Of course, if you combine all these technologies, you're able to quickly ensure behavioral norms in any context. Think of prisons and schools. I mean, I went to a high school with four thousand students, and only twenty kids were troublemakers. I could imagine if teachers were wearing retinals, and could see the red-coded students from a mile away—I mean, that would eliminate most trouble. And then the sensors would pinpoint any antisocial behavior."

Now Stenton was leaning back in his chair, his thumbs in his belt loops. He'd relaxed again. "It occurs to me that so much crime and trouble is committed because we have too much to track, right? Too many places, too many people. If we can concentrate more on isolating the outliers, and being able to better tag them and follow them, then we save endless amounts of time and distraction."

"Exactly sir," Finnegan said.

Stenton softened, and, looking down at his tablet, seemed to be seeing what Mae was seeing on her wrist: Finnegan, and her program, were immensely popular. The dominant messages were coming from victims of various crimes: women and children who had been abused in their homes, saying the obvious: *If only this had been around ten years ago, fifteen years ago. At least,* they all said in one way or another, *this kind of thing will never happen again.*

When Mae returned to her desk, there was a note, on paper, from Annie. "Can you see me? Just text 'now' when you can, and I'll meet you in the bathroom."

Ten minutes later Mae was sitting in her usual stall, and heard Annie enter the one next door. Mae was relieved that Annie had reached out to her, thrilled at having her so close again. Mae could right all wrongs now, and was determined to do so.

"Are we alone?" Annie asked.

"Audio's off for three minutes. What's wrong?"

"Nothing. It's just this PastPerfect thing. They're starting to dole out the results to me, and it's already pretty disturbing. And tomorrow it goes public, and I'm assuming it'll get even worse."

"Wait. What did they find? I thought they were starting in the Middle Ages or something."

"They are. But even then, it's like both sides of my family are these blackhearted people. I mean, I didn't even know the British *had* Irish slaves, did you?"

"No. I don't think so. You mean, white Irish slaves?"

"Thousands of them. My ancestors were the ringleaders or something. They raided Ireland, brought back slaves, sold them all over the world. It's so fucked up."

"Annie—"

"I mean, I know they're sure about this because it's cross-referenced a few thousand ways, but do I look like a descendent of slave owners?"

"Annie, give yourself a break. Something that happened six hundred years ago has nothing to do with you. Everyone's bloodline has rough patches, I'm sure. You can't take it personally."

"Sure, but at the very least it's embarrassing, right? It means that it's part of me, at least to everyone I know. To the next people I see, this'll be part of me. They'll be seeing me, and talking to me, but this will be part of me, too. It's mapped this new layer onto me, and I don't feel like that's fair. It's like if I knew your dad was a former Klansman—"

"You're completely overthinking it. No one, I mean no one, will look at you funny because some ancient ancestor of yours had slaves from Ireland. I mean, it's so insane, and so distant, that no one will possibly connect you to it. You know how people are. No one can remember anything like that anyway. And to hold you responsible? No chance."

"And they killed a bunch of these slaves, too. There's some

story about a rebellion, and that some relative of mine led some mass slaughter of a thousand men and women and children. It's so sick. I just—"

"Annie. Annie. You've got to calm down. First of all, our time's up. Audio's going back up in a second. Secondly, you just cannot worry about this. These people were practically cavemen. Everyone's cavemen ancestors were assholes."

Annie laughed, a loud snort.

"Promise me you won't worry?"

"Sure."

"Annie. Don't worry about this. Promise me."

"Okay."

"You promise?"

"I promise. I'll try not to."

"Okay. Time."

When the news of Annie's ancestors went out the next day, Mae felt at least partially vindicated. There were some unproductive comments out there, sure, but for the most part the reaction was a collective shrug. No one cared much about how this connected to Annie, but there was new and possibly useful attention brought to the long-forgotten moment in history, when the British went to Ireland and left with human currency.

Annie seemed to be taking it all in stride. Her zings were positive, and she recorded a brief announcement for her video feed, talking about the surprise in finding out this unfortunate role some distant part of her bloodline played in this grim historical moment. But then she tried to add some perspective and levity to it, and to ensure that this revelation wouldn't dissuade others from exploring their personal history through PastPerfect. "Everyone's ancestors were assholes," she said, and Mae, watching the feed on her bracelet, laughed.

But Mercer, true to form, was not laughing. Mae hadn't heard from him in over a month, but then, in Friday's mail (the only day the post office still operated), was a letter. She didn't want to read it, because she knew it would be ornery, and accusatory and judgmental. But he'd already written a letter like that, hadn't he? She opened it, guessing that he couldn't possibly be worse than he'd been before.

She was wrong. This time he couldn't even bring himself to type the Dear before her name.

> Mae,
> I know I said I wouldn't write again. But now that Annie's
> on the verge of ruin, I hope that gives you some pause.
> Please tell her she should cease her participation in that
> experiment, which I assure you and her will end badly. We
> are not meant to know everything, Mae. Did you ever think
> that perhaps our minds are delicately calibrated between
> the known and the unknown? That our souls need the
> mysteries of night and the clarity of day? You people are
> creating a world of ever-present daylight, and I think it will
> burn us all alive. There will be no time to reflect, to sleep,
> to cool. Did it occur to you Circle people, ever, that we can
> only contain so much? Look at us. We're tiny. Our heads

are tiny, the size of melons. You want these heads of ours
to contain everything the world has ever seen? It will not
work.

Mae's wrist was popping.

Why do you bother, Mae?

I'm already bored.

You're only feeding Sasquatch. Don't feed Sasquatch!

Her heart was already thumping, and she knew she shouldn't
read the rest. But she couldn't stop.

I happened to be at my parents' house when you did
your little idea meeting with the Digital Brownshirts.
They insisted on watching it; they're so proud of you,
despite how horrifying that session was. Even so, I'm glad I
watched that spectacle (just as I'm glad I watched *Triumph
of the Will*). It gave me the last nudge I needed to take the
step I'd been planning anyway.

I'm moving north, to the densest and most uninteresting
forest I can find. I know that your cameras are mapping out
these areas as they have mapped the Amazon, Antarctica, the
Sahara, etc. But at least I'll have a head start. And when the
cameras come, I'll keep going north.

Mae, I have to admit that you and yours have won. It's
pretty much over, and now I know that. But before that
pitch session, I held out some hope that the madness was
limited to your own company, to the brainwashed thousands
who work for you or the millions who worship around the
golden calf that is the Circle. I held out hope that there

were those who would rise up against you people. Or that a new generation would see all this as ludicrous, oppressive, utterly out of control.

Mae checked her wrist. There were already four new Mercer-hating clubs online. Someone offered to erase his bank account. *Just say the word,* the message read.

But now I know that even if someone were to strike you down, if the Circle ended tomorrow, something worse would probably take its place. There are a thousand more Wise Men out there, people with ever-more radical ideas about the criminality of privacy. Every time I think it can't get worse, I see some nineteen-year-old whose ideas make the Circle seem like some ACLUtopia. And you people (and I know now that *you* people are *most* people) are impossible to scare. No amount of surveillance causes the least concern or provokes any resistance.

It's one thing to want to measure yourself, Mae—you and your bracelets. I can accept you and yours tracking your own movements, recording everything you do, collecting data on yourself in the interest of . . . Well, whatever it is you're trying to do. But it's not enough, is it? You don't want just *your* data, you need *mine*. You're not complete without it. It's a sickness.

So I'm gone. By the time you read this, I'll be off the grid, and I expect that others will join me. In fact, I *know* others will join me. We'll be living underground, and in the desert, in the woods. We'll be like refugees, or hermits, some unfortunate but necessary combination of the two. Because this is what we are.

I expect this is some second great schism, where two humanities will live, apart but parallel. There will be those who live under the surveillance dome you're helping to create, and those who live, or try to live, apart from it. I'm scared to death for us all.

Mercer

She'd read the note on camera, and she knew that her viewers were finding it as bizarre and hilarious as she had. The comments were popping, and there were some good ones. *Now the Sasquatch will return to his natural habitat!* and *Good riddance, Bigfoot*. But Mae was so entertained by it that she sought out Francis, who, by the time they saw each other, had already seen the note transcribed and posted onto a half-dozen subsites; one watcher in Missoula had already read it while wearing a powdered wig, the background filled with faux-patriotic music. That video had been seen three million times. Mae laughed, watching it twice herself, but found she felt for Mercer. He was stubborn, but he was not stupid. He was not beyond hope. He was not beyond convincing.

The next day, Annie left her another paper note, and again they planned to meet in their adjoining stalls. Mae only hoped that since the second round of major revelations, Annie had found a way to contextualize it. Mae saw the tip of Annie's shoe under the next stall. She turned off her audio.

Annie's voice was rough.

"You heard it got worse, right?"

"I did hear something. Have you been crying? Annie—"

"Mae, I don't think I can handle this. I mean, it was one thing to know about the ancestors in jolly Olde. But there was a part of me that was thinking, you know, that's fine, my people came to North America, started anew, put all that in the past. But shit, Mae, knowing that they were slave owners *here,* too? I mean, that is fucking stupid. What kind of people am I from? It has to be some disease in me, too."

"Annie. You can't think about this."

"Of course I can. I can't think of anything else—"

"Okay. Fine. But first, calm down. And second, you can't take it personally. You have to separate yourself from it. You have to see it a bit more abstractly."

"And I've been getting all this crazy hate mail. I got six messages this morning from people calling me Massa Annie. Half the people of color I hired over the years are now suspicious of me. Like I'm some genetically pure intergenerational slave owner! Now I can't handle having Vickie work for me. I'm letting her go tomorrow."

"Annie, you know how crazy this all sounds? I mean, besides, are you sure your ancestors *here* had black slaves? The slaves weren't Irish here, too?"

Annie sighed loudly.

"No. No. My people went from owning Irish people to owning African people. How's that? Couldn't keep my people from owning people. You also saw that they fought for the Confederate side in the Civil War?"

"I saw that, but there's millions of people whose ancestors fought for the South. The country was at war, half and half. "

"Not *my* half. I mean, do you *know* the chaos this is wreaking on my family?"

"But they never took all this family heritage stuff seriously, did they?"

"Not when they assumed we were *blue*bloods, Mae! Not when they thought we were *Mayflower* people with this unimpeachable lineage! Now they take it *really* fucking seriously. My mom hasn't left the house in two days. I don't want to know what they find next."

What they found next, two days later, was far worse. Mae didn't know, ahead of time, precisely what it was, but she did know that Annie knew, and that Annie had sent a very strange zing out into the world. It said *Actually, I don't know if we should know everything.* When they met in the stalls, Mae couldn't believe Annie's fingers had actually typed that sentence. The Circle couldn't delete it, of course, but someone—Mae hoped it was Annie—had amended it to say *We shouldn't know everything—without the proper storage ready. You don't want to lose it!*

"Of course I sent it," Annie said. "The first one anyway."

Mae had held out hope that it was some terrible glitch.

"How could you have sent that?"

"It's what I believe, Mae. You have no idea."

"I *know* I don't. What idea do you have? You know what kind of shit you're in? How can you of all people espouse an idea like that? You're the poster child for open access to the past and now you're saying . . . What are you saying, anyway?"

"Oh fuck, I don't know. I just know I'm done. I need to shut it down."

"Shut what down?"

"PastPerfect. Anything like it."

"You know you can't."

"I'm planning to try."

"You must *already* be in deep shit."

"I am. But the Wise Men owe me this one favor. I can't handle this. I mean, they've already quote-unquote relieved me of some of my duties. Whatever. I don't even care. But if they don't shut it down I'll go into some kind of coma. I already feel like I can barely stand or breathe."

They sat in silence for a moment. Mae wondered if she shouldn't leave. Annie was losing her hold on something very central about herself; she felt volatile, capable of rash and irrevocable acts. Talking to her, at all, was a risk.

Now she heard Annie gasping.

"Annie. Breathe."

"I just told you I can't. I haven't slept in two days."

"So what happened?" Mae asked.

"Oh fuck, everything. Nothing. They found some weird stuff with my parents. I mean, a lot of weird stuff."

"When does it go live?"

"Tomorrow."

"Okay. Maybe it's not as bad as you think."

"It's so much worse than you can imagine."

"Tell me. I bet it's fine."

"It's not *fine*, Mae. It's anything but *fine*. The first thing is that I found out my dad and mom had some kind of open marriage or something. I haven't even asked them about it. But there are photos and video of them with all kinds of other people. I mean, like, serial adultery on both sides. Is that *fine*?"

"How do you know it was an affair? I mean, if they were just walking next to someone? And it was the eighties, right?"

"More like the nineties. And trust me. It's definitive."

"Like sex photos?"

"No. But kissy photos. I mean, there's one with my dad with his hand around some woman's waist, his other hand on her tit. I mean, sick shit. Other pictures with Mom and some bearded guy, a series of naked photos. Apparently the guy died, had this stash of photos, they were bought at some garage sale and scanned and put in the cloud. Then when they did the global facial-rec, ta-da, Mom's naked with some biker guy. I mean, the two of them just standing there sometimes, naked, like posing for prom."

"I'm sorry."

"And who *took* the pictures? There's some third guy in the room? Who *was* that? A helpful neighbor?"

"Have you asked them about it?"

"No. But that's the better part of it. I was about to confront them when this other thing popped up. It's so much worse that I don't even care about the affairs. I mean, the pictures were nothing compared to the video they found."

"What about the video?"

"Okay. This was one of the rare times the two of them were actually together—at night at least. This is from some video taken at some pier. There was a security camera there, because I guess they store stuff in the warehouses there on the water. So there's a tape of my parents hanging around this pier at night."

"Like a sex tape?"

"No, it's much worse. Oh fuck, it's so bad. Mae, it's fucking so twisted. You know my parents do this thing every so often—they sort of have a couples night where they go on some bender? They've told me about it. They get stoned, drunk, go dancing, stay out all night. It's on their anniversary every year. Sometimes it's in the city, sometimes they go somewhere like Mexico. It's like some all-night thing to keep them young, keep their marriage fresh, whatever."

"Okay."

"So I know this happened on their anniversary. I was *six years old*."

"So?"

"It's one thing if I hadn't been born— Oh shit. So anyway. I don't know what they were doing beforehand, but they show up on this surveillance camera around one a.m. They're drinking a bottle of wine, and kind of dangling their feet over the water, and it all seems pretty innocent and boring for a while. But then this man comes into the frame. He's like some kind of homeless guy, stumbling around. And my parents look at him, and watch him wandering around and stuff. It looks like he says something to them, and they sort of laugh and go back to their wine. Then nothing happens for a while, and the homeless guy's out of the frame. Then about ten minutes later he's back in the frame, and then he falls off the pier and into the water."

Mae took in a quick breath. She knew she was making this worse. "Did your parents see him fall?"

Now Annie was sobbing. "That's the problem. They totally did. It happened about three feet from where they were sitting.

442

On the tape you see them get up, sort of lean over, yelling down into the water. You can tell they're freaking out. Then they sort of look around, to see if there's a phone or anything."

"And was there?"

"I don't know. It doesn't look like it. They never really left the frame. That's what's so fucked up. They see this guy drop into the water and they just stay there. They don't run to get help, or call the police or anything. They don't jump in to save the guy. After a few minutes of freaking out, they just sit down again, and my mom puts her head on my dad's shoulder, and the two of them stay there for another ten minutes or something, and then they get up and leave."

"Maybe they were in shock."

"Mae, they just got up and left. They never called 911 or anything. There's no record of it. They never reported it. But the body was found the next day. The guy wasn't even homeless. He was maybe a little mentally disabled but he lived with his parents and worked at a deli, washing dishes. My parents just watched him drown."

Now Annie was choking on her tears.

"Have you told them about this?"

"No. I can't talk to them. They're really disgusting to me right now."

"But it hasn't been released yet?"

Annie looked at the time. "It will be soon. Less than twelve hours."

"And Bailey said?"

"He can't do anything. You know him."

"Maybe there's something I can do," Mae said, having no idea what. Annie gave no sign she believed Mae capable of slowing or stopping the storm coming her way.

"It's so sick. Oh shit," Annie said, as if the realization had just passed through her. "Now I don't have parents."

When their time was up, Annie returned to her office, where, she said, she planned to lie down indefinitely, and Mae returned to her old pod. She needed to think. She stood in the doorway, where she'd seen Kalden watch her, and she watched the CE newbies, taking comfort in their honest work, their nodding heads. Their murmurs of assent and disapproval gave her a sense of order and rightness. The occasional Circler looked up to smile at her, to wave chastely at the camera, at her audience, before returning to the work at hand. Mae felt a surging pride in them, in the Circle, in attracting pure souls like this. They were open. They were truthful. They did not hide or hoard or obfuscate.

There was a newbie close to her, a man of no more than twenty-two, with wild hair rising from his head like smoke, working with such concentration that he hadn't noticed Mae standing behind him. His fingers were typing furiously, fluidly, almost silently, as he simultaneously answered customer queries and survey questions. "No, no, smile, frown," he said, nodding with a quick and effortless pace. "Yes, yes, no, Cancun, deep-sea diving, upscale resort, breakaway weekend, January, January, meh, three, two, smile, smile, meh, yes, Prada, Converse, no, frown, frown, smile, Paris."

Watching him, the solution to Annie's problem seemed obvious. She needed support. Annie needed to know she wasn't alone.

And then it all clicked. Of course the solution was built into the Circle itself. There were millions of people out there who no doubt would stand behind Annie, and would show their support in myriad unexpected and heartfelt ways. Suffering is only suffering if it's done in silence, in solitude. Pain experienced in public, in view of loving millions, was no longer pain. It was communion.

Mae turned from the doorway and made her way to the roofdeck. She had a duty here, not only to Annie, her friend, but to her watchers. And being witness to the honesty and openness of the newbies, of this young man with his wild hair, made her feel hypocritical. As she climbed the stairs, she assessed her options and herself. Moments ago, she'd purposely obfuscated. She'd been the opposite of open, the opposite of honest. She'd hidden audio from the world, which was tantamount to lying to the world, to the millions who assumed she was being straightforward always, transparent always.

She looked out over the campus. Her watchers wondered what she was looking at, why the silence.

"I want you all to see what I see," she said.

Annie wanted to hide, to suffer alone, to cover up. And Mae wanted to honor this, to be loyal. But could loyalty to *one* trump loyalty to *millions*? Wasn't it this kind of thinking, favoring the personal and temporary gain over the greater good, that made possible any number of historical horrors? Again the solution seemed in front of her, all around her. Mae needed to help Annie and re-purify her own practice of transparency, and both could be done with one brave act. She checked the time. She had two hours until her SoulSearch presentation. She stepped onto the roofdeck, organizing her thoughts into some lucid statement. Soon she made her way to the bathroom, to the scene of the crime, as it were, and by the time she'd arrived, and saw herself in the mirror, she knew what she needed to say. She took a breath.

"Hello, watchers. I have an announcement to make, and it's a painful one. But I think it's the right thing to do. Just an hour ago, as many of you know, I entered this bathroom, ostensibly under the auspices of doing my business in the second stall you see over here." She turned to the row of stalls. "But when I entered, I sat down, and with the audio off, I had a private conversation with a friend of mine, Annie Allerton."

Already a few hundred messages were shooting through her wrist, the most-favored one thus far already forgiving her: *Mae, bathroom talk is allowed! Don't worry. We believe in you.*

"To those sending your good words to me, I want to thank you," Mae said. "But more important than my own admission is what Annie and I talked about. You see, many of you know that Annie's been part of an experiment here, a program to trace one's ancestry as far back as technology will allow. And she's found some unfortunate things in the deep recesses of her history. Some of her ancestors committed serious misdeeds, and it's got her sick about it all. Worse, tomorrow, another unfortunate episode will be revealed, this one more recent, and perhaps more painful."

Mae glanced at her bracelet, seeing that the active viewers had nearly doubled in the last minute, to 3,202,984. She knew that many people kept her feed on their screens as they worked, but were rarely actively watching. Now it was clear her impending announcement had the focused attention of millions. And, she thought, she needed the compassion of these millions to cushion tomorrow's fall. Annie deserved it.

"So my friends, I think we need to harness the power of the Circle. We need to harness the compassion out there, of all the people out there who already know and love Annie, or who can empathize with Annie. I hope you can all send her your good wishes, your own stories of finding out about some dark spots in your family past, and make Annie feel less alone. Tell her you're on her side. Tell her you like her just the same, and that some distant ancestor's crimes have no bearing on her, don't change the way you think about Annie."

Mae finished by providing Annie's email address, Zing feed and profile page. The reaction was immediate. Annie's followers increased from 88,198 to 243,087—and, as Mae's announcement was passed around, would likely pass a million by the end of the day. The messages poured in, the most popular being one that said *The past is past, and Annie is Annie*. It didn't make perfect sense, but Mae appreciated the sentiment. Another message gaining traction said, *Not to rain on the parade, but I think there is evil in DNA, and I would worry about Annie. Annie needs to try doubly hard to prove to someone like myself, an African-American whose ancestors were enslaved, that she's on the path of justice.*

That comment had 98,201 smiles, and almost as many frowns, 80,198. But overall, as Mae scrolled through the messages, there was—as always when people were asked for their feelings—love, and there was understanding, and there was a desire to let the past be the past.

As Mae followed the reaction, she watched the clock, knowing she was only an hour away from her presentation, her first in the Enlightenment's Great Room. She felt ready, though, with this Annie business emboldening her, making her feel, more than ever, that she had legions at her back. She also knew that the technology itself, and the Circle community, would determine the success of the demonstration. As she prepared, she watched her bracelet for any sign of Annie. She had expected some reaction by now, certainly something like gratitude, given that Annie was no doubt inundated by, buried under, an avalanche of goodwill.

But there was nothing.

She sent Annie a series of zings, but heard no reply. She checked Annie's whereabouts, and found her, a pulsing red dot, in her office. Mae thought, briefly, about visiting her—but decided against it. She had to focus, and perhaps it was better to let Annie take it all in, alone. Certainly by the afternoon, she would have taken in and synthesized the warmth of the millions who cared for her, and would be ready to properly thank Mae, to tell her how, now with the new perspective, she could put the crimes of her relatives in context, and could move forward, into the solvable future, and not backward, into the chaos of an unfixable past.

"You did a very brave thing today," Bailey said. "It was brave and it was correct."

They were backstage in the Great Room. Mae was dressed in a black skirt and a red silk blouse, both new. A stylist orbited around her, applying powder to Mae's nose and forehead, Vaseline to her lips. She was a few minutes away from her first major presentation.

"Normally I would want to talk about why you'd chosen to obfuscate in the first place," he said, "but your honesty was real, and I know you've already learned any lesson I could give you. We're very happy to have you here, Mae."

"Thank you, Eamon."

"Are you ready?"

"I think so."

"Well, make us proud out there."

As she stepped onto the stage, into the bright single spotlight, Mae felt confident that she could. Before she could get to the lucite podium, though, the applause was sudden and thunderous and almost knocked her off her feet. She made her way to her appointed spot, but the thunder only got louder. The audience stood, first the front rows, then everyone. It took Mae great effort to quell their noise and allow her to speak.

"Hello everyone, I'm Mae Holland," she said, and the applause started again. She had to laugh, and when she did, the room got louder. The love felt real and overwhelming. Openness is all, she thought. Truth was its own reward. That might make a good tile, she thought, and pictured it laser-cut in stone. This was too good, she thought, all of this. She looked out to the Circlers, letting them clap, feeling a new strength surge through her. It was strength amassed through giving. She gave all to them, gave them unmitigated truth, complete transparency, and they gave her their trust, their tidal love.

"Okay, okay," she said, finally, raising her hands, urging the audience into their seats. "Today we're going to demonstrate the ultimate search tool. You've heard about SoulSearch, maybe a rumor here and there, and now we're putting it to the test, in front of the entire Circle audience here and globally. Do you feel ready?"

The crowd cheered its answer.

"What you're about to see is completely spontaneous and unrehearsed. Even I don't know who we'll be searching for today. He or she will be chosen at random from a database of known fugitives worldwide."

On-screen, a giant digital globe spun.

"As you know, much of what we do here at the Circle is using social media to create a safer and saner world. This has already been achieved in myriad ways, of course. Our WeaponSensor program, for example, recently went live, and registers the entry of any gun into any building, provoking an alarm that alerts all residents and the local police. That's been beta-tested in two neighborhoods in Cleveland for the last five weeks, and there's been a 57 percent drop in gun crimes. Not bad, right?"

Mae paused for applause, feeling very comfortable, and knowing what she was about to present would change the world, immediately and permanently.

"Fine job so far," said the voice in her ear. It was Stenton. He'd let her know he would be Additional Guidance today. SoulSearch was a particular interest of his, and he wanted to be present to guide its introduction.

Mae took a breath.

"But one of the strangest facets of our world is how fugitives from justice can hide in a world as interconnected as ours. It took us ten years to find Osama bin Laden. D. B. Cooper, the infamous thief who leapt from an airplane with a suitcase of money, remains on the lam, decades after his escape. But this kind of thing should end now. And I believe it will, now."

A silhouette appeared behind her. It was the shape of a human, torso and up, with the familiar mug-shot measurements in the background.

"In seconds, the computer will select, at random, a fugitive from justice. I don't know who it will be. No one does. Whoever it is, though, he's been proven a menace to our global community, and our assertion is that whoever he or she is, SoulSearch will locate him or her within twenty minutes. Ready?"

Murmurs filled the room, followed by scattered applause.

"Good," Mae said. "Let's select that fugitive."

Pixel by pixel, the silhouette slowly became an actual and specific person, and when the selection was finished, a face had emerged, and Mae was shocked to find it was a woman. A hard-looking face, squinting into a police camera. Something about this woman, her small eyes and straight mouth, brought to mind the photography of Dorothea Lange—those sun-scarred faces of the Dust Bowl. But as the profile data appeared beneath this photo, Mae realized the woman was British and very much alive. She scanned the information on-screen and focused the audience on the essentials.

"Okay. This is Fiona Highbridge. Forty-four years old. Born in Manchester, England. She was convicted of triple murder in 2002. She locked her three children in a closet and went to Spain for a month. They all starved. They were all under five. She was sent to prison in England but escaped, with the help of a guard who she apparently seduced. It's been a decade since anyone's seen her, and police have all but given up on finding her. But I believe we can, now that we have the tools and the participation of the Circle."

"Good," Stenton said into Mae's ear. "Let's focus now on the UK."

"As you all know, yesterday we alerted all three billion Circle users that today we'd have a world-changing announcement. So we currently have this many people watching the live feed." Mae turned back to the screen and watched a counter tick up to 1,109,001,887. "Okay, over a billion people are watching. And now let's see how many we have in the UK." A second counter spun, and landed on 14,028,981. "All right. The information we have says that her passport was revoked years ago, so Fiona is probably still in the UK. Do you all think fourteen million Brits and a billion global participants can find Fiona Highbridge in twenty minutes?"

The audience roared, but Mae didn't, in fact, know if it would work. She wouldn't have been surprised, actually, if it didn't—or if it took thirty minutes, an hour. But then again, there was always something unexpected, something miraculous about the outcomes when the full power of the Circle's users was brought to bear. She was sure it would be done by the end of lunch.

"Okay, everyone ready? Let's bring up the clock." A giant six-digit timer appeared in the corner of the screen, indicating hours, minutes and seconds.

"Let me show you some of the groups we have working together on this. Let's see the University of East Anglia." A feed showing many hundreds of students, in a large auditorium, appeared. They cheered. "Let's see the city of Leeds." Now a shot of a public square, full of people, bundled up in what appeared to be cold and blustery weather. "We have dozens of groups all over the country, who will be banding together, in addition to the power of the network as a whole. Everyone ready?" The Manchester crowd raised their hands and cheered, and the students of East Anglia did, too.

"Good," Mae said. "Now on your mark, get set. Go."

Mae drew her hand down; next to the photo of Fiona Highbridge, a series of columns showed the comment feed, the highest-ranked appearing at the top. The most popular thus far was from a man named Simon Hensley, from Brighton: *Are we sure we want to find this hag? She looks like the Scarecrow from Wizard of Oz.*

There were laughs throughout the auditorium.

"Okay. Time to get serious," Mae said.

Another column featured users' own photos, posted according to relevance. Within three minutes, there were 201 photos posted, most of them close corollaries to the face of Fiona Highbridge. On-screen, votes were tallying, indicating which of the photos were most likely her. In four minutes it was down to five prime candidates. One was in Bend, Oregon. Another was in Banff, Canada. Another in Glasgow. Then something magical happened, something only possible when the full Circle was working toward a single goal: two of the photos, the crowd realized, were taken in the same town: Carmarthen, in Wales. Both looked like the same woman, and both looked exactly like Fiona Highbridge.

In another ninety seconds someone identified this woman. She was known as Fatima Hilensky, which the crowd voted was a promising indicator. Would someone trying to disappear change their name completely, or would they feel safer with the same initials, with a name like this—different enough to throw off any casual pursuers, but allowing her to use a slight variation on her old signature?

Seventy-nine watchers lived in or near Carmarthen, and three of them posted messages claiming they saw her more or less daily. This was promising enough, but then, in a comment that quickly shot to the top with hundreds of thousands of votes, a woman, Gretchen Karapcek, posting from her mobile phone, said she worked with the woman in the photo, at a commercial laundry outside Swansea. The crowd urged Gretchen to find her, there and then, and capture her by photo or video. Immediately, Gretchen turned on the video function on her phone and—though there were still millions of people investigating other leads—most viewers were convinced Gretchen had the right person. Mae, and most watchers, were riveted, watching Gretchen's camera weave through enormous, steaming machines, coworkers looking curiously at her as she passed quickly through the cavernous space and ever-closer to a woman in the distance, thin and bent, feeding a bedsheet between two massive wheels.

Mae checked the clock. Six minutes, 33 seconds. She was sure this was Fiona Highbridge. There was something in the shape of her head, something in her mannerisms, and now, as she raised her eyes and caught sight of Gretchen's camera gliding toward her, a clear recognition that something very serious was happening. It was not a look of pure surprise or bewilderment. It was the look of an animal caught rooting through the garbage. A feral look of guilt and recognition.

For a second, Mae held her breath, and it seemed that the woman would give up, and would speak to the camera, admitting her crimes and acknowledging she'd been found.

Instead, she ran.

For a long moment, the holder of the camera stood, and her camera showed only Fiona Highbridge—for there was no doubt now that it was her—as she fled quickly through the room and up the stairs.

"Follow her!" Mae finally yelled, and Gretchen Karapcek and her camera began pursuit. Mae worried, momentarily, that this would be some botched effort, a fugitive found but then quickly lost by a fumbling coworker. The camera jostled wildly, up the concrete stairs, through a cinderblock hallway, and finally approached a door, the white sky visible through its small square window.

And when the door broke open, Mae saw, with great relief, that Fiona Highbridge was trapped against a wall, surrounded by a dozen people, most of them holding their phones to her, aiming them at her. There was no possibility of escape. Her face was wild, at once terrified and defiant. She seemed to be looking for gaps in the throng, some hole she could slip through. "Gotcha, kid-killer," someone in the crowd said, and Fiona Highbridge collapsed, sliding to the ground, covering her face.

In seconds, most of the crowd's video feeds were available on the Great Room screen, and the audience could see a mosaic of Fiona Highbridge, her cold hard face from ten angles, all of them confirming her guilt.

"Lynch her!" someone outside the laundry yelled.

"She must be kept safe," Stenton hissed into Mae's ear.

"Keep her safe," Mae pleaded with the mob. "Has someone called the police—the constables?"

In a few seconds, sirens could be heard, and when Mae saw the two cars race across the parking lot, she checked the time again. When the four officers reached Fiona Highbridge and applied handcuffs to her, the clock on the Great Room screen read 10 minutes, 26 seconds.

"I guess that's it," Mae said, and stopped the clock.

The audience exploded with cheers, and the participants who had trapped Fiona Highbridge were congratulated worldwide in seconds.

"Let's cut the video feed," Stenton said to Mae, "in the interest of allowing her some dignity."

Mae repeated the directive to the techs. The feeds showing Highbridge dropped out, and the screen went black again.

"Well," Mae said to the audience. "That was actually a lot easier than even I thought it would be. And we only needed a few of the tools now at the world's disposal."

"Let's do another!" someone yelled.

Mae smiled. "Well, we *could*," she said, and looked to Bailey, standing in the wings. He shrugged.

"Maybe not another fugitive," Stenton said into her earpiece. "Let's try a regular civilian."

A smile overtook Mae's face.

"Okay everyone," she said, as she quickly found a photo on her tablet and transferred it to the screen behind her. It was a snapshot of Mercer taken three years earlier, just after they'd stopped dating, when they were still close, the two of them standing at the entrance to a coastal trail they were about to hike.

She had not, before just then, once thought of using the Circle to find Mercer, but now it seemed to make perfect sense. How better to prove to him the reach and power of the network and the people on it? His skepticism would fall away.

"Okay," Mae said to the audience. "Our second target today is not a fugitive from justice, but you might say he's a fugitive from, well, friendship."

She smiled, acknowledging the laughter in the room.

"This is Mercer Medeiros. I haven't seen him in a few months, and would love to see him again. Like Fiona Highbridge, though, he's someone who is trying not to be found. So let's see if we can break our previous record. Everyone ready? Let's start the clock." And the clock started.

Within ninety seconds there were hundreds of posts from people who knew him—from grade school, high school, college, work. There were even a few pictures featuring Mae, which entertained all involved. Then, though, much to Mae's horror, there was a yawning gap, of four and a half minutes, when no one offered any valuable information on where he was now. An ex-girlfriend said she, too, would like to know his whereabouts, given he had a whole scuba apparatus that belonged to her. That was the most relevant message for a time, but then a zing appeared from Jasper, Oregon, and was immediately voted to the top of the scroll.

I've seen this guy at our local grocery. Let me check.

And that poster, Adam Frankenthaler, got in touch with his neighbors, and quickly there was agreement that they had all seen Mercer—in the liquor store, in the grocery, at the library. But then there was another excruciating pause, almost two minutes, where no one could figure out quite where he lived. The clock said 7:31.

"Okay," Mae said. "This is where the more powerful tools come into play. Let's check local real estate sites for rental histories. Let's check credit card records, phone records, library memberships, anything he would have signed up for. Oh wait." Mae looked up to see two addresses had been found, both in the same tiny Oregon town. "Do we know how we got those?" she asked, but it hardly seemed to matter. Things were moving too quickly now.

In the next few minutes, cars converged on both addresses, their passengers filming their arrival. One address was above a homeopathic medicine outlet in town, great redwoods rising high above. A camera showed a hand knocking on the door, and then peering into the window. There was no answer at first, but finally the door opened, and the camera panned down to find a tiny boy, about five, seeing a crowd at his doorstep, looking terrified.

"Is Mercer Medeiros here?" said a voice.

The boy turned, disappearing into the dark house. "Dad!"

For a moment Mae panicked, thinking that this boy was Mercer's—it was happening too quickly for her to do the math properly. He already has a son? No, she realized, this couldn't be his biological child. Maybe he'd moved in with a woman who had kids already?

But when the shadow of a man emerged into the light of the doorway, it was not Mercer. It was a goateed man of about forty, in a flannel shirt and sweatpants. Dead end. Just over eight minutes had elapsed.

The second address was found. It was in the woods, high up

a mountain slope. The main video feed behind Mae switched to this view, as a car raced up a winding driveway to stop at a large grey cabin.

This time the camerawork was more professional and clear. Someone was filming a participant, a grinning young woman, knocking on the door, her eyebrows dancing up and down with mischief.

"Mercer?" she said to the door. "Mercer, you in there?" The familiarity in her voice was momentarily unnerving to Mae. "You in there making some chandeliers?"

Mae's stomach turned. She had a sense that Mercer would not like that question, the dismissive tone of it. She wanted his face to appear as soon as possible, so she could speak to him directly. But no one answered the door.

"Mercer!" the young woman said. "I know you're in there. We see your car." The camera panned to the driveway, where Mae saw, with a thrill, that it was indeed Mercer's pickup. When the camera panned back, it revealed a crowd of ten or twelve people, most of them looking like locals, in baseball hats and at least one in camouflage gear. By the time the camera arrived back at the front door, the crowd had begun to chant. "Mercer! Mercer! Mercer!"

Mae looked at the clock. Nine minutes, 24 seconds. They would break the Fiona Highbridge record by at least a minute. But first he had to come to the door.

"Go around," the young woman said, and now the feed followed a second camera, peering around the porch and into the windows. Inside, no figures were visible. There were fishing poles, and a stack of antlers, and books and papers in piles by dusty couches and chairs. On the mantel, Mae was sure she could see a photo she recognized, of Mercer with his brothers and parents, on a trip they'd taken to Yosemite. She remembered the photo, and was sure of the figures in it, because it had always struck her as strange and wonderful, the fact that Mercer, who was sixteen at the time, was leaning his head on his mother's shoulder, in an unguarded expression of filial love.

"Mercer! Mercer! Mercer!" the voices chanted.

But it was very possible, Mae realized, that he was on a hike or, like some caveman, out collecting firewood and might not return for hours. She was ready to turn back to the audience, call the search a success, and cut the demonstration short—they had, after all, found him, beyond the shadow of a doubt—when she heard a shrieking voice.

"There he is! Driveway!"

And both cameras began to move and shake as they ran from the porch to the Toyota. There was a figure getting into the truck, and Mae knew it was Mercer, as the cameras descended upon him. But as they got close—close enough for Mae to be heard—he was already backing down the driveway.

A figure was running alongside the truck, a young man, who could be seen attaching something to the passenger-side window. Mercer backed into the main road and sped off. There was a chaos of running and laughter, as all the participants assembled at Mercer's house got into their cars to follow him.

A message from one of the followers explained that he'd put a SeeChange camera on the passenger window, and instantly it was activated and appeared on-screen, showing a very clear picture of Mercer driving.

Mae knew this camera had only one-way audio, so she couldn't speak to Mercer. But she knew she had to. He wouldn't know, yet, that it was she who was behind this. She needed to assure him this wasn't some creepy stalking expedition. That it was his friend Mae, simply demonstrating their SoulSearch program, and all she wanted was to talk to him for a second, to laugh about this together.

But as the woods raced past his window, a blur of brown and white and green, Mercer's mouth was a terrible slash of anger and fear. He was turning the truck frequently, recklessly, and seemed to be rising through the mountains. Mae worried about the ability of the participants to catch up to him, but knew they had the SeeChange camera, which was offering a view so clear and cinematic that it was wildly entertaining. He looked like his hero, Steve McQueen, furious but controlled while operating his heaving truck. Mae briefly had the thought of some kind of streaming show they could create, where people simply broadcast themselves driving through interesting landscapes at high velocity. *Drive, She Said,* they could call it. Mae's reverie was interrupted by Mercer's voice, filled with venom: "Fuck!" he yelled. "Fuck you!"

He was looking at the camera. He'd found it. And then the camera's view was descending. He was rolling down the window. Mae wondered if it would hold, if its adhesive would trump the strength of the automatic window, but the answer arrived in seconds, as the camera was shaved off the window, its eye swinging wildly as it descended and fell, showing woods, then pavement, then, as it settled on the road, sky.

The clock read 11:51.

For a long few minutes, there were no views of Mercer at all. Mae assumed that at any moment, one of the cars in pursuit would find him, but the views from all four cars showed no sign of him at all. They were all on different roads, and their audio made clear they had no idea where he was.

"Okay," Mae said, knowing she was about to wow the audience. "Release the drones!" she roared in a voice meant to invoke and mock some witchy villain.

It took agonizingly long—three minutes or so—but soon all the available private drones in the area, eleven of them, were in the air, each operated by its owner, and all were on the mountain where, it had been surmised, Mercer was driving. Their own GPS systems kept them from colliding, and, coordinating with the satellite view, they found his powder-blue truck in sixty-seven seconds. The clock was at 15:04.

The drones' camera views were now brought on-screen, giving the audience an incredible grid of images, all of the drones well spaced, providing a kaleidoscopic look at the truck racing up the mountain road through heavy pines. A few of the smaller drones were able to swoop down and get close, while most of them, too large to weave between the trees, followed from above. One of the smaller drones, called ReconMan10, had dropped through the tree canopy and seemed to attach itself to Mercer's driver-side window. The view was steady and clear. Mercer turned to it, realizing its presence and tenacity, and a look of unmitigated horror transformed his face. Mae had never seen him look like this before.

"Can someone get me on audio for the drone called Recon-Man10?" Mae asked. She knew his window was still open. If she spoke through the drone's speaker, he'd hear her, know it was her. She received the signal that the audio was activated.

"Mercer. It's me, Mae! Can you hear me?"

There was some faint sign of recognition on his face. He squinted, and looked toward the drone again, disbelieving.

"Mercer. Stop driving. It's just me. Mae." And then, almost laughing, she said, "I just wanted to say hi."

The audience roared.

Mae was warmed by the laughter in the room, and expected that Mercer would laugh, too, and would stop, and would shake his head, in admiration for the wonderful power of the tools at her disposal. What she wanted him to say was, "Okay, you got me. I surrender. You win."

But he wasn't smiling, and he wasn't stopping. He wasn't even looking at the drone anymore. It was as if he'd decided on a new path, and was locked into it.

"Mercer!" she said, in mock-authoritative voice. "Mercer, stop the car and surrender. You're surrounded." Then she thought of something that made her smile again. "You're surrounded . . ." she said, lowering her voice, and then, in a chirpy alto, "by friends!" As she'd known they would, a burst of laughter and cheers thundered through the auditorium.

But still he didn't stop. He hadn't looked at the drone in minutes. Mae checked the clock: 19 minutes, 57 seconds. She couldn't decide whether or not it mattered if he stopped, or acknowledged the cameras. He'd been found, after all, hadn't he? They'd probably beaten the Fiona Highbridge record when they'd caught him running to his car. That was the moment they'd verified his corporeal identity. Mae had the brief thought that they should call off the drones, and shut down the cameras, because Mercer was in one of his moods, and wouldn't be cooperating—and anyway, she'd proven what she intended to prove.

But something about his inability to give in, to admit defeat, or to at least acknowledge the incredible power of the technology at Mae's command . . . she knew she couldn't give up until she had received some sense of his acquiescence. What would that be, though? She didn't know, but she knew she'd know it when she saw it.

And then the landscape passing beside the car opened up. It was no longer woods, dense and moving quickly. Now there was all blue, and treetops, and bright white clouds.

She looked to another camera-view, and saw the view from an overhead drone. Mercer was driving on a bridge, a narrow bridge connecting the mountain to another, the span rising hundreds of feet over a gorge.

"Can we turn the microphone up at all?" she asked.

An icon appeared, indicating that the volume had been at half-power, and was now at full.

"Mercer!" she said, using a voice as ominous as she could muster. His head jerked toward the drone, shocked by the volume. Maybe he hadn't heard her before?

"Mercer! It's me, Mae!" she said, now holding out hope that he hadn't known, until then, that it was her that was behind all this. But he didn't smile. He only shook his head, slowly, as if in disappointment most profound.

Now she could see another two drones on the passenger-side window. A new voice, male, boomed from one of them: "Mercer, you motherfucker! Stop driving, you fucking asshole!"

Mercer's head swung to this voice, and when he turned back to the road, his face showed real panic.

On the screen behind her, Mae saw that two SeeChange cameras, positioned on the bridge, had been added to the grid. A third came alive seconds later, offering a view of the span from the riverbank far below.

Now another voice, this one a woman's and laughing, boomed from the third drone: "Mercer, submit to us! Submit to our will! Be our friend!"

Mercer turned his truck toward the drone, as if intending to ram it, but it adjusted its trajectory automatically and mimicked his movement, staying directly in sync. "You can't escape, Mercer!" the woman's voice bellowed. "Never, ever, ever. It's over. Now give up. Be our friend!" This last entreaty was rendered in a child's whine, and the woman transmitting through the electronic speaker laughed at its strangeness, this nasal entreaty emanating from a dull black drone.

The audience was cheering, and the comments were piling up, a number of watchers saying this was the greatest viewing experience of their lives.

And while the cheers were growing louder, Mae saw something come over Mercer's face, something like determination, something like serenity. His right arm spun the steering wheel, and he disappeared from the view of drones, temporarily at least, and when they regained their lock on him, his truck was crossing the highway, speeding toward its concrete barrier, so fast that it was impossible that it could hold him back. The truck broke through and leapt into the gorge, and, for a brief moment, seemed to fly, the mountains visible for miles beyond. And then the truck dropped from view.

Mae's eyes turned, instinctively, to the camera on the riverbed, and she saw, clearly, a tiny object dropping from the bridge overhead and landing, like a tin toy, on the rocks below. Though she knew this object was Mercer's truck, and she knew, in some recess of her mind, that there could be no survivors of such a fall, she looked back to the other cameras, to the views from the drones still hovering above, expecting to see Mercer on the bridge, looking down at the truck below. But there was no one on the bridge.

"You doing okay today?" Bailey asked.

They were in his library, alone but for her watchers. Since Mercer's death, now a full week ago, the numbers had remained steady, near twenty-eight million.

"I am, thanks," Mae said, measuring her words, imagining the way the president, no matter the situation, has to find a medium between raw emotion, and quiet dignity, practiced composure. She'd been thinking of herself as a president. She shared much with them—the responsibility to so many, the power to influence global events. And with her position came new, president-level crises. There was Mercer's passing. There was Annie's collapse. She thought of the Kennedys. "I'm not sure it's hit me yet," she said.

"And it might not, not for a while," Bailey said. "Grief doesn't arrive on schedule, as much as we'd like it to. But I don't want you to be blaming yourself. You're not doing that, I hope."

"Well, it's sort of hard not to," Mae said, and then winced. Those words were not presidential, and Bailey leapt on them.

"Mae, you were trying to help a very disturbed, antisocial young man. You and the other participants were reaching out, trying to bring him into the embrace of humanity, and he rejected that. I think it's self-evident that you were, if anything, his only hope."

"Thank you for saying so," she said.

"It's like you were a doctor, coming to help a sick patient, and the patient, upon seeing this doctor, jumps out of the window. You can hardly be blamed."

"Thank you," Mae said.

"And your parents? They're okay?"

"They're fine. Thank you."

"It must have been good to see them at the service."

"It was," Mae said, though they'd barely spoken then, and hadn't spoken since.

"I know there's still some distance between you all, but it will collapse with time. Distance always collapses."

Mae felt thankful for Bailey, for his strength and his calm. He was, at that moment, her best friend, and something like a father, too. She loved her own parents, but they were not wise like this, not strong like this. She was thankful for Bailey, and Stenton, and especially for Francis, who had been with her most of every day since.

"It frustrates me to see something like that happen," Bailey continued. "It's exasperating, really. I know this is tangential, and I know it's a pet issue of mine, but really: there'd be no chance of that happening if Mercer was in a self-driving vehicle. Their programming would have precluded this. Vehicles like the one he was driving should frankly be illegal."

"Right," Mae said. "That stupid truck."

"And not that it's about money, but do you know how much it'll cost to repair that bridge? And what it already cost to clean up the whole mess down below? You put him in a self-driving car, and there's no option for self-destruction. The car would have shut down. I'm sorry. I shouldn't get on my soapbox about something so unrelated to your grief."

"It's okay."

"And there he was, alone in some cabin. Of *course* he's going to get depressed, and work himself into a state of madness and paranoia. When the participants arrived, I mean, that guy was far past gone. He's up there, alone, unreachable by the thousands, millions even, who would have helped in any way they could if they'd known."

Mae looked up to Bailey's stained-glass ceiling—all those angels—thinking how much Mercer would like to be considered a martyr. "So many people loved him," she said.

"*So* many people. Have you seen the comments and tributes? People wanted to help. They *tried* to help. *You* did. And certainly there would have been thousands more, if he'd let them. If you reject humanity, if you reject all the tools available to you, all the help available to you, then bad things will happen. You reject the technology that prevents cars from going over cliffs, and you'll go over a cliff—physically. You reject the help and love of the world's compassionate billions, and you go over a cliff—emotionally. Right?" Bailey paused, as if to allow the two of them to soak in the apt and tidy metaphor he'd conjured. "You reject the groups, the people, the listeners out there who want to connect, to empathize and embrace, and disaster is imminent. Mae, this was clearly a deeply depressed and isolated young man who was not able to survive in a world like this, a world moving toward communion

468

and unity. I wish I'd known him. I feel like I did, a little bit, having watched the events of that day. But still."

Bailey made a sound of deep frustration, a guttural sigh.

"You know, a few years ago, I had the idea that I would endeavor, in my lifetime, to know every person on Earth. Every person, even if just a little bit. To shake their hand or say hello. And when I had this inspiration, I really thought I could do it. Can you feel the appeal of a notion like that?"

"Absolutely," Mae said.

"But there are seven-odd billion people on the planet! So I did the calculations. The best I could come up with was this: if I spent three seconds with each person, that's twenty people a minute. Twelve hundred an hour! Pretty good, right? But even at that pace, after a year, I would have known only 10,512,000 people. It would take me 665 years to meet everyone at that pace! Depressing, right?"

"It is," Mae said. She had done a similar calculation herself. Was it enough, she thought, to be *seen* by some fraction of those people? That counted for something.

"So we have to content ourselves with the people we do know and can know," Bailey said, sighing loudly again. "And content ourselves with knowing just how many people there are. There are so many, and we have many to choose from. In your troubled Mercer, we've lost one of the world's many, many people, which reminds us of both life's preciousness and its abundance. Am I right?"

"You are."

Mae's thoughts had followed the same path. After Mercer's

death, after Annie's collapse, when Mae felt so alone, she felt the tear opening up in her again, larger and blacker than ever before. But then watchers from all over the world had reached out, sending her their support, their smiles—she'd gotten millions, tens of millions—she knew what the tear was and how to sew it closed. The tear was not knowing. Not knowing who would love her and for how long. The tear was the madness of not knowing—not knowing who Kalden was, not knowing Mercer's mind, Annie's mind, her plans. Mercer would have been saveable—would have been saved—if he'd made his mind known, if he'd let Mae, and the rest of the world, in. It was not knowing that was the seed of madness, loneliness, suspicion, fear. But there were ways to solve all this. Clarity had made her knowable to the world, and had made her better, had brought her close, she hoped, to perfection. Now the world would follow. Full transparency would bring full access, and there would be no more not-knowing. Mae smiled, thinking about how simple it all was, how pure. Bailey shared her smile.

"Now," he said, "speaking of people we care about and don't want to lose, I know you visited Annie yesterday. How's she doing? Her condition the same?"

"It's the same. You know Annie. She's strong."

"She *is* strong. And she's so important to us here. Just as you are. We'll be with you, and with Annie, always. I know you both know that, but I want to say it again. You'll never be without the Circle. Okay?"

Mae was trying not to cry. "Okay."

"Okay then." Bailey smiled. "Now we should go. Stenton

awaits, and I think we could all," and here he indicated Mae and her watchers, "use some distraction. You ready?"

As they walked down the dark hallway toward the new aquarium, radiating a living blue, Mae could see the new caretaker climbing a ladder. Stenton had hired another marine biologist, after he'd had philosophical differences with Georgia. She'd objected to Stenton's experimental feedings and had refused to do what her replacement, a tall man with a shaved head, was about to do, which was to combine all of Stenton's Marianas creatures into one tank, to create something closer to the real environment in which he'd found them. It seemed like an idea so logical that Mae was glad that Georgia had been dismissed and replaced. Who wouldn't want all the animals in their near-native habitat? Georgia had been timid and lacked vision, and such a person had little place near these tanks, near Stenton or in the Circle.

"There he is," Bailey said as they approached the tank. Stenton stepped into view and Bailey shook his hand, and then Stenton turned to Mae.

"Mae, so good to see you again," he said, taking both her hands in his. He was in an ebullient mood, but his mouth frowned, briefly, in deference to Mae's recent loss. She smiled shyly, then raised her eyes. She wanted him to know that she was fine, she was ready. He nodded, stepped back and turned to the tank. For the occasion, Stenton had built a far larger tank, and filled it with a gorgeous array of live coral and seaweed, the colors symphonic under the bright aquarium light. There were lavender anemones, and bubble corals in green and yellow, the strange white spheres of sea sponges. The water was calm but a slight current swayed the violet vegetation, pinched between nooks of the honeycomb coral.

"Beautiful. Just beautiful," Bailey said.

Bailey and Stenton and Mae stood, her camera trained on the tank, allowing her watchers a deep look into the rich underwater tableau.

"And soon it will be complete," Stenton said.

At that moment, Mae felt a presence near her, a hot breath on the back of her neck, passing left to right.

"Oh, there he is," Bailey said. "I don't think you've met Ty yet, have you, Mae?"

She turned to find Kalden, standing with Bailey and Stenton, smiling at her, holding out his hand. He was wearing a wool cap and an oversized hoodie. But it was unmistakably Kalden. Before she could suppress it, she'd let out a gasp.

He smiled, and she knew, immediately, that it would seem natural to her watchers, and to the Wise Men, that she would gasp in the presence of Ty. She looked down and realized she was already shaking his hand. She couldn't breathe.

She looked up to see Bailey and Stenton grinning. They assumed she was in thrall of the creator of all this, the mysterious young man behind the Circle. She looked back to Kalden, looking for some explanation, but his smile didn't change. His eyes remained perfectly opaque.

"So good to meet you, Mae," he said. He said it shyly, almost mumbling, but he knew what he was doing. He knew what the audience expected from Ty.

"Good to meet you, too," Mae said.

Now her brain splintered. What the fuck was happening? She scanned his face again, seeing, under his wool cap, a few of his grey hairs. Only she knew they existed. Actually, did Bailey and Stenton know that he'd aged so dramatically? That he was masquerading as someone else, as a nobody named Kalden? It occurred to her that they had to know. Of course they did. That's why he appeared on video feeds—probably pre-taped long ago. They were perpetuating all of this, helping him disappear.

She was still holding his hand. She pulled away.

"It should have happened sooner," he said. "I apologize for that." And now he spoke into Mae's lens, giving a perfectly natural performance for the watchers. "I've been working on some new projects, lots of very cool things, so I've been less social than I should have been."

Instantly Mae's watcher numbers rose, from just over thirty million to thirty-two, and climbing quickly.

"Been a while since all three of us were in one place!" Bailey said. Mae's heart was frantic. She'd been sleeping with Ty. What did that mean? And Ty, not Kalden, was warning her about Completion? How was that possible? What did *that* mean?

"What are we about to see?" Kalden asked, nodding to the water. "I think I know, but I'm anxious to see it happen."

"Okay," Bailey said, clapping his hands and wringing them in anticipation. He turned to Mae, and Mae turned her lens to him. "Because he'd get too technical, my friend Stenton here has asked me to explain. As you all know, he brought back some incredible creatures from the unmapped depths of the Marianas Trench. You all have seen some of them, in particular the octopus, and the sea-horse and his progeny, and most dramatically, the shark."

Word was getting out that the Three Wise Men were together and on camera, and Mae's watchers hit forty million. She turned to the three men, and saw, on her wrist, she'd captured a dramatic picture of their three profiles as they all looked to the glass, their faces bathed in blue light, their eyes reflecting the irrational life within. Her watchers, she noticed, were at fifty-one million. She caught the eye of Stenton, who, with an almost imperceptible tilt of his head, made clear that Mae should turn her lens back to the aquarium. She did, her eyes straining to catch Kalden in some acknowledgment. He stared into the water, giving away nothing. Bailey continued.

"Until now, our three stars have been kept in separate tanks as they've acclimated to their lives here at the Circle. But this has been an artificial separation, of course. They belong together, as they were in the sea where they were found. So we're about to see the three reunited here, so they can co-exist and create a more natural picture of life in the deep."

On the other side of the tank, Mae could now see the caretaker climbing the red ladder, holding a large plastic bag, heavy with water and tiny passengers. Mae was trying to slow her breathing but couldn't. She felt like she'd throw up. She thought about running off, somewhere very far away. Run with Annie. Where was Annie?

She saw Stenton staring at her, his eyes concerned, and also stern, telling her to get herself together. She tried to breathe, tried to concentrate on the proceedings. She would have time after all this, she told herself, to untangle this chaos of Kalden and Ty. She would have time. Her heart slowed.

"Victor," Bailey said, "as you might be able to see, is carrying our most delicate cargo, the seahorse, and of course his many progeny. As you'll notice, the seahorses are being brought into the new tank in a baggie, much as you would bring home a goldfish from the county fair. This has proven to be the best way to transfer delicate creatures like this. There are no hard surfaces to bump against, and the plastic is far lighter than lucite or any hard surface would be."

The caretaker was now at the top of the ladder, and, after a quick visual confirmation from Stenton, carefully lowered the bag into the water, so it rested on the surface. The seahorses, passive as always, were reclining near the bottom of the bag, showing no sign that they knew anything—that they were in a bag, that they were being transferred, that they were alive. They barely moved, and offered no protestation.

Mae checked her counter. The watchers were at sixty-two million. Bailey indicated that they would wait a few moments till the water temperatures of the bag and the tank might be aligned, and Mae took the opportunity to turn back to Kalden. She tried to catch his eye, but he chose not to take his eyes away from the aquarium. He stared into it, smiling benignly at the seahorses, as if looking at his own children.

At the back of the tank, Victor was again climbing the red ladder. "Well, this is very exciting," Bailey said. "Now we see the octopus being carried up. He needs a bigger container, but not proportionately bigger. He can fit himself into a lunchbox if he wanted to—he has no spine, no bones at all. He is malleable and infinitely adaptable."

Soon both containers, those housing the octopus and the seahorses, were bobbing gently on the neon surface. The octopus seemed aware, to some degree, that there was a far bigger home beneath him, and was pressing itself against the base of his temporary home.

Mae saw Victor point to the seahorses and give a quick nod to Bailey and Stenton. "Okay," Bailey said. "It looks like it's time to release our seahorse friends into their new habitat. Now I expect this to be quite beautiful. Go ahead, Victor, when you're ready." And when Victor released them, it *was* quite beautiful. The seahorses, translucent but tinted just so, as if gilded only slightly, fell into the tank, drifting down like a slow rain of golden question marks.

"Wow," Bailey said. "Look at that."

And finally the father of them all, looking tentative, fell from the bag and into the tank. Unlike his children, who were spread out, directionless, he maneuvered himself, determinedly, down to the bottom of the tank and quickly hid himself amid the coral and vegetation. In seconds he was invisible.

"Wow," Bailey said. "That is one shy fish."

The babies, though, continued to float downward, and to swim in the middle of the tank, few of them anxious to go anywhere in particular.

"We're ready?" Bailey asked, looking up to Victor. "Well this is moving right along! It seems we're ready for the octopus now." Victor opened the bottom of the bag, splitting it, and the octopus instantly spread itself up like a welcoming hand. As it had done when alone, it traced the contours of the glass, feeling the coral, the seaweed, always gentle, wanting to know all, touch all.

"Look at that. Ravishing," Bailey said. "What a stunning

creature. He must have something like a brain in that giant balloon of his, right?" And here Bailey turned to Stenton, asking for an answer, but Stenton chose to consider the question rhetorical. The slightest smile overtook the corner of his mouth, but he did not turn away from the scene before him.

The octopus flowered and grew, and flew from one side of the tank to the other, barely touching the seahorses or any other living thing, only looking at them, only wanting to know them, and as he touched and measured everything within the tank, Mae saw movement again on the red ladder.

"Now we have Victor and his helper bringing the real attraction," Bailey said, watching the first caretaker, now joined by a second, also in white, who was manning some kind of forklift. The cargo was a large lucite box, and inside its temporary home, the shark thrashed a few times, its tail whipping left and right, but was far calmer than Mae had seen it before.

From the top of the ladder, Victor arranged the lucite box on the surface of the water, and when Mae expected the octopus and seahorses to flee for cover, the shark went absolutely still.

"Well, look at that," Bailey marveled.

The watchers spiked again, now to seventy-five million, and climbed frenetically, half a million every few seconds.

Below, the octopus seemed oblivious to the shark and the possibility of it joining them in the aquarium. The shark was utterly frozen in place, perhaps negating the tank's occupants' ability to sense him. Meanwhile, Victor and his assistant had descended the ladder and Victor was returning with a large bucket.

"As you can see now," Bailey said, "the first thing Victor is doing is dropping some of our shark's favorite food into the tank.

This will keep him distracted and satisfied, and allow his new neighbors to get acclimated. Victor has been feeding the shark all day, so it should be well satisfied already. But these tuna will serve as breakfast, lunch and dinner, in case he's still hungry."

And so Victor dropped six large tuna, each ten pounds or more, into the tank, where they quickly explored their environs. "There's less need to slowly acclimate these guys to the tank," Bailey said. "They'll be food pretty soon, so their happiness is less important than the shark's. Ah, look at them go." The tuna were shooting across the tank in diagonals, and their sudden presence chased the octopus and seahorse into the coral and fronds at the bottom of the aquarium. Soon though, the tuna became less frantic, and settled into an easy commute around the tank. At the bottom, the father seahorse was still invisible, but his many children could be seen, their tails wrapped around fronds and the tentacles of various anemones. It was a peaceful scene, and Mae found herself temporarily lost in it.

"Well, this is plain gorgeous," Bailey said, surveying the coral and vegetation in lemons and blues and burgundies. "Look at these happy creatures. A peaceable kingdom. Seems almost a shame to change it in any way," he said. Mae glanced quickly to Bailey, and he seemed startled at what he'd said, knowing it was not in the spirit of the present endeavor. He and Stenton exchanged quick looks, and Bailey tried to recover.

"But we're striving here for a realistic and holistic look at this world," he said. "And that means including *all* of the inhabitants of this ecosystem. So I'm getting an indication from Victor that it's time to invite the shark to join."

Mae looked up to see Victor struggling to open the container's bottom hatch. The shark was still holding still, a marvel of self-control. And then he began to slide down the lucite ramp. As he did, for a moment Mae was conflicted. She knew this was the natural thing to happen, his joining the rest of those with whom he shared his environment. She knew that it was right and inevitable. But for a moment, she thought it natural in a way seeing a plane fall from the sky can seem natural, too. The horror comes later.

"Now, for the last piece of this underwater family," Bailey said. "When the shark is released, we'll get, for the first time in history, a real look at how life at the bottom of the trench really looks, and how creatures like this cohabitate. Are we ready?" Bailey looked to Stenton, who was standing silently next to him. Stenton nodded brusquely, as if looking to him for the go-ahead was unnecessary.

Victor released the shark, and, as if it had been eyeing its prey through the plastic, mentally preparing its meal and knowing the precise location of each portion, the shark darted downward and quickly snatched the largest tuna and devoured it in two snaps of its jaws. As the tuna was making its way, visibly, through the shark's digestive tract, the shark ate two more in rapid succession. A fourth was still in the shark's jaws when the granular remains of the first were being deposited, like snow, onto the aquarium floor.

Mae looked then to the bottom of the tank and saw that the octopus and the seahorse progeny were no longer visible. She saw some sign of movement in the holes in the coral, and caught sight of what she thought was a tentacle. Though Mae seemed sure that the shark couldn't be their predator—after all, Stenton had found them all in close proximity—they were hiding from it as if they knew it, and its plans, quite well. Mae looked up and saw the shark circling the tank, which was now otherwise empty. In the few seconds that Mae had been looking for the octopus and seahorses, the shark had disposed of the other two fish. Their remains fell like dust.

Bailey laughed nervously. "Well, now I'm wondering—" he said, but stopped. Mae looked up and saw that Stenton's eyes were narrow and offered no alternative. The process would not be interrupted. She looked to Kalden, or Ty, whose eyes hadn't left the tank. He was watching the proceedings placidly, as if he had seen it before and knew every outcome.

"Okay," Bailey said. "Our shark is a very hungry fellow, and I would be worried about the other occupants of our little world here if I didn't know better. But I do know better. I'm standing next to one of the great underwater explorers, a man who knows what he's doing." Mae watched Bailey speak. He was looking at Stenton, his eyes looking for any give, any sign that he might call this off, or offer some explanation or assurance. But Stenton was staring at the shark, admiring.

Quick and savage movement brought Mae's eyes back to the tank. The shark's nose was deep in the coral now, attacking it with a brutal force.

"Oh no," Bailey said.

The coral soon split open and the shark plunged in, coming away, instantaneously, with the octopus, which it dragged into the open area of the tank, as if to give everyone—Mae and her watchers and the Wise Men—a better view as it tore the animal apart.

"Oh god," Bailey said, quieter now.

Intentionally or not, the octopus presented a challenge to its fate. The shark ripped off an arm, then seemed to get a mouthful of the octopus's head, only to find, seconds later, that the octopus was still alive and largely intact, behind him. But not for long.

"Oh no. Oh no," Bailey whispered.

The shark turned and, in a flurry, ripped its prey's tentacles off, one by one, until the octopus was dead, a shredded mass of milky white matter. The shark took the rest of it in two snatches of its mouth, and the octopus was no more.

A kind of whimper came from Bailey, and without turning her shoulders, Mae looked over to find that Bailey was now turned away, his palms against his eyes. Stenton, though, was looking at the shark with a mixture of fascination and pride, like a parent watching, for the first time, his child doing something particularly impressive, something he'd hoped for and expected but that came delightfully sooner.

Above the tank, Victor looked tentative, and was trying to catch Stenton's eye. He seemed to be wondering what Mae was wondering, which was whether they should somehow separate the shark from the seahorse, before the seahorse, too, was consumed. But when Mae turned to him, Stenton was still watching, with no change of expression.

In a few more seconds, in a series of urgent thrusts, the shark had broken another coral arch and extracted the seahorse, which had no defenses and was eaten in two bites, first its delicate head, then its curved, papier-mâché torso and tail.

Then, like a machine going about its work, the shark circled and stabbed until he had devoured the thousand babies, and the seaweed, and the coral, and the anemones. It ate everything, and deposited the remains quickly, carpeting the empty aquarium in a low film of white ash.

"Well," Ty said, "that was about what I imagined would happen." He seemed unshaken, even buoyant as he shook Stenton's hand, and then Bailey's, and then, while still holding Bailey's hand with his right hand, he took Mae's with his left, as if the three of them were about to dance. Mae felt something in her palm, and quickly closed her fingers around it. Then he pulled away and left.

"I better head out, too," Bailey said in a whisper. He turned, dazed, and walked down the darkened corridor.

Afterward, when the shark was alone in the tank, and was circling, still ravenous, never stopping, Mae wondered how long she should remain in place, allowing the watchers to watch this. But she decided that as long as Stenton remained, she would, too. And he stayed for a long while. He couldn't get enough of the shark, its anxious circling.

"Until next time," Stenton said finally. He nodded to Mae, and then to her watchers, who were now one hundred million, many of them terrified, many more in awe and wanting more of the same.

In the bathroom stall, with the lens trained on the door, Mae brought Ty's note close to her face, out of view of her watchers. He insisted on seeing her, alone, and provided detailed directions for where they should meet. When she was ready, he'd written, she need only leave the bathroom, and then turn and say, into her live audio, "I'm going back." It would imply she was returning to the bathroom, for some unnamed hygienic emergency. And at that moment he would kill her feed, and any SeeChange cameras that might see her, for thirty minutes. It would provoke a minor clamor, but it had to be done. Her life, he said, was at stake, and Annie's, and her parents'. "Everyone and everything," he'd written, "is teetering on the precipice."

This would be her last mistake. She knew it was a mistake to meet him, especially off-camera. But something about the shark had unsettled her, had left her susceptible to bad decisions. If only someone could make these decisions for her—somehow eliminate the doubt, the possibility of failure. But she had to know how Ty had pulled all this off, didn't she? Perhaps all this was some test? It made a certain sense. If she were being groomed for great things, wouldn't they test her? She knew they would.

So she followed his directions. She left the bathroom, told her watchers she was returning and, when her feed went dead, she followed his directions. She descended as she had with Kalden that one strange night, tracing the path they'd taken when he'd first brought her to the room, far underground, where they housed and ran cool water through Stewart and everything he'd seen. When Mae arrived, she found Kalden, or Ty, waiting for her, his back to the red box. He'd taken off the wool hat, revealing his grey-white hair, but he was still wearing his hoodie, and the combination of the two men, Ty and Kalden, in one figure, repulsed her, and when he began walking toward her, she yelled "No!"

He stopped.

"Stay there," she said.

"I'm not dangerous, Mae."

"I don't know anything about you."

"I'm sorry I didn't tell you who I was. But I didn't lie."

"You told me your name was Kalden! That's not a lie?"

"Besides that, I never lied."

"Besides that? Besides *lying about your identity*?"

"I think you know I have no choice here."

"What kind of name is Kalden, anyway? You get it off some baby-name site?"

"I did. You like it?"

He smiled an unnerving smile. Mae had the feeling that she shouldn't be here, that she should leave immediately.

"I think I need to go," she said, and stepped toward the stairs. "I feel like this is some horrific prank."

"Mae, think about it. Here's my license." He handed her his driver's license. It showed a clean-shaven, dark-haired man with glasses who looked more or less like what she remembered Ty looked like, the Ty from the video feeds, the old photos, the portrait in oil outside Bailey's library. The name read Tyler Alexander Gospodinov. "Look at me. No resemblance?" He retreated to the cave-within-a-cave they'd shared and returned with a pair of glasses. "See?" he said. "Now it's obvious, right?" As if answering Mae's next question, he said, "I've always been a very average-looking guy. You know this. And then I get rid of the glasses, the hoodies. I change my look, the way I move. But most important, my hair went grey. And why do you think that happened?"

"I have no idea," Mae said.

Ty swept his arms around, encompassing everything around them, the vast campus above. "All this. The fucking shark that eats the world."

"Do Bailey and Stenton know you're going around with some other name?" Mae asked.

"Of course. Yes. They expect me to be here. I'm not technically allowed to leave campus. As long as I'm here, they're happy."

"Does Annie know?"

"No."

"So I'm—"

"You're the third person who knows."

"And you're telling me why?"

"Because you have great influence here, and because you have to help. You're the only one who can slow all this down."

"Slow what down? The company you created?"

"Mae, I didn't intend any of this to happen. And it's moving too fast. This idea of Completion, it's far beyond what I had in mind when I started all this, and it's far beyond what's right. It has to be brought back into some kind of balance."

"First of all, I don't agree. Secondly, I can't help."

"Mae, the Circle can't close."

"What are you talking about? How can you say this now? If you're Ty, most of this was your idea."

"No. No. I was trying to make the web more civil. I was trying to make it more elegant. I got rid of anonymity. I combined a thousand disparate elements into one unified system. But I didn't picture a world where Circle membership was mandatory, where all government and all life was channeled through one network—"

"I'm leaving," Mae said, and turned. "And I don't see why you just don't leave, too. Leave everything. If you don't believe in all this, then leave. Go to the woods."

"That didn't work for Mercer, did it?"

"Fuck you."

"Sorry. I'm sorry. But he's why I contacted you now. Don't you see that's just one of the consequences of all this? There will be more Mercers. So many more. So many people who don't want to be found but who will be. So many people who wanted no part of all this. That's what's new. There used to be the option of opting out. But now that's over. Completion is the end. We're closing the circle around everyone—it's a totalitarian nightmare."

"And it's my fault?"

"No, no. Not at all. But you're now the ambassador. You're the face of it. The benign, friendly face of it all. And the closing of the Circle—it's what you and your friend Francis made possible. Your mandatory Circle account idea, and his chip. TruYouth? It's sick, Mae. Don't you see? All the kids get a chip embedded in them, for safety, when they're infants. And yes, it'll save lives. But then, what, you think they suddenly remove them when they're eighteen? No. In the interest of education and safety, everything they've done will be recorded, tracked, logged, analyzed—it's permanent. Then, when they're old enough to vote, to participate, their membership is mandatory. That's where the Circle closes. Everyone will be tracked, cradle to grave, with no possibility of escape."

"You really sound like Mercer now. This kind of paranoia—"

"But I know more than Mercer. Don't you think if someone like me, someone who invented most of this shit, is scared, don't you think you should be scared, too?"

"No. I think you lost a step."

"Mae, so many of the things I invented I honestly did for fun, out of some perverse game of whether or not they'd work, whether people would use them. I mean, it was like setting up a guillotine in the public square. You don't expect a thousand people to line up to put their heads in it."

"Is that how you see this?"

"No, sorry. That's a bad comparison. But some of the things we did, I just—I did just to see if anyone would actually use them, would acquiesce. When they did buy in, half the time I couldn't believe it. And then it was too late. There was Bailey and Stenton and the IPO. And then it was just too fast, and there was enough money to make any dumb idea real. Mae, I want you to imagine where all this is going."

"I know where it's going."

"Mae, close your eyes."

"No."

"Mae, please. Close your eyes."

She closed her eyes.

"I want you to connect these dots and see if you see what I see. Picture this. The Circle has been devouring all competitors for years, correct? It only makes the company stronger. Already, 90 percent of the world's searches go through the Circle. Without competitors, this will increase. Soon it'll be nearly 100 percent. Now, you and I both know that if you can control the flow of information, you can control everything. You can control most of what anyone sees and knows. If you want to bury some piece of information, permanently, that's two seconds' work. If you want to ruin anyone, that's five minutes' work. How can anyone rise up against the Circle if they control all the information and accesss to it? They want everyone to have a Circle account, and they're well on their way to making it illegal not to. What happens then? What happens when they control all searches, and have full access to all data about every person? When they know every move everyone makes? If all monetary transactions, all health and DNA information, every piece of one's life, good or bad, when every word uttered flows through one channel?"

"But there are a thousand protections to prevent all of this. It's just not possible. I mean, governments will make sure—"

"Governments who are transparent? Legislators who owe their reputations to the Circle? Who could be ruined the moment they speak out? What do you think happened to Williamson? Remember her? She threatens the Circle monopoly and, surprise, the feds find incriminating stuff on her computer. You think that's a coincidence? That's about the hundredth person Stenton's done that to. Mae, once the Circle's complete, that's it. And you helped complete it. This democracy thing, or Demoxie, whatever it is, good god. Under the guise of having every voice heard, you create mob rule, a filterless society where secrets are crimes. It's brilliant, Mae. I mean, you are brilliant. You're what Stenton and Bailey have been hoping for from the start."

"But Bailey—"

"Bailey believes that life will be better, will be perfect, when everyone has unfettered access to everyone and everything they know. He genuinely believes that the answers to every life question can be found among other people. He truly believes that openness, that complete and uninterrupted access among all humans will help the world. That this is what the world's been waiting for, the moment when every soul is connected. This is his rapture, Mae! Don't you see how extreme that view is? His idea is radical, and in another era would have been a fringe notion espoused by an eccentric adjunct professor somewhere: that all information, personal or not, should be known by all. Knowledge is property and no one can own it. Infocommunism. And he's entitled to that opinion. But paired with ruthless capitalistic ambition—"

"So it's Stenton?"

"Stenton professionalized our idealism, monetized our utopia. He's the one who saw the connection between our work and politics, and between politics and control. Public-private leads to private-private, and soon you have the Circle running most or even all government services, with incredible private-sector efficiency and an insatiable appetite. Everyone becomes a citizen of the Circle."

"And that's so bad? If everyone has equal access to services, to information, we finally have a chance at equality. No information should cost anything. There should be no barriers to knowing everything, to accessing all—"

"And if everyone's tracked—"

"Then there's no crime. No murder, no kidnapping and rape. No kids ever victimized again. No more missing persons. I mean, that alone—"

"But don't you see what happened to your friend Mercer? He was pursued to the ends of the earth and now he's gone."

"But this is just the pivot of history. Have you talked to Bailey about this? I mean, during any major human turning point, there's upheaval. Some get left behind, some *choose* to be left behind."

"So you think everyone should be tracked, should be watched."

"I think everything and everyone should be seen. And to be seen, we need to be watched. The two go hand in hand."

"But who wants to be watched all the time?"

"I do. I *want* to be seen. I want proof I existed."

"Mae."

"Most people do. Most people would trade everything they know, everyone they know—they'd trade it all to know they've been seen, and acknowledged, that they might even be remembered. We all know we die. We all know the world is too big for us to be significant. So all we have is the hope of being seen, or heard, even for a moment."

"But Mae. We saw every creature in that tank, didn't we? We saw them devoured by a beast that turned them to ash. Don't you see that everything that goes into that tank, with that beast, with *this* beast, will meet the same fate?"

"So what exactly do you want from me?"

"When you have the maximum amount of viewers, I want you to read this statement." He handed Mae a piece of paper, on which he'd written, in crude all capitals, a list of assertions under the headline "The Rights of Humans in a Digital Age." Mae scanned it, catching passages: "We must all have the right to anonymity." "Not every human activity can be measured." "The ceaseless pursuit of data to quantify the value of any endeavor is catastrophic to true understanding." "The barrier between public and private must remain unbreachable." At the end she found one line, written in red ink: "We must all have the right to disappear."

"So you want me to read all this to the watchers?"

"Yes," Kalden said, his eyes wild.

"And then what?"

"I have a series of steps that we can take together that can begin to take all this apart. I know everything that's ever happened here, Mae, and there's plenty that's gone on that would convince anyone, no matter how blind, that the Circle needs to be dismantled. I know I can do it. I'm the only one who can do it, but I need your help."

"And then what?"

"Then you and I go somewhere. I have so many ideas. We'll vanish. We can hike through Tibet. We can bike through the Mongolian steppe. We can sail around the world in a boat we built ourselves."

Mae pictured all this. She pictured the Circle being taken apart, sold off amid scandal, thirteen thousand people out of jobs, the campus overtaken, broken up, turned into a college or mall or something worse. And finally she pictured life on a boat with this man, sailing the world, untethered, but when she tried to, she saw, instead, the couple on the barge she'd met months ago on the bay. Out there, alone, living under a tarp, drinking wine from paper cups, naming seals, reminiscing about island fires.

At that moment, Mae knew what she needed to do.

"Kalden, are you sure we're not being heard?"

"Of course not."

"Okay, good. Good. I see everything clearly now."

BOOK III

TO HAVE GOTTEN so close to apocalypse—it rattled her still. Yes, Mae had averted it, she'd been braver than she thought possible, but her nerves, these many months later, were still frayed. What if Kalden hadn't reached out to her when he did? What if he hadn't trusted her? What if he'd taken matters into his own hands, or worse, entrusted his secret to someone else? Someone without her integrity? Without her strength, her resolve, her loyalty?

In the quiet of the clinic, sitting next to Annie, Mae's mind wandered. There was serenity here, with the rhythmic hush of the respirator, the occasional door opening or closing, the hum of the machines that kept Annie alive. She'd collapsed at her desk, was found on the floor, catatonic, and was rushed here, where the care surpassed what she could have received anywhere else. Since then, she'd stabilized, and the prognosis was strong. The cause of the coma was still a subject of some debate, Dr. Villalobos had said, but most likely, it was caused by stress, or shock, or simple exhaustion. The Circle doctors were confident Annie would emerge from it, as were a thousand doctors worldwide who had watched her vitals, encouraged by the frequent flittering of her eyelashes, the occasional twitch of a finger. Next to her EKG, there was a screen with an ever-lengthening string of good wishes from fellow humans from all over the world, most or all of whom, Mae thought wistfully, Annie would never know.

Mae looked at her friend, at her unchanging face, her glistening skin, the ribbed tube emerging from her mouth. She looked wonderfully peaceful, sleeping a restful sleep, and for a brief moment Mae felt a twinge of envy. She wondered what Annie was thinking. Doctors had said that she was likely dreaming; they'd been measuring steady brain activity during the coma, but what precisely was happening in her mind was unknown to all, and Mae couldn't help feeling some annoyance about this. There was a monitor visible from where Mae sat, a real-time picture of Annie's mind, bursts of color appearing periodically, implying that extraordinary things were happening in there. But what was she thinking?

A knock startled her. She looked beyond Annie's prone form to find Francis behind the glass, in the viewing area. He raised a tentative hand, and Mae waved. She would see him later, at an all-campus event to celebrate the latest Clarification milestone. Ten million people were now transparent worldwide, the movement irreversible.

Annie's role in making it possible could not be overstated, and Mae wished she could witness it. There was so much Mae wanted to tell Annie. With a duty that felt holy, she'd told the world about Kalden being Ty, about his bizarre claims and misguided efforts to derail the completion of the Circle. Remembering it now, it seemed like some kind of nightmare, being so far under the earth with that madman, disconnected from her watchers and the rest of the world. But Mae had feigned her cooperation and had escaped, and immediately told Bailey and Stenton about it all. With their customary compassion and vision, they'd allowed Ty to stay on campus, in an advisory role, with a secluded office and no specific duties. Mae hadn't seen him since their subterranean encounter, and did not care to.

Mae had not reached her parents in a few months now, but it would be only a matter of time. They would find each other, soon enough, in a world where everyone could know each other truly and wholly, without secrets, without shame and without the need for permission to see or to know, without the selfish hoarding of life—any corner of it, any moment of it. All of that would be, so soon, replaced by a new and glorious openness, a world of perpetual light. Completion was imminent, and it would bring peace, and it would bring unity, and all that messiness of humanity until now, all those uncertainties that accompanied the world before the Circle, would be only a memory.

Another burst of color appeared on the screen monitoring the workings of Annie's mind. Mae reached out to touch her forehead, marveling at the distance this flesh put between them. What was going on in that head of hers? It was exasperating, really, Mae thought, not knowing. It was an affront, a deprivation, to herself and to the world. She would bring this up with Stenton and Bailey, with the Gang of 40, at the earliest opportunity. They needed to talk about Annie, the thoughts she was thinking. Why shouldn't they know them? The world deserved nothing less and would not wait.

ACKNOWLEDGMENTS

Thank you to Vendela, to Bill and Toph, to Vanessa and Scott, and to Inger and Paul. To Jenny Jackson, Sally Willcox, Andrew Wylie, Lindsay Williams, Debby Klein, and Kimberly Jaime. To Clara Sankey. To Em-J Staples, Michelle Quint, Brent Hoff, Sam Riley, Brian Christian, Sarah Stewart Taylor, Ian Delaney, Andrew Leland, Casey Jarman, and Jill Stauffer. To Laura Howard, Daniel Gumbiner, Adam Krefman, Jordan Bass, Brian McMullen, Dan McKinley, Isaac Fitzgerald, Sunra Thompson, Andi Winnette, Jordan Karnes, Ruby Perez, and Rachel Khong. Thank you to everyone at Vintage and Knopf. Thank you to Jessica Hische. Thank you to Ken Jackson, John McCosker, and Nick Goldman. Thank you to Kevin Spall and everyone at Thomson-Shore printers. Also: San Vincenzo is a fictional place. Certain other small liberties with Bay Area geography were taken in this book.